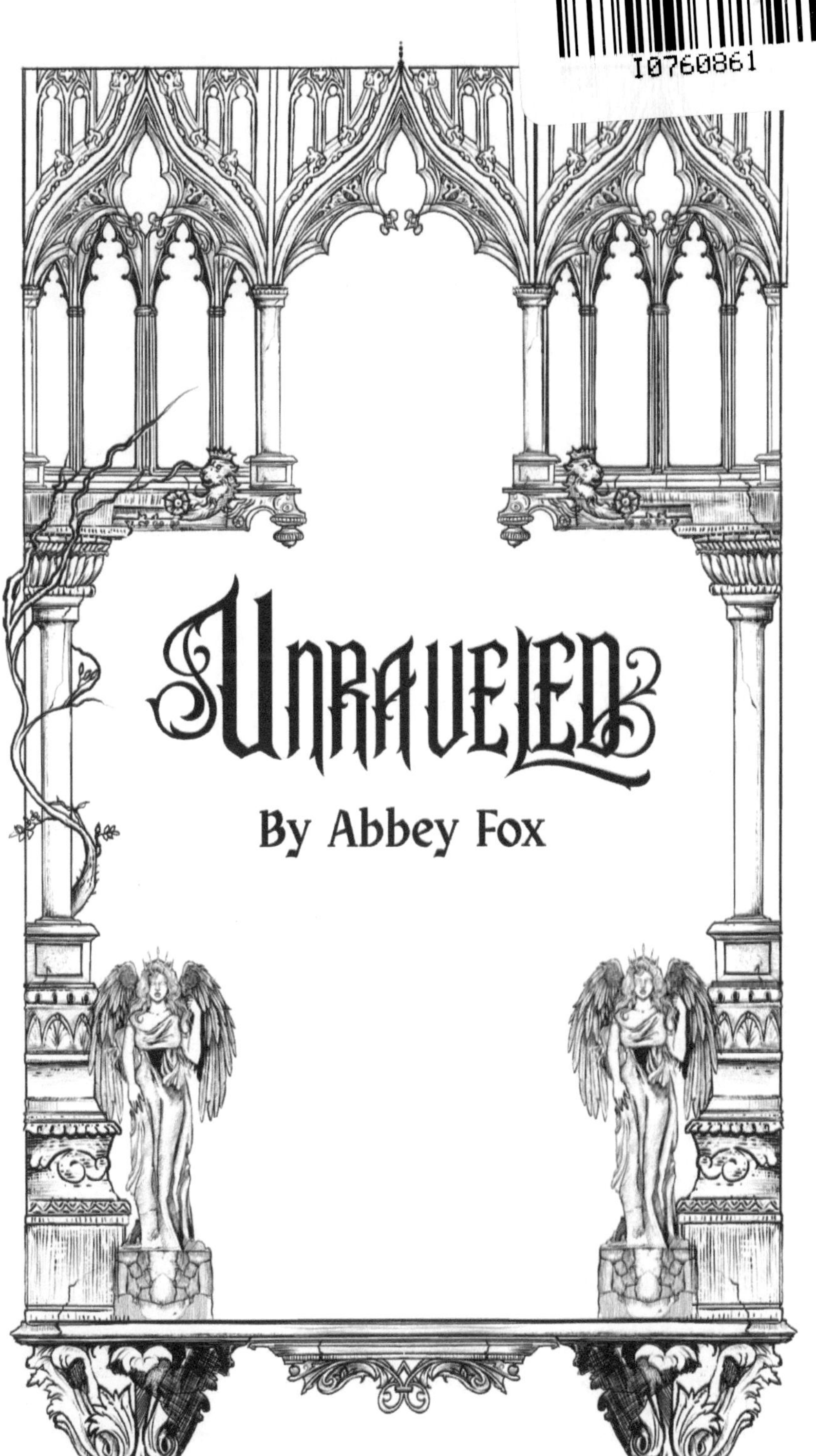
Unraveled
By Abbey Fox

Unraveled
Published by The Wild Rabbit LLC
www.abbeyfox.com

World map design:heathersouliere

World map shading: Camila Lohr a.k.a. Abbey Fox

Character art and cover illustrations: Camila Lohr a.k.a. Abbey Fox

Illustration of kiss: Camila Lohr a.k.a. Abbey Fox

Editor: Anna Corbeaux @corbeauxeditoralservices

Illustration of couple with magic and books: jjflorentina

Illustration of couple embracing: Natalia Sorokina - jwitless.art

All suffering originates from craving, from attachment, from desire.

Edgar Allan Poe

TRIGGERS

Please be advised this book is for adult audiences only. It contains strong language; explicit, consensual sex scenes; and violence typical for the genre. There is also a bit of a horror element, manipulation and kidnapping.

Playlist of songs that inspired me...

Breathe - Tommee Profitt, Fleurie
You Belong To Me - Cat Pierce
The Death Waltz - Tobias Lilja
The Fight - Silly Boy Blue
I Found - Amber Run
Love and War - Fleurie
Where Is My Mind - Safari Riot, Grayson Sanders
Where's My Love - SYML
Start a War - Klergy, Valerie Broussard
Solitude - M83, Felsmann + Tiley.

THE CITY OF EPONDE
PENUMBRA

THE CROSSROADS
THE CITY OF HEDRUM
KINGDOM OF APHELION
FAIRHOPE

I had a dream black feathers rained from a stormy sky, leaving pools of poisoned ink over the land.

From the darkness, a beast appeared, with sharp teeth and magic, bringing death to us all.

But I didn't run from him. Instead, I welcomed him with open arms.

Because he's death . . . and death has been hunting me all my life.

CHAPTER 1

There are three rules I must follow if I want to survive the Wild Hunt:

One, don't wander the streets after nightfall, especially during the blood moon.

Two, don't leave the house without Mother's protective amulet.

Three, never look a fae in the eye.

That is . . . if I ever find a fae wandering our little city. I scoff at the thought, shaking my head at the memory of my father's voice.

After all, it's been a decade since the fae disappeared from our world, leaving behind the beasts of the Hunt.

The wood groans under my shifting feet as I balance on the narrow shelf. Exhaling a shaky breath, I stretch toward the bookshelf on the other side of the aisle.

Almost there. Sweat beads on my temple, and my fingers tremble as I trace the worn leather binding of the forbidden grimoire. The book's magic sparks at my fingertips, wrapping around my wrist as it shifts toward me on the wood surface.

My heart jolts at the movement, and even though I've been

coming here for a week to study its pages in my spare time, its power never ceases to surprise me.

I wrap my hand around the spine and pull the book out. Losing my balance could mean death, or a couple broken bones. But I'm tired of living in fear.

Gaining the ability to defend Irene from the beasts that took our father is worth it—even if it means breaking a few rules.

The room spins as I shift my gaze to the ground. I'm at least fifteen feet up, climbing bookcases I shouldn't even be looking at let alone borrowing books from.

I press my lips together in an effort to stay silent and adjust my grip on the shelf to bring the heavy, magical grimoire to my chest. Breathing raggedly, I wait for my heart to stop trying to escape my body.

Perhaps Irene is right, and I have a death wish. But the threat of the blood moon every three months can make a sane person mad.

My amulet vibrates as it does when another librarian approaches. Which means I have little time to get my myself somewhere inconspicuous.

I climb with practiced ease, bringing the book with me as I descend shelf by shelf, until my bare feet hit the frigid floor.

The stone of my amulet is glowing now, illuminating the narrow corridor and the two shelves looming over me. I swallow the bitter taste of fear and rush toward my discarded boots as I tuck my necklace back under the thick layers of my cloak.

Whatever magic is inside my mother's amulet, it's never led me astray.

I shove a foot into my soft leather boot, and it's a welcome reprieve from the cold. As fast as I can, I run, holding the grimoire with one hand and my remaining boot with the other.

Tomorrow, I'll have to return it to the towering bookcases

filled with the rest of the old tomes, before any of the elder librarians notice it's missing.

I glance at the now-familiar embossed leather that binds the grimoire. Every time I borrow this one, it's harder to give it back. The spells within its pages are too alluring, not from this world. But it's more than that. The book begs me to not let it go.

With no windows or lamps of any sort around me, muscle memory guides me across the circular room. I lock the iron gates with the help of a spell I learned months ago, using magic I'm not supposed to wield.

Oh well, it's not like anyone's watching me. Sighing, I walk down the slim steps leading to the main floor. Usually, I wouldn't dare to read this out in the hall. Right now, though, all but the assigned guardian—have left for the night. I place my book on the polished reading table and tug on my other boot. The sunrays of the late afternoon spill across the floor, casting lengthy shapes of gold and pink. I have an hour at most before I have to run home.

Magic has a particular old parchment smell. The power held in these pages also smells of leather and something woodsy I can't place. My heart soars as the book's glowing yellow energy snakes to my fingers, around my wrist, and into my arms.

The passages are written in a language I shouldn't understand, but somehow, and against all odds . . . I do. The first time I gazed upon this grimoire, I was confused. How had the strange symbol-like letters become something I could read? Like the book was whispering the words right into my mind.

I can't tell anyone about this. It's forbidden for me to so much as *be* in that part of the library, never mind study the grimoires. I know people would think I'm crazy. No one would believe me if I told them the books talk to me.

Time slows, then speeds up. I blink at the darkness surrounding me. I blink again and notice the red glow seeping from the largest window. The air thickens, a crawling sensation slithering over my skin as I close the grimoire.

"No, no, no . . ." I move between bookcases standing tall like columns and reach for the windowsill.

As one of the few people in the city with an affinity for weaving small traces of magic, I'm in tune with the phases of the moon, and it's never caught me off guard.

I push an errant strand of hair behind my ear, and the warmth of my breath fogs the glass as I press my cheek to the window. The moon hangs in the air, glowing in shades of pale pink. It mocks me. Even though the fae are gone, the ancient power of the unseelie is approaching the veil.

I should've been out of here at least two hours ago. I jump back and turn when a shrill voice startles me.

"Mia, what are you doing here?" A petite woman with a curvy figure dashes from the farthest staircase across the massive room toward me.

Harper wears librarian regalia much like I do. A red cloak that reaches the floor contrasting against the simple white dress underneath. The dim light catches on the librarian's emblem stitched with gold thread on the front of the cloak. A shield between two olive branches, and in the center, a stack of books with a glowing star floating above.

With Knowledge, Power

The words are embroidered inside scrolls at the bottom of the crest. It's the motto we librarians live by as we study ancient writings seeking the reason for this blood moon phenomenon.

"I lost track of time." Dust motes float in the air, tickling my nose, and I choke back a cough. Reaching over the wooden bench, I slide the forbidden grimoire from the table and shield it from view under my cloak.

Harper clicks her tongue and glances at the sky behind me. "You know, curfew starts at sunset during the full moon. Especially the blood moon. You don't want to be caught outside if—"

"If a fae breaks through the veil to prowl the streets of Penumbra?" I say, repeating the words I've heard a dozen times before. "I know."

The legends we were told as bedtime stories say the blood moon exists because the god Cronus, who loved a fae named Amelia, cast a spell. The fae once lived among the gods, but the fae were so wicked, they were kicked out of the deities' realm and into ours.

Every three months, the spell Cronus cast on the moon thins the veil dividing the realms enough for the gods and spirits to roam the land of mortals.

So he can find his fae lover among the riders of the Wild Hunt.

"The fae might not come here anymore, Mia, but even though they're gone, they left behind their hungry monsters." Harper grunts, her disdain for the unseelie—and the fae's beasts—clear in her tone. Her blue eyes settle on me, and the strain in her jaw eases. "I'm the guardian of the library tonight, and only I can stay. You know that. It's on the schedule."

I lower my face to hide the flush on my skin and tighten my grip around my stolen book. I'm not ready to let it go, not yet. But that doesn't matter because a warning spell will alert the head librarian if someone—me—were to take a grimoire out of the building. I have to leave it behind.

"I live close by," I say, walking to the lockers where we keep our belongings. "I should be home in no time."

Placing the book inside my locker, I ignore the fingerlike traces of the grimoire's magic. It holds on to me. Beckoning me to not let it go. I sigh, lock the padlock, and whisper a spell that will guard it from everyone but me.

The flicker of a gas lamp hanging from the wall reminds me how late it is.

"Actually—" Harper's breath stutters out as she meets me in the middle of the room, her eyes search my face. "It might be best if you stay the night. No one has to know."

"Alana will know." I straighten the cloak over my shoulders, the soft fabric gliding over my tan skin. "*Only one librarian may stay in the building when the cursed moon presses upon us,*" I parrot, something that's been drilled into my mind ever since I ascended to guard the grimoires.

The elders believe the magic of the librarians can call the beasts toward the books. One person's power is too small to detect, but multiple clustered together in one place, well, we'd be a magnet for them.

Harper clenches her jaw, shaking her head. Her silver hair flows out from under the hood of her cloak. "Can't you feel it, Mia? I'm practically vibrating with anxiety. Something is happening tonight, and the veil is too weak to hold it back. *Stay.*"

I reach for Harper's hand. It's cold and damp in my grasp. "I'll get you in trouble if I do . . ."

We stare at each other in silence, understanding passing between us.

Harper should've found me before nightfall. It's the guard's duty to ensure all librarians are out of the building before sunset. Guilt makes my stomach churn. Perhaps she checked but couldn't find me because I was in the forbidden area.

This is my doing, and I won't drag her down with me.

Harper swallows and dips her gaze to the floor. "I messed this up, however, I insist. If a beast makes it past the veil tonight, I won't be able to forgive myself if it takes you."

"I'll be fine. I'm three blocks from home." With that, I drop Harper's hand and head toward the grand staircase that leads to the bottom level.

The heels of my boots click over the polished marble floors, echoing in the quiet. The pressure of what's coming grows, and the surrounding bookcases only increase my sense of being trapped.

"The veil is cracking. I don't know what they are doing to keep the shield up, but whatever it is, it's strange—and weak. Isn't your sister one of them? Has she said anything about it?" Harper's voice is harsher than before.

My steps slow to a stop, and I turn toward the smaller woman behind me, raising a brow. It isn't a secret Irene's one of the scientists in charge of maintaining the veil that protects the city.

But it never ceases to amaze me that once every three months, without fail, the town grows weary of the people keeping us safe. It's been a year since a beast made it through, but just the same, the tension growing in the streets is palpable.

"Much like us, she isn't allowed to speak of what goes on there," I say, and continue on to the main doors. I've wasted enough time and need to keep moving. "We all do the best we can, and it's worth remembering, no one is perfect at their duties."

Harper's cheeks bloom bright red, noticeable even in the darkness. "I didn't mean to malign your sister's good work . . ."

Even if my relationship with Irene is far from ideal, she and the grimoires inside this library are all I have left of the life I had before everything happened.

"I better go now, or I might not make it . . ."

A murmur goes over and around me, hushed words in another language. Goose bumps lift from my skin as I slowly turn back toward the double doors.

It moves past me, a cyclone of magic carrying the faint scent of frankincense and rain on an early winter day. The wind pushes the red hood covering my dark hair back, and a loose stack of parchment by the tables flies off in disarray.

Panic paralyzes me as adrenaline rushes through my veins like molten fire. The beasts have come. I push the doors open as the veil cracks right above the library's metal roof. A fissure extending like a spiderweb over the shield, invisible to everyone in town that wasn't trained to see how magic affects their surroundings.

"They're here." Harper's skin grows gray with every passing second as something comes down from the sky.

A man?

A fae? Impossible.

He doesn't look like a beast from this distance. His back is wide and tapers to a narrow waist. A humanlike being that sends a shiver skittering down my spine.

He moves over the city as if searching, and behind him, the moon shines a brighter shade of red. Like the shield dulled it before, and now, I can see its true color.

A halo of gold magic outlines his figure, and his powerful wings keep him in one place for longer than a mindless beast—if that's what he is—should linger. His attention snaps toward the library, as if called by my staring.

I let out a trembling breath and steady myself against the doorframe.

The cool stone under my palm matches the ice in my veins. Time stills as his whole body tilts, and when he dips closer to the street, the angles of his face catch the light.

It's a beast—except not like any I've seen before.

I've caught the eye of a predator, and my mind and body know it. I can't run home, and going back into the library could spur him to attack, fed by the thrill of the chase.

He's going to take me.

Harper's fingers dig into my arm as she pulls me back to the library. "We can't be out here. The wards aren't as strong on the street."

The first alarm bell goes off, then another, then hundreds follow suit. All at once, they ring and warn the citizens a beast has broken through the veil. The winged creature flinches at the sound and turns away from us.

Time stills as he studies his surroundings with renewed interest.

He dives from the sky into the city, gliding over the empty streets. And this close, I can make out the feathers covering every inch of his body and part of his face. I pull my arm from Harper's grasp and follow his retreating shape.

He blends with the darkness, and anxiety smothers me when I notice where he's headed. The scientist quarters. A building as tall as the library itself, with an enormous glass dome, from which a ray of light shoots into the air.

The veil is the only thing protecting us most days from the dangers awaiting in the forest.

He isn't hunting for prey.

This beast is not mindless like the rest. He has come for the scientists or for the machine. My sister is in danger.

CHAPTER 2

"No, Mia. Stay!" Harper screams behind me.

I don't stop running.

Would I prefer to remain in the safety of a magically protected building? Yes. But I can't lose Irene . . .

If someone in my family is going to be hurt by a beast this night, it has to be me. I'm the rule breaker, the eldest. I promised Father I would protect her, no matter what. Even though she is a competent twenty-one-year-old woman, to me, she will always be the child with large brown eyes and frizzy hair.

The city's familiar stench of sewage, oil from the gas lamps, and the crispness of the early winter night surrounds me as I run down the street in the darkness. Something else lingers in the air, however, different from what I'm used to. A sweet humidity seeping into my clothes and dampening my skin. It's the forest trickling into the city through the hole in the veil.

I haven't been out of Penumbra since my family moved here twenty years ago, and I remember little of the outside world. But the clean scent of the forest lures me in. A call to safety, even if that's a foolish notion, since magical beasts hunt those grounds.

Penumbra comprises a circular net of cobbled streets and narrow sidewalks, connecting the library to the other main buildings in town. The scientist quarters and city hall are as magnificent as the library, and together they form a triangle in the city's heart.

I rush down the uneven steps toward the main road and stumble over the last few when my feet tangle in the length of my cloak. Catching my breath, I scan for the predator. Some of the tension in my shoulders eases as I find my surroundings empty. Other than the trash skittering over the ground, I'm utterly alone.

Even if it's rare for multiple beasts to break through the veil and into the city at once, there have been occasions in the last five years when they've managed. I shudder, remembering the bald, grayish skin that sags around their necks. Or the milky-red gaze that was so similar to my father's blood . . .

The alarm bells are loud, and pain bursts in my ears, pulling me out of my memories. I have no time to mourn my father right now. All I can do is try my best to not lose my sister at the hands of another beast.

Downtown, homes and businesses made of bricks and light-colored mortar stand wall-to-wall against one another. Their old wooden shutters bang open and shut in the unusual breeze, and the screeching of hinges is loud enough to be heard even over the alarm.

"Stop!"

I freeze and turn around in the darkness, searching for the source of the warning call. A man stands on the flat roof of a nearby tower. He's a silhouette, but he stands next to a bell. A night guard wearing silver armor.

"You don't want to go that way. A beast flew in toward the center of town!" The dim gas lanterns barely illuminate his hand as he points toward where I'm headed.

"I know," I say, though I'm certain he can't hear a word. Not with the surrounding noise, or how his ears must be ringing since he was banging on metal to warn the citizens of danger.

I resume my run before he says much else, choosing alleyways to find cover. I'm not so foolish to assume the beast is sentient enough to know the scientist quarters keep the veil up. But the elders taught me to follow my gut, for magic seldom lies.

I know this part of town like the back of my hand. A network of asymmetrical pathways leading to the plaza next to Irene's work. Steam rises from the ground as my boots splash stagnant water over my stockings. I spot the building as I exit the alleyway. The door is grand and forged in iron. Unlike the library's uneven staircase of beige-and-gray marble, this building's front entrance is machined almost to perfection.

The air burns my throat as I push my body harder and run across the road, hoping the shadows of the night shield my red cloak from view.

I take the steps two at a time, and my calves scream with exertion. Not even the noise of the bells, which drown out all else, can hide the explosion coming from above. I duck for cover, tucking my body under the archway over the front door. I turn my face to the sky, and the previously thin cracks in the veil expand; the gaps grow larger, stretching rapidly across the dome of magic.

My skin turns cold as the same winged black shape circles over the building, magic enveloping him in a shield of gold. He can cast the type of spells most people fear, and they're unlike anything I've ever seen.

A ray of light shoots from his extended arm, and the white energy of the veil stutters.

Usually, the beasts are mindless, hungering only to take a human away to the forest. He is a bird of prey, weakening our only defense against the lot of them. Soon enough, we'll be drowning in a sea of creatures. Unless we stop him.

This is why I've broken the librarian's code of sorcery and studied the forbidden spells no one else dares to look at.

The doors of the scientist quarters are locked from the inside, and while that alone should deter me from entering, my sister is in there. And I won't let another beast take a member of my family without fighting back.

I've known there would come a time when I'd need to be brave, strong—daring. And I feel those things as I reach for the polished red stone of my amulet; it lights up under my touch and whispers a question in my head. Not with words, but feelings. It wants to know what I desire.

I was not born with magic like the fae, or even like the sorcerers from the outside world. We librarians have borrowed power, lent to us by the grimoires we keep.

I hope my borrowed magic is enough to let me in. The unraveling spell leaves my lips as if I've used it many times before. I haven't.

Never use a spell out in the open. One of the many vows I took when I ascended. And I'm sure it's one I will break again by the night's end.

The door clicks and slowly swings open with a squeak. I enter the building, and the ground shakes beneath my feet with a new explosion. Waves of golden magic hover over the polished floor as a large iron chandelier right over my head waves in the air like a pendulum. It screeches a warning to move away.

"Hello?" I step over the debris scattered across the floor and away from the chandelier's drop zone. The staircase spirals down from several floors above, opening wide at the far end of the room.

I shout again. "Irene?"

The place is desolate, as one would expect during a blood moon. Flickering lantern light casts an orange hue over the otherwise colorless space.

While most citizens return home for the night, scientists stay in these quarters, maintaining the veil. My youngest sister hasn't come home for the last year. I don't expect today to be any different.

I don't let go of my amulet as I climb the stairs, recalling spells that might help me in the case of an ambush.

The room is quiet even though I know the bells still ring outside, and the distinct sound of soles over tile flooring startles me. I see him before he sees me. A tall man with gold hair tied back into a low ponytail. He wears a white shirt with sleeves rolled to show muscular arms, and long trousers tucked inside tall black boots.

"Good evening," I say, and he's a blur of glinting brass in the dim light as he trains a pistol on me. I lift my arms with my palms forward, breathing raggedly. "I'm human and unarmed."

Anyone who can wield magic is never truly unarmed.

He hesitates before lowering his gun. "How did you make it past the doors?" His dark gaze with a hint of amber travels from the top of my head down to the filthy hem of my dress.

If he learns I used magic to break in, he might report me to the elders and then I'll be punished.

"The door was unlocked." I shrug. "I want to make sure my sister is alright."

His lips thin. "Your sister . . . ?"

"Irene."

He searches my face with renewed interest. Slowly, his brows unknot, his eyes lighting with recognition. "Ah, so you're the infamous Mia. I didn't know you were a librarian. Isn't it forbidden to use spells to barge into a restricted establishment?"

"I didn't—" I fight the urge to fidget, lifting my chin in the air. "I couldn't wait for someone to let me in . . . There's a beast outside."

He allows me to step closer and hums at my answer. Even though the uneasiness in my gut increases with every step I take, I push myself forward. He returns his weapon to the worn leather holster on his belt and studies the room. I doubt he can see the threads of magic snaking over the walls and floor or he would look more panicked than he does.

"Where is she?" I ask.

"She is . . . occupied."

The building trembles again, this time hard enough that I have to hold on to the nearest wall while it shakes and rolls.

"Take me to her."

The man crosses both arms over his chest at my command, lifting a brow.

I clear my throat and add, "Please."

"Look, darling, I don't allow random people near the machine, even if they are the sister of one of my scientists. Frankly, I don't have the time to protect you if the beast were to come in, nor escort you to a safe place. So stay—or leave. I don't care. One of the lower rooms will do until this shit blows over."

"I'm not leaving without making sure Irene is safe. So lead me to her or get out of my way." I keep my face neutral as he blinks at my tone and words.

I get the distinct impression no one speaks to this man with any sort of authority. Too bad I have to be the first one, and on such a night as tonight.

He glares at me. "So, what do you plan on doing if I take you to her, Mia? Use one of your parlor tricks to stop the beast?"

I take a deep breath, and the yellowed pages of the forbidden grimoire flash in my mind. A spell weaving in my thoughts as if I'm reading it for the first time. Sometimes, librarians' "parlor tricks" scare the citizens in Penumbra even more than the threat of beasts and fae. It makes us different—closer to what awaits outside the veil. A wolf hidden under a sheep's skin.

"Skylar, the beast is tearing the veil apart, and we've run out of energy—" A familiar voice has both of our heads snapping in her direction.

Irene's steps slow as her eyes meet mine from down the hall, and her brows wrinkle as she studies me. She wears brown trousers with a white shirt tucked into the high waistline. Is this their uniform?

Her hair is still as long as I remember it, black and styled to the side in a long braid. "Mia? What are you doing here?"

I walk past the man—Skylar—and reach for her hand, already feeling the pit in my stomach loosen. She's safe for now.

"She broke in," Skylar says, waving his hand in my direction.

"I suppose that's something she would do," Irene says, and her face falls.

I never expected a warm welcome from my sister. We are far from a loving duo, but still . . . "What are you saying?" I straighten where I stand and let the mask of indifference fall over my face. It's better than glaring at both of them like I want to.

"You're supposed to be the sensible one, Mia, but with every passing day, you become more reckless."

I stiffen as pain blooms in my chest. It takes extreme self-control to resist reaching for my amulet. I crave the calm it provides me. "I saw the beast heading this way and wanted to make sure you were alright . . ."

Irene's eyes soften, but the tightening in her lips warns me she's about to say something I won't like. "You shouldn't be out during the blood moon when a beast is on the prowl. Have you thought about what would happen to me if it hurt you?" She shakes her head, wiping her shiny forehead with her forearm. "You can't stop a beast so powerful with your trickery and illusions."

My cheeks warm and my gaze flashes back to Skylar, and to his growing smirk. Thankfully, my ire dampens whatever sadness lingers inside me.

"Can you blame me?" I whisper, hoping only she can hear. "We lost our father a year ago to a beast right outside."

The building shakes again, and the faint sound of screaming in the distance pierces the weird silence around us.

"That's hardly an excuse," Irene says as she glances apologetically at Skylar. "I'll get her into my room and be right back."

I pull away from her. "I can help you strengthen your wards to buy you enough time to leave this building before it collapses. That's why I came here."

"You think we would let the veil fall?" Skylar scoffs, already moving toward the screaming. "I keep telling the mayor the librarian program is useless, a waste of our city's resources. This proves my point."

Irene reaches for my arm again and tries to pull me in the other direction, but I don't move. I'm not hiding in a room waiting for the beast to take her away, even if she treats me like I'm a blight on her life.

"Mia, I can't deal with you right now. I won't let the beast tear down the veil or everyone will die," Irene says past tight lips. But then she pauses, looking at me with something akin to hope shining behind her eyes. "Unless . . . you can use one of those new spells you've been learning to stop it?"

Skylar freezes mid-stride and slowly turns to face me.

Oh. I shouldn't have told her about the grimoires when we met for dinner last month.

I take one long step away. "No."

"You can, can't you?" She shortens the distance between us, and her previously closed expression lights up. "You told me you were learning them to defend us in an emergency, Mia. This is it! I need you."

"No," I repeat, and my skin crawls under the cotton layers of my dress. It's true I'm learning from the forbidden texts in case I need a powerful enchantment to protect *her*. But somehow, this doesn't feel like my choice, more like being pressured to attack rather than defend.

"I can't use those spells out in the open, or to harm any living creature. Only in a self-defense situation. I never said I would attack a beast."

"You can wield such a spell?" Skylar drawls, suddenly back to where he'd been standing before.

Golden magic weaves around us, thicker now, and invisible to their eyes.

Panic grips me tighter, but I force my gaze away from the walls. "Even if I can, I won't. Not unless it's in self-defense."

"The beasts that took Father will be upon us tonight if you don't, Mia," Irene says, those big brown eyes I can't say no to wide. "The one flying above us is breaking our only defense against them. There's no extra energy we can tap to rebuild the veil. If he breaks it, it will stay broken until the blood moon passes."

I swallow and plead with her without words, but the walls of my resolve are crumbling brick by brick.

"The Wild Hunt is coming. Imagine all the families that will lose it all, like we did. These are people only *you* can help."

I shake my head, but I know deep inside, she already won. Hate now flows in my veins, even as memories of my father's smile, how it brought crinkles to the corners of his eyes, warm my insides. The morning before the beast took him from us, he'd promised me a game of scribbles that night. He was smart, like my sister, and also worked in this building.

The scientists protect the city, while I foolishly guard the ancient spells of long-forgotten races. My vision blurs, and I take a sharp breath to calm myself.

My job in this city is worthless, I've been worthless, but tonight I can be different . . .

"Doesn't Father deserve justice?" Irene reaches for my hand,

and I wipe rogue tears from my face with the other, still holding my amulet.

"Yes, he does." And there it is, the real reason I borrowed forbidden writings. I almost forgot it in my panic. He deserves my vengeance.

Tonight, I will break my vows and use a forbidden spell to stop him.

He won't see me coming.

CHAPTER 3

I FOLLOW IRENE AND SKYLAR THROUGH A MAZELIKE SERIES OF LONG corridors. My breath stutters out of me as I cross my arms to shield my body from the surrounding cold.

The building trembles once again, and I fear it'll collapse at any moment. What kind of magic does the beast possess to take down a magical structure like the veil?

Steam clouds my vision as we step inside the machine room. Based on everyone's sweaty faces, I expect it to be a furnace, but it's even colder than out in the streets.

There's a distinct ticking, like a clock, somewhere in the background.

Tick, tick, tick.

The team hustles around us, distracted by their own tasks. They wear similar clothing to my sister and Skylar, simple brown woolen trousers and white shirts. A few have masks over their faces, made of brass and aged leather.

I'm speechless. Not at their strange getups or the building so massive it could rival the library. But at the feeling of . . . death, lingering in this place.

Cold. Slimy. Unwelcome and wrong.

"The beast is gone." A woman's shout breaks through the loud hissing of steam. I can't place her with my limited vision of the crew, nor can I see the infamous machine.

"Maybe he gave up and is searching for a victim instead?" another person says, rushing out of the mist while their eyes scan the wooden crates next to me.

The steam thins, and now, I can see a pyramid made of bronze that looms over every inch of the room. Different-sized panels cover the entire geometric shape, along with gears that click a mechanical rhythm. Around it, walkways wide enough to fit a person wrap the pyramid's body, and a scientist tightens a tube caked in a viscous substance to the wall.

I blink and shift my gaze to another using a pulley to haul a sack of clinking metal parts over the side of the pyramid. This is not what I thought it would be.

I pause just before I step in a pool of liquid that's run off from a hose nearby, and wrinkle my nose at the dark color. Burgundy, maybe even purple, and smelling of rotten meat.

"Don't stop working to fix whatever that monster destroyed. We haven't seen the last of it. I fear it knows what we have here. I'm not sure how, but we have to stop it before it succeeds at ripping apart what's left of the veil. For our people," Skylar says from the entrance of the room. He tucks a strand of golden hair behind his ear, his dark brown eyes fix on me, and my stomach hollows.

He's speaking to me, maybe sensing I'm on the edge of backing away from this madness. His scrutiny is intense and makes me squirm. I reach for the hood of my cloak and pull it forward farther so it covers my face in its entirety.

A ray of light stutters and then shoots into the sky from the pyramid's point, blinding me as I look through the glass dome over us.

The hair of my arms stands on end, lifted by static. Then, the scent hits me like a wall of decay, burned hair, and alcohol.

I search the room for the source and find a man in a jumpsuit using leather straps to pull a dead person out of a bronze chamber connected to the pyramid. I stumble back and crash into a broad, warm body.

“Easy there,” Skylar whispers against my ear, his hands steadying my floundering steps. His touch is hot like coals on fire, and when I try to move out of his grasp, he tightens his hold.

I’m too distracted to ask him to release me. All I can focus on is the body’s gray skin pulling into the crevices between ribs and wrapping tightly over the thick bones of kneecaps.

“W-what are you doing here?” I gasp and shove him away as horror settles in the pit of my stomach. A bitter taste drenches my palate and my lips quiver.

“We’re protecting our people, which is more than I can say for you, librarian . . .” Skylar moves past me, gesturing at the body. A bald, ratlike face. Bone structure that’s more angular than a human. Its blank eyes stare at nothing, red irises hazed by death.

Not the corpse of a person, but a beast. Somehow, I don’t feel better about it.

“Mia, are you alright?” Irene says, with the same placating tone Mother used when we were upset as children. Whatever she’s trying to accomplish, it only disturbs me further.

Who could be okay with this? How can all these people be so casual around a dead being? I gag, in spite of my empty stomach, but calm my body before I’m sick over my only good pair of boots.

“Nevan, we have company. Get that thing out of sight.”

The man drops the dead beast from the leather strappings. He glances in our direction warily, wiping the sweat that drips from his bald head, before he rushes to pull out a large canvas sheet and drape it over the body. As if that makes everything better. I look away so I don't fixate on the dark spots already staining the fabric.

How many times have they done this, hidden a corpse from a visitor?

"I was upset the first time I saw a dead monster as well." Irene walks into my line of sight with a tentative smile. She mistakes my horror, and seems to believe it's at seeing a corpse.

Why is there a beast in the middle of town? Why were they keeping it in that chamber?

I cover my lips and wheeze.

"I assume this is the first time you've encountered a beast?" Skylar shoves his hands into his pockets and rocks from the balls of his feet to his heels and back. It's a carefree movement that doesn't match his calculating expression.

Of course it's not, though I'm usually safe inside my home when they break through the veil. My blood turns cold, and I shiver when my mind supplies me with the screech of the beasts as they hunt the streets.

"It's not that," Irene says. "Mia has a soft spot for animals . . ."

My hackles rise, and I'm not even sure why I'm feeling defensive. Both things can be true. I like animals, and I also believe in our survival. "They are predators, but so are we, and many other creatures out in the world."

I always wondered what goes on in this room, what the machine is like. But now that I'm here, the only thing I can focus on is the body abandoned in the corner, with a dirty tarp on top of it.

"The one that killed our father looked like that one." Irene's voice has me jumping where I stand. I glance back at her with growing unease. She would know as they were together when it happened. It's hard to forget my father's blood stained the sidewalk for weeks before I gathered enough courage to wash it away.

"I just— I can't believe you have a dead being here."

"Beast. Call it what it is. It helps. You're human and feel empathy. It's why it's shocking to see them dead for the first time. But remember, they aren't like us or even like other animals in the forest." Irene's voice trembles as she points in the direction of the forest outside, and the voices in the room grow quiet. "They're despicable and evil. They take us from our homes. Sometimes they gut us in the streets and don't even eat us."

"What are you doing with them? Does the mayor know what's happening here?"

"Of course she does. She funds our initiative, as it's the only thing keeping us safe from the Hunt," Skylar says. "To simplify it so you can understand, the machine gathers their core energy and uses it to keep the veil running."

I purse my lips to hold back an insult. I might not be a scientist, but I'm not an idiot, either. "So you use the beast's magic. I can understand how that works." Probably better than they can, for I can use magic when neither of them can.

It makes sense, and yet, I'm not fully buying the goodness of their intentions.

"Do they feel it?" I ask, because torture isn't something I could ever agree with, no matter how horrible the one receiving it is. "Are they alive when the machine is . . . using them?"

Irene opens her mouth, but Skylar beats her to it. "It takes their energy. Like the nectar from a flower, and we are the bees."

"You aren't answering my question."

"We aren't the animals here." Skylar's smile is pleasant enough. His straight teeth and handsome face have Irene under a spell. He straps a handheld crossbow the size of my two palms to his belt. The polished-redwood and aged-brass details on the handle stand in contrast to the black grease smeared on his fingertips.

I'm not sure I believe them, which is not good as I need confidence in them if I'm going to use magic against the powerful monster ripping our veil to shreds.

The building trembles again as the machine sputters. When the building shook before, I assumed it was the beast's doing. A scientist rushes to replace one vial with a new one. It's a long bottle, filled to the brim with a thick, glowing golden liquid that sloshes against the glass. As soon as it glides into place, the ray of light shooting from the top of the pyramid renews, bright and vigorous.

Even though I can't see it, I can feel the veil growing stronger. How often do the scientists go into the forest to hunt for beasts to feed this machine? Does the veil weaken every time they change bodies in the chamber, allowing a beast in? Or do the beasts break through regardless, like the flying one did earlier, but on a much smaller scale?

It's been a year since a beast crossed the veil—or so we've been told. I remember the night Father was killed like it happened yesterday. But how many truly cross every three months during the blood moon? That corpse isn't a year old.

"We are going to the west tower, so we are close, but hidden. When the monster comes back to attack the dome again, you can cast your spell to kill it."

"I won't do anything unless you answer my questions." I point toward the forgotten corpse in the corner. "Was it conscious? Had it hurt anyone before you captured it?"

"It's nothing you need to concern your pretty head with, darling." Skylar's voice is all politeness, but his flaring nostrils reveal a horrible temper. "We don't have time for this, but I promise after we're done, I will answer all your questions. Otherwise, how will the people of Penumbra feel when they find out you could have saved their children but instead allowed the veil to fall?"

It's official. I don't trust this man. His condescending words might be worse than the way he stares at me. “I don’t care about opinions. Librarians have our own set of laws to abide by. I’ve already said hurting the beast will break one of those laws. I was ready to do so if it meant saving Irene, but after what I’ve seen here . . . I require more of an explanation.”

“We follow the laws,” Skylar agrees, and a pit settles in my stomach at the wicked glint in his gaze. “Which is why I might need to report you to the head librarian. Using magic to break into the scientist quarters goes against your laws, too, doesn’t it?”

Even Irene stops breathing as we stare at each other in silence.

“Skylar . . .” Irene speaks, but stops when he raises a hand.

“The mayor and her council know we need the energy of a magical beast to maintain the veil. Their own essence repels them. We capture them during the blood moon, before they can take any of our citizens to be killed.” Skylar gestures to the corpse. “That one tried to take a six-year-old girl with it a few months ago. We barely made it in time to save the child.”

I turn to my sister, who nods, and the corners of her lips dip into a grimace. “It’s true, I was there.” She reaches for me, her small hand grasping my shoulder. “Do you remember that our father, who was a good man, helped create this machine?”

I can’t breathe as his face flashes in my mind. Then I remember how my fingers cracked open as I struggled to clean his blood from the concrete.

“If you help us, Mia, then you’re here with a formal invitation, which makes your previous . . . mishap a necessity for the greater good.”

I always defend the scientists to everyone who doubts their worth. My father was a scientist, and my sister still is. Yet here I am, refusing to help the only way I can when it truly matters. But my respect for their work only goes so far, especially now that Skylar’s laid this threat in front of me. Even if their intentions are for the good of the people, I’m being forced to perform. Or else.

"I won't kill the beast," I warn.

"It's alright, Mia. You just have to help us stop him from destroying the veil. That's all." Irene's smile eases some of my wariness.

Will I be able to cast a spell strong enough to put the beast to sleep? I hope so.

As the dead creature is being dragged away, its feet catch on a hose on the floor. The tarp slides and reveals part of its leg. Instead of the familiarity of a human foot, there are claws in its place.

It shouldn't matter that they aren't human, I should want to protect their lives regardless, but it matters tonight. I have to choose between them or us, and the choice is easy. "Alright, I'll do it."

Irene beams at me, and I wish I could match her enthusiasm.

"Great," Skylar says. "I brought you to the machine room, so you could see for yourself what goes on here. We aren't ashamed of what we do."

"For our father," Irene whispers to me, and I nod, the weight lifting from my chest.

Hate doesn't have a place in the life of those who wield the borrowed power of the grimoires. But knowledge sometimes breaks even our most deeply embedded promises. They took my father, who was kind and the rock in my world after my mother disappeared. He didn't deserve to go the way he did . . . and neither did the 120 other Penumbrians who've been taken by the beasts even with the veil's protection.

I'm ready for my revenge.

CHAPTER 4

Skylar and Irene take me to the west side of the building, and I clutch my amulet. The waves of magic lying dormant within the stone pull at something in my stomach.

We climb a spiral staircase, dozens of steps up into a narrow tower. My breath billows in front of my face as the air grows colder the farther up we go. The red light of the moon bathes the upper steps as we pass a tall, pointed window.

"Is the necklace a magical amulet or a lucky charm? You're holding it like a lifeline." Skylar looks back at me with a raised brow and focuses on my hand. And what's within it. "I thought only sorcerers used such objects to harness their magic."

He's far too interested, and it makes my skin crawl.

I grunt noncommittally and drop my gaze. I'm not feeling chatty, and I never show my amulet to anyone, let alone speak about it.

"It's a family heirloom and belonged to our grandmother." Irene tucks a long strand of black hair behind her ear, doing her best to match his grueling pace, but her heavy breathing gives away how tired she is. "Nanny was rumored to be one of the first librarians . . ."

I inhale sharply, and my blood flares hot, my cheeks heating. First, we never met our grandmother. Second . . . "Irene! That's my private business."

She glances back and looks almost apologetic, but still, I glare at her. Amulets are rare. Coveted. Mine is embedded with a beautiful gem that originated in the fae lands, far beyond the veil, where humans should never go.

My father gave it to me when I turned twenty and showed an affinity for wielding magic. A small amount. Nothing like the sorcerers I've read so much about, who could cast spells to end wars and who could fight the fae when they still walked this world. Their magic was the kind a person like me yearns for.

I can't create dragons out of fire, but I can light a few torches and candles, and tonight, I'll wield a forbidden ball of energy to stop the birdlike beast attacking our city.

"Calm down, I don't care about magic trinkets, much less a stone that'd be a paperweight for someone like me." Skylar waves his hand over his shoulder, dismissing me. He doesn't even look back this time, instead just exits through a wide archway and onto the upper landing.

I follow him onto the empty rooftop, which is surrounded by a four-foot-tall stone wall with a decorative pillar at each corner.

Irene stays behind, leaning on a rounded column of the open archway we came through. She clasps her hands in front of herself and pins me with her doe eyes. "I'm sorry. I know you hate when I talk about the necklace. But I don't understand all the little details that make it *extraordinary*." She puts air quotes around the last word, and my annoyance burns bright once again.

"Your non-apology is as refreshing as always," I say, not hiding the bite in my tone.

I allow myself to mourn the relationship Irene and I had when we were younger. We used to be best friends and always stuck together. We'd spend hours out on our rooftop counting stars, planning how one day we would leave Penumbra and explore the world. But all of that was before my magic wedged itself between us. Before she put this place first . . . and before Father died. Still, I'll never stop fighting to protect her, even if we aren't the same.

"You don't have to worry about us, Mia. Skylar is right. The necklace won't work for someone who has no magic—it wouldn't do anything."

She would know, she's stolen it from me many times before. She wanted to study it, to replicate the protection it provided me, to share it with everyone. If only it worked that way . . .

"I don't trust him. You can justify whatever you're doing down in that horrid room however you want, but you're killing beasts to use their magic. And my necklace is *not* a paperweight, no matter what he says," I hiss, not caring if Skylar hears me.

"So I keep hearing . . . You can save your lecture for a time when we don't have a beast flying over us. You came here to help me—help us—and that's what's important."

I nod and move toward the edge of the rooftop, where Skylar awaits. The bells ring loudly, echoing through the city at an alarming rate. I know he's out there, even if I can't see him prowling in the darkness.

My heart pounds as I take in the beauty of Penumbra at night. I know what Irene said is true, and there's no reason to fight about something so minuscule when a beast is here. I'm diverting my attention to something else because what I have to do feels wrong, even though I've been studying and preparing for months.

I inhale deeply to ease my heavy breathing and step closer to Skylar. He's loading his pistol and doesn't lift his gaze even as he says to me, "Before you ask, I intend to kill this beast today, whether you like it or not."

He lifts his gun and inspects it before aiming in the general direction of the dome where the ray of light shoots into the sky.

"Irene will hide over there." He points to one side of the tower where supply crates are piled high, covered in tarps. "And I'll be over there." He shifts his hand in the other direction, to the ornate spires and the flying buttresses that support the stone walls of the building. He'd have to walk across the tarnished copper rooftop if he wanted to actually hide from view.

"Once you cast your spell, run back inside the way we came and hide in any room down there. Don't come out unless we come to get you."

"I'm not leaving Irene here with the beast," I say. She's the reason I'm here. "Even if my spell fails, I'm not useless. In fact, I've trained to wield weapons for years."

I eye his gun and swallow thickly. I guess I never got a handle on how to use a gun.

"Darling, do as you're told," Skylar says, and his lips tilt into a smile that doesn't reach his eyes. I open my mouth to tell him what to do with his condescending words, but he continues on. "If you stay here, it will force me to defend you instead of subduing the beast. Irene is a decent shot, but I don't trust she can handle the beast on her own. Plus, if she's worried about your well-being, she'll be useless to me."

Irene takes a sharp breath, though she says nothing to defend herself, and it makes the flare of anger running through me burn hotter. I'm one breath away from walking out and facing my fifteen weeks in jail for breaking into this place.

I place my hands on my hips, tapping my foot on the stone floor, and match his glare. "For your information, I know how to cast more than one spell. I might save *you* instead."

We stare at each other, and his expression shifts from cool indifference to curiosity. "Is that so? Well, he's coming. Better be ready." He laughs, pointing to the sky. It's a blend of red and deep blue shades, and a black dot moves toward us.

My stomach sinks as I stumble toward the wall that marks the edge of the rooftop.

Up here, darkness shrouds us, and I know the beast hasn't seen me yet, for he flies toward the dome. Placing my hands on the cold stone and breathing deep, I center my focus on the pages of the grimoire.

The old, scripted sorcery flashes through my mind, my skin tingling as my amulet warms over my chest.

I open my eyes, and my heart lurches. The beast is flying so close, I can distinguish the long shapes of his black wings.

He extends one of his hands, and from his fingertips, a massive ray of golden power shoots out, swirling rapidly toward the veil. The beast's spell collides with it, and a wave of pressure blows the hood of my cloak back. It smells of something familiar, mixed with the bitterness of burning metal.

Lightning crackles around the beast's spell, and the veil flickers off and on, fluttering like a bird's heartbeat. The domed shape enhances the shrieks of the beasts in the forest, and while I can't see them, I know they're out there, waiting for it to break so they can feast on us.

The iron beams of the building's dome move with the onslaught, and an intense wind shatters some of the glass beneath it. Metal screeches as it scrapes against metal.

I stretch my arms wide, and my hands prickle as I recall the words of spells written in languages I don't know, reaching for the whispers the grimoire shared with me. My power doesn't come from my head or my heart. It comes from somewhere in my stomach, slowly pouring out as waves of magic circle my fingers. I close my eyes and ignore something exploding in the distance.

The alarms of the city grow louder, thundering in my ears.

I press my lips together and force myself to focus back on the memory of the pages of the forbidden book I read hours ago. The surrounding noises fall away.

The words of a great spell flash through my mind, and my skin heats. I've never used a forbidden spell out in the open. Especially one that feels like destruction—like this one does.

I remember the spell vividly, and I don't need to speak the words aloud. I simply focus on the sensations inside me, and magic surges around my wrists and arms.

I open my eyes again, and every inch of my body heats and burns, bringing tears to my cheeks. I direct my hands toward the beast and throw the attack across the rooftop. It's bright blue, opaque, and it crackles like electricity. It moves so fast, the beast doesn't have time to dodge out of the way.

He stumbles back with a flutter of wings that gets lost in the night, barely catching himself before he spirals down. He shifts his attention from the veil to me, breathing with difficulty, though what the spell did to him is . . . unclear. All I know is what I felt from the magic itself.

It was meant to consume all his energy. To drown him in a deep sleep. But the beast is awake. And angry.

"Run!" Irene shouts in the distance. And I want to, but I'm paralyzed, like I'm under a strange enchantment.

The beast charges at me. His golden power trailing him like fairy dust. Lead weighs my arms as I slowly lift them to grasp my necklace. A burst of furious energy rushes through me when I wrap my fingers around the red stone, vanishing whatever spell nearly froze me. I regain the function of my limbs little by little until I'm able to sprint toward the stairs.

A shot rings out, but I don't turn back. The air burns in my throat as I push my body to move faster and try to recall any other spells from the book. None come to mind as another shot echoes off the stone walls around me. The beating of his wings sends debris flying across the floor, and the warm air from his body sinks through the layers of my clothes. Tendrils of magic raise the hair on the back of my neck like static. I scream when the finger-like threads grip my shoulders, extending down my back, slowing me.

More shots, desperate now, but the beast is still behind me. He growls, and my blood turns to ice.

He doesn't sound like a normal beast—at least not any I've heard before.

I've never excelled at wielding fire, but it's the only spell that comes to mind. Ready to attack as the smoke dissipates, I turn around. He's close enough I can see his eyes, gleaming like they're made of liquid gold.

Every thought I had vanishes, and I'm left balancing on a precipice of emotions I can't place.

His face resembles a human, with pale skin framed by black hair that turns into feathers trailing down his neck, and growing longer over his broad shoulders and the expanse of his massive wings.

He reaches toward me, and the dim light catches the tips of his pointed claws.

Bang, bang.

When has a beast looked so human before? My subconscious mind knows the answer even before I can fully accept it. For I know deep within myself.

Something inside my chest tears free, leaving behind a hollow sensation that spreads like a disease, and magic freezes my movements.

Another shot booms, and this time, the bullet grazes his arm.

The beast flinches, glaring across the distance to where Irene is running toward us. I can't warn her off. He moves so fast it doesn't matter. A spell of his own bursts out of his hand as he points at my sister. So fast, I don't know if she can escape it.

I yell so loud it tears at my vocal cords until they give out. The beast is six feet away from me, like no bullet hurt him. He shows no pain, no remorse. Just red, unabashed anger.

His teeth are long and sharp as he snarls at me, his arms outstretched.

My energy is depleted and I can't cast another spell to defend myself. And I know one thing for certain.

He is going to kill me.

CHAPTER 5

The beast's magic wraps me in a cocoon. Like a bird of prey, he cuts through the air, reaching for me with the sharp talons that must serve for his hands. His arms coil around my body, and he plucks me from the rooftop as if I'm weightless.

"L-let me go!" My tongue feels thick from his magic, the words coming out slow and slurred.

Bullets cut through the sky, and the beast swoops over the edge of the building, his wings tucked close. We plummet through the air, hugging the outside wall.

I can barely breathe.

The cold bites my skin, leaving it numb, as the cobblestone gets closer and closer. I can't hold on to anything, but my muscles tense as I prepare for impact.

Fuck. I'm going to die on the same street my father did.

The beast spreads his wings, and my body jolts as we level out to soar through the air, only ten feet away from the road below.

"Stop screaming," he says sharply.

My heart lurches to my ears, and I stare at him, unblinking. Since when can beasts speak?

At the sound of his voice, something pulls in my gut, like a string wrapped around the center of my being, sending molten heat through my veins.

I would recognize the lingering notes of old parchment anywhere. Magic? It has to be, and it burns as much as it feels pleasant, like bathwater that's a little too hot.

I don't have the luxury of thinking about it beyond that, not when he is taking me away from Penumbra and the safety of the veil.

Does the high-pitched sound of my screams bother him? I test my tongue on the roof of my mouth. It feels normal and I may be able to form words again.

"What will you do if I don't stop? Are you going to eat me?" I ask, unable to hide the sarcasm in my tone.

He meets my glare, and everything around me quiets.

But I can't stop, not even if his magic has taken my limbs hostage. "We both know you're already planning on doing that, so I'll scream as much as I please—unless you let me go."

He tilts his head to the side and lifts a brow. "And if I let you go, little human, will you stop screaming?"

I nod, trying to not let my expression show the spark of hope blooming inside me. Perhaps this beast can be reasoned with.

"I enjoy making deals," he says, and his lips tilt into a slow, wicked smile. "If I let you go, and you don't scream, then you will be free."

Before I can ask him what he means, his arms uncoil from around my body and I drop. A scream rips past my lips, drowning out even the sound of air rushing past as I free-fall.

From the corner of my eye, I spot a blur of darkness trailed by gold. The beast cuts through the night as if he's made of nothing but shadows and scoops me up before I hit the ground.

Bile burns the back of my throat as I gasp for air. His scent is all around me, earthy, like pine needles and moss. And I hate that I don't hate it.

"You screamed the entire way," he declares before clicking his tongue, giving me a clear view of his sharp white teeth. His voice sends shivers down my spine. "Now be quiet."

I try to push him off. To speak. But every inch of my body is now completely frozen, again.

Shivering in his arms, I take in his features. From the feathers fanning out from the middle of his high cheekbones—iridescent black like spilled oil, stark against his pale skin—to the golden markings, like glowing tattoos, stretching from his eyes down to his jaw.

He flies faster toward the crack I saw him carve in the veil. From here, with the frigid wind burning my ears and the loud beating of his wings, I can't even hear the bells ringing in the distance.

The red glow of the blood moon shines over the treetops that are the home of the beasts. I've never left Penumbra, not even before the veil existed to protect us from them. Though admittedly, I remember little of my youth.

My stomach hardens as I focus back on his face, on his thick lips, trying to find the sharp teeth that will cut through me once we're clear of the veil. Is he going to devour me while I'm still alive? Beasts have done so to others before.

His canines are slightly elongated but hardly enough to truly tear through me. Perhaps he's planning to drop me from the sky, like he did before?

He glares at me sideways, surely called by my staring. My blood grows colder.

I turn away. My thoughts race as I study the sprawling city below. If I don't escape now, I'll die a horrible death out there like so many others have. But I can't move to hold on to the beast, much less fight him.

The library comes into view through the thick mist. Its spires stretch toward us. An ember of my power comes to life, simmering underneath my skin. I'm not a helpless damsel; I can wield flames and study magic in languages I don't know.

I can escape him.

Spells are simple, threads of magic woven together, and I've spent years studying them. If I push aside my fear, I could unmake the one paralyzing me.

Some magic threads are the glue that binds more powerful strands together, and that binding can make a weapon. The beast's spell can't be that different from what I've been training for.

I take a deep breath, ignoring his tightening grip on me. I want to live. And to go back to the library, to the grimoires that feel like home. Minutes separate me from my fate, and I must unravel his spell before he realizes I might know how to break free.

Chasing the magic threads takes much longer than I expected. At first, I feel their humming energy. Then, I chase the pull of his power and the warmth it offers.

When I open my eyes again, the tight threads of red-and-orange magic wrapped tightly around my body are visible to me. From here, the crack in the veil is massive. This beast must be extremely powerful if he could do that on his own.

The air shifts, and suddenly, we're crossing the city's edge, moving beyond the threshold and into another realm. A foul stench claws at my senses, the reek of decaying flesh clinging to my nostrils. The veil smells like death.

Nausea builds in my stomach as the forest greets us. The pine trees are eerily beautiful, unlike anything I've ever seen. The moonlight bathes everything with a touch of red, like the gods are bleeding over the treetops.

A thick white mist covers the ground, and I need to time my escape right if I'm to survive the fall.

My teeth chatter with the cold, calling his gaze back to me and sending a fresh wave of fear through my veins.

"Why are all humans so fragile?" He glowers at me. His lips—strangely human for something so otherworldly—thing slightly as we shift in the air toward the trees, catching the warmer air beneath.

Even in the freezing night, I feel the fire of my anger bloom in my chest once again. Fragile? Sure. And that probably means he considers me harmless as well.

The hum of my amulet reminds me with a small voice who I am. I close my eyes and reach for the threads of his spell. At first they zap me with an intensity I recoil from, and for once, I'm grateful he paralyzed my body so I can't physically react to the pain.

My skin tingles as my power seeps into my veins, loosening the beast's grip inch by inch. I hold my breath, fearing he'll feel my limbs twitch as I regain control.

"Where are you taking me?" I ask.

The beast looks at me like answering would be a waste of the air he breathes.

We descend through the night, the branches of ancient trees brushing under us. Our proximity to the ground makes my heart hammer with hope; it's now or never.

Summoning every ounce of my latent power, I conjure a fire spell from deep within, feeling the raw energy heat my palms as embers fly from my fingertips.

The beast's face snaps to my hands. "What are you—?"

I scream, knowing the sound will be unwelcome, and unleash my flames upon his chest. His brows arch as a strained noise escapes his lips and his arms shift around me, his long talons digging into my flesh.

The smell of singed feathers is strong, and I slam my elbow into his stomach. He curls forward with a gasp and releases me.

I twist in midair, extending my arms as I call forth gusts of wind to buffer my descent. My amulet glows bright red, warm to the touch.

The world spins in a dizzying kaleidoscope of green and black, leaves and twigs snapping around me with each wild turn of my body. Pain rips through me when the branches scratch and tear my clothes, and I grunt. With a bone-jarring thud, I crash into a massive branch that knocks the air from my lungs. It's wider than me, and its rough bark bites into my skin.

For a precious few seconds, I dangle above the ground, gasping for air and trying to quell the dryness that claws at my throat. Then, with trembling limbs, I climb down the tree's trunk, glancing to the sky where the beast searches for me.

CHAPTER 6

I drop to the ground from a low-hanging branch, and my legs collapse under my weight. The forest debris cushions my fall. The sleeves of my dress are tattered and torn, and the fabric sticks to the scrapes on my elbows.

I'm free.

I swipe at something wet dripping over my face, and pain pulses from the top of my cheekbone to my jaw. I wince and lift my hand to inspect my fingers, now drenched in red.

The cut is deep enough I may need stitches, and it could get infected unless I find a healer soon. Judging by how far the beast flew, it might take me a couple of days to walk back to the city.

Adrenaline pulses through me as I scramble to my feet. Everything hurts, from my face to my bruised ribs and sore legs. A branch cracks, and I turn where I stand as mist billows from my parted lips, but there's nothing but trees.

The forest canopy is so thick I can barely see the night sky above. Squinting in the darkness, I try to find anything that will guide me home. My father spent the last three years of his life teaching Irene and me how to navigate these woods. This—being kidnapped by a beast—was always a possibility we needed to know how to escape from.

While he had detailed maps of the area and took us out to study the stars, I've never set foot in the forest before. I couldn't climb out there to get a better view of the constellations.

And Father never accounted for a beast who could speak, let alone fly through the skies.

I have my amulet's magic, and while I'm drained from using it to escape, if I had to use it again, I could.

I stand still, trying to listen for something that might give me a clue of where I should go. The Dagen River cuts through the forest and provides water to Penumbra. I could follow it south and get back home. And if the flying beast can use my scent to find me, I should be able to lose his trail that way.

I reach for my necklace, and the stone pulses in my grasp. Its gentle humming warms my icy fingers.

Thump thump.

It glows with the same rhythm as my heartbeat.

I turn toward the distinct crunching of leaves, and my hair stands up as I feel something watching me. Crawling closer and hidden from view. Adrenaline dulls the ache in my body as I duck under a low-hanging branch and reach for the small dagger I strapped around my leg before I left the library.

My fingers are numb, but still, they tighten around the polished bone handle. I step forward and away from the noise, following the gentle pull of my amulet. Whatever is out there, lurking in the shadows, is waiting for the perfect moment to strike.

I keep my steps light over the wet, mushy ground. The longer I remain in the dark, the more my surroundings become clear to me. Something scurries right in front of me, and I barely hold back a scream. It looks like a small dog, but its weird spindly legs snap with jagged movements as it crawls over the ground like a spider.

I gasp, jumping back to get some distance from the beast in front of me. The red light of my amulet's stone buzzes brighter, illuminating my surroundings.

The beast has a long, slender snout with patchy black hair. I hold my dagger high with a trembling hand as its red eyes pin me down. With a snarl, it opens its enormous jaws, showing me rows of jagged teeth dripping with venom.

It could be worse. This isn't the biggest beast out here. I can handle him. I think those words again and again, but not even my inner voice sounds confident.

I take a backward step in the other direction, away, and hear a hiss from the side. And then another behind me. The hairs on my arms stand on end as I glance back to find another beast crawling from between tree trunks. They all look the same. I'm being hunted by a pack.

The beast in front of me takes one slow jerky step forward, and then it leaps. I duck, barely avoiding its snapping jaws. Sharp teeth rip through the layers of my cloak and graze the skin of my arm.

Pulling back with a cry, I kick at the beast's head as it bites my boot. My ankle twists at a weird angle, and pain ricochets through me. Spinning around, I bury my dagger in the head of one of the beasts. It collapses, dead, its black blood splattering my fingers.

Retrieving my blade from the bone takes all my strength, but it hardly matters when the third beast jumps from the shadows and bites into my arm. I scream and drop my dagger to the darkened ground.

The beast's rotten breath fans over my face as its sharp teeth dig deeper into my forearm, ripping through fabric and muscle. It smells like a decaying body, and bile rises in my throat. This is how I die. Devoured by animals—by monsters of nightmares.

I would've preferred the flying beast eat me than these creatures. At least he smelled nice. My delirious mind supplies the most useless information as I try to ignore my building despair.

No. I can't die wishing for another beast to eat me instead. I have surely gone mad. My eyes blur with tears, exhaustion, and fear. I don't know where one emotion begins and the other ends.

With my uninjured hand, I call for the fire spell to burn hotter. My skin blisters as the flames lick my fingers. The two small beasts that remain yelp, scurrying back into the shadows. Their muzzles ripple when they snarl at me.

I turn around and call off my spell. The amulet is scalding my chest, and I know without a doubt I have pushed it too far. I search for my blade in the darkness but can't find it under the layers of fallen leaves and sticks, and my sense of urgency is making my movements jerky.

A massive shape barrels into my side, knocking the wind from my lungs. I hit the ground hard, and my world spins over me. A new, much larger beast's fetid breath fans across my face.

"Get off me!" I snarl, and my magic scorches my veins, but nothing comes out of my hands. I'm bleeding so much, dark spots dance over my vision, though not so much that I can't take in the creature's form.

Its skin is gray like death, eyes hollow and milky with a white haze that barely obscures a red iris. It's bald, its face looks almost human, but it lacks lips and its teeth jut out of bleeding gums.

I lose my breath. This one is heavy, and with my wounded arm, I can't hold it off. I cry out, twisting my torso as I try to get away from underneath its armpit.

Its claws dig into my flesh, drawing lines of fire across my sides. Pain laces my scream, mingling with fury as I struggle beneath its weight.

I plead with the amulet to give me one last push, for magical objects like these—or the grimoires of the library—are living, with a power I don't fully understand. But it has dimmed, its magic spent the same as my strength. The creature recoils at something howling in the trees, a scream perhaps?

I can't tell. My ears are drumming with my pounding headache. Yet its grip doesn't falter as it drags me deeper into the forest, where not even the moonlight reaches.

"Help . . ." I force the word through my torn vocal cords. My plea is lost in the void.

Mist swirls around my ankles as I'm hauled through the underbrush, my mind racing with the tales of those who ventured into the forest and barely escaped with their lives.

Panic gnaws at me as I push off the ground, ignoring my injuries, and strike out at the beast with my fist. I'm sure it hurts me more than it, but losing my dagger and spending my magic left me without any other defense.

The creature snarls in pain but only tightens its grip on me.

A shadow descends from above so fast it's merely a blur until it crashes into the beast, forcing it to loosen its grasp on my leg. They intertwine in a mass of blackness, and I inch away, dragging myself over the ground, trying to put as much distance between them and me as humanly possible.

I need time to hide somewhere and recharge. I track the massive wings and black feathers, and I know who this is.

His magic is a storm of golden light that bathes the area with such intensity it burns my nostrils.

The winged beast from Penumbra glances over his shoulder and meets my gaze. His face twists with something I can't place, and now more than ever, he looks more beast than man. The spell he throws at the bald creature that attacked me erupts in a plume of yellow and black.

The creature disintegrates right in front of my eyes. Cell by cell, it becomes ash.

I raise my chin as the beast slowly straightens. His golden

markings flow thickly over his cheeks, like tears made of molten metal dripping to his chin.

He moves toward me with steps strangely fluid for a monster.

I press my back against a tree, and I know I can't escape him again. He is so large, with massive shoulders that narrow to a small waist. Feathers cover every inch of his body. From his chest to his feet—no, not feet, but claws.

He extends his hand, and his brows pinch in the middle as he studies me. "Come now, Monster, you have played enough." His voice is a low rumble that stirs something deep within me.

"Monster?" I echo. "Have you seen yourself in a mirror?"

"As a matter of fact, I haven't in a while." He tilts his head as he speaks. His gaze does not waver. "I don't have time to waste in this place. This is your last warning. Come willingly and save some of your dignity."

"Fuck you," I snarl, my hands trembling with both fury and exhaustion. I don't even feel pain anymore. "I will fight you until the end."

My words hang between us, charged with my promise and his steely resolve. I knew he would come for me even if I wasn't injured or tired. Beasts don't cease their hunt, not even after their prey gets away the first time.

"If you think I'll give you another opportunity to escape . . ." His voice is gravel wrapped in velvet, distorted somehow, different from how he sounded before. It's as if each syllable dragged itself from the depths of his throat, scraping past those elongated, razor-sharp teeth that gleam with his golden magic.

I recoil back into the tree. But the world blurs, and space folds around us as he closes the distance with unnatural speed. He is upon me before I can think of an incantation strong enough to paralyze him.

Not that I could, even if I had any energy left.

His arms—like iron shackles—wrap around me, sending a jolt

of pain through my body. I'm going to be sick, and I hope it would be all over him.

"Ah," he murmurs, almost to himself, the ferocity melting from his face to reveal something unreadable underneath. "You're hurt worse than I thought." His golden gaze flicks over my shoulder to where the ashes of the bald creature remain, a neat pile on rotting leaves.

Disbelief threads through my fatigued mind. Is he concerned? Impossible. And yet, I can't shake the odd feeling that this beast might not eat me tonight.

The sweet scent of pine envelops me as he kneels at my feet. How can all the other beasts feel like death, but he, in contrast, be so . . . alluring?

I despise it—despise him—for making me so powerless. With all the strength I can muster, I push against his chest, my hands sliding over the sleek texture of his velvet coat of plumage. "Don't touch me!" My voice comes out hoarse, but at least I sound defiant, not afraid.

The beast doesn't seem to hear, nor care about, my demands as he stands fluidly. He turns toward a sound in the distance, a clicking of jaws, and it's approaching.

Then he reaches for me and lifts a brow when I flinch. "More lunargyres are coming. Unless you want to be their dinner, I suggest you cooperate."

What the hell is a lunargyre? Is that what he calls the beasts?

The dry blood on my cheek cracks as I peel my lips over my teeth into a new snarl. "I would rather take my chances with the stupid beasts than you."

"That's enough now. You're mine, Monster, and no other beast will have you tonight," he says in a low, commanding tone. His words send a rush of warmth through my body I can't decipher, but whatever it is, it has no business being there.

Then he reaches for me so fast I don't have time to move away

—not in my current condition. His touch is as light as a moth's wing as he brushes one long finger across my forehead.

A sudden drowsiness cascades through me, heavy and irresistible. With laden lids, I glare at him, blinking slowly and trying to keep my eyes open, to resist whatever magic he used on me. When he lifts me from the ground, I can't fight him.

It's a similar spell to what he used back in Penumbra when he took me from the scientist quarters, but different.

"I don't want you to use your trickery on me again," he says, and surely, that apologetic look is only in my imagination.

He leaps gracefully onto one of the thickest branches overhead, and it groans under our weight. I clutch at his shoulders, hating how soft his feathers are under my hands.

"I'm not yours," I whisper, more to myself than him.

But he tilts his head and observes me in silence before jumping to another branch, and then another, until we break through the canopy to where the air is fresh.

"I tried to leave you behind tonight, after you burned me," he admits, not looking at me as he leaps into the sky.

"And w-what do you expect from me? A thank-you?" The spell is making me stutter. I narrow my gaze at him.

He smirks, and the expression transforms his features. It's almost like he's slowly losing some of the feathers on his face. "Why yes, a thank-you would be appreciated. After all, I put my life at risk to save you by entering the forest during the blood moon."

My lips part. "A-are you mad? Y-you are kidnapping me from my city, against my will!"

He shrugs and looks away. "Only after you tried to kill me."

True, but I'm not about to agree with him. "Because you were trying to take down the v-veil!"

And if the veil failed, Penumbra's citizens would be at the

mercy of the creatures that almost killed me tonight. Whatever guilt churned within me for shooting at this beast vanishes.

While he had saved me, it's also his fault I was in danger in the first place. He went into our city and tried to get innocents killed.

The pleasant expression on his face changes into something horrible. It matches my feelings exactly. I suspect this beast hates me as much as I do him.

When he looks at me again, the magic lulling me to sleep grows thick enough I can taste it on the back of my tongue. Blackberry and vanilla.

Fear courses through me, and my vision dulls at the edges.

"Go to sleep, Mia."

And then, darkness takes me.

CHAPTER 7

I'm not dead and it wasn't a dream. A beast of nightmares took me from my home.

My eyelids are heavy when I open them, like I've been asleep for days—months even. The only reason I know I'm alive is because every cell in my body fires with pain.

The surrounding room is dark, with tall ceilings and bleak wallpaper. My blurry vision does little to gather more details. I'm not in the forest anymore, but I'm far from home.

I hold in the groan that almost spills past my lips and shift my body over the soft surface I lie on. It smells smoky, like a campfire in the woods and fine tobacco.

Blinking rapidly, I take quick breaths in an attempt to ease the pain in my side. I'm keenly aware I should remain still—and quiet—to figure out where I am and why I'm alive.

There's something cold and wet running down the side of my torso and sticking to my dress. I don't think I've got it in me to check how bad my injury is, so I focus on everything but that.

Other than the sound of a crackling fire, I'm surrounded by silence. I tilt my head and find I'm lying on a tufted couch of forest-green velvet. In front of me, there's a massive fireplace crafted of black marble.

Wooden bookcases line most of the walls, and the scent of leather fills the room. A study, perhaps? No matter, at least the familiarity of books around me soothes my soul.

There are magical grimoires in this place, and they whisper to me. I struggle to find the threads of their power under the layers of my pain. Their voices are far from gentle. It's almost like these specific tomes don't want to speak with me but are disgruntled by everything around them. I reach for my amulet and . . . it's gone.

Did I drop it back in the forest? I grip the sofa and push myself up with shaking arms, searching the tile floor around me. The room begins to spin. Where did it go?

Loud steps come from outside the wooden doors, stopping me before I rise from where I sit. The doorknob twists, and I lie back down in the same position I was when I woke, doing a remarkable job at ignoring the pain shooting from my wounds.

The door cracks open, bringing in the frigid winter breeze. A spicy-fruity scent wafts in, reminding me of roses.

"You know what this means, Ash. She can't stay."

I shut my eyes right as I glimpse the beast's massive wings. They block what little light might seep in from the outside.

"I know." The beast's voice rumbles as their steps move inside. The door closes behind them, and the room grows warm again. "It's not like I had a choice."

My heartbeat thrashes in my ears, and my thoughts run wild. Who is the second voice, and why did the beast bring me to this place?

"You are perfectly capable of ignoring the pull of the blood moon. You've been doing it for a decade. What made it different this time?" the first voice says.

My lips tremble as the ache becomes too much to ignore. I put it away in a little box inside my mind, where it can't invade my every thought. I need to remain aware of what is happening if I'm to escape whatever fate the beast has planned for me.

"It's different because she attacked me with . . . peculiar magic." The beast's voice lowers at the end, like he isn't sure he should speak this aloud. Silence takes over the room, and my breath is loud as I wait for one of them to speak.

"I begged you not to go to that hellish town," the first voice says with a tone of resignation I can't understand. Why would he care whether the beast went anywhere? And who are they?

"Tell me, Finley, since you're so wise: What is going to happen if the sacrifices continue?"

Sacrifices? Could the beast be referring to what Skylar and Irene are doing in that tower? Is that why he targeted the building? Or is it something else? The silence extends long enough I almost give up my pretense of being unconscious and peek at them.

"Did you consider what will happen to the humans once their little shield comes down? The lunargyres will swarm that place."

"So be it."

My breath hitches. They stop speaking again, but this time the silence is broken by the rustle of fabric. A rug muffles the stomping of big, clawed feet as they close in on me.

Fuck. He must know about the scientists taking beasts.

I need to get back to Penumbra and let Irene know. Whether he knows that their magic powers the veil is unclear. But he's ready to condemn my city to make them stop.

I try my best to look like a good, unconscious prisoner. My amulet is nowhere near me. Without it, I can't cast spells. Sweat prickles the back of my skull.

"You can stop pretending, Mia. We know you're awake," the beast says.

I blink my eyes open, and his massive body casts a shadow over me. He must stand almost seven feet tall.

"How do you know my name?" I push my body against the back of the sofa and hiss as pain wakes down my side. My vision blurs again, and I bite on my lip to prevent myself from crying out.

I can't show him I'm weakened by my condition. It would make me easier prey. Perhaps he doesn't know I lost my necklace and I'm as defenseless as any unarmed human.

After all, magic is a rare gift, and very few can master it without an amulet.

The beast tilts his head, stepping closer to me until his knees touch the edge of the sofa. "The other woman on the rooftop called you by that name right before she shot me."

I meet his eyes, and warmth spreads through me. It's the same warmth I felt earlier when he broke through the veil. A sense of belonging.

I hate how my heart sputters at hearing my name from his lips, so I say, "Well, you don't get to call me that."

His gaze is bright, even as it narrows on me. It's then I notice he's wearing clothes, unlike earlier in the evening.

He shrugs. "I guess I enjoy calling you Monster. It suits you."

"I'm not a monster," I snarl, and anger blurs the edges of my pain. "You are."

A slow smile tilts his lips. It's cold and calculating and does nothing to ease the dread spreading through my body. "Did no one teach you manners, Little Monster?"

My lips part and close again. "You're the one calling me Monster—" I stop myself from continuing this useless argument and change tack. "Let me go."

He crosses his arms and looks amused as he says, "I don't think so."

Gods, I hate him.

"What is this place, and why did you bring me here?" Unsteadily, I start to stand, ignoring my wounds and fear. My vision darkens as I attempt to take in my surroundings, and shock surges in my chest as he catches me right before I fall face-first to the ground.

He's more gentle than I expect as he helps me settle back. "You're injured," he says coldly, like he can't believe he needs to remind me of the fact.

When our eyes meet, I feel the same pull in my gut as I did before.

He steps away from me like I burned him. "I tried to stop the bleeding, but healing magic is not my calling."

Heal me? Why would he want to heal me? Is this some sort of sick game? "If you're not going to eat me, then why am I here?"

"Are you that eager to be devoured?"

"No." My cheeks burn, and I know he doesn't mean it as anything carnal. I'm not even sure why my mind went there.

"Then be thankful I don't crave humans, Monster," he says, and his eyes glow a little brighter.

I jump at the sound of a male clearing his throat. Finley—if I remember correctly—walks from behind the beast's body and stops beside him, like they're old friends inspecting an injured animal.

"I'm sorry I scared you," Finley says with a small smile, "but while this conversation is riveting, we don't have time."

I gape at the newcomer; he's human. At least half a head shorter than the beast, Finley has a slender build and long, dark blond hair that falls in soft curls over his ears, blending almost seamlessly with the golden tone of his skin.

A conventionally attractive man. The kind of dangerous beauty Irene would fall head over heels for. Next to the massive winged beast, Finley looks like a harmless beacon of hope.

"She smells strongly of blood," he says to the beast and looks down at my body. Not in a predatory way, but a clinical one. "Let me heal her, and you can talk later. That's why you brought me here."

I try to catch the coppery scent of blood, but I can't move much, let alone smell whatever Finley is referring to. In the back of my mind, I know I should protest that it's not the beast who gets to decide whether I'm healed by a stranger or not.

But why would I stop them from saving me? It's the only way I'll be able to escape.

During my time in the library, I studied the art of healing in the old grimoires. My wounds must be deep enough to risk an infection, and if I'm to travel back to Penumbra by foot, I need all my strength.

Finley kneels in front of me, holding a small leather case full of potions and bandages. He reaches for me, and I push back and away from his touch.

My heart hammers in my chest, and my mind whirls with what-ifs. Why am I alive, about to be healed by a magical human?

"I will not hurt you, Mia. Quite the contrary. If I don't treat the lunargyre wounds, they will fester and you risk losing your arm."

His words have the desired effect, and I sit still as he rolls up the tatters of my dress's sleeves and begins cleaning the scrapes left behind by the beast's teeth.

I hold my breath when he presses the first cotton swab to the gashes on my skin. It burns like alcohol but has a strange reddish tint. Like the light of the blood moon spilling in through the lancet windows.

"You seem to be taking this well," Finley says, pointing at my bloodied arm. He is studying me like I'm a curiosity that needs to be unraveled.

"A cut to my skin is not new to me," I say, but don't elaborate. The scars on my body from my parents' training spring to mind. They started teaching Irene and me to wield swords and daggers as soon as we entered our teen years. A way to defend ourselves from the beasts—or any trouble that may come.

"The lunargyres' claws contain a poison that stops your blood from coagulating," Finley says, and his brows pinch in the middle as he throws me an apologetic look. "It makes it very hard for your body to heal itself before you bleed to death, or infection takes you."

"Great." I close my eyes and try to push the pain back, but tears still streak down my face and my breath shakes. It's hard not to scream as Finley scrapes deep into my wounds, wiping away anything that might remain from the creature's claws. "What's a lunargyre?"

Finley glances at the beast with a silent question that goes unanswered as he—Ash—walks over to a nearby bookshelf.

The Beast picks up a crystal bottle of amber liquid and pours some into a glass. Then he returns to the sofa where I sit. "A lunargyre is what we call the creatures affected by the sickness in this land." He trails off, staring into the distance. "Some lunargyres are rabid all the time, like the one that attacked you. Some are lucid, but lose their minds at night during the blood moon."

"But multiple beasts attacked me, not just one . . ."

"There are many types of beasts in the forest, and while I didn't see what came before, I can tell you the one I took care of was a lunargyre. Many are bald, with humanlike bodies and red eyes."

Like the one that killed my father. I swallow thickly, and the pain makes my throat shake. I won't cry in front of them, not from pain . . .

When I thought they were going to kill me, it was easy to ignore the little details. Like the fact that Ahs's wearing an elegant black coat, neatly embellished with golden thread. He's covered in black feathers of different sizes. And there is something magical about his eyes; even the darkness of his lashes appears deeper than the shadows of the room.

The beast looks a lot less like a lunargyre and more like something from old scriptures. Like an ancient being designed by the gods with a beautiful human face and a tragic story.

He doesn't meet my gaze as he extends the drink toward me. "This will help with the pain."

While a bit of liquid courage wouldn't be bad, I'm not about to drink a stranger's alcohol. Especially when these strangers are my enemies. I've sort of accepted this might be my last night in this world, but I will not die on their terms.

No. I'll be the most insufferable person they've ever met. I push the glass away. Our fingers graze, and a spark rushes up my arm.

Ash pulls his hand from me and glares, as if that was my doing. "What are you?"

"What do you mean?"

"Clearly, you're human," he says, gesturing at my body with detached interest, "but somehow you cast multiple fire spells and a shyene."

Am I supposed to know what he's talking about? "Shyene?"

"The spell you used back on that rooftop when you tried to kill me." He takes an exasperated breath, like I'm the most annoying thing he's ever met.

Mission accomplished.

"I wasn't trying to kill you," I say past gritted teeth, and direct my attention back to Finley as he pours a new potion over my arm. "I was trying to stop you from taking down the veil and killing hundreds of innocent people."

The potion fizzes over the cut, first tickling and then dulling the rest of the pain. Finley pauses, and he tilts his head back to meet Ash's gaze. They share a silent conversation, and I'm woman enough to admit I'm dying to know what this is all about.

"Those in Penumbra are hardly innocent," Ash says, and takes a sip of the drink I refused.

An ember of guilt kindles in my chest as I remember the

corpse the scientist dragged out of the machine. I shake it away. We have to do whatever we can in order to protect the ones we love. The children who are innocents, and the hardworking families who make our city beautiful.

Humans know the difference between right and wrong. Many have families, friends, and futures. The raging beasts that attacked me in the forest don't. They kill without mercy, like the one who disemboweled my father and left his body behind.

I refuse to feel guilty.

"I really need to know what you are, Monster," Ash says.

"Why would I tell you anything?" Heat bursts in my stomach at him calling me that damn name. I curl my lips back from my teeth and snarl. "You tried to destroy my home and haven't told me a single thing about where I am or what's happening."

"If I answer one of your questions, will you tell me what you are?"

A rush of adrenaline surges through me as I nod. I'm going to get an answer, and I have to ask him the right question . . .

"I brought you to my home in the Kingdom of Aphelion," Ash says, not waiting for me to speak.

"Wait, I didn't get to ask my question!"

"But you did. You asked me where I brought you, and I answered." His stupid side smile is back as he crosses his arms over his chest, swirling the drink in the glass he offered me before in lazy circles. Gods, I hate it.

"I asked before we agreed on anything. You know I would've asked a different question." I glare at him and then at Finley, who quietly wraps my arm with clean bandages.

This was a trick all along. A play on words to get what he wanted by giving me very little. But it's something. If we flew to Aphelion, it would have taken most of the night. The Orenda Forest lies between Penumbra and here. My breathing slows, and I feel myself sink into the sofa. It will take me weeks to get back home on foot.

My hopes dwindle faster than the fire in the fireplace. Aphelion . . . the Kingdom of the Fae. Or it was before all of them disappeared. I thought nothing remained of this place, but this room definitely feels like something. These aren't ruins, but a warm home with dark wallpaper and beautiful marble floors.

I blink rapidly and look at the beast, then at the floor, and back to his beautiful-yet-deadly face. Otherworldly. Is he fae? Even wearing a fancy coat, he can't hide his clawed feet or his massive stature. A body unlike anything depicted in the books I studied.

No, not fae.

Is he the reason the fae are gone, then? A demon, perhaps? Did he kill them and take their home—and kingdom—as a trophy?

"I'm waiting for your answer, Little Monster," he says. And his cocky grin widens, showing two sharp canines that turn my breath to ash in my throat.

Two can play his game. I was raised with a younger sibling; I know well how to play with words. "I'm a librarian," I say, matching his smile.

"A librarian?" His face falls, and he glances back at Finley, who shakes his head and mumbles something under his breath I can't decipher. "That's simply not enough. It's not the answer I seek."

"And yet, it's the one you get. Next time, ask a better question."

Finley chokes on a laugh and attempts to hide it with a cough. Not even the dull pain from my side can take this win away from me.

Two things I know for sure. First, the beast will not kill me . . . yet. He is healing me for some unknown reason. And second, he's interested in me because I can use magic. Which means I'm one wrong answer away from leading him to what gave me that power. The grimoires and my amulet.

I need to find my necklace so I can escape before I accidentally tell him what we have in Penumbra. Plus, I have to warn Irene there's a larger, smarter beast—one who might be a demon or even a fae—who knows what the scientists are doing.

Ash opens his lips to speak, and a guttural screech pierces the night, interrupting him. My blood turns to ice. I know that noise well. I've lived for years fearing the beasts that come to Penumbra every blood moon. Somewhere outside, the lunargyres are hunting.

A curse leaves Ash's lips, and he's already moving toward the door, finishing the amber liquid with one gulp.

His magic flares in a golden halo around his body as he pauses a moment before exiting. "See that she's healed, Finley, or the lunargyres will swarm the castle by morning."

Castle . . . So it's true. We are in the old fae realm, and my life just got a lot more complicated.

CHAPTER 8

I'm left alone with Finley, who cleans the wound in my torso with a gentleness I don't expect from someone who works for a beast. My cheeks burn, and I clutch at what remains of my dress as he cuts through my corset with sharp shears, slicing through the boning like it's butter.

"I'm sorry about this." His expression turns apologetic. "I'm sure this is uncomfortable for you, but we don't have a female healer in the castle."

"I'm fine." I'm not. "You healing me isn't the worst thing that's happened to me tonight."

I can barely breathe as he sutures my torn flesh, the pain making my toes curl back. I sweep my gaze around the room, trying to find something to distract me. Anything.

An enormous statue takes up most of a corner. A life-size female with dainty pointed ears protruding from waves of expertly sculpted hair. Her figure arches forward as if stuck in a dancer's pose. Her slender arms extend to the ground, her hands hovering over the tile floor. Two massive white wings tilt down, framing her back and hiding her face.

I glance to Finley, my vision blurring with unshed tears. Now that Ash is gone, I can feel how ill I've become. Whatever spell the beast used to help me must work better if he's near.

"That's a fine cloak you're wearing," Finley says, and his magic hums through me, dulling some of the pain as he pushes the curved needle through layers of my skin once again.

I've lost count of how many stitches I have, but I know it's more than fifteen. I blacked out for a moment before, and only recently woke again when he went through a particularly sore spot.

"Yes. But it's not good for this weather." I'm trying to remain awake. While Finley is helping me and doesn't seem like he wants to take advantage of my condition, I can't trust him.

"I noticed there's an emblem embroidered on the back. What's it for?"

"I won't give you the answer the beast wants, Finley."

He chuckles, shaking his head with an honest smile. "Am I that obvious?"

"Yes," I say, but can't help the small grin tugging at my lips.

His expression sharpens at my words, and then he inspects the red fabric draping over my legs and part of my torso. "So . . . in Penumbra, the librarians can use magic?"

"What makes you say that?"

"I'm guessing it's the emblem of the library you work at. There are traces of a spell woven into the fabric of your cloak, likely to protect you from the weather—even if poorly so."

My mouth falls open and my cheeks warm. "I put the spell on myself." I sigh with resignation. "I could never master that one . . ."

Alarms are ringing inside my ears. I never expected this man to put everything together so fast. After all, *librarian* is not a synonym for *magic user*. Only in Penumbra do we use the power of the old scriptures.

"If you say so," he says, but judging by his expression, he knows he hit a bullseye.

"Why are you helping the beast keep me here?"

Finley ties one last suture but remains quiet. I don't think he's going to say anything else.

"Did he also steal you away from your home?" I whisper, like the walls are listening.

"In a way . . ." Finley shakes his head, and amusement takes over the somberness that previously shone behind his features. Then he sobers. "I'm here because I must be. Because Ash is my best friend and my allegiance is to him."

I frown. His posture is stiff as he shoves his medical tools back into the case. Its worn leather creaks as he opens it wide and pulls out a large roll of cotton bandages.

"Am I wrong to assume you won't tell me why I'm still alive—or why I'm here?"

"You assume correctly," he says. "I should get you to your room before you freeze to death in this icebox."

"My room?" I take his offered hand, and he helps me stand like a newborn fawn, shaking and trying not to lose what remains of my supper. "Is that another word for dungeon?"

"You aren't a prisoner, Mia."

"What do you call being held against a person's will?"

"Fine." He sighs, rubbing the back of his neck. "But you aren't sleeping in the dungeons. Now, we should get going. The sun's almost out."

There's a slight shift to his tone. I wouldn't have noticed the hitch in his breath if the room wasn't so quiet.

"Finley," I plead. "I know Ash is your friend, but surely you can see this isn't right. Help me escape?"

I stood too fast and now everything spins around me. He steadies me by my elbows, and his touch is warm with a spike of magic that eases my vertigo. His brows scrunch in the middle as he looks at me with pity. I hate it, and I want to not like Finley, even though he's been kind to me.

"If I do, you'll die in the forest before midday. I can't help you get all the way home because you know too much. It'll take your people less time than you think to get here to try to kill Ash . . ."

My lips part as I try to come up with an argument, but the image of the beast in the machine takes my words away. I can't promise my people won't come. Not when Ash is so powerful he can destroy the veil. And honestly, I don't know why I should care.

"I won't tell them anything, I promise. I have magic and can protect myself."

Except I don't have my amulet, and without it, I'm nothing but a regular human. I press my hand to my stomach where the pressure of magic churns. Probably the remnants of something I took.

"Not during the blood moon," he says, leading me out of the study and into a wide, dark hall.

Windows line one side, with metal details swirling like vines and casting long shadows on the polished checkered floor. Our steps echo as we cross the space, and the chill of the winter morning seeps under the layers of my torn dress.

I hug myself, trying to bring some heat back into my shivering body. I've never experienced this kind of cold. It's like the kiss of death. I swallow and glance at the paintings lining the other wall. Dark hues of burgundy, forest green, and raw umber in a variety of still life of dying flowers.

"This is . . . cheery," I say, quickening my steps to catch up to Finley, who's left me behind. I don't want to be alone here. "So, why is Ash so interested in the spell I used, or that I can do magic?"

"Who says he is?" Finley opens the door at the end of the hall. Its black metal hinges screech, and dust rains on us as we cross the threshold into a big, circular room.

My mouth falls open as I take in my surroundings. From the wide staircase hugging the wall, its banister beautifully sculpted to depict nature. To pictures framed in gold lining the upper half of the walls, from the top landing to the high ceiling, and arranged around a massive window letting in the gentle light of the approaching morning.

It's not the grandness of this place that takes my breath away but the roses growing from every column, the vines climbing to the vaulted ceilings and covered with black blooms.

How can these flowers be alive in the middle of winter? When it's so cold? My body is stiff with it. I stop moving to inspect the black leaves and even darker petals.

Magic clings to the surface. Around every stem and spine. The sort of power I can feel deep in my bones. They call me to come closer. To touch.

"Those aren't regular roses," Finley says from the bottom of the steps. He's gripping the baluster with white knuckles, and he looks impatient. "Come on, Mia, I really need to get you into your room."

I nod and force myself to move. His urgency is odd, and likely not good for me.

"Why are we in such a rush?"

"Because there are times during the day that walking these halls is dangerous for us." He signals for me to walk in front of him, and blue magic swirls around his fingers.

"For us, humans?"

"Yes. Especially those of us with magic. Mages, sorcerers"—he pauses long enough that I turn back to look at him—"librarians . . . take your pick."

"The art of sorcery is dead, it doesn't exist anymore . . ." I whisper, and immediately press my hand to my parched lips, horrified the words made it out. I'm so tired—hurting and afraid. My filter is long gone.

I've spent the better part of the last five years of my life studying old grimoires written by sorcerers. Wishing I could wield my magic like they once did.

"In Penumbra, maybe. But out here in the world, our race is very much alive."

It takes us a long time, due to my slow pace, to climb three floors before Finley takes a turn down a new hall. I can't help but gawk at the roses as they grow thicker the farther up we go, fully covering old paintings and furniture. Their scent surrounds us as we walk a narrow corridor lined with doors but no windows.

The size of this place makes me numb in a way the cold hasn't. I'm not even sure how I could find my way out of here before someone found me.

"Is Ash the king of the beasts?" I ask, wanting to fill in the silence but not expecting an answer. Finley fishes a ring of skeleton keys out of his cloak's pocket, and uses one to unlock a door that's the same deep green as his clothes.

My palms sweat as my new prison cell comes into view. It's massive, with high ceilings and a large crystal chandelier hanging over the bed.

Finley strolls in, and the candles light in succession with a spike of his magic. Then, he turns to the fireplace in the corner, and swirls of green power burst out of his hand and toward the old, moldy wood lying there.

My arms hang limp on either side of my body as I follow him, taking in the grand space, bigger than the bottom floor of my townhouse.

"Why am I here? Why did Ash take me? At least tell me something before you lock me in."

He tugs at one of the velvet drapes with a lot more strength than closing a curtain would need. When he nods, I can breathe.

"Alright, Mia. I'm sure you know what the lunargyres do every blood moon."

How could I not?

"Well, like the lunargyres, the moon compels Ash to hunt for a human. Now, he usually ignores the call, but tonight, something was different."

"Because I used my magic on him?" I drag a finger over the dressing table, leaving a trail through the thick dust. No one has been in this room in ages. "So, is he the king?"

Finley stares but doesn't answer. Instead, he opens his healing case, fishes out three vials of a dark red potion, and places them on the table. "Take this later in the morning to help with pain. Someone will bring you food."

I take in the rest of the room and the plants in each corner. The roses aren't as massive as the ones in the halls, but they still reach the ceiling. There aren't many blooms here, just a couple—and while they're clearly a magical flower, I can't help but like them.

My eyes drop to the bed. I could try to escape as he leaves, but I know—like he does—that there's no way I could run all the way to Penumbra with my injuries.

"If anything happens, and I mean *anything*, there's a bell beside your bed. This is my wing, and my bedroom is not too far." Finley picks up his case from the ground and walks toward the door, turning before he steps out to say, "I don't know how much you know of the lunargyres, Mia, but tonight—and for the next three days—they will be active. Please, try to stay and rest. Escaping won't end well for you."

CHAPTER 9

I OPEN MY EYES TO THE WIDE CEILING ABOVE. GRAY LIGHT POURS through the windows and into my new prison, catching on every dusty surface and the cobwebs accumulated in the corners.

I thought this was all a terrible nightmare. After all, it wouldn't be the first time I dreamed of beasts falling from the sky. Of death . . .

My lips tremble, and it takes all my strength to not break down.

The mural on the ceiling depicts vines and dark-colored flowers wrapping around the gray stone beams. I blink again and my vision clears. It's not a painting, but roses, like the ones I saw earlier.

Something damp drags over the side of my arm, and warm air blooms over the wet spot. My gaze snaps down to meet four glowing amber eyes staring out from blackish-purple fur.

I slam into the cushioned headboard and scream so loud something in my throat tears. A horse— No, a wolf the size of a horse stands by my side. A beast on four legs, with two long bushy tails that swish through the air. Light swims around its body like twinkling fireflies.

I'm paralyzed. The bitter taste of fear coats my tongue. I follow the wolf's movements as it approaches me. Sniffs the blankets over my legs. Steps closer, pressing its heavy snout to my arm.

A cry leaves my parched lips, and adrenaline blurs the edges of my panic as I jump out to the other side of the bed, reaching for the dagger that I usually keep on my nightstand. Of course, it isn't there. This isn't my bedroom at home, and I dropped my weapon in the forest last night.

I grip at a candelabra that sits on the table and wave it in front of myself. "Stand back. I don't want to hurt you, but I—will." My voice cracks, and I don't know why I'm talking to the beast. It's not like it will listen to me, and if it's like the lunargyres in the forest, it wouldn't care even if it did.

But this wolf feels different somehow. Like something out of a textbook I've seen before, though I can't quite place it.

The wolf doesn't move, and its eyes follow me as I round the bed toward the door. Surely, after he cared for my wounds, Finley will come help me if he hears me scream?

"Finley, there is a beast in the room!"

The wolf tilts its head, blinking rapidly before sitting back on its hindquarters. It snorts in my direction, as if protesting my choice of words—as if it understood me.

I have gone mad.

We stare at each other, unblinking. My breathing slowly eases, and my arms relax in front of me. "Are you going to hurt me?"

The wolf huffs and lies down, placing its head on top of its two front paws as its curious eyes follow me.

I walk toward the windows. I can't hear Finley outside, and I can't stay here and wait for this wolf to change its mind and eat me. If what I suspect is true, and Ash plans to go back to Penumbra and finish what he started yesterday, I must get back.

Everyone in the city is in danger. Somehow, I know without a doubt that he will succeed next time.

Between the two windows, there's a polished wooden dressing table, caked with dust and topped with knickknacks that are of no use to me. I rummage through the contents of the first drawer. Slips, ribbons, and lacey things. I don't know whose room this was before, nor do I care.

The candelabra shakes in my hand, and I pull it close when I hear the wolf shift toward me.

I might be imagining things, but I swear the creature's eyes narrow at me. "I like wolves," I say, feeling crazier than before, "but you have four eyes. And I'm a prisoner here, so I can't just trust you."

The second drawer is full of the same things, and I shut it when I see an insect with a stinger crawling around inside. Good to know I won't be opening that drawer ever again.

I step to the window closest to the door. The handle doesn't move, and judging by the gentle vibration coming from it, a spell keeps it locked.

I groan again, holding my injured side as I walk around the dressing table and try the second window. Locked.

"I don't suppose you have magic and can help me open this thing," I say to the wolf.

Its ears perk up, and it raises its head. Mist lifts from its fur to crawl across the floor toward me. Panic renewed, I press my body against the wall, my breath hitching as my lungs freeze.

The wolf's magic doesn't reach for me, however. Instead, it wraps around the window lever, and the metal shrieks. My lips part as the wolf's aura darkens. Glowing dots of light twinkle around it, a living night sky right in front of me.

The glass shakes behind me, and I hear the handle screech as it turns. But I don't move a muscle. My eyes remain glued to the beast. I've lived my entire life in Penumbra, surrounded by humans, but through the grimoires I've learned about ancient beings. I've read about beasts with auras of night.

This wolf has to be one of the sacred spirits of the gods, brought to the lands of mortals by the fae eons ago and rumored to live among the royal fae.

My blood runs cold. Yesterday, I thought Ash might be fae. That perhaps he was cursed, since he acted so different from the lunargyres outside. But I brushed it off. It was easier to imagine him being a monster who took over the ruins and feasted on the old race.

But what if the fae hadn't disappeared? What if they were cursed and turned into beasts?

My mouth is so dry I can barely swallow. Ash is a beautiful beast. His face is a gift of symmetrical angles and a very straight nose. His eyes—ones I foolishly looked into—shine with ancient magic.

I press my fingers against the frigid window. The early winter air filters in through the opening, seeping through the layers of my borrowed dress.

Never look a fae in the eyes.

The wolf huffs again, and its purple tongue lolls out, its mouth twisting into something akin to a smile. The room smells musky, and the scent tickles something in the back of my mind. Familiar, yet strange.

Movement outside my window calls me. I reluctantly pull my eyes from the ancient wolf spirit and take in the massive rosebushes climbing the outside wall, thousands of black blooms standing in contrast to the shiny, deep green leaves.

My heart squeezes at the sight of it. No rose could climb this high unless it was aided by magic. I've stumbled on something bigger than myself, and I'm working against a powerful foe. I'm one bad decision away from getting eaten by beasts, or worse, being held prisoner for the rest of my life by a cursed fae.

If only I had my amulet, I could use a wind spell to get myself out of here. Fire to defend myself, like I did yesterday.

In the courtyard, broken pavers litter the ground. The overgrown trees have lost all their leaves, and a dried fountain rests in the middle.

Beyond that, there are buildings. A stable? Perhaps horses are still living there. I can't make it to Penumbra by myself with a cursed fae on my heels. I must be faster than he can run—or, as it happens, fly.

Making up my mind, I hoist myself onto the window ledge, hoping Finley won't come in. I'll run to the stables and get a horse before they catch me. Blood loss and pain have made me delusional, but how different is that from normal?

"Are you alright?" It's Finley's voice, and the door handle dips.

I reach for the rose cane. It's as thick as one of my thighs, and its thorns are sparse enough that I won't get pricked if I'm careful. The spirit lifts its head, wagging its tails hard enough they slap over the stone floor. The moment my fingertips brush the stem, energy surges from the plant through my arm and straight into my heart.

The blooms around the window turn from black to blood red. With a gasp, I pull my hand back, and the scent of magic wafts around me. It smells of old and new. Of dewdrops in the early morning.

The wolf whines and stands to its full height, looming over everything around me, eyes on the petals as they begin shifting color even inside my prison.

Then the spirit disappears in a puff of mist just as the door cracks open, and I meet Finley's eyes across the room. He's wearing an olive-green cloak and his hair is brushed back, revealing the sharp angles of his cheekbones and his rounded ears. He freezes, and panic etches his features. "Step down from the ledge, Mia."

I shake my head, swallowing deep as I take hold of the plant once again. Icy droplets of rain pad at my exposed skin, but with the adrenaline rushing through me, I can ignore their bite. "Ash thinks he owns me because I stared into his eyes. That's why I'm not dead, isn't it?"

Finley's face shifts from worry to understanding as he steps into the room. "Why don't you come inside and we can talk about it?"

"No, thank you. The elders in my city told me enough." I peel my lips back from my teeth and tighten my grip on the rose. My fingers are numb, and I should've grabbed a coat before climbing up here, but it's too late now.

I looked the king of the fae in the eyes, and now, I'm his human pet. A thing for him to torment and do with as he pleases.

"He will always find you. You're tethered to each other, and it's better if you remain here."

I can't wait a moment longer. This might be my only chance to escape, and Finley is stalling me with information he was unwilling to share last night. I ignore the sharp pain from my injuries and climb out the window, holding tightly to the climbing bush even as the wind blows my hair into my face.

My hand slips, and I struggle to find purchase on the rose vines. Energy drums under my palms, vibrating through me and igniting something beneath my skin.

Finley's hard-soled boots click over the floor as he rushes across the room, and his blond mop of hair peeks over the windowsill. I meet his eyes again.

"How did you open the window?"

"The spirit helped me," I say, seeing no reason to lie as I continue my descent.

Finley pauses, apparently lost in thought, and his brows pinch in the middle. Then, he moves to climb out after me but stops when he sees the first red rose. His eyes widen with horror as they move over the roses that have changed.

I was so caught up in my escape, I hadn't realized most of the blooms out here are now deep shades of blood red instead of black.

"Are you able to climb down to safety, or do you need help?"

My lips part as I struggle to find the right words. Why does he care—or better yet, why isn't he trying to stop me? These men are endlessly puzzling.

"Yes?"

"Fuck, Mia," he says, and I meet his gaze over the rose's stems. His face hardens with an emotion I can't place. "I have to go. If Naheli let you out, I hope she keeps you safe. You can't outrun Ash. He isn't human, and he's powerful, even now. Stay inside the castle. It's for your own good."

I show him my middle finger and continue making my way down, using the massive thorns to climb. Everything is slick with rain, and my wounds are screaming with the effort.

It feels like I've been holding on to this plant for years. Arms shaking with strain, I continue to move. My hands slip. I fall a few feet before just barely catching myself, and I manage to keep my grip on a longer stem. By some miracle, I don't even hurt myself on any of the thorns.

I spot a balcony to my left; I didn't see it before with the thickness of the foliage. Leaping onto it, I rush to hide under the roof and away from the weather. My teeth chatter as I try to rub some warmth back into my bones. Behind me, there are two locked doors. I consider shattering the glass and letting myself in that way, but the noise will call unwelcome attention to me.

I'll have to brave the climb.

Something shifts in the corner, and in the shadows cast by the massive columns that hold up the roof, mist forms the shape of the spirit, Naheli—is that what Finley called her?

The spirit sits unmoving, watching me. Just like before, she's not trying to eat me but studying me with a strange curiosity that makes the hairs on my arms stand up. I move to climb onto the rosebush again, and the moment I touch the plant, magic sings through me, similar to what I feel when I wear my amulet.

I don't have time to think about everything Finley said. If Ash can sense me, or if Finley went to get him, I can't stay here gawking at the red roses around me, wondering why they're turning.

A howl pierces the air. It sounds like a dozen souls crying all at once.

Gooseflesh breaks out over my skin, and my head snaps toward the wolf spirit, who's still howling to the sky like a siren. I don't know how I know, but I know she's calling *him*.

The king of the fae. I can't believe I foolishly tethered myself to him. I feel him before I see him. Dread settles in my stomach, and I turn just as Ash swoops down. In the gray daylight, he stands in contrast.

I narrow my gaze at the wolf and climb faster, and the thorns shift away from my stomach, avoiding pricking me. My heart drums as I slip again, but this time, I catch myself with less trouble. Fear doesn't register in my mind. I don't have time for that.

The beating of Ash's wings pushes cold air against my back.

The golden swirls of his aura shift around him like liquid metal, and I tighten my hold around the stem, willing myself to keep my grip.

"Where do you think you're going, Monster?"

CHAPTER 10

My chest caves in, and everything closes in around me. I shut my eyes and breathe around the feeling. Ash got me—again—and perhaps it was foolish to try to escape, but how else am I supposed to survive this? How can I warn my sister, the only person I have left, if I'm trapped here?

I hate feeling powerless. Finley told me the lunargyres would feast on me, but if I don't go back, they'll feast on Penumbra's citizens the minute Ash tears down the veil.

"Go away." My voice trembles as I speak, and I glare at him over my shoulder.

His wingbeats send my hair flying over my face. The scent of pine and frankincense mixes with the rose musk, and I grip the bush harder, pushing down my fear. And my body's reaction to him, which I refuse to acknowledge any more than I already have. His body heat sears my skin through the thin layer of my slip as he flies closer. A welcome reprieve from the icy wind.

"Do you know what you've done?" His voice is deep as his arms cage me into the rosebush. His breath against my neck raises gooseflesh across my skin.

My blood sings at his nearness, and I slam those feelings back behind a wall inside my mind. It's a flimsy wall that I must strengthen if I'm to survive this.

"I've done nothing but try to escape your crumbling castle," I snap, and even as the words leave my lips, I know that's not entirely true. My mind feeds me images of Finley's panicked expression when he noticed the roses were turning red.

I did something else, though not intentionally.

"How did you get out of your room, Monster?" Ash's grip tightens around my waist, and a pleasant heat radiates from every point he touches.

I turn toward Naheli; she sits on the balcony, in the same corner as before, and is looking at me like she's expecting me to follow his orders. The traitor . . . This is what I get for trusting anything that's tied to the beast behind me.

"Did she let you out?" Ash whispers, and I turn just as he glances at the wolf. His lips tighten. "Please tell me you have nothing to do with this, Naheli . . ."

The spirit whines and tilts her head in that cute way that got me to trust her, and Ash mutters something in another language. He doesn't sound happy. The wolf slowly vanishes into the shadows. Her eyes are the last thing to disappear, and they stare at me until they, too, are gone.

He wraps his arm tighter around me, and I hold on to the plant like my life depends on it, drinking in the soft pull of its magic. It feels like the roses are holding on to me as much as I'm holding them.

"Let go, Mia."

My traitorous heart stumbles over the velvet notes of his voice, and how my name sounds on his lips. Gods, what's happening to me? "What will you do if I don't?"

He places his other hand on the wall, next to my face, and all the blooms on that side wither to brown mush. Whatever warmth was inside my body dies as fear takes over.

This is better, right? Fearing the beast is a normal reaction. I gulp, fighting to swallow the thickness in my throat. "If you wanted me dead, you would have killed me already."

His lips thin, but his touch on my body remains gentle. "Perhaps I'll change my mind." His expression hardens. "You have a lot to lose, Monster. Let go of the plant."

"You don't scare me," I lie. I know baiting him is foolish, but he ignites the rebellious side of me I hate the most.

"I'm not playing this little game." Something rattles in his chest, deepening his voice. "I'll put you to sleep like I did in the forest."

I really don't want that. I don't want him to touch me, let alone lock me in that room. At least if I stay awake, I can ask him questions. Perhaps this time he'll tell me what he intends to do with me. Now that I know who he is, maybe I can bargain for more.

While I know little about the fae, I know they like to strike deals. Surely, I can get out of here for a price?

I let go, Ash twists me in his arms so he's cradling me like I'm his bride, and we fly away over the misty castle grounds.

The first lunargyre I spot is roaming through the courtyard like a ghost. Partially hidden by the fog and blending into the drab surroundings, it's almost invisible to my human eyes.

More clicking noises reach us in the open air. I can't tell if there are a couple of beasts roaming the space, or a dozen. If Naheli hadn't tattled on me, I would've died today. But why help me escape my room in the first place?

I hold on tightly to Ash's shoulders when he swoops under an archway that leads into a long hall held up by a sequence of rounded columns. Roses climb everywhere. Some blooms are still black, and others have shifted. The haunted beauty of this place takes my breath away.

"I don't have to tell you what would've happened if you had been successful, do I?" Ash says, turning his sharp gaze on me. "Do you enjoy constantly putting your life in danger?"

"Constantly?" I stare at him in disbelief. "You don't know me."

In the daylight, his beautiful fae features are so clear. His glowing eyes strip me down, and the bond we formed tugs on my stomach. I'm so fucked, and I know near nothing about how to unravel my ties with him.

"I don't need to know you to understand your character."

I open my lips to retort, but he continues speaking over me.

"You attacked me with a spell you could barely control. Then, you lit me on fire to escape *while we were in the air*. And today, you were almost a tasty treat for a lunargyre because you attempted to escape into a kingdom you know nothing about."

My cheeks heat. "I didn't see the beasts roaming the courtyard from the room's window." And honestly, I'm desperate.

"You're a menace to yourself—and to everyone here." His frown eases right before his plush lips tilt into a crooked smile. A beautiful disaster framed by a mixture of raven hair and feathers. "Perhaps that's what I should call you. Menace. Though I have to admit, I've grown fond of Monster. I think it suits you."

"You don't seem like someone who thinks too hard." I glare at him, ignoring the fluttering of my stomach at his widening grin. "Where is my amulet? I know you took it from me."

"And how would you know that?"

I don't. But what else could've happened to it? I press my lips tight and wield the only weapon he hasn't taken from me. Knowledge. "A fae king would recognize a magical artifact. It isn't a stretch to conclude that you took it."

It happens fast. His eyes widen with horror, and for the briefest moment, his arms loosen around me. A heartbeat and gravity pull me down. He catches me before I have time to scream, and I cling to his shoulders with all the strength left in my arms. If I'm pulling feathers from the back of his neck, he doesn't complain.

We glide through the air to the end of the hall where it spills into a round chamber surrounded by archways and the castle's overgrown gardens.

His throat bobs as he swallows. "How did you figure it out?"

"Like it's hard?" My voice echoes off the domed ceiling as Ash lowers us to the ground. The minute my feet hit the stone floor, my legs nearly buckle under my weight. "Return my necklace to me, I'll leave, and you won't have to worry about me messing with anything else in this castle . . . like what happened with the roses."

Studying me like he's seeing me for the first time, he uncoils his arms from around me. "If it were that easy, Monster, I would've done it already. But you knowing who I am changes nothing."

My body might miss his heat, but I'm glad for the space as I need it to regain a semblance of clarity. "Why not?"

"Because I'm bored, and you're a mystery I want to unravel." Anger rolls off him in waves. He eats up the small distance between us, and I have to steel my nerves to not cower. "Because you were foolish enough to unleash something in my castle this morning."

Curiosity swirls within me, and my mind urges me to step away from him. His canines are sharper—longer—than a human's, yet somehow, something tells me Ash won't hurt me.

Maybe he's right and I am reckless.

His breath hits my face. Fresh, like citrus and mint. I'm paralyzed by something grander, something I can't figure out. "You silly little human, stared right into my eyes and now you're mine."

"I'm not yours!" I hiss, pushing against his chest with all my strength. My fingers slide over his slick feathers, but he's an immovable object under my palms.

"Are you sure? Would you be willing to bet your life on it?" he asks, casting a shadow over me as his eyes settle on my lips. "Do you feel a pull toward me? Does your blood heat when you're near me?"

My heart sputters and I pull away, baring my teeth. Mist rolls through the open arches to either side of us. Thick enough, I can't even see the roses I know wrap around every column.

I open my lips to tell him I feel nothing of the sort, but my stomach rumbles instead. My cheeks warm as I shut my mouth and move away a few more steps, hating the way his lips curl in response.

One of his brows tilts up. "Are you hungry?"

"No." My stomach is so hollow, and it complains again at my response. So loud, I hear the silence that comes after.

I drape my arm over my torso, shielding myself from the cruelty I know is coming. I have heard so much about the fae. The malicious ways they play with and torture their humans. Perhaps any food he offers will make me go crazy.

A ghastly sound comes from my right, and then everything is a blur. A pale beast, the same shades of gray and white as our surroundings, leaps out of the mist. A long-clawed hand swipes toward me.

Muscular arms wrap around my stomach, and my gravity shifts as Ash pulls me into a cyclone of feathers and golden magic. His wings beat, and we glide across the hall toward a green door etched with gold. The lunargyre chases after us, growling as its nails click over the tile. A bald face with wrinkled skin, its white eyes rolling. Hundreds of razor-sharp teeth jut out from bleeding gums.

Not even with the power of Ash's wings can we get away fast

enough. The putrid scent of its breath blooms over my face, warm against my cheeks.

A scream echoes off the tall ceiling. It's me—I've been screaming the entire time, and my throat gives out as it tears. Ash pulls me behind his body so fast I stumble when my feet hit the ground. He lifts a hand toward the approaching monster, and translucent golden ribbons made of magic burst from his clawed fingers. Ash throws the lunargyre against a column. The sound of bones breaking and its screeches are all I hear.

"This is why you can't be out here." Ash's voice is deep. He tilts his face toward me, and something in his expression has gone dark. "Don't escape your chambers again, not unless you want to become their meal."

CHAPTER 11

"You're far too quiet . . ." Ash says, narrowing his gaze at me. "Why aren't you asking more questions?"

I'm too shaken by the encounter with the lunargyre to speak, let alone ask him anything. "Would you answer any if I did?"

"I suppose you've got to ask to find out."

I get the distinct impression this king is lonely. After all, we've been here for some time, and I haven't seen another living creature besides Naheli, Finley, and a bunch of raging monsters.

I follow Ash through the dark, serpentine hallways of the castle in complete silence. Thick velvet curtains keep away the gloomy morning daylight, and flickering light from melting candles illuminates the intricate paintings on the walls. Nature inspired but worn by age and the unforgiving traces of a spell.

Now that I have a vague idea of what's happening here, it's so obvious. Even this far from the gardens, rose canes climb over these walls. Perhaps Ash keeps the place dark so he can't see the blooms. I've yet to understand the correlation between the roses and the curse, but it can't be a coincidence.

Right now, I can barely seem to string two cohesive thoughts together. The fight has left me—at least for today. Had Ash not found me, I wouldn't have survived my escape, and that alone leaves a bitter taste on my tongue.

Not even the dull throbbing of my wounds is enough to bring me out of this stupor. I have never felt so utterly defenseless before. I guess I've never been in genuine danger either.

"Where is my necklace?"

"What a poor attempt at a question." An amused breath leaves his lips as he faces forward. "You know I'm never going to tell you."

Anger flares in my veins, and I fight my need to touch where the necklace usually rests against my skin, missing the warmth of the magic that always emanates from the stone.

The light from Ash's eyes illuminates the top of his sharp cheekbones. "What are you thinking, Little Monster?"

"I'm thinking: How can a brute beast, such as yourself, move so quietly on taloned feet?" Venom drips off each word as my lips thin over my teeth. I might not have his powerful magic, but I sure as hell won't make my company pleasant.

His expression hardens, and I count that as a petty victory in what was turning out to be a terrible day. Of course, I won't ever tell him he's also more graceful than anyone I've ever met.

"Now that's something I can answer," he says, failing to hide the annoyance tinting his tone. "I practiced. Perhaps you should follow my example, since you don't have the excuse of taloned feet to blame for your unrefined ways."

I whirl to face him, arms crossed. "What do you want from me? Why save me from the lunargyres when you clearly hate me? Why am I even in this castle? If you think I'm going to be a compliant pet for you, you can go to hell."

His steps slow. His eyes shimmer with delight. "I agree. You'd make a truly terrible pet. But why would you think I'd ever want that from you?"

“It’s what the fae do! You find it entertaining to hunt humans during your Wild Hunt, then you make us subservient to your wishes.”

“Do we?” He lifts a brow, and he’s all but laughing at me. “Go on, Monster, I find it amusing to learn about my kind’s history from a human.”

My cheeks warm, but I steel my spine against the urge to fidget under his intense scrutiny. “I looked into your eyes by accident, and you stole me from my home.”

We stand in front of a door painted the same green color as the one to my room. Ash reaches for the handle and pauses before opening it. “Did you also attack me by accident?”

I press my lips together, and the memories of the veil cracking under his power flash through my mind. Skylar demanded I stop the beast with my magic—something that was forbidden for me to use out in the open. “You were going to destroy the veil and kill hundreds—thousands—of people.”

“And how many of my people have yours killed?”

We stare at one another in a silence that extends for so long it makes my skin tighten. I open my mouth to answer but shut it without saying a thing. Doubting all I thought I knew. Like that the fae are gone, or the beasts are creatures of the Hunt, when they might be more.

If he is the cursed fae king, then the lunargyre might be his people. Gooseflesh chases across my skin. I remember the dead beast in the machine, and my stomach churns with nausea.

I study his features closely, trying to mask my horror, but I’m not sure I succeed. His jaw works, tight as he pushes the handle down to open the door. The metal hinges squeak, and a vast kitchen comes into view.

The pleasant smell of buttered rolls and roasted meat chases the traces of guilt-driven sickness out of me, and my thoughts narrow to the movement beyond the door’s threshold.

A beast stands in front of the burners. Spindly, long limbs catch the vast light spilling from windows on one side of the room. Pale arms covered by skin so thin I'm able to see the dark veins underneath. I hold still, my skin crawling as adrenaline pushes through my body, and I inch away. One step. I hold my breath. Then another.

"No need to run. Alaris won't hurt you," Ash says.

"But I thought all lunargyres are dangerous three days after the blood moon?"

"He hasn't turned rabid."

I blink in horror as the beast snaps his head toward me. His movements are choppy as he pauses in the middle of cutting an onion. Unlike the lunargyres outside, this beast's irises are hazel.

"You brought a visitor?" Alaris's voice is hollow and distant, and it sends chills down my spine. The lunargyre tosses his onions into a sizzling pan, then moves with uneven steps across the terracotta floors, slightly hunched over, and reaches for a spatula.

"Visitor?" I ask through thinning lips. "More like a prisoner."

"Prisoner doesn't have the same ring to it, though, does it?" Ash shrugs and strolls into the kitchen without a glance back. He pauses by Alaris, pats his bony shoulder, and continues on to a long wooden table at the end of the room. "I thought you were hungry?"

The smell of butter and pan-fried onions thickens around us, and my stomach growls loudly again. I'm too shocked to even feel embarrassed anymore. Alaris doesn't speak as I cross the room, nor does he attack me, but he stares with a thoughtful curiosity that wasn't there in the lunargyres I encountered before.

Ash awaits me, seated at the head of the table. He crosses one long leg over the other and leans back carelessly on a chair made of sturdy black wood. Though the furniture itself is large, his body makes it look small. He pops a piece of chocolate into his mouth and chews slowly while he watches me approach.

I eye the offerings in front of me with wariness. Glistening roasted meat, and a display of aged cheese and dried fruit. My mouth waters, and I peek at Alaris as he works on whatever is in the skillet with practiced ease.

Could I even eat something he made? I wrinkle my nose as I study his black veins, the baldness of his head, the long fingers that end in even longer nails. Alaris looks alarmingly like a naked mole, with the sharp teeth of a sea monster.

"If our food isn't to your liking, I can feed you stale bread and water to better suit your pet role," Ash says with more sharpness in his tone than he's used before, calling my attention back to him.

He's frowning at me, like my wariness of Alaris's cooking is the most offensive thing I've done so far. I shift uncomfortably where I stand, lifting my chin to stare him down through my eyelashes. "It's not that," I lie. "Are you trying to poison me?"

"Why would I save you to poison you half an hour later?" Ash is wearing an outfit similar to what he wore the night before. Black feathers cover his hands and poke out under his coat's lapels.

I shrug and take a seat. "Perhaps you'd like to see me suffer . . ."

"Don't give me ideas," he says, reaching for another piece of chocolate. "I guarantee you, your people aren't offering the lunargyres they capture a nice warm meal before they're killed."

Shame burns my cheeks. I know deep inside he's right. Even before I knew what I know now, it disturbed me what I found inside the machine room.

"Are you cursed? Is that why your people have turned into lunargyres that go into Penumbra when the fae used to ride the Wild Hunt?"

"Perceptive, and yes."

"Well, my people don't know about the curse, or that the lunargyres are fae . . ." I let my words trail off. My heart is beating so fast I feel lightheaded.

"Are you sure?" His eyes narrow, and I swallow deep as I watch him pile food on a plate before he slides it across the table toward me. "Do you think, in all these years, I haven't tried to reason with your mayor?"

I sit very straight, and whatever hunger I felt before is long gone. What was that my father used to tell me? The three rules I've been following ever since I became a librarian, ever since he gave me that stone.

Don't wander the streets after nightfall, especially during the blood moon.

Don't leave our home without my protective amulet.

Never look a fae in the eyes.

Did he know the beasts are fae?

Alaris pauses in front of the stove, blinking his bulging eyes slowly and taking in every word Ash says. After a moment, he places a large cast-iron pot over the orange flames and continues his task.

"We think you're all gone," I argue, quiet enough so only Ash can hear, and tear a chunk off the bread, eyeing the butter in front of me.

"Is that supposed to make it better? Should I look the other way and not destroy the veil because the citizens are ignorant? Let your people continue to kill mine?" Ash taps the wooden table. A smile twists his thick lips, but the gesture doesn't reach his eyes.

"N-no. What's happening is terrible. If you let me go, I'll talk to my sister. She's reasonable. She'll stop them from taking the lunargyres to feed the machine."

"Before the night we met, I never considered Penumbra anything I needed to worry about. It's far enough that the lunargyres shouldn't travel there." Glancing away, as if lost in thought, Ash takes a sip of his tea. "But someone was taking them—killing them—so I went to investigate and found the veil . . ."

"We have it to protect our people from yours. If you're able to put a stop to the lunargyres, then the veil will cease to be necessary," I say, and drop the bread onto my plate.

"If you believe that, then you are more naive than I thought."

I couldn't even argue with that. If the elders know the beasts are fae, but aren't discouraging the rumors of their race being dead, something's up.

"A beast killed my father in front of my sister a year ago, and it took a week for me to muster the courage to clean his blood and guts from the sidewalk," I say. "We aren't making up how the beasts kill us every blood moon."

"I don't deny that. But that doesn't mean the veil was created to protect your people from us. There is something they're protecting, but it's not your people."

The night we met, I got the impression Ash didn't think highly of humans. Of the people of Penumbra. At the time, I didn't understand why, but it makes sense now. I didn't know then that he was a cursed king of a failing kingdom whose subjects were being harvested by scientists.

I can understand where he's coming from, but that doesn't mean I'll sit here and eat buttery potatoes and wait for him to destroy my home.

My goal is still the same. I have to leave this place and warn the scientists he's coming. The kitchen door slams against the wall, and the pots hanging over the kitchen island shake with the force. Finley rushes in, and he's completely soaked, like he was just in a river.

His eyes shift nervously from me to Ash, and then across the room to where Alaris is drying his claws and limping away.

"Are the wards still standing?" Ash asks, and from the corner of my eye, I catch him placing a steaming sweet roll on my golden plate.

A ward? Like the ones the head librarian maintains around our building to protect the grimoires from thieves?

Our town attempted to use wards to repel the monsters—but we quickly learned wards didn't keep them from entering.

"Yes," Finley sighs, and sits next to me. He drags a hand over his dark blond hair, sending droplets of water falling to the table. His face is strained, exhausted. "There's a small tear on the west side. I patched it with the last yellow crystal. It should hold her back . . . for a time. But I'll have to leave for Hedrum in a few days to get supplies, just in case."

Hold her back? Is this a result of me touching the roses? Is that why Finley didn't chase after me? He had to inspect a possible faulty ward?

I bring the roll to my lips and chew slowly, unable to taste much as I process the new information. The town of Hedrum sounds familiar and pulls at a distant memory. Probably something I read in a grimoire.

"I'm sorry, Ash. Naheli let Mia out, and I wasn't prepared for that." Finley's grimace deepens, and his eyes flash to me.

Guilt churns in my stomach. How silly. I don't even know him or owe him anything—well, except for saving my life . . .

"Of course she did." Ash glances to the window where rain now pours down. His jaw tenses as he leans back in his seat. "That wolf has her own agenda."

"Is the crack related to me?" I ask before I can stop myself, and both their gazes fall on me. I fight the urge to squirm by reaching for my glass of water and taking a big gulp.

"I might answer that question if you tell me what you are."

"I already told you," I say, frowning. I'm thinking that whatever Ash believes I am is something else. Something I'm not. That must be why he's keeping me alive.

"A librarian?" Ash uncrosses his legs, looking at my barely touched food. I wonder if he's going to take it away now that I'm not giving him what he wants. "I'm older than you. A librarian keeps books. They don't cast magic the way you did."

"I had an amulet, which you took away."

"Where did you learn that spell?" He slowly stands, his body looming, casting a shadow across the table.

Finley stiffens by my side, and I tighten my hand around the butter knife. I know I can't do any true harm with something this dull, but I'll at least defend myself any way I can. "The amulet . . ."

"Stop!" Ash slams a hand down on the table, and all the dishes rattle. "An amulet can't teach you a fae spell that's been in my family for a century."

I feel the bite of food I swallowed come back as I shrink in my seat. "I don't know any fae spells."

"I recognize it because I wrote it." He lowers his face until his breath blooms across my cheeks.

The room spins around me, and I can't breathe. Remembering how I asked my necklace to let me into the forbidden area of the library. How many of those books should have been illegible to me? I didn't recognize the language, but I could still understand it.

"You call yourself a librarian because you are amongst books," he says, settling back. "And you read one of our stolen grimoires, didn't you?"

I raise my chin but don't say a word.

"The real reason the veil exists, Monster, is not to protect your people. It's hiding my stolen texts from me."

"That's a lie . . ." My voice cracks. Is he telling the truth?

No other grimoire I read outside that forbidden place had that same magic. None beckoned me like those did.

"Ash . . ." Finley begins, but quiets when Ash sends him a warning look.

I press my whole body into the chair. Trying to get away, even though there's something wrapped around my guts tethering me to him.

Ash's sharp teeth catch the light of the rainy day just as thunder rolls above us. And right now, he looks much less like the king of the fae and more like a monster.

He grips the armrest of my chair, and the wood groans under his strength. "So you see, Mia, you aren't a librarian. What you are is a thief."

CHAPTER 12

"Never look a fae in the eyes, Mia," my father whispered. "They will see it as a challenge and will never let you go."

"The fae are gone," I said with a laugh, watching him as he pulled something out of his pocket. He was acting strange that morning and waited for Irene to leave for work before he spoke with me.

A long necklace hung from his thick fingers. The red stone caught the light coming from the kitchen window.

I was told ever since I was little that the magical amulet had been in my mother's family for centuries. To be inherited by the firstborn. Me. Father had been wearing it for as long as I could remember, always keeping it hidden under his clothes.

He didn't need to say a word; I knew what he was trying to do. But giving me that necklace could put him in danger. He'd been working on perfecting the veil for years, and that meant going into the forest where the beasts hunted. I rarely ventured out of the library, let alone left Penumbra.

"Take it, pumpkin. I never meant to hold on to it for this long. It doesn't belong to me." A smile pulled on his lips, and the corners of his

eyes wrinkled with age. His hair was too white for someone as young as he, stress stealing his youth far too early.

"You need it more than me," I said, but presented my palm. When the amulet hit my skin, a jolt of electricity surged through me. With a hiss, I attempted to pull back, but my father held me in place with his other hand. Something crawled across my fingertips, tickled my palm, and stretched up my arm. Magic warmed my heart.

A shot of euphoria seized my lungs as the amulet tugged at something inside me and whispered a greeting.

"Now that you've begun your training as a librarian, you must carry this with you at all times." Once it was clear I wouldn't drop the amulet or try to stand, he placed a hand over mine, encouraging me to close my fist around the stone.

"I'm not supposed to have something this powerful inside the library. It's forbidden for humans to hide an amulet." I parroted what the head librarian, Alana, had told us in the initiation.

"To hell with them. This is not theirs to collect. It has been in your mother's family and, as the eldest daughter with magical affinity, it's yours. Protect yourself from the magic sleeping in those grimoires, Mia. Don't take it off or leave this house without it. And by the gods, don't let anyone see it."

Knock, knock.

"Dad, I forgot my keys!" Irene's voice came from the street.

We turned to the door, and Dad looked panicked as he took the pendant from my hand and draped it around my neck.

"Hide it from view at all times, Mia. Don't let anyone touch it, not even Irene."

Knock, knock.

I struggle to open my swollen eyes against the brightness of the candles burning around me. My head pounds with the migraine I've been fighting for a week, ever since Ash revealed the forbidden grimoires were his.

I spent the better part of my time locked inside this room, telling myself he lied. But under the webs of my rage, I know Ash was telling the truth.

Humans didn't write what's inside those grimoires. They are forbidden for a reason, and I sneaked in to study them instead of asking for permission, because I knew if I asked, they would deny me.

Knock, knock, knock.

I groan, wearily lifting my head to turn toward the majestic door across the room. "Go away, Finley, I already said I'm not hungry!" I shout with a voice roughened by my crying.

How can I leave this place to warn Irene of what's coming—of what we are doing—when I don't know what's right and wrong? When I can't fully trust what I've been taught.

"Oh, it's not Finley. It's Morgana." The voice coming from the other side of the door is feminine, marked by a light accent. "The king sent me to fit you with new clothes and help you run a bath."

I lift a brow and eye the tight-fitting dress I've been wearing since yesterday. I found it in the back of the dresser, and it's one size too small for me. I can't wear my librarian dress anymore, not after Finley cut it to treat my wounds. Plus, it's caked with dirt and blood. And my old slip is ripped and filthy after my failed escape attempt.

"I can run the bath myself," I say.

I hear the distinct sound of a heavy sigh and a body pressing against the door. "The king is quite upset you escaped a few days ago, and sent me to ensure your room is—safe. I can't leave until I come in and make sure all is well."

Does that mean Finley left for Hedrum already and won't be coming to check on me today? I guess the blood moon has passed now . . .

“I don’t think I can open the door.” Not without Naheli’s help.

“Oh no, that’s not how the spell works. It will allow you to open the door and let me in. It just won’t let you out.”

I sigh and roll out of the bed, tiptoeing my way over the frigid floor and across the room. When I touch the handle, it’s warm enough to give me pause, and I pull my hand away. A warning, perhaps?

Should I not open the door?

“Miss?” The female voice comes again.

Surely, Ash wouldn’t send anyone here to hurt me, right? He might hate me, but he’s saved my life multiple times.

“How do I know you’re here to help me?”

She laughs, and it’s so melodic, almost like chimes. “Alright, what can I do to prove His Majesty sent me?”

I press my back against the door and eye the red roses by my side. Waves of magic hug the stems, brightly colored. “I don’t know . . .”

There’s a pause, and then I hear the distinct shifting of fabric on the other side. Perhaps the sound of her dress? “His Majesty told me beasts destroyed your white dress in the forest. He said lunargyres out there hurt you, and that your boots have holes and need repairing.”

I look to the place I left my boots, right under the dressing table, and frown. Those are my best shoes. I open the door and find a female lunargyre standing on the other side. A bubble pushes me back, just like she said. She’s a lot less bald than any of the other beasts I’ve seen so far and greets me from across the threshold with a demure smile before dipping into a curtsy.

“You don’t have to do that.” I try to stop her, but she’s already straightened and is pushing into the room, holding a tray of food that smells just as delicious as Alaris’s kitchen. A black mask covers most of her face, and her wavy blond hair flows like a cascade of gold behind her back.

Morgana places the tray at the bottom of my bed. "I know the mask is strange," she says, dragging a finger along the edge of it. "But I'm afraid my face isn't what it used to be, and I don't want to frighten you."

Her eyes are brown with a trace of gold speckles. Not white or red. That settles some of my nerves.

"I really thought I was going to have to beg you to let me in." She chuckles, then eyes me from my filthy bare feet to the top of my messy hair. Her brows dip right before she points at the dressing table. "There should be a comb in there."

My cheeks warm as I close the door behind her and step toward the food. "There is, but I can't find a mirror anywhere." I can't fully place her expression with the mask hiding most of her features.

"Ah, yes. Of course. I'll try to bring one when I come back with your new dresses. It must be a lot for a human girl like yourself to take all of this in." As she speaks, she inspects the room with increasing curiosity. Her eyes fix on the climbing rose in the corner, now blooming bright red. "I've never been to this room before . . ."

It almost feels like she isn't talking to me, so instead of waiting in here, I go into the bathing chamber. It's almost the same size as the bedroom, with polished tiled floors arranged in a beautiful design of black-and-white marble.

On one wall there's the tub with aged-brass pipes jutting from the floor and ending with a curved spigot. It's the most lavish washroom I've ever been in, and not even the library has this much marble everywhere. Just thinking about that place makes my migraine return.

How many of my fellow librarians know we are holding stolen books?

"We have similar bathrooms in Penumbra. I can run it myself," I say, gesturing at the tub as I turn to face the cursed fae who just entered the room behind me. Her feet, like Ash's, are light enough I can barely hear them.

Morgana hums but makes herself busy, laying a couple of fluffy towels on a wooden stool and turning the water on, letting it run until it's steaming as it pours into the large pool-like tub.

"Are you here because Finley's gone?" I ask.

Her eyes widen. "I—uh—yes. He left before sunset. It's easier to travel the forest at twilight, in the morning or evening, since most of the mindless beasts are slumbering."

I stop breathing, glancing at the window to my right and over the treetops where the sky is neither dark nor bright.

"I shouldn't have said that." Morgana's face hardens as she dumps bathing salts and oils into the water, turning it milky with added minerals. The wonderful scent of it fills the room, like lavender and roses. "But please don't think of leaving. Plenty of beasts that live in the castle aren't affected by twilight. Myself included."

I nod and step into the water with my slip still on. Gods, I'm so filthy, and my sore muscles relax with the scalding heat of the bath.

When I arrived here, Finley seemed eager to get me inside my room. Ash left right before twilight—perhaps he was going to slumber. Maybe his magic faded at that time of the day and it made the wards weaker—easier to escape.

Was that why Finley wanted to get me in here? So the few beasts who remained awake wouldn't get to us?

"Is Hedrum far?" I change the subject, hoping Morgana doesn't get suspicious and run to tell Ash she gave me a clue of when I might escape without him being the wiser.

"A couple of days if the horses are healthy and the weather cooperates, a week at most," she says and beckons me to her. "Come, I have an affinity for making clothes, but I also love to work with hair. If you let me, I can sort out the knots."

After some consideration, I nod, scooting over the smooth surface of the bath and settling in one corner, where Morgana kneels and works on my hair. Her fingers end in sharp tips, which she uses to massage my scalp and work through the tangles.

I have four days, minimum, before Finley returns to the castle. I trace my fingers over the healing wound on my side and along the bumps of stitches that line the bottom of my ribs.

I suck in a breath, and Morgana pauses, craning her long neck over my shoulder. "Did I hurt you?"

"No, I'm sore, that's all."

The plan is already weaving together in my mind. If Ash is in fact sleeping at twilight, I can try to find my amulet then. Once I have it, I'll take some food from Alaris's kitchen, steal a horse, and leave this place.

But in a castle this big, how will I ever track it down? Perhaps I can start in the first place I was after I arrived. The study with the statue in the corner.

Morgana hums and pours warm water over my head with a ladle, again and again until none of the suds remain. "I've heard a whisper in the castle that the roses changed color when you touched them," she says, calling my attention back to her. Unease grows in my stomach, and she grabs the towel to hand to me. "Are you a sorceress?"

I laugh, shaking my head. "I don't have magic on my own like a sorcerer would. Just an affinity to wield magic lent to me by other things."

Morgana nods and turns around, giving me privacy to take off my wet slip, dry myself, and step into my new clean one. Then she spends the next ten minutes measuring every inch of my body. When she leaves, sunrise is peeking through the curtains.

CHAPTER 13

The day crawls to an end as the dull light of a stormy sunset signals the magical hour of my escape. I reach for the double doors and open them to the dark hall.

The enchantment is still in place, keeping me locked in this room. I hum and study the emptiness beyond. The rain ceased, but it remains cool and gloomy, even for this time of year.

Can I unravel this bubble of magic without my amulet?

Ever since he stole my necklace, I haven't felt magic—not unless I was touching one of those climbing roses. I freeze and slowly turn to the corner, where the creeping branches stretch over the wall and above the door.

Can I use the roses to harness magic?

I take a leaf and my heart booms in my ear. I feel its power fluttering like a bird's delicate heart, humming under my fingertips.

"I want to leave this room," I whisper.

The leaves move with a breeze I can't feel, then the first threads of power emerge from the stems and reach for me. It tells me it's dangerous, but slowly, it reveals the spell to me.

The bubble that keeps me inside is no longer invisible to my eyes.

I draw back, wheezing with the effort of unmaking the enchantment from where I stand in the corner, still holding the leaf between my fingers.

Free of the room and rushing down the halls, I keep my feet light over the rugs. My breathing is loud—too loud. I'll call all the slumbering beasts to me if I can't calm down.

I tighten my hold on the rose vine that guides me through the never-ending maze. The stems are at least an inch thick, and the thorns shift away from my touch, leaving behind small traces of magic. There is no time to obsess over something I can't understand. But the questions still swirl in my head.

Why?

Why could I escape my prison by asking this plant to help me?

Why are the roses turning red with my touch?

Why would an ancient spirit let me out when the result would weaken the wards around the castle?

The delicate petals of the rose shift from black to a bright crimson. The transition is smooth, leaving behind gentle trails of magic that appear light blue and yellow.

Closing my eyes, I force my thoughts back to my mother's pendant and focus on the safety it provides me, the familiarity of its weight, the power it allows me to wield.

The rose cane drums under my fingertips, guiding me forward. Through the web of tightly wound magical threads that wrap around the castle walls and the roses, I can feel the familiar beating of my artifact.

I'm getting closer.

And Morgana was right, the beasts are slumbering. This almost feels too easy.

I don't let go of the plant until the stems thin out and stop near the familiar study's door, where Finley stitched my wounds.

That night I didn't notice roses growing outside, which could mean they're expanding—or that I was too traumatized to notice them.

As I push the door open, and I expect something to pop out of the shadows to snatch me.

After making sure the room is truly empty, I step into its darkness, closing the door behind me. The sun is peeking out, and I have fifteen minutes at most. I rush to the desk. It's the most logical place to hide a magical necklace away and out of sight.

I fumble through the drawers, sifting through quill tips, old ink pots, and disheveled plumes. The amulet isn't here.

My heart hammers in my throat as I pull a new drawer open, my eyes flashing to the door, expecting the beast to come barreling in at any moment.

My mother's necklace hums at me—a warm energy in clear contrast to the chill of the morning. It's close, but I'm not used to tracking magic across a room in this way and can't place it clearly.

Shadows stretch through every inch of the study, and it looks so much darker than earlier in the week. I try to ignore the phantom ache in my ribs.

The air is heavy with the musk of old books and the distinct scent of pine that reminds me of Ash.

I yank open a second drawer and move its contents aside. Scrolls, leather ribbons, and a letter opener. My hand shakes as it hovers over the blade. I pick it up and slide it under the layers of my slip, right between my breasts.

The edges of my new weapon aren't sharp, but it's pointy.

I move to the other side of the desk and pause when the distinct sound of rock scraping rock pierces the dreary, silent space.

Jerking up, I inspect the study. It's empty.

Everything appears the same as when I entered . . . right?

"Naheli?" My voice trembles as I glance at the shadowed

corners, expecting the ancient spirit to morph out of one. Nothing happens. She's not here.

I'm going mad.

Yet every single hair on my body stands on end as I stare unblinkingly at the sculpture in the corner. Something *is* different. The beautiful fae is just as she was before, but there, behind the massive wings that cover her face, there's a soft red light highlighting her stone feathers. My mother's amulet.

But instead of relief, dread sinks into me, and I'm unable to move a muscle to cross the space to retrieve it.

The early evening moonlight rolls across the statue's surface.

I attempt to push aside the irrational fear inside me, and my natural instinct demanding that I run away. I take a step around the desk, and then, the sound of stone scraping again. A shiver races up my spine, and I stare in horror as the statue comes alive.

Her movements are impossible. They defy reality. As if she were flesh instead of marble, a beast unfurls before me. Her massive white wings stretch outwards, framing a body of haunting beauty and a face of nightmares.

I stumble back against the wall of books behind me, gasping as the creature takes a hesitant step forward, as if testing the weight of her body and the limits of her mobility.

In the center of her naked chest, the silver of my necklace shines against her pale skin. The stone glows red with the rhythm of my heartbeat.

Thump, thump, thump.

With a trembling hand, I pull my small blade out of my dress. Red irises that burn through the milkiness of her eyes follow my every move.

A snarl leaves her throat, lips parting to reveal rows of jagged teeth protruding from bleeding gums.

Perhaps she isn't rabid, like the beasts roaming the castle's courtyard. Perhaps . . . she's like Alaris in the kitchen, or like

Morgana. I'm frozen, unblinking, while fear rushes through my body.

She lunges across the room without warning. Her movements are eerily silent and too fast for a thing of her size.

I scream and bolt. The desk behind me splits under her weight as she crashes over its thick wood to slam against the bookcase to my right. It collapses on impact, wood splinters from the broken bookshelves raining down on us. Artifacts fall and shatter on the ground, and I jump over them. Leather-bound tomes hit my shoulders and head, no matter how much I try to duck on my way to the door.

The air shifts, warm and humid. The statue is far too close.

I reach with my empty hand for the handle, but a claw snags on the edge of my dress, yanking me back. I turn, barely keeping my balance, and swing my stolen letter opener at her face. She is undeterred and unharmed.

My eyes meet hers. Red is all I see right before she collides with me and my blade bounces off her smooth stone skin.

We tumble to the floor, and the adrenaline tingling through my body keeps me from fainting. I strike at her again and again. My knuckles split, and my blood stains her white face.

The scent of her sour breath fans over my cheeks, making my stomach churn.

I tighten my grip on the hard surface of her, fighting with all my strength to push her body off mine, but she doesn't move an inch. The pressure of stone pressing down against every soft part of my body is too much. The weight of her steals my air.

The lunargyre snaps her jaws at my hands and my face, and drool slides down my cheek, blending in with my tears.

Pain radiates from my old wound as stitches tear open and my muscles strain to keep her vicious teeth away from my face. I'm barely holding on.

This is how I die.

Something deep inside my stomach stirs as my amulet, hanging from her long neck, swings closer to my heart. Heat flows through my veins with a familiar magic. A power that surges, making my skin tight and hot. It claws at my insides, demanding to be unleashed.

A cry leaves my lips, and my elbows shake with tension. Confusion clouds my panicked thoughts. I don't understand where the pressure in my stomach originates from. The depths of my gut? Or is it from the amulet hanging so close, though still out of reach?

The power lurks hotter inside my body, but I can't wield it—not unless I can snatch my stone from her.

"Nera!" A deep male voice booms from the hall outside, and the door blows open a second later.

A tempest of gold ink and black mist bursts into the room just before Ash's body collides with the white-marble beast, sending them both tumbling to the ground and away from me. A pile of feathered wings tangles in a whirlwind of snarls and claws.

They move too fast for me to follow as I crawl back until my back hits whatever's left of the bookcase behind me and then scramble to my feet, all without tearing my eyes from the beasts.

I should leave now. I only have minutes at most before one of them is dead and the other hunts me down.

With bated breath, I do my best to track Ash's maneuvers. A blur of flowing, intricate movements as he avoids the marble beast's attacks with impressive precision.

He weaves around her lunges, his own strikes aimed to slow her down but not kill. I press my lips together and edge along the wall toward the door. My heart drums in my ears.

What if I leave and he dies while saving me? It's his fault I'm here—and I hate him. I shift toward the door with more purpose, but my muscles clamp down, refusing to move.

I don't care. But the words don't sound true, even in my head.

"Stop." His breathy voice echoes in the room, breaking through the loud growling of the white beast. My feet obey, even though I'm not sure if he's talking to me or her. What did he call her? Nera?

Each time Ash's fists connect with the marble beast's body, a harsh clack reverberates in the chamber, mixing with the rasp of his labored breathing. I look through the rubbish on the ground around me, trying to find something to use as a weapon to help him. Ash isn't using his magic like he did with the other beasts. He seems slower. Like he isn't giving this fight his all. Like . . . he doesn't want to hurt her.

Ash tackles her to the ground, drawing my eyes even as I crouch and pull at one of the desk's legs. The wood groans as I yank and twist to remove it from the fragments of the old desk. It's heavy, and just what I need.

Ash hisses in pain and grips the beast by the shoulders, pushing her away from his body as she continues to struggle inside the cage of his arms.

"Fuck, Nera. Come back to me." His voice holds an edge of panic as the lunargyre snarls at him. She's rabid. Whatever he's trying to see in her face is gone.

The white beast pushes him back, tearing one of her hands from him, and her sculpted wings unfurl, even crushed under both her weight and his. She lets out a bone chilling screech before her already-sharp claws elongate slowly.

Even in the dim light, her red irises burn bright with hate. She pushes him off, and leaps onto him with the same speed as before, but now golden magic trails her movements, so similar to Ash's that I'm taken aback.

A guttural roar tears from Ash's throat when her pointed nails dig into his chest, piercing past black feathers and coming out bright gold.

Blood?

A scream shakes the room, louder than theirs combined. It takes me a moment to realize it's me. I'm the one who's screaming. I don't pause to analyze why my skin feels cold and clammy. Why my mind detaches from my body as I jump over the fallen desk, carrying the desk's leg like it weighs nothing. Why I swing it at the white beast, power singing through my veins. Why I can't see anything in the moment before it makes contact with her face, before she even looks at me.

Crack.

My weapon hits her chin, hard, and her eyes roll to the back of her head. The stone in my necklace shines brightly against her skin. Glowing faster and faster, matching her heartbeats—or my own. I can't be sure.

Swirls of my power wrap around her like ropes right before she hits the ground.

My vision sharpens on Ash as he clutches his chest and gasps for air.

I let the shattered wooden leg fall to the ground. He's staring up at me from the floor with those beautiful pools of gold he has for eyes.

I kneel by him, pressing my hand tightly over his, staving off the flow of blood that stains his pale fingers. Pale, because right now they aren't covered by feathers or claws.

I don't know why I'm so scared. "Tell me what to do."

He swallows and slowly sits up, groaning in pain. His lips have turned a pale shade of mauve, and he looks sickly, unlike the days before. He stares over my shoulder, where the white beast lies, still struggling with the magical bindings that I put around her.

"Go to my—room. Mia." He points to the door with gold-stained fingers. I never knew the fae bleed gold. "It's not safe here."

I open my lips to tell him I won't be leaving him here to get carved up by that beast. His words register in my mind, and the whys become heavier.

Too many questions, and too few answers.

I clear my throat but keep my distance from him. "She has my amulet," I say, glancing at the white beast pointedly.

Ash stills. "Ah—you tied her down?"

I shrug, because frankly I don't know what the fuck I did, but I won't let him know that. "You need help. Perhaps Finley can—"

"He's not here." His throat bobs and he moves to stand.

I knew Finley isn't here, and was wondering where he keeps his medical supplies, but I couldn't tell Ash how I learned that without getting Morgana in trouble.

Ash's brows wrinkle and he glares at me, like I'm the one who tore a hole through his chest, not the one to save him.

"My office is destroyed." He waves at the surrounding mess. "You shouldn't have left your room, Monster."

Ungrateful bastard.

"A thank-you for saving your life would suffice . . ." I snarl, crossing my arms. How stupid would it be to get my necklace now? I could leave while he's injured, but then again, whatever magic my amulet has, it's what's holding the dangerous lunargyre to the ground.

Ash is silent, and just when I think he won't say a thing, he whispers, "Thank you."

My heart rate doubles in speed when I meet his gaze. Now that the adrenaline pumping through my veins is gone, and the impending doom of a beast killing us has passed, I notice what he's wearing.

A loose white shirt with puffed sleeves that gather around his wrists. He clutches his shoulder, and blood stains the fabric, spilling way too fast for comfort. Ash flicks his wings, as if he's testing that he can still move them. Then he takes a tentative step toward the white beast.

"It's not safe here right now. Go to my room. The beasts won't enter. It's the first door to the left. Wait for me there." As he steps away, he leaves a trail of blood behind him.

And I shouldn't care. If he dies, it will set me free of whatever has tethered me to him. I should celebrate on my way out of here.

I stare at the torn fabric where his shoulder meets the wide planes of his muscular chest, and I know I can't. He's hurt because of *me*.

"You're losing a lot of blood," I say. "Do you need me to do anything?"

Being a librarian in Penumbra means dealing with magical books, which sometimes leads to accidental injuries. Basic healing skills are part of the coursework and some of the first lessons we go through.

Ash's pale lips quirk into a half smile. His eyes dance with amusement. "Are you worried about me, Monster? It takes more than this to kill me." I can see the clear pain in his features, even as he turns away from me and back to the white statue. He's wearing black trousers that skim his toned legs, and his bare feet leave bloodied footprints over the polished marble floors. Feet, *not* talons.

Perhaps he isn't as injured as I thought.

"Is that statue spelled to protect your office? Because that seems a bit excessive if it hurts you as well . . ."

"She isn't spelled by me." There is clear annoyance in his tone, but I'm not sure whether it's directed at me or someone else.

"Is she a lunargyre?" Her eyes are red. I shiver as I follow him when he kneels beside the beast. "But I thought they were bald and only went feral during the blood moon?"

"Not all lunargyres look the same, or hold the same patterns. Some snap back into a more coherent state during the day, even during the three days of the blood moon—"

"Like Alaris?"

He nods. "Alaris usually comes to his senses during the day, though nothing is guaranteed."

"But there are others who remain feral?"

"Yes." His hand shakes as he touches the white statue's stone cheek. A careful, loving gesture. "You almost became breakfast for one of them the other day."

Oh, I remember that too well. "What about her?"

"She's been stuck in a slumbering state for weeks now, since days before the blood moon arrived."

There's so much sorrow in his inflection that I hold my breath and swallow my other questions. Was this beast a lover? A friend? A sister?

"Why did you leave your room?"

I could say I knew about twilight, and that I was determined to escape him. That I thought the halls would be safer somehow, now that the blood moon is gone. But instead, I remain quiet.

His gold eyes pin me down. He looks far too pale and so unlike the strong fae from before. "A week ago, you talked about saving the people you love back in that dumpy city of yours. How are you going to save your sister from me if you're dead?"

The lunargyre blinks rapidly, her milky irises slowly transitioning from red to a bright rose gold. They shine with the same unnatural intensity as his. "Ash?" The voice coming from her lips is sweet, and it quakes with panic. "Did I—hurt you?"

CHAPTER 14

A beast's screech echoes from the hall outside the office. It's not too close yet, I hope, but the sound alone sends a rush of adrenaline through my veins all the same.

Ash is losing blood too quickly, and he must realize it because he allows me to unravel the spell binding the white beast to the ground.

"I must have gone mad," I mutter under my breath, extending my fingers over the glowing stone of my mother's necklace, pulling at the threads of magic like I have been for the last ten minutes.

They both ignore me, something they're quite good at doing. Ash leans against the backrest of a green couch. He is too quiet, and that alone is unsettling.

"Do you even know what kind of magic you used, or do you make a habit of doing things you don't understand?" Nera glares at me as she struggles briefly with the tightening ropes of light, though they keep her from moving much.

I press my lips tight and try to smother the guilt churning through me by welcoming the healthy dose of annoyance that replaces it. "Had I not done it, you would've killed your brother."

I know they're siblings with a certainty I don't have about anything else right now. And while neither of them told me so, being this close to Nera allows me to see the similarities in their features, especially now that she isn't trying to kill me.

They have the same proud mouth, a thick lower lip, and elegant brows. Their eyes are enormous and equally breathtaking, with a metallic shine that makes them each feel like a piece of prized jewelry.

"I wasn't going to kill him . . ." She sounds defensive but unsure. Her eyes cut to Ash, whose face tilts to the ceiling as he breathes slowly. I try to ignore the pool of blood staining the elegant green velvet of the seat.

"Perhaps next time, don't steal other people's belongings, and you won't be under such a spell." I glance down at my mother's amulet, which still rests on Nera's chest.

No matter how many times Ash or I have tried to retrieve it in the last half hour, it's like the silver chain has become a part of Nera.

"It wasn't her fault." Ash finally breaks his silence, though the deep rumble of his voice sounds weak and unlike himself, at least what I've seen of him. He opens his eyes slowly, and his brow furrows as he shifts his weight on the couch. "She was in a magic-induced slumber, and while in it, the stone was likely alluring to her. Are you able to unravel the spell to set her free?"

"Well, I've never used magic like this before. I don't know how to undo it . . ." Heat flares in my cheeks at my admission. Honestly, I don't know what's worse, admitting I acted rashly to save my enemy or that I don't know what the hell I'm doing with my magic.

"I knew it," Nera groans, and lets her head hit the hard floor twice.

"Somehow, you undid the enchantment that was supposed to keep you inside your room." Ash's expression heats with annoyance as he stares at me, unblinking. "How did you get out, Monster? I know Naheli wasn't with you this time."

I pull my hands away from where they hover over Nera's chest. I could admit I used the roses and whatever power coursed through them. But if he's planning on locking me back in that room, I don't want him to know how I did it and take away whatever little freedom I gained.

All this time I've thought that my amulet lent me power, or the grimoires, or the roses. What if it wasn't those things, but me, all along? Unraveling a spell feels like cutting fabric with very sharp, small shears. I could try to do the same now, even if the amulet refuses to come with me.

"How do I know she won't attack us again once she's free?" It's a fair question, and not one we've discussed yet.

"I can't be sure, but I can guarantee you I'll put her to sleep if I see her reverting." Ash waves a bloodied hand in Nera's general direction, who glowers at me. She always looked beautiful, like a perfectly carved sculpture, and now her beastly features have receded somewhat.

I'm still not sure . . .

"Look, she's out of her feral state, and I haven't seen a beast lose their mind unless we are closer to the next blood moon. We should be fine for now."

I study his face, looking for lies hiding in plain sight, but find nothing. While I don't trust the king of beasts, I also know he's bleeding on that couch because he saved me. I doubt he'd lie and have me killed for nothing. I nod and resume what I was attempting before. Except this time, my heart is beating slower. I feel myself settle down, my weight lighter upon my thighs as I let my eyes close.

Ignoring Nera's sharp words and glares helps, and the familiar tug of magic from the stone calls to me. I focus on that power, on how it hovers beneath my fingers, pulling them down and embracing them like lukewarm water.

Hello, dear old friend, I say to the amulet in my head, remembering all the years I've worn it under the layers of my librarian's cloak, how it led me to the forbidden grimoires and alerted me when others were coming.

It hums its response, but while it greets me, I can feel deep in my bones its reluctance to come with me. To let go of Nera. It desires to remain with her.

My eyes prickle as emotions swirl inside me, twisting in my gut. I promised Father I would protect this jewelry. That I would keep it with me always. But right now, I'm not sure it belongs to me anymore . . .

"What's happening?" Ash's voice breaks through the chaos in my mind.

I don't trust my voice to not break if I dare to speak, so instead I clear my throat and ask the necklace to release the ropes around Nera and let her go.

It doesn't take long for the enchantment to tear around my fingers. The warmth of my old amulet retreats, and when I open my eyes, the red swirls around Nera's body snap and loosen, like an elastic that has stretched too thin.

Nera sits, rubbing each thin wrist with the other hand. Her long nails crawl over the stone of her skin, and the scraping noise pebbles my skin with gooseflesh. I rush to my feet and take a long step away from her, feeling exposed as two predators' eyes follow me and without my traitorous necklace for help.

"I won't hurt you, human," she says, and gets off the ground, completely dismissing me. She's at least half a head taller than I am and tests the movement of her wings before stepping toward Ash. "Can you fly? Walk? We need to get you to Finley, now. He'll know what to do."

"He isn't here, Nera, and it takes more than a stab wound to kill me," Ash growls, pushing her hand away. "Take Monster to my room. She isn't safe here."

"It isn't just a stab wound, Ash. You well know a lunargyre's claw is poison, especially to you. If Finley isn't here, then I have to get you the potion, right? You need it."

"I said I'm fine." Ash stands with one fluid motion. His face shifts from pale to sickly green, and his skin shines with sweat. "See?"

"You look half dead now. Congratulations, brother."

"Help me get the human into my room, then when she's safe, get the potion from Finley's study and bring it to me."

"Have you seen the amount of blood you've lost? You know well I can't help you with bandages, much less sew you up. If you're unconscious and can't suture yourself, then you'll bleed out before I get back with the potion. A human life is not more important than yours," Nera says, panic coloring her tone. Her eyes shift to me and narrow briefly. "No offense."

"None taken. I'm not a king . . ." I shrug, and my dark hair sticks to my sweaty skin. It's sweltering in this room, humid, and the scent of blood claws at my nostrils. "I—can help?"

I don't know why I'm so worried about him. My hate for him still lingers in my heart. But guilt feels stronger now, and I can't help but think he's in this position because of my actions.

Sure, he took me from Penumbra, but I attacked him first. He warned me to not leave the room, and I did anyway. Not that I regret trying to escape or save Irene. But that doesn't take away the fact that he's bleeding, apparently poisoned by the same venom that almost killed me days ago. Because of me.

Ash tilts his body forward, his lips hovering near Nera's face as he whispers something I can't hear. Nera's brows lift as her eyes meet mine, and her face softens, like she's seeing me for the first time.

Curiosity morphs features carved in stone, mirroring my own. What did he say to her?

"What's your name, human? I bet it's not Monster, like Ash has been calling you."

"It's Mia."

"Well, Mia. It seems I can't leave you here, for your human scent will attract the lunargyres to you. It's why I rose from my slumber." She shakes her head as if it's clouded, and I wonder if I should be worried about her reverting to the mindless beast she was before.

What did she look like when she was made of flesh and bone? The curse seems to affect everyone in different ways. "What did you tell her, Ash?"

"That you know where our stolen grimoires are and can use fae magic," he says, still pressing one open palm to his bleeding chest.

"Right . . ." Nera's eyes cut to him, a crease appearing between her brows. A strange sight for a being made of marble to change so drastically, like she's being sculpted right in front of my eyes. A sigh leaves her hard lips. "Let's get you both into his room, then you can help me with his bandages."

"I don't know much about healing, much less anything with poison," I admit, feeling overwhelmed by Ash's complexion and the pools of gold blood everywhere.

Nera glances down at her hands and her long nails that are still stained with Ash's blood. Sharp enough to be blades. "I can't bandage him, because my nails won't retract for another week—if I'm lucky."

She moves to help Ash walk, but his withering expression makes her pull her hands back.

"I can walk on my own," he says, stepping in front of us and limping over fragments of the old door and the tomes scattered on the ground.

CHAPTER 15

His chambers are the size of my entire townhouse back in Penumbra. I don't know what I expected to find here, but this isn't it. The room isn't dark, or impersonal, or full of gaudy decor meant for a king.

Its walls lack ancient weaponry and artifacts. There isn't even an oil painting of his ancestors hanging from the walls. The reality is nothing like what the human monarchy usually has in their castles—from what I learned studying royal history, anyway.

I wander into the room, unsure of what to do with myself as I take in my surroundings. A tree grows from one corner. Its massive trunk has to be at least twenty feet around. In the base, there's a hole in the shape of an arch, and underneath it, a bed, where an ancient spirit that looks like a black wolf lies.

Naheli lifts her head, and her four yellow eyes meet mine from the shadows. A galaxy moves inside her body, power so old I can't comprehend. She whines and lies back down, her brows shifting as she tracks my movements.

I wrap my arms around my chest as magic presses in around me, inside me, with every breath I take. It tastes familiar, like sweet berries and citrus. I tighten my grip on the billowing sleeves of my gown, wondering if Naheli stole the warmth away from my body.

"Don't look so scared, Monster. She likes you."

I jolt at the sound of Ash's voice and freeze when he shrugs off his shirt to reveal light golden skin wrapped tightly over his sculpted chest. The washboard of muscles in his stomach flexes as he discards his soiled shirt to the side.

I follow the dark feathers fanning down his abdomen, lightly covering the distinct V-shape below his navel, right before they get lost under the waistband of his black trousers. My throat dries instantly, and whatever cold I felt before is replaced by a sweltering sensation that rushes through me like wildfire. Something wicked unravels inside my body, and my stomach flips as heat unfurls between my thighs.

I can't even hear the wind rustling the leaves of the gods-damned tree in this room, let alone think, over the thundering beat of my heart. Except, I hear the distinct sound of a throat clearing, and when I lift my eyes to meet Ash's, I feel like I'm going to die. Of embarrassment and desire.

It's a spell, surely, because there is no way I'm feeling this intense attraction to him naturally. My enemy. A beast.

Ash lifts a brow, and his eyes dance with amusement like he can read my every single mortifying thought on my face. "Do you see something you like?"

"You wish," I scoff. Well, I try, but the words come out breathy instead. "I don't know about fae customs, or how long you've been living here alone, stuck as a beast, but it's improper to undress in front of a stranger . . . At least warn me first."

"You didn't strike me as a maiden, Monster." A dark chuckle filters into the room. "Is that a requirement to be a—librarian?"

I get the distinct impression he's trying to distract himself from the pain he's feeling right now by teasing me. His wound is oozing dark gold blood. Blue and purple veins fan out from three small punctures between his pec and shoulder.

Had Nera struck two inches to the left, she would have hit his heart. The fight leaves me at once, and I press my lips tight as I step closer to him to get a better look at what he's doing.

"Romantic entanglements are discouraged, because they cloud a person's judgment and can make protecting the grimoires a secondary priority," I parrot the head librarian's words from the first day we ascended to be Librarians.

In the back of my mind, I know I shouldn't share something so intimate with him, but keeping Ash distracted with something as trivial as my sex life—or lack thereof—seems like the right thing to do.

Something else nags at the back of my mind as I mull over what I just said. If the powerful stolen grimoires belonged to the fae, were they keeping us from making connections with others so we wouldn't share what we found there? So no one would suspect Penumbra stole something we shouldn't have?

"Didn't it get lonely?" Ash moves to the bed, picking up a brass box of medical supplies on his way. His eyes fix on me with burning curiosity as he sits on the edge.

Sometimes it did, but I'm not about to admit that to him. "I'm not one for one-night entanglements, even though Irene keeps encouraging it."

"Ah. The sister," he says, looking away from me right before he empties a clear vial of liquid over his mottled skin. He hisses in pain, clamping his jaw tightly as if to suffocate a scream.

The wound may no longer be bleeding as profusely as before, but Ash is looking sicker, even though he's talking a lot more. I don't think that's a good sign.

"How far is Finley's room?" I ask.

"Near yours. It's an absolute nightmare. I wouldn't know

where to even start searching for the potion." Ash pulls a needle and a spool of black thread out of an emerald velvet pouch.

Dread claws at my throat as I watch him clean the sharp object with a trembling hand. Then he attempts to thread the needle, but the hole is too small and his fingers don't hold still.

"Here, let me do it," I say, and reach for his hand. His skin is cool to the touch.

"Are you sure you can do this?"

"It can't be that difficult if you can do it . . ."

The corner of his lip twitches, and he lets go of the needle as I examine the purplish skin once again. Dark feathers hug the sides of his ribs and shoulders, getting thicker as they hide behind his back and blend with his majestic wings. Ash's legs ease around me as I step closer. His scent envelops me. Pine, leather, frankincense, and a hint of mint all blend with the heavy fragrance of alcohol and blood.

I take a deep breath and focus on the three wounds I must close, hoping Nera will be back soon with that potion, so I can put some distance between us and then obsess over everything that happened today alone in my room.

I lower the sharp object to his wound but his hand shoots up, stopping me before I pierce his skin. "Wait."

The minute his fingers touch my hand, electricity rushes through me from the point of contact. It takes my breath away. Ash's face morphs with horror, and he snatches his hand back, like he felt it too.

He swallows deeply and turns toward the spirit resting on the bed. "Naheli."

The wolf shoots up. Her four eyes blink at different times, and then she hops off the bed, fairy dust trailing behind her, and trots across the room toward a cabinet on the other side.

A bar, I realize, when the light of the fireplace catches the crystal bottles on top. The spirit stands on her hind legs and picks up a bottle with her massive mouth. Like this is something they have done before.

One second Naheli is by the bar, the next she's a blurred shape of stars and swirls of darkness, and then she's beside Ash. Drool stretches from the top of the bottle as he takes it from her. His nose wrinkles, but he quickly wipes the bottle off with his trousers, opens it up, and takes a healthy swig of the smoky-smelling whiskey.

Naheli's purple tongue lolls out as she pants. Her eyes are intelligent, following every single one of our movements. Ash continues drinking, on and on, until he's put away half the bottle. He meets my gaze, and alcohol hazes his eyes. "Alright, Monster, I'm all yours now."

A breath escapes me at once, and it takes me longer than I care to admit to gather my strength. I bring the needle back to his chest and get to work.

"Have you sewn anything before?" His face scrunches as I tie the first knot.

"I patched a dress or two and can guarantee you my skills are not what you desire." I smile, wickedly. Rejoicing in the way his face falls.

"Great, just what I need. A crooked scar to go along with losing my gods-damned mind," he mutters under his breath, and leans back while his arms wrap around his body.

Is he referring to the fact that he will eventually lose his mind because of the curse? Or something else?

"Do you always mope about with strangers when you're drunk?" I frown at the teasing in my voice.

I don't want to flirt with him, but it's hard when compassion clouds my judgment, and I can admit I find him alluring. I take in the beauty of the toothy, drunken smile that stretches across his face, even though it doesn't quite reach his eyes.

"Only when they're as lovely as you—even if you can't stitch a straight line to save me from a terrible scar."

Heat flushes my face, but I keep my lips tightly shut as I loop one more stitch around the first wound and cut the string. There's no need to obsess over what he just said. He's drunk and has lost a lot of blood. I don't even like him . . . I mean, I find him attractive for a bird, but there is nothing else going on in there.

I stitch up the last two wounds and silence falls between us. Awkward and heavy with tension.

"Why didn't you get your stone earlier? I wouldn't have stopped you," he admits. Naheli whines again and plops to the ground beside Ash. I almost forgot she's here.

When I meet his gaze, my chest tightens and I turn away, pressing my lips together as I swipe over his wound with a bit of wet gauze. I put it away, pick up the clean wrappings, and unravel them. I feel like I might say nothing, it hurts too much, but I surprise myself when the words spill out.

"It didn't want to come with me." It sounds so stupid when I say it out loud, because why would I speak of a thing like it has feelings?

Surely he will mock me now for the rest of eternity.

"It changed alliance?"

"Is that even a thing? It's been in my family for generations. It shouldn't . . . I never thought objects could do something like that." I wrap the white gauze around his torso and shoulder, making sure it's tight enough to stay in place while he sleeps.

"It doesn't happen that often, but Nera has a gift with artifacts. They always respond to her, though tying herself to a strange necklace can be problematic." His face turns with worry, and perhaps some of his previous intoxication evaporates.

"Why did she do it then?" I wish my voice didn't sound so accusatory, but I can feel my father's disappointment in me, even though he hasn't been alive for a while.

"Her affinity is chaotic when she's under the effects of the blood moon."

"It was my mother's," I admit, not sure why I'm being so candid with him. Perhaps it's because I haven't slept at all, or the near-death experience we shared has somehow made me delusional enough to feel like we connect somehow. "My father gave it to me before he died, and he made me promise I'd protect it, and not let anyone see it."

Ash's eyes soften as he studies me in silence. I'm sure my failure is written across my face.

"You don't need the amulet to wield magic, Monster."

It's what Finley said before, though at the time I didn't believe him. But after what I did in the study with Nera, I'm starting to.

I grin and flatten my hand across his shoulder, smoothing the bandage over his skin before pinning it in place. "Why are you being so nice?"

"Perhaps I'm drunk." He drags one of his hands through his hair, glaring at the discarded bottle on the floor. Dark wavy locks stand in disarray, and he closes his eyes and leans back. "Or maybe I'm grateful you saved my life."

I shouldn't feel worried he's nodding off, especially when he drank almost an entire bottle of whiskey on his own in record time. But Nera isn't back yet with the potion, and I can't help but wonder if this is the poison's doing.

"Well, you have saved me from the lunargyres two times already. It seems only fair that I return the favor."

"Three times."

"Huh?"

"I saved you three times. Once in the forest, once in the courtyard, and once today when Nera almost got you," he explains, counting them on his fingers.

"Right," I say bitterly, and shove all the medical supplies back into the box. "She isn't a bird-beast like you. Does the curse present differently for everyone?"

"Nera started like me—just a lot of feathers. For a time, I was hopeful the curse would spare her from the worst of it. But five years ago, her body began shifting to stone. Three months ago, during the last blood moon, she lost herself completely, much like you saw, and became a—"

Ash doesn't have to say it, because I read the words in his horrified expression. A rabid lunargyre.

"Why was she in your office if she's dangerous even to you?"

"Because I can put her into another deep slumber if I have to. I don't want her to be frozen like an actual statue, but it'd be worse if she went outside and was captured by your people."

Ash trapped her in a magical sleep to save her from my sister. I look away from him as shame takes all of me. He'll do anything to protect Nera. Like I tried to do for Irene.

"Is she the reason you stormed into Penumbra a week ago? It had nothing to do with the stolen grimoires, did it? But everything to do with Nera."

"For her—and my people." His jaw tightens before he speaks. "I'll storm that city, destroy the veil, and recover what's mine."

"If you release me and tell me what grimoires you need, I'll bring them back to you," I promise, and when Ash stares at me, I think he understands I'm speaking my truth.

"I was being honest with you when I told you I didn't want you here, Monster. But I can't let you go either. An ancient bond tethers you to me, has ever since you met my gaze. And it's one I'm bound to follow. If you leave, I'll come to get you, even if I want to let you go. My nature demands it and overrules any rational thought I may have on the matter."

"And there's no end to it?"

He hesitates and then sighs, loudly. "You'll be mine until the end of our lives, or the next Séance happens, which will be in a century—or so."

Mine. I hate that word. Hate that alongside the dread tightening around my lungs, there's also a small part of me rejoicing at being his. What the hell is wrong with me?

"The Séance?" I drawl. Thinking back to my old studies. "The meeting with the ancient spirits? You can't be serious."

"I'm afraid I am." When he looks back at me, a shadow of remorse shines behind his eyes. "Taking humans and their souls was a practice my ancestors started when they wanted to ride the Hunt across the human lands. I haven't participated in a long time, but we can only change the rules when we meet with the ancient spirits and the seelie court. Of course, that hasn't happened in three hundred years."

"Is there any way for you to let me go without waiting for this meeting?"

I have read hundreds of books about the fae and the history of the world. In my twenty-five years of life, I spent a significant amount of time learning all manner of exciting things about lost civilizations. I know the fae like to bargain. Anything that might allow them to change their hand for the better. A chance to be cunning.

They don't like to lose. But I bet I can entice him with a better arrangement. They usually can't say no—or so the writings say.

"Can I buy my freedom?"

Ash tilts his head, the haze of drunkenness clearing from his eyes. He stares at me for so long, I think he might not answer me at all. But when he speaks, his voice is rough and sends a shiver down my spine. "There is a way, but I don't think you'll like it . . ."

"Try me."

"You must give me one hundred souls."

I drop my hands to my sides and stare at him, at a loss for words. "One hundred . . . How could my soul be worth that many?" Panic seizes me inch by inch until I can't breathe past the knot that's grown in my chest.

"I didn't make the rules, but I'm bound to tell you the stipulations. Let me make one thing clear: I don't want your soul tethered to mine, much less one hundred more. I didn't live most of my life avoiding the Hunt for this to happen. So you'll stay and drop this nonsense."

"What if I help you with the curse? Would that be enough to let me go?"

He growls deeply, and I can hear steps coming down the hall outside his room. "I don't think you know what it takes, what you're offering."

I take a stuttering breath and meet his golden gaze. He is too beautiful, and deadly. I should heed his words and live the rest of my life in peace—until he loses his battle with the curse and a mindless beast kills me. "Would you release my soul if I help you break the curse?"

He straightens where he sits and reaches for the discarded shirt he tossed to the side earlier. Perhaps I'm imagining the waves of golden magic that radiate from him.

"It'll make it harder for me to let you go . . ." he mutters, and stands, wincing as he seems to have forgotten Nera stabbed him less than an hour ago.

"What do you mean?" I wring my hands, still feeling the stickiness of his blood between my fingers, and step away from the bed to follow behind him as he moves toward the massive windows. I'd never have expected this place to be so lived-in and human—so normal.

"If you break it"—he pauses, and his brows knit in the middle as he reaches for the gauzy curtains fluttering in the frigid breeze—"you will release more than one hundred of my people, and so you'll be free."

"You have a deal." A smile tugs at the corner of my lips as I extend a hand to him.

Ash turns to me and looks at it like snakes are curling around my fingers.

"If I'm connecting all the pieces of this massive puzzle correctly, then you're running out of time. It's why Nera turned feral, isn't it? It's why you ended up in Penumbra even though you've been cursed for a while. You're desperate. What do you have to lose?"

"You don't know . . ." Ash's face loses whatever little color he regained. The door to his room swings open, revealing Nera's marble body.

Ash clasps my hand with his, and a cyclone of gold magic envelops me, wrapping over both of our forearms and extending up our shoulders to seal our bargain with a brand over each of our hearts. I'm afraid I will never cease to smell like him, even if I succeed.

"Be thankful, Monster, that I didn't feed you to Naheli for all the mess you've brought into my life." He pulls his hand away.

The wolf lifts her head from the floor. A deep rumbling breath leaves her, and then her purple tongue rolls out of her mouth. She blinks her four eyes and lies back down, wagging her two tails rather heavily over the tile floor.

"I'm terrified," I say flatly, and turn to pat the wolf's enormous head. Her hair is coarse and cool under my fingers.

"What did I miss?" Nera asks, stepping forward, a pink potion in her long claws.

I press my hand to my chest and feel the warmth of our deal buzzing under my skin. I no longer have to run away to be free.

CHAPTER 16

Knock, Knock.

A rhythmic tapping pierces through the deep layers of my dreamless mind. Distant, yet close. I stir reluctantly, chasing the remnants of sleep and the warmth that seeps from my covers, beckoning me back into slumber.

Someone speaks from the other side of the door. I don't care who's here, all I want is to sleep just a little longer.

"Go away!" I mumble into the down feathers of my pillow. The cool silk of the cover is soft against my cheeks.

The knocking continues, and I blink my eyes open. My vision clears to the soft light that spills through the window. I sit on my bed, rubbing the sleep from my face, when my eyes meet a dark shape of galaxies resting at my feet.

Naheli lifts her head, blinking her four yellow eyes before a massive grin splits her face and she pants her good morning.

"What—?" Sleep roughens my voice, and I don't know why the spirit is here, nor can I ask when whoever is outside my room has little patience. I grunt loudly and scoot off my bed. Could this be Morgana? I hope whoever it is hears my displeasure, so next time they'll leave the food on the floor and leave me be.

My tiredness evaporates when I yank the door open, because I don't see a maid, nor my new gowns. Instead, outside my chambers, the king himself leans against the doorframe. He straightens to his full height, casting a shadow over me as his gold eyes travel from the tips of my bare toes to the top of my bedhead. His perusal is slow, like a caress that trails over my poorly covered body through my sleep gown.

The mortifying thought breaks through, and my face goes up in flames as I take a step back and attempt to cover myself behind the door.

"I thought you were Morgana," I say, and cross my arms over my chest to hide whatever remains visible of my breasts through the sheer layers of my chemise.

"Who?" Ash blinks a dazed expression off his face, then he turns away abruptly, hiding his blushing cheeks as he focuses somewhere outside my room. He clears his throat. "Get dressed, Monster, we have somewhere to be."

"What— Where? I would much prefer going back to sleep now. I was up all night and all day yesterday."

"We're training, so get into something you can move around in that's not . . . what you're wearing now."

I step away from the door, gripping the handle and moving to close it. Ash's hand shoots up and blocks it before I'm successful at shutting him outside.

He's looking past my shoulder at the wolf still resting on the bed. "Naheli, you traitorous mutt."

The spirit's ears shift around, but she doesn't even lift her head from the mattress. Just snorts loudly.

I grin, glancing back at Ash, unable to hide my triumph. "Are you jealous, Ash, king of beasts?"

"Mia." His eyes pin me down with an intensity I'm not prepared to face. "You have no idea."

Something else quickly replaces the heat of embarrassment I felt before. My mouth goes dry, and I forget what I was about to say or do. My name spilling from his lips sounds like something I'm not supposed to hear, forbidden, and my poor twisted heart has no defense against it.

"Get dressed. I'm not a patient man." And with that, he closes the door and leaves me inside this sweltering room.

No one has ever offered to train me in magic before. I shake off my shock and dress as quickly as I can before I rush out of the room. If Ash wrote that grimoire . . . I can barely hold in my excitement about what I may learn today.

"You're training me?" Incredulity that seeps into my tone as I catch up to him.

"Seems like the logical next step, since you're going to help me with my . . . situation." He looks pointedly into the courtyard through the large windows to my left. The three sculptures I spotted earlier drift across the dilapidated space. Lunargyres that look much like Nera. Their hissing vibrates almost as loud as our footsteps.

"I didn't think those were—" I begin, rubbing my hands over the gooseflesh that lifted on my arms. I shift away from the windows and closer to Ash. Like the mass of his body might protect me from being seen.

"They blend rather beautifully with the stone outside." Ash stops at an impressive set of doors, and gold swirls of power wrap around each of his fingers before the lock clicks. The two panels swing open in unison, revealing only gaping darkness in the room ahead.

"The one that attacked me before wasn't made of rock." It looked like a bald mole, much like Alaris in the kitchen.

"The high fae transition to stone, while low fae change to a more animalistic lunargyre." He pauses, gesturing for me to enter the room. "The sculptures blend with the garden. It makes them deadlier."

His words don't match the true devastation in his expression. I feel sick thinking about it, remembering the dead beast the scientist dragged out of the machine. I haven't thought about it in a while, but the image seldom leaves me.

"And about the training, it's an insurance policy on my part, to keep you from dying. Especially since you seem to enjoy danger."

I could have told him I didn't, but that would be a fat lie. Proven by the actions that brought me to this very moment. Or by the fact that I'm truly considering stepping into that dark room, where beasts could be hiding. "What if I use my newly gained skills to escape you?"

"Then you'd better run fast, Monster, because I like the chase." He disappears in the darkness.

As soon as I step inside, I can't see anything around us except for tall columns that catch the dim gray light from the hall. Ash steps around me, rolling his sleeves up over his forearms, revealing his pale gold skin and the contrasting peppering of small feathers on his forearm.

He looks different from the night I met him. Now he looks a lot more like I imagine the fae did once upon a time. The plumes are a reminder: A curse still lingers inside him, around us all.

I force my attention away from the newly revealed skin of his arms, and from the memories of how he looked last night when I stitched him up.

"I trust you're feeling well enough to train me?" Are we practicing my fencing skills, or does he intend to test my handle on magic? I guess it's safe to assume it might be the latter.

"Why? are you worried about me?" His eyes dance with humor.

"No," I say. "Are we supposed to train in the dark?"

"Yes. The lunargyres lurk in the dark corners of the castle. It seems wise for me to teach you how to read the small shifts of energy that might help you figure out where they are."

I nod, glancing around as my eyes adjust to the lack of light. There are pockets where the sun spills from small skylights in the ceiling to catch on surfaces around the room. A table here. A pillar holding a vase there.

"As you now know, many of our lunargyres appear to be sculptures. It's important for you to read the way magic shifts around you. It might help you stay alive."

"Aw." I smile at him as I throw his own words back. "If I didn't know better, I'd think you worried about me."

"To my own misfortune . . ." Judging by the slight pinch between his brows, he's as displeased by the revelation as I am by my concern for him. "But make no mistake, I have the animalistic need to protect what belongs to me."

I open my mouth to tell him I don't belong to anyone but myself, but he strolls away, waving a hand over his shoulder as if to dismiss my future comeback. "I'm going to disappear into the shadows now. Your job is to find and stop me before I get you."

"And what do I get if I do?"

He laughs, like I asked the most ridiculous thing he's ever heard. Perhaps he doesn't remember that I saved him yesterday.

"Your incentive should be getting to survive. To walk out in the halls without one of us having to keep you safe. If you don't stop me today, we will meet here every morning until you can."

"So, if I find you, I'll be able to explore the castle on my own?"

"Yes. Most of the lunargyres in the halls aren't feral yet, but it's best to be careful."

"And outside, in the courtyard?"

"Don't go there unless one of us is with you."

"In that case, I'm ready. Are you going to give me a training dowel?"

"Where's the fun in that?" He lifts a brow as he finishes rolling up his sleeves and cracks his neck to either side.

"How else am I going to stop you?"

"I'm sure you'll come up with something," he says right as he disappears between two columns. The shadows of the room swallow him whole, and I'm left alone. Only the sound of my heavy breathing remains.

There is no way I can detect him in this vast room without my amulet. Back in the library, the forbidden grimoires spoke to me when I touched them. Same with the roses. I guess I could walk through this open area trying to feel my way around, but I doubt that's what Ash is looking for.

My heart drums in my ears, and blood rushes into my head. Panic coats the back of my tongue, tasting bitter and wrong. I take a tentative step forward, not knowing where to look.

"Start moving around, Monster. There is nothing worse than being a sitting duck when a predator is on the hunt." His voice comes from everywhere and nowhere at once.

I try to find him, to discern the shape of something familiar, like a wing or strands of hair, that might let me know where he is.

But I can't tell how deep the room is or where the nearest wall might be. How low the ceiling is from where I stand. Only that there is a deafening silence that remains in his apparent absence. I take another step forward. The click of a heel echoes mine. I turn, following the sound, unsure if it's him approaching or if it's the sound of my own steps going around and around, intensified by a spell.

There's magic I'm supposed to sense, and there is no way I'll be able to do it if I let myself spiral into a panic attack. I take a deep breath and focus on finding a familiar gentle buzz of power. It should feel similar to when I'm near my mother's necklace.

The subtle scent of pine needles and leather come with the shift of air right before his words break the silence. "If you don't breathe, you're going to pass out." His breath washes over my neck, warm, sending a shiver down my spine. I spin, swinging my arms around, trying to smack him.

A chuckle pierces the space, but I find nothing but stale air around me. I whirl again and meet Ash's gaze on the other side of the room. His smile is a sliver of white teeth that catch what little illumination is around us.

How could he be behind me one second and all the way over there the next?

"Don't rely on your human senses. Feel the trace of magic I leave behind, nothing else," he says, then whooshes back into the shadows.

The question must've been written all over my face, even from where he stood a moment ago. How did he know I would follow his scent? It doesn't matter.

I told Skylar the night Ash took me, I'm not powerless. It's about time I believe it too. Inside my mind, hiding in my memories, are all the strange spells I paged through once upon a time.

I could never really understand what the texts said as they were written in old languages, perhaps even in the tongue of the fae. But I could feel the meaning and what each spell would do. Ash doesn't know this, but I once read a revealing spell. A casting that shows what one is searching for.

A mixture of exhilaration, adrenaline, and fear takes ahold of me as I debate whether I should use it now. Could I, even if I wanted to, without the amulet? Would my magic answer me?

Taking a deep breath to calm my erratic emotions, I focus on the memories of reading that spell. On how it felt when the grimoire's power graced my skin. Surely a revealing spell wouldn't cause harm. It shouldn't do anything other than show me where Ash is hiding, which is what he tasked me with.

I can almost smell the scent of freedom as I picture the words —the feelings—in my mind. I recall the warmth of the grimoire's magic wrapping around my fingers as I paged through it. Blocking out all distractions is easy since I can't see much.

My skin glows in sputtering tones of gold, and when I reach my hands out in front of myself, I empty my thoughts, except for those of what lies within the room. I want to see every dark corner and crevice where he might be.

A wave of bright yellow light explodes from my hands. I hear a distinct pained sound from somewhere in the distance, though I can't tell if it's me. The exhilaration I felt before vanishes, and panic takes over my body. The spell doesn't stop. My skin burns, and I'm blinded by the light as it continues pulsing through me.

I shut my eyes, but inside my head, I can see every detail of the room. The roses that climb the walls in every direction. Broken furniture piled up by the walls. Dusty curtains hastily closed over boarded windows.

Ash is running—no, flying toward me, cutting through the space with the precision of a bird of prey as I flounder back two, three steps. My back hits a column, and something wet runs down my cheeks.

A high-pitched scream pierces the room, tearing through my eardrums. I press my hands to them, trying to drown out the sound right as something heavy crashes into my side. We tumble onto the hard ground, and a cocoon of dark feathers wraps around me, sheltering me from the bright light that continues shining on.

"What the fuck are you thinking, Mia?" I can hear his snarl far from me. My head hurts so much, but I welcome the reprieve from the brightness inside his protective embrace. Even if everything hurts. "The grimoire didn't seem dangerous when I studied it."

I didn't intend to say that out loud, but I'm too scattered to really make much sense of anything.

"What does that mean?"

When I open my eyes, Ash is pinning me to the ground with his significant weight. Our faces are close—too close—and my thoughts clear instantly. I feel the quickness of his breath against my skin, and his scent is exhilarating.

The brightness of the revealing spell fades slowly, and the room returns to darkness. He eases his body off me and gets to his feet.

"I-I guess the training is officially over," I whisper. My heart is still beating so fast. I gather my strength to get up, but my arms feel heavy.

Ash snaps his fingers, and light flickers on in every candelabra and lamp around us.

I swallow thickly. "I found you. Does that mean I won?"

He looks anything but pleased when he gestures to me where I still lie on the floor. "I literally took you down. I asked you to focus on the trace of magic I leave behind, not to use enchantments you don't understand."

"I tried, but I felt nothing." I'm fed up with feeling like a failure everywhere I go. Like I disappoint everyone that matters. Irene, my father—him. Too many emotions swirl inside me, and my head threatens to split open with the migraine that follows.

"Did you?" he asks. "Or did you give up trying because you thought you couldn't do it?"

I wince and fight the urge to shield myself from his scrutiny.

Ash sighs, making his way back to the double doors we came in through. "I hoped my assessment of your nature wasn't correct, and you wouldn't be irresponsible enough to do something so idiotic."

I frown and follow him. "So was this a test to get me to perform a forbidden spell, like I did the night we met?"

"The spell isn't forbidden. When used properly, it reveals hidden items. Even if they are spelled to remain so or the room is dark. But you are an untrained human, and using fae magic like that could kill you."

I fight the need to hug my body to warm myself against the

chill crawling over me, the shame of being the way I am. Irene has been telling me I've become impulsive, but I always told myself I was doing it for her. To protect her. But I never intended to cause harm to others, like almost killing Ash, much less myself.

The spell left me drained.

"You don't know what kind of magic you learned, what enchantments you're unleashing upon others. It's the first rule of spell casting, Monster, to never use magic you don't understand. Your precious librarians should've taught you that."

I want to defend myself. He's no one to tell me what to do or how I should've been taught magic. But I was never taught these. I stole moments with forbidden books and somehow, against all odds, I learned.

We weren't allowed to use this sort of power, and I'm not sure people like Harper even could. One librarian wasn't dangerous. We did parlor tricks, like Skylar so gracefully pointed out. But I craved more. I wanted to make a difference and learn the truth.

Shame weighs me down as we leave the dark room. I missed the chance to learn something new, like detecting magic waves, when I defaulted to old habits.

"Where are we going?" I ask Ash as we head a different direction from where we came.

"The library. There's something I need you to do."

CHAPTER 17

My heart might leap out of my chest at any moment as I take in a magical library that could rival the one in Penumbra. Rich, dark green bookcases extend up three stories high. There must be hundreds of thousands of books in here. So many tomes bound with leather I wouldn't be able to read them in my lifetime. And their scent is like coming home.

I step into the room, twirling around, my arms clasped against my chest. My cheeks hurt as I smile and take everything in.

"What do you think?" I hear Ash beside me, and I nod, taking in the beautiful landscape painted on the ceiling.

"It's breathtaking."

These grimoires are all magical, like the ones forbidden back home. I feel it deep within my bones as their aged parchment sings to me.

"How did you realize you were missing grimoires when you have this many?" I ask, and the moment I meet his gaze, I realize he's staring at me with an emotion I can't place. Or perhaps I'm too scared to do so.

Longing—desire?

His gold eyes have turned near black by the time he shifts them away from me.

"Because I needed them." He clears his throat and stalks forward, the long tail of his coat billowing, leaving trails of his intoxicating scent behind. "Having so many is why they could steal them right out from under my nose. I imagine they took one at a time, and I only realized they were gone years after the curse was in place."

If—when—I earn some semblance of freedom inside this castle, I will come here every day. I need to really start putting into practice what Ash was trying to teach me earlier, just so I can finally study magical grimoires in peace. Alone. Without having to hide.

Ash stops in front of a massive tapestry that hangs from a brass rod on the wall to the right of us. It tells a story, from the top of the scroll to the bottom. The colors were probably vibrant once upon a time but now are muted by age.

I step forward and take in every beautiful detail like a starved woman in front of a feast. Magical beings and fae riding horses, boars, and elk. I recognize this image. I've seen it before in the encyclopedias we study as children. It shows the blood moon shining behind a mess of spirits similar to Naheli. And so many bodies sprawled everywhere. Dead humans.

It's of a time when the fae came to our human towns to hunt for slaves.

I step past Ash and study every shape and horned beast like I'm seeing them for the first time.

"Do you know what this is, Monster?"

I tilt my head toward him, blinking rapidly before I nod. "The Wild Hunt. We are shown a reproduction of this exact image when we're young—and we're told to never look the fae in the eyes. My father repeated it to Irene and me the nights the moon was reddest."

His lips quirk at the same time his brow tilts up. “Funny how you ignored every warning.”

I huff a breath and continue my inspection of the tapestry. “Perhaps you should have warned me what you were before I bound us to each other, since you apparently didn’t want a human tied to you.”

“Should I have screamed the warning when you were attacking me with your spells? Or perhaps when your friends were shooting at me?”

I don’t turn to look at him, instead I gesture vaguely at the tapestry. When I realize there are two familiar faces in the chaos, I freeze.

Ash is riding a black elk. His eyes are so gold, they shimmer with the candlelight around us. Beside him, running next to his mount, is the wolf that was sleeping in my bed this morning. The air lodges in my throat, and I must have stopped breathing.

“This was the day I met Naheli,” he says. “And the last time I took part in the Hunt.”

A sudden heaviness expands inside my stomach as I face him.

Ash barely glances my way before turning abruptly away from me. “Wait here,” he says, storming past a statue nestled between two bookcases and up a narrow staircase that leads him to the second story of shelves.

Now alone in the darkness of the bottom floor, I step forward to get a better look at the grimoires closest to me. Their imprint of magic sings the loudest, and my fingers ache to flip the pages and learn ancient things.

The room is exquisitely decorated. The door moldings are of fine-carved wood depicting flowers and leaves, stained deep forest green. Tapestries hang from the few walls that aren’t covered in books, and busts of fae stand on tall pedestals.

I walk by those with special care, studying each face like it might attack me at any moment. I even try my best to sense traces of magic from them, like I do with the grimoires. But these aren't lunargyres, they're simple marble sculptures. Unmoving and unalive.

This might be the only place in the castle without roses, and I wonder— A flash of white to my right makes me pause. Inside a dark alcove, a statue shifts slightly with a rumbling snarl.

My heart leaps into my throat and I jump back, screaming as I grab a grimoire from the bookcase next to me and throw it at the lunargyre with all my strength. The book hisses in response, followed by a little screech of offense as it hits the beast's head with a thump.

"Ouch," Nera says, her nose scrunched. Her rose-colored eyes blink rapidly before she smiles, mischievous and showing her very sharp teeth. "You were so afraid."

Adrenaline makes my hands shake as the same energy I felt back in Ash's studio rushes through my body, hot and demanding to be unleashed.

I hear the flapping of wings right before an enormous shadow descends from the second floor and Ash lands in a crouch.

His eyes are severe, like he's readying himself for a fight. Then he meets his sister's gaze and eases. "Nera, don't you have better things to do than terrorize the human?"

"No, I truly don't." Her laughter is harmonious even as it is cruel. And the remnants of my fear go up in flames as anger takes over.

"I could've hurt you," I storm over to collect the grimoire from where it lies on the ground. This one is not happy when I pick it up again, and it burns me as I rush to put it back where it was before. I shove my shaking hands into the pockets of my dress to hide my glowing fingertips.

Nera opens her mouth, not looking apologetic in the slightest, but Ash speaks before she can. "She can hurt you, Nera, and if she does when trying to defend herself, it will be your own damn fault if you revert to a mindless lunargyre. She knows how to wield old spells I haven't seen in a long time."

Nera tilts her head and studies me with renewed interest. "Fine. I'm sorry, Mia. I was just having a little fun. You were so cautious with the other statues, it was hard to pass up the opportunity."

Her apology feels sincere. It's been such a long time since anyone played with me just for fun. It feels strange, but nice.

"I would like you to read this," Ash says, showing me the small book he holds in one hand. "This book comes from the seelie court. We have a few of their tomes. A handful of fae on our continent can understand their language." He moves to a table in the middle of the room, and we sit close enough to the windows to read without the need for candlelight.

"You are letting the human read the seelie king's diary? I thought that belonged to me, since he's my betrothed?"

"Wait, you're marrying the seelie king? Aren't you all enemies or something?" Surely I read that somewhere.

Ash says, "Enemies is a strong word—"

"Yes, we are. But when I was promised to him, we were on better terms."

"You promised your sister to a fae you hate?"

Ash takes a deep breath and interlaces his fingers on the table. He levels me with a glare and nods to the forgotten book in front of me. "Read, Monster. That's why we're here. Not for you to judge our customs."

"But, why would you do that?"

"Yes, brother, I'm dying to know." Nera rests her small chin in her hands, batting her lashes rapidly.

"Don't encourage her," he growls. "I doubt Monster would understand, with her very limited human knowledge of how the fae work."

"If you don't tell her, I will. Though my account may reveal certain aspects of our nature, like fated—"

"I didn't promise her to anyone," he blurts out. An expression of genuine panic flickers over his face, there one second and gone the next. "I would never do that to her. It was written in the stars."

"What?" I almost laugh, but the both of them look so serious, I sober immediately.

"A prophecy, Monster. Humans also have those."

True, but I've never heard of one that was taken seriously before. They're more a myth than anything else.

Ash leans back in his chair and brushes invisible fluff from the lapels of his coat. "My father promised Nera's hand to King Aberon's son after a soothsayer foresaw that her union with the crown prince would prevent a calamity that would destroy the seelie."

"I wasn't born yet, but Father saw the opportunity to strike a mutually beneficial deal," Nera says, far too relaxed for someone who was offered around like cattle for auction. "It was the only way he could convince the king of the seelie to ride the Wild Hunt so Ash could get his spirit companion. They don't believe in the Hunt or the genuine connections we form with the ancient beings."

"That is . . ." *awful*. I'm glad the word remains inside my mouth.

Nera taps her long fingernails over the wood table, like she's talking about the weather. "Don't look so horrified. It won't happen. Have you seen me? I'll be dead before he comes to claim his bride."

"But I thought you just said your nails will be back to normal soon, and you aren't rabid anymore."

There's a flash of hurt behind Nera's eyes, though she's so quick to hide it she must be an expert. "It's only a matter of time until I don't snap back to my old self after a blood moon, and with how things have been going for me, I probably only have one left. Three more months." She shrugs like she doesn't care. No one in this library believes her act. "It doesn't matter either way, Mia, the curse will take me either by making me mad or by turning me into stone until I won't be able to move anymore, to eat—to *live*."

Horror settles in the pit of my stomach. I hate that she's talking about fading into the curse like there isn't a way out.

I glance back at the tapestry and take in the fine details woven together to create the beautiful masterpiece. Naheli runs beside Ash. Every single star inside and around her body is stitched with silver thread. I study Ash's sword, which he swings at a man whose head is flying somewhere else. Humans are running, screaming. It's almost like I'm there, watching the Hunt unfold in front of me.

I clear my throat, hoping my voice doesn't break with how overwhelmed I feel. It would be better to change the subject. "So, you've met him before? The king?"

Nera shakes her head. "No, not in person at least." Her expression turns more severe, and she looks away, perhaps regretting telling me the truth. "But enough about me. Why are we here?"

"Ash and I made a deal yesterday," I say, and lean back against the smooth leather backrest of the plush, burgundy chair.

"Oh?"

I shrug, keeping my hands busy with the small book. "I will help you break the curse, and if I do, he will set me free. I'm guessing that's why I'm learning all about the Hunt and Ash has deemed it necessary that I read this strange diary."

"Something like that . . ." he says, looking away from us, his jaw ticking. "I might have drunk too much whiskey and gone half mad to make this deal."

"I see." Nera's brows arch, and I'm still amazed her face can be so expressive even though it's all stone. It doesn't even make a sound, but it feels like it should. “Well, this should be interesting. I’ll stay here and see what you two get up to.”

“Are you bored, dear sister?”

“If the curse doesn’t kill me, the monotony of every passing day in this place will.” Her mouth tilts into a slow smile, and she lowers her body into a chair beside me. The wood groans and bends. I hear a crack, but just as I expect Nera to fall to the ground, Ash waves a hand and gold magic shoots from his fingers, wrapping around the chair and preventing it from collapsing under her considerable weight.

“Please, stop destroying the little furniture we have left. Use your magic, Nera. It will help you maintain your sanity.”

“You know I can’t. Not anymore.”

“You’re just choosing not to because it’s difficult to accept the curse has dampened it and it’s not as it was.”

“You don’t know anything.” Nera’s nostrils flare ever so slightly, but a heartbeat later, a mask of indifference falls upon her face and the hurt is gone. She turns to me, rolling her rear over the chair to push it to its limits. “I admit, I’m curious how this will all pan out. I guess no human has survived in our kingdom as long as you, Mia. Not since the curse began. How are you planning on helping us?”

“Well, this is all new to me, and frankly, I didn’t think this through when I made the deal with your brother last night.”

“Shocking,” Ash says, tapping his fingers on his chin. “You don’t seem like an impulsive person at all.”

I glare at him. “Well, I don’t have a lot of choices, and I don’t like to not be in control over my future. So, please tell me more, anything I can use to break this, for example: Who cursed you? A warlock, a sorcerer—an angry family member?”

There is always a fail-safe woven into the layers of a curse so it can be broken. The laws of magic require balance. It must be the reason beasts come to Penumbra on every blood moon. They usually try to take a human away, so perhaps one of us is destined to break it. And here I am, in the perfect place at the perfect time.

Nera and Ash stop moving—stop breathing. They sit rigid in their chairs, stares burning a hole in my face. The intensity makes my skin crawl. Their lips remain shut tightly. Ash is pale, looking almost like his sister, another statue sitting in an ocean of books.

"You can't talk about who put the curse on you, can you? That's why you've been showing me clues. Perhaps if I figure out who did it, I can break it?" I study their shocked expressions and rejoice in this little win. "I take it I'm close to the truth?"

"Oh, she is good," Nera croons in delight. "Let's keep her."

I frown at the white beast and her delicate features. "I'm not a pet for you to keep."

She sobers and nods, her previous mocking expression gone, replaced by something more serious that makes her look much older. "You're right. And we both know that. Isn't that true, Ash?"

"What's that you're trying to accomplish, Nera? Perhaps you should go before I lose my temper and put you back to sleep."

I blink, confused. Not sure if I should be offended, curious, or both. It's probably best to not ask questions or get hung up on whatever silent conversation they're having in front of me. Who cares if they don't like me? The feeling's mutual. This is nothing but a transitional place for me.

"Why do the lunargyres come to Penumbra? The city is far, at least a week away. I'm sure there are other towns near the castle that also house humans."

Not that I want the beasts to torment and kill those humans like they have so many of us.

"The citizens of Penumbra have made it so. They stole from me, and the lunargyres can sense traces of fae magic in the city. A connection that perhaps feels like home and ties us to Penumbra. So they flock there and take humans to bring to me."

I nod, opening the grimoire he handed me and feeling little

fibers of magic cling to the palm of my hand. A soft, but somehow fiery, greeting. "They kill most of the people they take, though. Have they ever succeeded at delivering a human here?"

The siblings trade a sad look before Nera speaks. "They are mindless beasts by the time they get there. No human can survive a feral lunargyre."

But they keep coming for more, and the bloodshed won't end until the curse is broken. I don't have a lot of time to help Penumbra, nor Nera, who is more beast than fae.

I page through the book and smile as its magic grips at my fingers. I've never seen this language before, but the parchment greets me. The aura hovering over the pages is light red.

"What do you see?" Ash asks, and the surrounding silence is almost absolute.

I drag my finger over the elegant swirls that make words I can't discern. "Just letters . . ."

His sigh sounds distinctly relieved, and the wood of Nera's chair groans under her weight as she leans over the table.

Well, this was uneventful. I move to close the grimoire, but its magic whispers. It asks me with a deeper voice if I want to know its secrets; it holds knowledge of passages inside the castle. Not this castle, but one across the continents, where the nights are long and large lizards breathe fire.

My eyes widen and I slam the grimoire closed, pushing it toward Ash while perspiration accumulates on my temples.

"What—what did you read?"

"I can't read it." I shake my head "Can lizards breathe fire?"

Nera gasps and presses her hand over her lips.

Ash pulls the book back. "*When did you learn to speak the languages of the fae?*"

I stare at him as panic rushes through my body, because he isn't speaking the common human tongue. I stand up so fast my chair tumbles to the ground. But I need some distance from them.

The way words sound out of his lips is wrong. His inflection goes high and low, while the sounds form elegant, strange phrases. Words I shouldn't understand, but I do.

My skin tightens, and I want to get out of here and hide somewhere I can think over the seemingly insignificant details of my experiences to figure out what this could mean.

He stands fast and rounds the table toward me. His scent chases away every rational thought I have. "Mia?"

I jump at the sound of my name on his lips. Gods, I hate that I like it. Monster is much safer.

"I-I don't know when . . . how . . ." I try to see through the confusion clouding my thoughts, but everything is muddy. A shiver runs down my spine, and my heart pounds faster. I can't say anything coherent, so I glance at the tome on the table and the strange letters it contains.

Nera leans forward, her eyes wide as her face shifts with a mixture of horror and hope. Hope for what?

"Well, your understanding of our language explains how you're able to cast enchantments from the stolen texts. It explains what you truly are, Monster."

"And what's that?"

"Not human. Whoever made you believe that lied to you. You have fae blood."

CHAPTER 18

"There's nothing useful in this one either," I groan. Dust billows out from between sheets of thin parchment as I close the grimoire and push it away.

It's been more than a week of constant reading, and I've found all kinds of interesting—yet useless—spells, from ward-weaving to the breaking of enchanted locks.

I sigh, kneading my fingers into the stiff muscles of my neck, and glance at Naheli's semitransparent head and the twinkling lights dancing within her body as she lies under my feet. She's been by my side the entire time.

"I've never had a dog, nor any sort of pet, for that matter. Not that I'm saying you're a pet, but I'm not sure I'll be able to leave you here when I go home. Do you think Ash will notice you're gone?" I say, and the wolf snorts loudly, wagging her tails.

My lips tremble as I try to force a smile.

Home. Will I ever go back? Do I even want to return to a city where things aren't what they seem?

The reality of my nature becomes more apparent the longer I sit at this table.

How can I have fae blood running through my veins?

Needing some air, I head for a window that takes up most of the wall, arching at the top with lattices dividing it into neat diamond shapes. A wet snout presses against my palm. Naheli sits next to me, tilting her head as she studies me with an eerie stillness. Her curiosity pricks my mind, a tingling sensation that feels strangely invasive.

Her body always glows in blues and purples. But right now, when she is trying to communicate *something*, her power waves around her, reaching for me like the grimoires do.

My vision hazes, and I can't focus on what's in front of me anymore.

She wonders why I'm here by this window instead of combing through pages upon pages of old fae writings that have nothing to do with the curse.

I almost laugh at the obviously sarcastic tone in those thoughts. So much like Ash, I wonder if she's actually him and not a spirit at all.

"I don't know how I'm going to do this," I admit out loud, and the heaviness in my chest thickens. Watching the rain fall does nothing to relieve the need to be outside, feeling the wind on my face. "I don't know if I can break this curse, Naheli. There has to be at least a hundred thousand books inside this place. How can I break the curse before the next blood moon takes Nera?"

I think of the princess and the way she was the night we met. Mindless, hungry, and murderous. My heart aches for her and the hope that shone in her face days ago when we sat here last.

"I don't even know where to start, and Ash's hints aren't doing enough. I need more guidance."

Naheli stares at me and tilts her head down. A small nod while her four eyes pin me in place.

I fight the need to fidget under her scrutiny. Then she turns and walks away. Slowly at first, then she's trotting toward the wall with the tapestry. When her pace turns into a gallop, my adrenaline spikes. The room shifts into darkness, and a night sky explodes over my surroundings.

It smells like moss and morning dew. When she's about to collide with the wall, she blends with the shadows and disappears. I gape at the spot she'd been, my mouth hanging open. Of course she can do that. I've seen her appear from the shadows before.

She's gone, and this is a simple reminder of a type of magic I don't understand. When Naheli returns, she brings me a grimoire, its leather cover stained deep blue. Embossed in the center is an eight-point star with the gold foiling nearly worn off.

When I hold it in my hands, it clings to me, and the need to pore over the pages burns through me. There's something familiar about it that's unlike any other book that's ever spoken to me. I never want to let it go.

Turning to Naheli, I hug the book to my chest, like she might take it away at any moment. "Could you take me outside so I can read it? Somewhere the lunargyre won't hurt me?"

It seems unlikely, getting to walk the grounds. I've already accepted there's little chance I'll get to before I break the curse.

Naheli yelps by the door, tilting her head and showing me her sharp, white canines. I follow her out to the courtyard, where I sit on a stone bench near the back door to the kitchen.

The book of stars speaks to me about omens and old prophecies. But its pages keep secrets, even as they are warm under my touch and a welcomed reprieve from the chill of the winter afternoon.

When the castle gates open, I've been reading for so long I can no longer feel my rear, and I'm nearly drunk on the magic inside the grimoire. I close it and follow a covered wagon, pulled by massive winged beasts, as it crosses through the thick mist that divides the courtyard from the wilderness beyond.

The black fence peeks out behind the heavy fog like swirling fiddleheads reaching for the sky. The sun is hiding behind dark gray clouds that haven't parted, though it stopped raining.

Finley huddles in the front seat, holding the reins loosely in his gloved hands. Despite the hood of his cloak shrouding his features, I can feel his eyes burning into me.

He steers the carriage across the castle grounds and over large tree roots that have broken through the paved stones circling the fountain in the center. He slows down twenty feet away, by the side door.

I shift on the stone bench I've been sitting on since Naheli and I came outside. It was still drizzling then, and the layers of my cotton dress are damp beneath me. But even though I'm cold, there's no way in hell I'd go back inside right now.

Not unless a lunargyre attacks me. But so far, they've kept their distance, and I'm certain that has everything to do with Ash's spirit.

I reach for the wolf resting beside me, scratching under her ear as we watch Finley walk to the back of the carriage, which is filled with baskets and fabrics, and unpack the goods he brought from somewhere far away.

I tuck the book under my arm and walk over to him with a tentative smile. Last time I saw him, he'd been trying to work on the castle wards and had to leave in a rush to buy something to strengthen them.

He raises a brow at me after he inspects the tome I tried to hide, then goes back to his task. "I assume the king allowed you to borrow one of his books?"

"Hello to you too, Finley. It has been a while. I'm happy you're safe."

He hums a noncommittal response, unloading a basket full of red and green apples, so shiny and fresh my mouth immediately waters. With a smile, he hands me one and begins to load a smaller cart with bags of grains and nuts and rounds of cheese. "Well, did he? Or did you sneak past his wards again and steal it?"

"Will you believe me if I say he gave me permission to go over the grimoires?"

He stops, wiping his shiny face with his forearm before resting against the wagon. He looks at me openly, and for the first time since I met him, he seems to be amused more than anything else. "I doubt he let you have the book you're holding."

I tighten my grip on the aforementioned grimoire, tucking it farther into the layers of my cloak and away from Finley's prying gaze. Just in case he gets any ideas about trying to take it away from me.

"Can you read it?"

"I can understand some of it . . ." It's an oversimplification of what happens when I'm near magical objects.

I don't want to explain how they whisper to me, and sometimes I understand their voices. Or that most of the time, I see the halos of their presence, the very thing Ash has been working with me on for the last three days. Though he's spoken little to me since he told me I'm part fae, our training hasn't stopped.

"It's interesting you're out here in the courtyard with the lunargyres, and Naheli by your side." Finley scratches at the stubble on his chin. It's much longer than when I last saw him. "She rarely likes people, much less humans."

Ha. Joke's on him since I'm not human—apparently.

I reach for the necklace that's no longer there. I can't defend myself from the beasts as easily as I could've had the damned thing not abandoned me. Naheli wags her tails at Finley when he extends her a piece of jerky he pulls out of his cloak.

"She seems to like you."

"It took me years to earn her affections, and she's still apprehensive about it."

Warmth spreads in my stomach, and I scratch the wolf's head, right behind her ears where she likes it most. Something I discovered this morning. "I asked her to bring me out here so I could read and focus."

The wolf whines when I stop petting her and presses her head against my stomach, nearly making me fall.

"She lets you pet her?"

I nod and Finley's smile cracks across his face, making him appear much younger, and for a moment I wonder about his age. I know the fae live much longer than humans. But Finley isn't one of them.

He narrows his gaze at me, but returns to his previous task. "A lot seems to have happened since I left."

I shrug and take a bite of the apple. Its perfect flavor of sweet and sour coats my tongue. We never get apples in Penumbra. They come from the mountain range, so far and unreachable they're a luxury my family could rarely afford.

"How did you convince Ash to let you out here?"

"I promised to help him break the curse."

Finley's foot catches on an uneven rock, and the basket he's holding tips over, sending potatoes rolling over the wet ground. I put the book aside on a surface of the wagon and crouch to help him pick up the vegetables scattered in the mud.

"He told you about the curse?"

"It was easy to figure out when I was getting attacked by lunargyres left and right," I say. "Plus, I met Nera."

"Did she hurt you?"

"No, she hurt him."

His face falls, and he stands quickly, already rushing for the door.

Before he enters the castle, I shout, "He's fine now."

"Nera's nails are poison to Ash."

"I know. But he's fine, I promise."

Finley stops right at the door, his hand already extended to the handle. Then he slowly turns to me, his expression unreadable. "What if you're out here and they're both dead inside?"

I stare at him and realize there's no reason for him to believe I wouldn't hurt Ash now. It's something that still shocks me—my strange feelings for the fae king.

I toss a couple potatoes into the basket and point at Naheli sitting by my side. "Would she be here if I killed Ash?"

Finley's eyes cut to the wolf, and his posture visibly relaxes. "No, I guess she wouldn't."

"Exactly. They're both fine. The whole situation with Ash being poisoned led me to understand what's happening here."

I want my freedom, but not at the expense of the fae.

"Why, if you can leave, did you come back?" I ask. "You're clearly a magical human, but why live here, surrounded by the curse and the beasts? Don't they attack you?"

"The lunargyres are most dangerous during the blood moon. It's why I was in such a rush to get you into your room the night you arrived. I'm able to defend myself from them out here in the courtyard, since most are slowed down by their stone bodies."

"Nera isn't slow . . ."

Finley takes a sharp breath. I almost forgot he didn't see my meeting with the princess. "Nera is one of the royals, and her power makes it so the curse doesn't hold her back the same . . ."

"That still doesn't answer my question. Why are you here, helping Ash?"

He's quiet for long enough I don't know if he's going to answer me, but then his rough voice breaks the silence. "I'm a victim of the Wild Hunt, like you."

"What?" It comes out on a stuttered breath. I open my mouth to continue, but can't say anything else.

"I come from a small town of mostly humans and had never seen the fae before. I'd heard of them, of course, but usually they didn't go east of Hedrum." He shrugs. "I was naive, a fool who didn't understand the rules of the blood moon. When word came to town that the Hunt was possibly riding through, I thought it would be great to linger in the market and see if I could improve my magical skills."

"How would being outside during the Hunt improve your skills?" I study his face and find he doesn't seem angry about my questions, nor resentful when thinking back to that time.

"The fae ride alongside ancient spirits." Finley gestures widely at Naheli, who seems more interested in a lunargyre who's been encroaching on our space. This one is made of stone and stained with mold and moss. A male fae, with impressive wings frozen wide open.

Perhaps I should be worried, but somehow I feel, maybe foolishly, that Naheli wouldn't let me get hurt.

"And you searched for the Hunt because you wanted to see a spirit?" I guess I can't blame him. A part of me is drawn to the idea as well.

Naheli huffs, as if reading my thoughts and finding them idiotic.

"No, I wanted power, Mia." Finley smiles, but it doesn't quite reach his eyes. "Sometimes the spirits lose fragments of their magic, and if a sorcerer were to catch it—well, I can only imagine the kind of power they could gain."

My eyes widen as I stare at him, not knowing what I expected to hear. I guess him admitting he got caught by the Hunt because he was ambitious wasn't it. I don't know what to say to that, so instead I ask something else. "Was it Ash, or Nera?"

Finley laughs. "Nera hasn't taken part in the Hunt yet. She's young for a fae."

"And how old are you?"

"You don't hold back, do you?" The tightness in his jaw tells me he's ready to move on from this conversation.

I stare at Finley's irises and the striations of gold that radiate from his pupils. Muted yellow tones, similar to Ash's. Before, I thought they were amber, but they're actually light brown, with gold streaks. "Your eyes . . ."

"It's one of the marks that ties me to the king. When a human stares into a fae's eyes, ours change color to match theirs. It's a branding of sorts, and it dates back centuries. It signals the bond, and it used to be a great source of pride."

"Who could be proud of that?"

"Me?" He sounds defensive, and pink tints his cheeks. "It comes with perks. Being tied to a high fae gives us humans an unusually long life, which was particularly enticing in a time when we died young from sickness and war. For a sorcerer like myself, it's meant decades to study magic, and perfect it. It also heightened some of my senses, making me more powerful. A young Finley thought it was the best thing that could have happened to me."

"And current Finley?"

"Well, the curse is not ideal, like you mentioned . . ."

I press my fingers to my eyes, horrified. There aren't any mirrors around the castle, and I haven't seen my reflection anywhere but in my bathwater every night.

"If you're wondering about your eyes, they're dark brown. Unlike mine, I'm guessing they remained the same."

"Really?" Why do I feel disappointed? Something is wrong with me.

"Yes. So, if you're going to help Ash break the curse, then I'll do my best to help you with what I can."

I nod and reach for my borrowed grimoire. "Will this lead me to an answer?"

Finley eyes the book warily. "I have gone through every book and diary in the library, searching for anything that could release him, and that book wasn't there, Mia."

My cheeks warm, but I don't turn to look at Naheli. No matter what, I won't be the one to get her in trouble. Even though I doubt an ancient spirit could get reprimanded in any way that matters.

Just then, the lunargyre who has been slowly inching closer leaps toward Finley with a ghostly snarl. Goose bumps rise over my skin, and it takes a second for Naheli's mist to envelop him inside a cocoon of stars and darkness. Then she flings him across the courtyard without moving a muscle.

Both Finley and I stare at the space where the statue landed, unmoving and at a loss for words.

He moves first, picking up the now-full basket beside me and loading it into his cart. "There's a better chance of finding something in your city's grimoires than here." He pauses, following my gaze to where the door of the kitchen swings open.

"Finley, I thought the mountain people ate you." Ash beams from the open door, walking toward us with his arms wide in greeting.

My heart rate doubles as I take him in. He's wearing different clothes from earlier when we trained. A dark blue coat with gold embellishments and a tall cravat a similar color to the feathers that still hug his thick neck.

I hold my breath and bring the book to my chest. The movements call his eyes, and his steps slow. His expression darkens as he takes me in. Out here, in the open.

"Monster, what are you doing here?"

My traitorous stomach flutters at his throaty tone. "Studying."

Ash glances at the wolf who remains by my side, her tongue lolling, and she greets him with a whine.

He brings two fingers to his temple and massages gently. "Naheli, I hope you're behaving."

"I don't think she is," Finley pipes in, reaching into the depths of his wagon and dragging out a heavy-looking crate of wine bottles. "I brought you the wine you requested. But I had to go through the Crossroads to avoid a confrontation . . ."

Confrontation with whom?

"I was afraid that was the case, but I'm forever thankful." Ash's lips quirk, but his face falls when he notices what I'm holding.

One second, he's far away, and the next, he's looming in front of me, his scent harassing my nostrils, and I can't get away.

"What's that you have?"

If I hold the book hard enough, could I stop him from ripping it away from me? My fingers go numb as I try to do just that, and I shift my body away from him. Naheli stands, blinks in both of our directions, looking at least two feet taller than she did before Ash arrived. Then she poofs away without so much as a glance back. That mischievous wolf is up to something.

"This book? I found it in the library," I lie through my teeth with the ease of someone who has been doing it for far too long. Something I had to practice often when stealing chances to study the forbidden grimoires.

"No, you didn't."

"I did. I was in the library all morning before Naheli brought me here."

Ash glares at me and takes another step forward. His breath warms my face, and I hate the way my body reacts to his closeness.

"I know well where that book was this morning, and it wasn't the library. Has anyone ever told you you're an insufferable pest that causes trouble wherever she goes?"

His cruelty lights something in my chest. A challenge I want to take, to prove him wrong. I'm flustered by his nearness, and a wave of pure desire courses from the top of my head down to my chest.

"You're the biggest ass I know, Ash." I tighten my lips and grip the book harder. I'm so close to finding something new. My curiosity demands answers.

He studies my face, pausing on my mouth, and his expression sharpens with the ferocity of a predator.

A breath catches in my chest, and my blood sings. "Don't look at me like that . . ." I whisper, hating the way my voice cracks on that last word.

His eyes crinkle with cold amusement. "And how am I looking at you?"

"Like you want me."

Finley gasps. I can't believe I actually said it.

My heart drums so fast I feel it in my throat. Ash looms over me with his massive, beautiful body. We stare at each other, and only the sound of the wind whistling past surrounds us.

"Don't flatter yourself," he says at last, and pulls the book from my hands. "This is off-limits."

The haze in my head is still too thick to make sense of what just happened. I watch him storm away from me, past Finley, who's staring intently at something inside his wagon, and across the open courtyard.

"Why?" I demand, rushing after him. I have never felt this need to read through a grimoire before. Not even the one I left in my locker in the city.

Not ever.

I fight the need to reach for the book again as wisps of its golden magic reach back for me. It whispers, and I can't discern its feelings from this far. "It can help me break your curse—"

"You won't look for this book again, Mia." Ash stops abruptly, and I barrel into his iron back. He whirls, meeting my gaze with a challenge in his own. "I know the contents intimately, because I wrote them, and there isn't a thing inside that will help you break the curse."

CHAPTER 19

The frigid air of the early morning burns my lungs as I sprint down the halls. I haven't run just because I can in a long time. I'm not fast, and my old boots and the layers of my nightdress make it harder to really gain speed.

But already the tension in my muscles eases. I can't catch my breath, but it doesn't hinder my pace. Ever since my first encounter with Nera, I've struggled with the sensation of energy trapped under my skin.

Moving my body and pushing it to its limits helps me, if not to ease the discomfort, at least to get some sleep. I can see my bedroom door as I turn the corner. Admittedly, going for a run in the hallways isn't my brightest idea, even if the beasts are slumbering.

I enter my room and shut the door, gripping the rose beside me as second nature and asking it to lock the wards back in place.

"I didn't know you were one of those strange people who like to run," a voice says from behind me.

I yelp and turn to find Nera walking out of the washroom. The morning sunlight spills past the gauzy curtains, casting white highlights over her marble skin.

"What are you doing here?" I press my back to the door and lift a hand to my chest, feeling my heart thundering under my palm. She doesn't look feral, but I didn't expect to find her in my room.

I left my door unlocked. What if instead of her, something else sneaked in? Something that wanted to kill me.

I follow her as she sits on the bed next to where Naheli peacefully sleeps, still taking up most of the space.

"One of the strangest things about losing my mind to the curse is that I can hear the lunargyres whisper . . ." She tilts her head up and meets my gaze. Her eyes are still that beautiful rose gold that shimmers like ground metal.

"They whisper to you?"

She nods, pressing her lips tightly together before she drags one hand gently over the wolf. Naheli's ears perk up, and slowly, she blinks her four eyes open. Her tails pat the mattress as she sleepily greets Nera.

Safe. I feel safer now that Naheli seems at ease. And perhaps I've gone mad.

"Most of the beasts that roam outside the castle have been gone for a long time, but I still recognize their voices. Many of them worked in the castle since before I was born." She shrugs a shoulder, but her expression is sad. "Either way, they whispered about a human running the halls. I came to make sure you were okay."

My stomach sinks like a stone, and I step forward, allowing myself to smile at the princess, who looks broken right now.

"Thank you, I'm—" I don't know if I should lie to her about the way I've been feeling. How it's driving me mad. Or how little sleep I've been getting. How crazy her brother makes me. How angry I am with my situation.

"I haven't been able to sleep much," I admit at last. "I've struggled with my magic lately, without my amulet."

"What do you feel?" Nera reaches for the glowing stone hanging around her neck. It almost looks like her heart is visible for everyone to see.

"It's like a fire that starts in the pit of my stomach and burns through my veins. I can't seem to find release."

She lifts a brow and stands from the bed, her lips tilting into a side smile that looks too much like Ash's. It takes all of me to not glower at her.

"Well, next time you want to go for a run, it's safer if you do it when we're all awake. And you should go with Naheli, Finley, or me—or even Ash." She lifts a hand toward my shoulder, but seems to think better of it and drops it to her side.

I wonder how lonely she feels. Perhaps she needs a friend that's not the two growly males that live here with her.

"I'll do that. I know I shouldn't have, but I couldn't sleep and felt like I was going to explode."

The burning hasn't eased off, even after the run. It's even stronger now, ever since Ash took away his book and was the biggest asshole ever. My complicated new feelings for the fae king, which are mostly still hate, are not something I'm ready to share with anyone, much less Nera.

"Mia, people with fae blood like you don't need an amulet to wield magic. I'm sure there's a part of you that's keeping it locked away for a reason. Maybe you don't even know why. But this"—she taps the red stone with her deadly fingernail—"is just a token that made you feel powerful. Perhaps it made it easier. But you don't truly need it."

Our relationship didn't start easy, but the warmth spreading in my chest, and the smile that takes over my face, is real. Nera is being kind. Even though I'm just a human with fae blood, and I tried to kill her brother, and then her. Of course, I was only trying to defend myself, and then him.

I feel we've come to an understanding. Perhaps it could build to a friendship? If I'm to remain here for the foreseeable future, I would like to have one of those.

Nera walks to the door with the same grace as always.

Silent.

Deadly.

As soon as she passes me, the gentle scent of blackberries and roses lingers behind, but then she pauses by the door, turning to meet my gaze. "I don't suppose you want to go to Eponde with me?"

"Eponde?"

"It's the largest fae town in our kingdom. It was the most prosperous too."

"Are there still fae living there?" I immediately regret my words when her face darkens.

"I'm afraid not. The lunargyres that didn't turn to stone abandoned their homes when they lost their minds and now live in the forest."

I shouldn't go but nod before I can talk myself out of it. "Will Ash stop us from going?"

"He doesn't have to know, and we'll be back before he notices we're gone. I overheard him and Finley talking yesterday about a fissure in our wards. He's going out to fix it this morning."

I remember the afternoon Finley said he had to leave to get the crystal from Hedrum. He mentioned that fissure.

"How will we know when he leaves? Are the lunargyres going to tell you?"

Nera narrows her eyes at me, tapping her foot on the floor. "Are you making fun of me?"

"No, I'm actually curious. I don't know enough about the curse or how your connection to everything works." I've barely accepted that somehow I can speak to the roses, the grimoires, and the necklace that's now, admittedly, permanently around Nera's neck.

Nera points with her chin at the wolf resting on my bed and smiles like a cat. "When Naheli leaves, then we know he's gone. He never goes to the edges of our land without her."

Naheli poofs out of my room mid-morning. One second, she's by my side, grooming her dark fur like a cat instead of a dog, and the next, she's gone.

I follow Nera through the halls, feeling almost naked without Naheli by my side. The excitement of getting to know the fae kingdom has me forgetting about the power that's been driving me crazy all morning.

That is, until Finley finds us on our way out of the castle. Apparently, Nera is not one to lie, and she tells him about our plans, even though she clearly doesn't intend to change them.

"Do you think that's a good idea, Nera? What happens if a beast wakes up and eats Mia for breakfast?"

Nera laughs dryly. "They've faded fully into stone, Finley. If only they could start moving again, then I wouldn't have to worry about what's happening to me, would I?"

"You know not all the stone lunargyres are completely asleep. Will, Carren, and Hane, they all turned, like you, and are still moving right outside." Finley points to the courtyard.

And now I know the names of the beasts that roam this place. The ones that don't look like bald moles but like garden decorations.

"I beg you to not go, much less take Mia with you. What would Ash say?" Finley's expression has morphed into panic. And perhaps he knows our minds are made up.

His eyes shift from the princess to me, as if he's looking for a more reasonable person. Has he met me? I wasn't so sure I wanted to see the devastation this kingdom suffered, but now I feel I should. Perhaps it will make me work harder.

I don't know what he expects me to do either way; I can't stop Nera from doing anything, and I'd rather go with her than let her meander through a ghost town on her own.

"This kingdom is not only Ash's. I'm their princess, and I've never been back to Eponde, not since the curse ran its course. I should have mourned with them, fought for them, not hidden here while I was also taken hostage."

I'm nodding along with her, and my eyes prickle with unshed tears. Nera was raised to rule, much like her brother. I can see it now.

"I beg you to reconsider."

"And I have decided. I'm going with or without my brother's permission," she says. "I don't know how much longer I have left. The next blood moon is just over two months away. I want to live a little, Finn, don't you?"

"Is this because of your birthday?" Finley asks. He sounds resigned.

Birthday?

"Of course it's because of my birthday," she groans, lifting her arms to the sky. "I've told Ash multiple times that I need to leave this castle. It's been a decade. I haven't left the grounds, not even before I showed traces of the curse, and I no longer care. I can't see my friends, my distant family. My people. They are all gone. The only thing I have is this castle and the two of you. But he left early this morning to strengthen the wards, and I can go to the city before he realizes I've gone."

"Wait, is today your birthday?" I don't know why and when I began to care about these people. I guess it happened slowly over the last few weeks. It would be much simpler if I were just trying to go back home, then worrying about them would be the very least of my problems.

"Not today, but in a week."

"What would you do on your birthday if there were no curse?" I ask, my smile tentative as I follow her down the hall.

Finley stays behind, glaring after us disapprovingly.

"I would love to go to Hedrum for a night. It's so beautiful in the winter. Have you ever been?"

I shake my head. I could never leave the confines of the veil, even though Irene did often, to gather supplies for the scientists. Now I know they were hunting for beasts to feed their machine. No wonder Ash calls me a monster. If I were the king and my people were being murdered that way, I would consider those behind it monsters too.

"They hold winter dances, and the food is delicious." She continues, not noticing the way my mood has soured. "It was one of my favorite places to go, and even though Hedrum used to be somewhere all races were welcomed, I would disguise myself as a human to not call unwanted attention when I wanted to have a little fun. Human men are eager in bed, but the fae have bigger cocks."

"Nera!" My cheeks burn, and I almost stumble to the ground.

Nera's laughter travels down the hall, her eyes shimmering with mischief.

I clear my throat and drag my sweaty hands over the skirt of my dress. Again and again, until I've calmed my racing heart. Not because of her comment, but because I almost kissed the ground. I'm not even wondering how big Ash's— Never mind.

It's hard not to remember the way he spoke to me the night I stitched him up. When he teased me about being a maiden and drunkenly called me beautiful. "I'm not used to talking about these kinds of things . . ."

"But I heard you have a sister."

"I do, but we aren't that close anymore." I look away, biting my bottom lip. "Actually, Irene and I have never been that close."

Is she also part fae? Does she know what I am, and is that why she kept her distance?

My heart squeezes at the possibility of being lied to like that. In the end, it doesn't matter; I don't love her any less.

"I always wanted a sister, but after my mother had me, she swore off being pregnant and never stopped taking the fertility-controlling brew." Nera pouts, then turns slightly at the sound of Finley's steps as he rushes to catch up to us. She leans closer to me, her expression turning conspiratorial. "Perhaps if this escapade goes well, and you master your trapped magic enough to help me with a glamour, we can leave for Hedrum next."

"That sounds like a terrible idea," I say with a laugh. "Which is my favorite kind of plan. So, sign me up."

"Really, Hedrum?" Finley asks, keeping his strides long and fast to remain by Nera's side. "Of all the places, that's where you want to go?"

"You know what happened the night I found out I couldn't call off my wedding after my father died?" Nera asks, staring at her long, clawlike nails with disinterest.

Finley pales, but I'm shaking my head, enthralled by the conversation.

"I went on a tirade, carried on all the way to Hedrum full of hate for my late father and with revenge in my heart. I wanted to reclaim what's mine. The old king promised my body to Sylas, and Ash couldn't break the deal as it was sealed with a blood vow. So, I did what any rebellious princess would do when faced with such a crossroad. I fucked strangers. All night long. It was wonderful, but I'm sure you understand, Finley, since you used to party there."

Finley's cheeks turn a deep shade of burgundy, and he looks away from us, muttering under his breath. "I told Ash having his little sister hovering around us all the time would come back to bite us, eventually."

It's almost cute how embarrassed he is, and I'm happy I'm not the only one acting like a bashful, innocent girl when speaking with Nera.

We make our way to the stables, crossing the courtyard toward the big black buildings that remain covered by fog. The lunargyres don't look our way.

"It has less to do with how you two behaved around me and more to do with how little time I have left to care about decorum."

"Nera . . ."

"Save it, Finley, I don't need your pity. What I need is to experience things, even if they are sad. I want to live while I still can."

His eyes soften before he nods. "Well, I guess if we're going to risk our lives, we might as well go in style and take the carriage."

CHAPTER 20

"Stay between Nera and me. It will mask your scent in case there are lunargyres around," Finley says as we follow the serpentine path toward the stables. Here, I no longer can smell the scent of roses and magic I've grown so accustomed to.

The gardens are breathtaking though, even in this cold season, with beautiful pathways made of broken stones and covered in moss.

The beasts don't attack Finley like they did yesterday, even though he's human. A sorcerer, but human. I study his wide back, round ears peeking out from under the soft curls of his light hair.

Pedestals stand on either side of us as we go under a wooden arch covered in roses. But unlike the ones in the castle, these roses are slumbering for the winter. Not magical, not unnaturally alive.

The blackwood stables impose over the surrounding area. Finley walks ahead of Nera and me, lifting his arms in front of himself as he mutters under his breath. I smell the magic before I see it bursting around us. My hair stands on end with static, and the ring on his finger glows green as the gates swing open.

A sorcerer's amulet—like the one I used to have.

When I was little, I asked my mother if she was a sorcerer in hiding. If not, why did she have the necklace? But she swore to me that she only had it because my grandmother gave it to her. That she had no magic. I don't know if I believe her anymore.

"Wait here while I get everything ready," Finley says, and disappears into the darkness as I wrinkle my nose at the distinct stench of hay and animal droppings lingering around us.

Finley rolls a carriage made of elegant, round shapes out of a stall. The massive winged creatures he attaches to the front could've been horses in a past life. Their coats are a shiny black that almost blends with the carriage, and their curious eyes glow red as they follow me.

The three of us climb inside and leave the castle grounds through an ornate gate. The wide road goes through a forest that feels infinitely gray, desolate, with spindly branches and falling leaves that float down to the ground. A thick layer of fog covers the gravel road, which at some point was packed tightly, but isn't anymore. We ride in silence while the chill of the later morning sneaks in through the crevices of the tight space we share.

"We can't stay in Eponde for long. The curse is heavy within the city, and being there might affect your deterioration, Nera."

She nods absently, holding the wispy curtain to the side and pressing her forehead against the window.

"Who is guiding the carriage?" I ask after a long moment, when my curiosity—and nerves—grow thick enough I find it hard to breathe. We roll over debris on the road, and I'm certain we could crash into something at any moment.

Finley steadies himself against the wall, pinning me with his gaze. "Me."

I try to mask my horror, but it comes through in a mess of shaky words. "But you're inside."

"I use magic, Mia." A smirk pulls his thick lips. "How much did they teach you in Penumbra? You're able to cast simple spells alongside some complex magic."

I consider telling him the complex spells he's referring to were not something anyone taught me. I was a rebellious fool trying to protect what was left of my family—or perhaps I was trying to prove to Irene, and myself, that I could be more than just a librarian in charge of old, magical books.

I wanted to protect others, so they didn't have to suffer like I did when I lost my father.

Finley shifts toward me, but the carriage shakes again and I cling to the seat, my skin growing clammy and cold.

"Our drawls are like horses, and have been trained to follow the road into the city ever since they were foals, Mia. You don't have to worry," Nera says with a tentative smile. "Finley has to do very little guiding with his spell. We are in excellent hands."

I feel like I should've known that. Because of my intense studying, I usually have the facts hiding up my sleeves. But here, I always seem to be floundering for answers left and right. I just keep saying and assuming the wrong thing. I'm not from the world of the fae, of course. How could I know these things?

But that's too long of an answer, and I don't want their pity. So instead, I remain silent.

"When you came into our kingdom, you called yourself a librarian. Are there more of you, and are they all able to use magic?" Finley asks.

I debate ignoring his questions, like I've been doing so far. But what am I gaining with secrecy? I can't leave the fae realm unless I help Ash break his curse, and I can't break his curse if I don't trust them . . .

"There are fifty of us, including the head librarian, twenty elders who have worked in the library for decades, and twenty-nine librarians like me, who I see infrequently. Most of us can only cast simple protective spells to keep the grimoires' magic controlled and strengthen the wards on the building. We also are trying to find more information about the blood moon, other than what the legend says about the god Cronus meeting his fae lover during the Wild Hunt."

"We can tell you about the blood moon, and the Hunt, if you're still curious . . ." Nera says.

I shift forward in my seat, my heart hammering in my chest as I nod.

Finley throws Nera a turbulent look I can't decipher, but she ignores it and continues talking. "The blood moon allows the fae, both the seelie and unseelie, to ride together and replenish the ancient magic we lose when we remain in the mortal lands. Since we aren't allowed to step into the lands of the gods anymore, it's the only way to keep magic in this world."

So the legend is true then . . . The god does actually come into our lands to ride with his lover every three months.

"Only during the blood moon can someone like me bond with a spirit like Naheli, and only a royal bonded to one can take the unseelie throne."

I let that part of his history sink in. Ash had to ride the Hunt one time to bond a spirit, and Nera was given away to the seelie so Ash could inherit his throne. In many ways, the fae are just as barbaric as I've been taught.

"Why take humans if it's about regaining magic and bonding with ancient beings?" I ask.

"Because fae become more animalistic during that time, and let's not forget, humans seek the Hunt."

"What?" I blink before glancing at Finley and remembering what he told me a day ago. He'd stayed out when he knew the fae were coming, hoping to gain power.

He clears his throat and peeks behind the curtain at the ruins of the fae city we're approaching. "Humans born during the blood moon are blessed with magic."

My mouth falls open as I catch on to the implication. "The blood moon makes a sorcerer?"

They nod at the same time, and Finley says, "Only if they are born on any of the three nights it lasts."

I let my body sink into my seat as I digest every morsel of this information. "So it has nothing to do with parentage?"

"Genetics do play a part, but there's a higher chance for a newborn to be blessed with the magic of the spirits if the Hunt rides close to your home the day the baby is born. So you can imagine all the humans, and their children, that were claimed by the fae for that very reason."

The carriage slows as we roll into the dead city. No life remains inside the tragically beautiful gray stone buildings that greet us on either side of the road. It's a pit of nothing, and it digs a matching hollowness into my stomach.

Finley helps me out of the carriage. Leaves float past, over what must have once been a busy street. Nature has reclaimed this place. No matter how much I rub my arms, I can't seem to bring the warmth back into my body.

"What are you thinking?" Finley asks me.

The knot in my throat makes it hard to speak as I take in the trees growing out from between the cobblestones. Climbing vines snake up the walls and into the open buildings. I swallow before I push the words out. "I am part fae, yet I feel lost in this world."

"Hybrids and fae have a complicated relationship. In a way, you were safer growing up away from this kingdom," Finley says.

The energy in my stomach flutters again, burning hotter just as wood shutters slam against the walls with a sudden gust of wind that howls past us. "A hybrid?"

Finley rubs his brow bone with one finger, looking miserable to be stuck in this city and talking about this. "It's what we call those who are of mixed blood."

"What do you mean by 'complicated relationship'?"

He makes way for Nera to exit the carriage onto the desolate street and sighs. "The fae are bound by the bond to care for their humans, but in fae society, it was expected for humans to remain servants. So when the offspring of forbidden relationships showed incredible power, some groups arose and riled up enough followers to track down the hybrids and kill them."

Was that why my parents hid in Penumbra?

"And so the first war of hybrids began." Nera cringes as she studies the drab surroundings of what once was the illustrious fae city of Eponde. A place I'd only seen in illustrations in books.

Ice rushes through my body as I stare at her—and at everything else—stuck in this horror. "Why?" The question leaves my lips before I can stop it.

This entire history lesson leaves me speechless, and the pressure in my stomach stirs again. I've been trying to ignore it all morning.

"Because the power some hybrids had could've challenged the position of power the fae held among other communities," Nera answers, misunderstanding my question.

I wasn't asking why things went wrong for the hybrids of old, though I guess that also crossed my mind. But I want to know why this destruction happened. Are all the fae cities the same, or just Eponde?

"Not all the high fae were on board, and many helped hybrids escape to find refuge from the Kingdom of Aphelion in nearby neutral cities like Hedrum and all the way south in Caliban. Many fae fled their homes with their humans. However, if they were found, those fae were tried for treason," Finley says as we pass under a streetlamp covered in spiderwebs and dust.

The farther into the city we go, the more I feel my power pushing against the insides of my body. Could the hybrids that escaped be responsible for the curse?

"I didn't expect this . . . emptiness," Nera admits by my side, hugging her body with both arms.

Finley slams an abandoned carriage door shut, and the sound echoes indefinitely down the long street. "This is what you wanted to see. The destruction of your people. Your little rebellious birthday present to yourself."

I watch as Nera swallows but straightens her back, glancing around with false detachment. "I wanted to see what's coming for me—for all the unseelie in hiding that may be affected by the curse."

Nera doesn't believe there's a way out of this mess.

Eponde isn't larger than Penumbra, but somehow, it feels vast and tiny at the same time. There are no birds singing. No children playing. The devastation holds on to every brick and cobblestone that lies in our path.

The first statue we encounter is of a fae woman with large wings and a slender figure completely bare of clothing. Like she went out on a stroll naked, and never came back.

Her arms are elegant, and her long claws catch the drab sunlight that sneaks past the thick cover of rain clouds. Her mouth is a horror of jagged teeth that could rival a creature from nightmares.

She looks so similar to the way Nera did the night I met her.

"Have you had enough now?" Finley asks from behind us. His expression is somewhere between compassion and resignation.

But Nera is staring at the fae woman with a consuming sadness that pulls at strings in my heart. The energy buzzing through me thickens, and a spark flies out of my fingers. I shove my hands into my pockets, taking deep breaths to calm myself.

I must focus on the icy wind hitting my face, how it smells like a winter morning and something old and sinister that holds on to the makings of the buildings.

"She won," Nera whispers, and the tears she's been holding

back finally drag down her face. “They destroyed us all with her help. Even those of us who got them out. Even those of us who fought for union. Even those that were innocent.”

She won . . . I tuck that little bit of information away in the crevices of my mind.

“I think it’s best if we return now. You had your—strange—fun, but this isn’t good for you. Nor for the curse.”

I open my lips to agree with Finley, but shut them again when I find more statues on the street ahead. Gray and blending with their surroundings but visible now that I know what to look for. Hundreds of them. My skin itches, and I can no longer push the power bursting inside me out of my mind.

There are always innocents on either side of a war, even one fought with secret curses and veils that slowly leech living beings dry. My energy burns hotter under my skin as my panic rises. But thankfully, neither Nera nor Finley seem to notice.

Ash’s reasons for attacking the scientist quarters are hard to ignore now.

I understand him, and that makes me hate him just a little less. Even though he’s still an asshole. But he has to be in order to save his sister—and perhaps he isn’t too late to save his people.

We walk down the city streets until my feet ache and my eyesight blurs with unshed tears.

I like Nera, even though we started our strange friendship with violence.

“Fine, we can go back.”

Magic buzzes through my veins, and I don’t feel my fingers anymore, but I continue walking between them, trying to calm my breathing and appear normal as I struggle to ease my anxiety.

A low fog hugs the road by the time we make it all the way back to the carriage, and something I can’t see spooks the monstrous horses.

The pressure in my gut builds, and I’m scratching my skin like my insides are clawing their way out. Everything itches, or burns, it's hard to know.

Nera glances at me. At first, her face is still sad. But then her brows pinch in the middle. "Mia, are you alright?"

I hate being part of the race who caused this. I don't know how to help them and break this curse. All I want to do is claim I'm fine, just a little cold, but the noise that comes out of me is something between a moan and a sob.

She steps forward, her stony hand wrapping gently around my shoulder, careful to not pierce me with her deadly nails.

I think I hear her saying something, but I can't be sure with the rushing of blood in my ears. Because behind her, there is an unbroken window, the glass shiny enough for a semblance of her reflection to peek through the layers of dust.

One where she doesn't look like a statue but a pale, beautiful fae with auburn hair that falls to the middle of her back. Behind her, there's a squirming, dark figure clinging to her body.

The curse?

I blink, and my skin crawls with the sensation of ants all over me. I cry out again and the dark figure snaps its shadowy gaze to me, and it's then that my magic bursts out in waves. My vision goes white and I'm falling.

Glass shatters. Finley urges Nera to get me back home. The carriage rumbles under me, and it makes the feeling of my bones melting worse.

We jolt to a stop, and the door creaks as it opens before the cool air from outside hits my face.

"Mia." Ash's voice is a rumble

And then my light envelops me, and everything around me fully disappears.

CHAPTER 21

"You took her to the city. What were you thinking, Finley?"

"For the last time, it wasn't his fault." Nera's voice barely registers over the beating of my heart. I snuggle closer to the coolness enveloping me, and the burning inside me eases.

Everything hurts, and through the webs of my cloudy mind, I remember. The light of my power wrapped around me back in Eponde, taking every ounce of my energy.

But . . . I'm not dead, at least.

"When was the last time anyone but you could stop Nera when she set her mind to something?" I hear Finley's voice in the distance, like he's rooms away. Maybe I'm dreaming this. "Not all of us can simply put a high fae—who's turning to stone—to sleep, nor do I want to."

I open my eyes when thunder cracks. Rain pads against the windows, and a dull headache beats any cohesive thoughts out of me. The scent of pine, leather, and frankincense assaults my senses. Somehow, the smells and shapes around me calm the adrenaline coursing through my body as I take in my surroundings.

Naheli is by my side. I know not because I can see her with my blurry vision, but her familiar warmth and the ease of her breathing soothes me. As my vision clears, the shapes of tree roots weave together, forming a dome shape over me. This is not my room.

My head spins when I sit up and take in Ash's chambers and the purple covers draped over my legs. Nera, Finley, and Ash are talking in hushed tones by the door. All I can see are their fuzzy shapes as they all turn in my direction at the same time.

"You're awake," Ash says, unfolding his arms from across his chest and striding toward me. He's wearing a white shirt with the sleeves rolled up, which lets me take in the light sprinkle of feathers that remain on his forearms.

"Why am I here?" I croak and shift closer to the edge of the mattress. It doesn't matter how much my body screams to remain here and rest, I need to be out of his bed. When my feet hit the ground, everything around me spins, forcing me to remain seated or I might lose the little food I've had.

Naheli's head presses against my shoulder, and she growls. A warning to remain seated. I'm not sure how I know this. I've stopped trying to make sense of it.

"It seems I need to lock you in my room if I'm to keep you safe, Monster. I can't even trust my family when I'm out."

My cheeks burn with embarrassment, anger—and desire. "I'm not staying here."

"Really?" He lifts a brow and steps closer, reaching for a glass of water on the nightstand, before handing it to me. "I have all night long to see how you will leave. This should be interesting."

There is a challenge in his eyes that pins me down, and my throat feels so dry I'm reaching for the water before I can talk myself out of it.

I have long accepted that I'm an impulsive person. Why stop

now? "I would like to know how you plan to stop me when you're slumbering?"

Ash's brows shoot up, and I hear Nera snickering in the background. Ash glares in her direction, and the buttons of his tailored shirt strain when he crosses his arms back over his chest. "Your loyalty is at a low point right now, Nerala."

Ash turns back to me, ignoring his sister. "I figured that's how you're escaping your room, but the question is, how did you learn about the slumber?" His eyes narrow as he watches me.

Morgana's face flashes in my mind. I haven't seen her—nor the dresses she promised—since that first morning. She's been leaving my food in front of my door, though I guess I don't technically owe her anything.

I bring the glass of water to my lips to prevent myself from dragging her into this mess, and the cool drink eases the burning in my throat.

I jut my chin up and don't elaborate further. We stare at each other in silence. His pupils enlarge right as his eyes dip to my lips. Thankfully, he is far from me. Not sure why it feels like that detail will save me from a true disaster, like throwing myself at him.

My heart soars, and heat pools in my stomach. The same ridiculous reaction I had before, when he took my book away, right before he told me he didn't want me.

His words sting as much now as they did when he said them.

"Do you know what almost happened to you today?" He leans on the bed, and the mattress dips as he puts pressure on the edge. "When you followed my little sister into our fallen city, did you think you might die?"

"What? No." Though I'm thinking of myself as the worst of weeds, that not even monsters and beasts can kill me.

"You're being an asshole," Nera hisses. "Sure, it was irresponsible to go to Eponde, and bring Mia, but I needed to see what happened there, and I thought perhaps she could get some ideas about how to help us."

"It looks to me like she almost killed herself with a power she has little control over."

I open my lips to protest, but the pressure in my stomach is a reminder that he's right.

Nera's usual graceful movements look so much slower as she steps closer to the bed, like her stone limbs weigh her down. And for once, I hear the marble scraping together. "I need to live before I'm gone. You can't stop what's happening to me. I've accepted it."

"I'm not giving up on you." Ash's raw pain taints his inflection. My throat closes as he moves toward Nera, lifting a hand and gently cupping her face. "We can't go to Hedrum. It doesn't matter what other suicide mission you're ready to drag Finley or Mia into"—Ash isn't looking at her. His eyes are fixed on me, and I find myself unable to look away—"I'm going to protect you until my last breath."

I have a feeling he wasn't only talking to his sister, and my blood burns again, but for a very different reason.

"It'll be my last breath, not yours," Nera rages and points at the corner of the room.

I gasp as I take in the rose vines that have overtaken the ceiling. I'm fairly certain those weren't there before.

"Even if I said yes, have you seen how we look? We don't fit in Hedrum, cursed as we are. If we go, you won't be able to enjoy your day. We can do something else. *Anything*."

"I may be young compared to you, Ash, but I have been listening during this last decade. I know our people are hiding behind glamours inside Aphelion. In small towns or even in our ruined cities. They are hiding in plain sight, and we can do the same. You and Finley can figure out an enchantment that will keep us hidden long enough. I get to decide how I spend my last weeks of sanity, and it's not inside this castle. You have the choice whether you're going to spend them with me or not. I'm done waiting, and I'll leave without you."

Ash presses his fingers to the bridge of his nose as Nera bolts for the door. The silence descends on those of us who remain.

He moves forward, picks up a golden plate from the night-stand, and places it on the bed beside me. Naheli lifts her head, sniffing at the food and eyeing it curiously.

"Eat, Monster, you used a lot of energy earlier."

"So what, now you're taking care of me?" I don't mean to sound snippy, but the way my traitorous heart somersaults keeps me on edge.

"It seems I have to—"

"Why?" I cut him off. Frustration seeping into my words as my hands shake. The water inside the glass I still hold sloshes over my fingers. "Why do you need to keep me alive when you clearly think I am— What was the word you used? Ah, yes, a pest."

If I hadn't been staring at him, I may have missed the subtle hitch of his shoulders as he winces. Like he isn't proud of his outburst from before.

"You called her that?" Nera's voice turns high-pitched from the door.

"I thought you were leaving after making your point?" he says to his sister, who huffs and exits the room. When he glances back to me, there is a softness to his brows. "I didn't put my best foot forward yesterday," he says, rubbing his temple. "I'm not used to having a human—let alone a hybrid—walking the castle and getting into my things."

It wasn't quite an apology, and I shouldn't care. All I have to do is find a way to unravel the curse so I can leave.

"If I'm actually going to help you, you need to be truthful with me." I hold my half-full glass between my thighs, and the layers of my full skirt do a somewhat-decent job of keeping it straight.

Then I reach for the food on my golden plate and take a slow bite of the buttery biscuit. The salty flavor coats my tongue, and I have to bite back a moan.

"I guess it's as good a time as any to talk about this." Ash scrapes his raven hair back with a groan and moves across the room, sitting on a massive wingback chair in the corner. "Ask your questions . . ."

"Did you know what I am?"

"Yes." He crosses a leg over his knee and leans back, draping both arms over the armrests. He is the perfect image of relaxation. "I suspected you were a hybrid the moment you used fae magic in Penumbra."

It's not surprising he knew, and it makes sense why he asked all those questions the night we met. Why he had so much hatred toward me, which I returned. But I didn't know the entire story then. I feel different now.

He continues, "It quickly became clear you didn't know what you are or what happened here."

"What gave it away? I could've been acting . . ."

He lifts a brow, like that's the most ridiculous thing he's ever heard.

Naheli shifts forward a bit, her snout inching closer and closer to my plate, her mouth making wet sounds as she salivates over my food. I shift the plate away from the gluttonous wolf. I might lose my old identity, my home, my bed, my sanity—since apparently I find the king of beasts insanely attractive—but I'm not losing my gods-damned biscuits.

The spirit's four yellow eyes meet mine, and I narrow my gaze at her in a challenge, then I quickly pick up the second biscuit and consume half of it in one bite.

"There are more where that came from, Monster. No need to fight Naheli for it."

"Shut up."

The grin that takes over Ash's face is wonderful. White teeth and fucking dimples.

There goes my stomach again, hollowing and flipping, which feels gloriously terrible when blended with the dull buzz of energy that remains trapped in there. I might be sick all over the floor.

"Either way, how would you have known I wasn't playing a game? Getting into the castle to make this curse more agonizing?"

Ugh. Who am I kidding? There isn't a way in the world I could be the mastermind behind that. I'm clearly floundering, even aside from finding out my whole life has been a lie.

"You were looking for the amulet, and couldn't control your magic without it." Finley steps into the room, digging his hands into his cloak pockets. "Nera told us earlier that you've been feeling a pressure building inside your body? That you can't get it out?"

"Yes, right here." I press my fingers to the middle of my stomach, where the knot of energy buzzes.

"Is that what happened in Eponde? You finally lost control?" Ash asks.

The memory of the dirty window and the shadow moving behind Nera bursts in my mind. I don't know if I've finally lost the last semblance of my sanity, or if I actually stumbled on something. I could tell him, but then again, can I trust any of them?

Taking a deep breath, I prepare myself to lie. "I saw a shadowy reflection behind Nera and got scared. That's when I lost control . . ."

Alright, so apparently I can't lie to him. Great.

I study their expressions, expecting them to change to recognition and excitement that perhaps I found something we can use, but they remain stoic. Nothing changes, not even a muscle twitch.

"I see . . ."

"That's all?"

"What do you want? Eponde is not a safe place. The dark magic of the curse attracts creatures that live in nightmares. It's hard to tell you what you saw without inspecting it myself," Ash says at last.

I slump on the bed and swallow the last bite of my food.

Finley tosses a log into the fireplace. "Going to Hedrum might be necessary beyond Nera's whims and wishes."

"How so?" Ash leans forward as the fire roars back to life, and the room warms again.

"We all know Mia doesn't need an amulet, yet her parents gave her one when she showed signs of magic. Isn't that true, Mia?"

I nod, holding onto each of his words like they are food for a starving woman.

"Continue . . ." Ash waves his hand in Finley's direction in a kingly manner that would have made me smile had they not been discussing my life.

"While we talked earlier, I got the impression all librarians use magic one way or another. Do any of them have artifacts like the one you had?"

The air lodges in my throat, and I know where Finley's line of questioning is taking us. Hybrids don't need amulets, while sorcerers, like him, do. I stare at the chunky silver ring on his finger. The green gem catches the light. "All the librarians use magic without amulets." I shift my body where I sit, moving the crumbs left on my plate with my finger.

"Did any of them ever mention anything about being hybrids?" Ash doesn't look surprised at all. I suppose he's known who had his grimoires all along. It was me who was unaware of everything.

"I don't . . . know." How many of my colleagues knew their nature? Surely the head librarian and all the elders must.

"I believe powerful sorcery is keeping Mia's magic locked, and it's only released when she's using an artifact," Finley says.

The room goes silent, and my forgotten vertigo returns. Everything spins, and I grip at the blankets tightly to ground myself. I used to be strong. Now I'm broken, tethered only by my will to save Irene, the fae—and myself.

"You think her parents were protecting her from the hybrids living in Penumbra? By what, trying to fool them into believing she could only access magic with her necklace?"

"No," I say, shifting forward and out of bed, ignoring Ash's protests and Naheli's annoyed huffs. "My father told me to never let them see my artifact. I was very careful."

Was I?

I got reckless during the last year while I attempted to learn ways to stop the beasts. While I mastered fire and wind spells. Irene knew about it, and that likely meant her friends in the scientist quarters did as well. Who else saw me?

"Artifacts allow sorcerers to wield magic," Finley says, and his amber eyes land on me. Pity fills them for the briefest of moments before he takes his hand out of his pocket and glances at the green ring on his thick fingers. "If I'm right, an artifact might be the only way she can access hers. A spell locks her power, and it was meant to fool most into believing she's a sorcerer, not a hybrid."

"Why would the hybrids need to be fooled if I'm one of them?"

"Because not all hybrids are trying to destroy the fae," Finley says, and then exchanges a meaningful look with Ash. "You need to tell her."

"Mind your own business, Finley."

"You made it my business when you went to Penumbra, even though I begged you not to."

"Tell me what?" I stand, shaking. Why is everyone keeping me in the dark?

Frustration grows within me like a sickness I can't stop. The burning sensation in my stomach returns with a vengeance.

A thread of magic pours from my fingers, shimmering white, and adrenaline moves through my body as I notice it escaping me. It's an uncontrolled spell that has no name, no meaning other than frustration. I can't pull it back inside me, fear takes over from anger, and the spell turns from white to blue. My skin glows on and off.

"Mia," Ash whispers, and it feels sweet and haunting. Like he's trying to calm a raging beast. Then in the fae tongue, he says, "*Naheli, help her.*"

The spirit leaps toward me. Her body enlarges, sending starlight around the room, blinding me, and all I can hear is the whooshing of my heart.

Her aura expands and wraps around me like a hug, soothing the burning inside me. Cool mist that shortly shifts to the smell of pine, leather, and frankincense. And when I open my eyes, I meet Ash's gaze as he embraces me, preventing me from collapsing to the ground.

Breathe. I read his lips and take a deep breath that eases the burning in my lungs.

Slowly, the room stops spinning, and I find myself relaxing in his grasp. Ash studies my face with pinched brows, and I think he's making sure I won't lose consciousness like in Eponde.

I nod, hoping he understands I'm fine, even though I'm too exhausted to speak.

"You should rest," he says, dropping his hands from around my waist, and I immediately miss the warmth they provided. He takes one long step away and shoves his hand into his trousers pocket. "Finley's right. We need to get you a new amulet until we figure out what's happening to you."

CHAPTER 22

When I wake up, there's a small mountain of flaky rolls on the side table, a dish with butter, and a jar of honey. I'm smiling before I can stop myself. I don't know how long I've been sleeping. A day?

A week?

I shift out of Ash's bed, and the silk of his sheets slides away from my crumpled dress. I'm feeling more rested than I have in a long time. A small win in a moment such as this.

I glance around the room to find that I'm alone. The fire is still going in that beautiful fireplace. The balcony's doors are wide open, letting in the gentle breeze of the evening.

The polished floor is cool under my bare feet, and I absently wonder who removed my boots and socks. I guess feeling embarrassed about any of them doing something so intimate, like caring for me, should be the least of my concerns. But I can't seem to make my heart listen.

"Hello?"

"We're outside, Monster." Ash's voice travels in, and my stomach flutters in response.

I step out to the balcony, and the air of the night envelops me, carrying the notes of mint and rose petals.

Ash sits on the smooth stone floor, petting Naheli's head. Neither of them looks at me as I join them. It's beautiful here. Rounded balusters keep us from the drop of at least a hundred feet to the gardens below. A light layer of moisture covers every surface, but the night spans over us. Indigo and violet, peppered with shimmering white dots, framed by the forest in the distance.

Ash looks at peace, unlike I've ever seen him before. Slightly hunched with his wolf resting her massive head on his lap. She is as breathtaking as the night sky above.

"I know Naheli and I are quite a sight to behold, but are you going to just stare at us or actually sit like a civilized creature?"

I glower at him. "You think a lot of yourself, don't you?"

He cocks his head in my direction. So completely at ease in himself and the way he looks—even with the remnants of feathers going down his ankles. I can't help but feel flustered and annoyed.

"I wasn't looking at you." Why am I still talking? "I was merely noticing that it isn't raining anymore. Ever since I arrived here, it's been one rainstorm after another."

Ash's eyes shimmer with delight at seeing me so awkward. At least he doesn't comment on it. "The curse's magic makes a perfect environment for dark creatures, and many of those who live in shadows bring storms."

I open my lips to ask about these creatures, and remember the shadow I saw in that reflection.

"The farther we get from the blood moon, the more it clears out."

I've been away from Penumbra and Irene for almost a month. I wonder if she thinks I'm dead, like our father.

I lean against the wall and slide my body slowly down it until I'm sitting on the cold ground. Rosebushes climb the columns on either side of the balcony that hold the roof up. The blooms have shifted from black to red.

From this position, I can better see the dark circles under Ash's eyes. I drink in his black pants and the loose shirt that hangs open over his clavicles, doing very little to hide his muscular chest.

I remember very little of the night after I lost control of my power in Eponde. Only our conversation back in his room, where I learned I may be under an enchantment. But the hours after that —they have been murky at best.

And even though I slept in his bed, I haven't seen him much.

"How long did I sleep for?"

"A day." He glances at the beautiful night in front of us. "I'm glad you're finally awake. I was getting concerned . . ."

"Who would have thought that the king of beasts would be worried about little ol' me? A hybrid who tried to kill him. And here I thought you hated me."

"It's a disaster," he says, leaning his head back to reveal the thick column of his throat. Naheli snorts, and her surrounding galaxy deepens, giving away her temper. Ash scratches behind her pointy ears. "It seems I'm destined to die surrounded by difficult females."

I chuckle and force myself to look at something that isn't him. "I've never slept for so long before . . ."

"It's likely your body was fighting whatever spell is keeping your magic locked and that drained you completely."

"So, you actually believe what Finley suspects?"

"He looks young, but he is over sixty human years old. He has seen many spells in his life, and is a great sorcerer. It makes sense." Ash lets out a long breath and turns to me. "I don't know where you came from, Monster, but your family went to great lengths to hide your nature."

"Sure," I bite out, and familiar anger bubbles in my gut. "They did such a great job of hiding me, I didn't even know what I am."

"Being a hybrid is dangerous in this world. It has been for a while . . . Your parents might have been hiding you from the fae at first."

"Except the fae have been gone for a decade."

"Yes, but there are other dangers besides my kind. For example, there's a different group of hybrids—a very dangerous one—that uses dark magic and wants to force others to join their cause."

"And you think the librarians are part of that group?"

"The hybrids who stole my books aren't innocents, and neither are those feeding my people to the veil."

Are they working together? It seems oddly coincidental that both are targeting the fae at the same time, but I'm not sure. It's not like the librarians work with the scientists. We are separate entities.

"I need to get my sister out of that town."

"Do you think she doesn't know?"

"I hope she doesn't," I admit, and press my lips tight as sorrow fills my heart. "She hasn't been the same since a lunargyre killed our father. She wants revenge, so perhaps she doesn't know the full truth."

I'm not even sure I believe that, but right now, when my entire life is falling apart, I need to hold on to something. Even if it's a ridiculous idea.

"I can understand that," Ash says. "If anyone hurt someone I love, I would burn the world down to avenge them."

I'm grateful he doesn't point out how unlikely it is that Irene is innocent.

"I haven't been entirely truthful with you, Monster." Ash opens his palms, and gold magic swirls around his fingers. The blue book he took from me days ago appears in his hand. Perfectly fitting there. Like it was made for him. Maybe it was.

I stare at the grimoire with bated breath, trying to school my features so Ash won't see my eagerness to get ahold of it again. I don't reach for it, not even when the book sings to me. The little wisps of its power reach closer and closer.

"What are you not telling me, then?"

He seems to consider it and flips quickly through the book, stopping on one particular page. "A long time ago, there was a prophecy that warned my people about the curse, and it's written here." Ash frowns before his eyes cut to me. I can barely see the shimmer of gold behind his thick, dark lashes. "I didn't want you to know about the prophecy, because it speaks of hybrids who would destroy my kingdom."

"Do you think I'm one of those hybrids?"

He inhales and shakes his head. "Surprisingly, no. At least not anymore."

I peek at the neat calligraphy marking the parchment as he reads: "*The hybrids will come under a blood moon to the unseelie halls.*" He speaks in the fae tongue, and the hairs on my arms stand up. Ash meets my gaze and continues from memory. "*Their eyes are a mix of human and fae with a power unlike anything we've seen before . . .*"

He hands me the grimoire, and I'm reaching for it before I can think twice. It hugs my fingers in greeting, its small voice singing through my veins, bringing warmth even on this chilly evening.

"You seem far too happy about this," he says dryly.

The smile that sneaks onto my face falls, and I blink through the haze of excitement that clouds my thoughts. "Sometimes magical items like this one speak to me in a way that's strange to explain. They aren't words, but feelings. This book is happy to be read by me. Even though I can't actually read what it says."

I study the symbols and words on the page.

Ash shifts closer and reaches for my hand. The moment we touch, electricity jolts through me. His eyes widen, and perhaps he felt the same. Hesitating, he shifts away, but not fully. His scent drives me mad. He's thinking of letting go—and I don't want him to.

Our gazes meet, and he moves my hand over the page as he recites in a voice that is honey to my ears.

"The hybrids will come under a blood moon to the unseelie halls. Their eyes are a mix of human and fae with a power unlike anything we've seen before."

He moves my finger over the paper. Gooseflesh races over my skin as my heart drums faster. I follow each line as he says it, and his voice feels so familiar, so like the one from the grimoire.

"A blackened rose will bring destruction to those who ride the Hunt. Only when the king who cries tears of gold loses all, will there come a new hope, and the one with the black rose will fall."

My eyes round and I stare at him, shocked. "Did you write this? Are you a soothsayer?"

"In the flesh." He frowns and shifts back to his old spot on the balcony floor. I immediately miss him near me. "The stars have been speaking to me since I was a young boy. It's a curse on its own. Everyone wants to know what happens in the future, but when it's something tragic, they sharpen their pitchforks."

"Is that what they did when you told them about this?"

He lifts a hand and waves it toward the castle grounds that expand beyond the rooftops. "No. My father forced me, his crown prince, to partake in the Hunt. Even though the prophecy clearly said it would bring on our downfall."

"The prophecy says the blackened rose will bring destruction." I stare at the rose canes growing over the wall, dread sinking in my stomach at the thought of how much I've been touching them. "Are these part of the curse then?"

"I've tried to destroy them multiple times." He doesn't even glance at them. "I still don't know why they sprout everywhere I go, even ten years later . . ."

I'm not interested in premonitions and prophecies. No matter what that book says, I'll help him. I care about Nera, Finley, Naheli —and him.

I hand him the book, and he sighs in relief as soon as it's back in his possession.

"This is where I keep all of my premonitions, and I believe whoever stole the grimoires from our library was trying to find this one. But they didn't know I keep it with me."

I blush as the memories of days ago flood my mind. How he reacted when he saw me with it. How angry he'd been that I somehow had it.

"It looks more like a diary than a book that holds visions of your kingdom's fate."

He smirks and relaxes back against the wall, crossing his arms over his knees. "That was on purpose. It's meant to look ordinary, and if unwanted hands get ahold of it, it will poison them. Only the king of the unseelie may glance at its pages."

"But I opened it, and I'm fine."

"A fact I'm still trying to figure out . . ."

I lower my gaze as shame weighs on my chest. "Naheli brought it to me," I admit. Ash clearly didn't want this to be read, not only because of what it contains, but because it could've killed me.

Something so powerful could be terrible in the hands of the wrong person, and I need to be more aware of what I am doing.

I glance at the wolf with a galaxy in her body. She barely

shifted an ear when I said her name, not ashamed of her actions whatsoever.

"I figured as much. No one else in the castle would've been able to access the safe."

"You two formed a powerful bond . . . Was that after the Hunt? Or during it? How did you convince her to stay?"

"The spirit is a gluttonous being. I just told her she could eat as many deer and geese as she wanted. Even an occasional human. She gladly stayed after that."

My brows shoot up, and horror swarms through my body.

"Close your mouth, Monster. I'm just playing with you." His chuckle begins as a slow roll, and deepens into a full belly laugh that breaks the gentle songs of the crickets below, and the hissing of the lunargyres that remain in the courtyard.

I hit the side of his arm with the back of my hand. "It's not funny." But there's hardly any heat in my words. Whatever shock and anger I felt before dissipates like sugar in water. I'm just getting used to his teasing moods, and I really like the way he laughs. I'm so fucked.

I should probably go back inside. It would be the sensible thing to do.

I run my hands over my skirt, smoothing any wrinkles. Afraid if I change positions or make too much noise, he'll stop smiling.

"She loves to eat deer, and it was the last thing I tried to bargain with that night. I was desperate, because she is extremely powerful. The Hellions, which is the type of spirit she is, are rarely seen roaming the mortal realms. But I think in the end, she wanted to be free. To live in our world. It's brighter here, and she loves the sunlight."

I bring my knees to my chest and wrap my arms around them. My cheeks hurt from smiling, and my heart feels strangely large as I imagine Naheli running through the forest as rays of sunlight pierce the thick canopy.

I love that he's sharing little details of his life with me. Even though a hybrid cursed him and his kingdom. Even though I'm part of the race that's to blame for what happened here. I wasn't part of the atrocities my people committed against his, just like he wasn't responsible for what the old fae did to the hybrids.

We were in the wrong place at the wrong time. But I'm still a hybrid. And he's still the king of the unseelie.

I'm woman enough to admit to myself that I like him. For better or for worse, he has become the one constant that I look forward to every day.

"And what do you get once you bond with a spirit?"

"My powers are exponentially amplified, and I can do things most fae can only dream of. Of course, now that I have to keep the kingdom's enemies from reaching the castle and the few people that remain conscious, we're both exhausted."

"What prevents other fae from bonding with a spirit and taking over the throne?"

"Oh, they've tried. But my bloodline possesses a magical trait that makes the bond possible. They call us the soul weavers. Whatever that means . . ." Rough laughter escapes his lips. Unlike the true, beautiful sound of before, this one is raw with pain. "When I was young, after I made the prophecy, I prayed a long-lost relative would come and usurp my father's throne so I didn't have to inherit a cursed land."

"Is that why Nera's prophecy sends her to the seelie kingdom? Because she can bond to a spirit that might save them?"

Ash's brows lift and he stares at me, jaw open for a moment before he can school his features. "You are intuitive, Monster, I give you that. And I assume that's the case, though the prophecy didn't reveal those details to me."

I mull over everything he's sharing and enjoy the breeze that hits my skin. It smells like a storm is brewing in the distance.

Then my world comes to a halt. I turn sharply to Ash. "You're Nera's soothsayer?"

"Of course I am." He sounds annoyed, though I'm not sure if it's more with himself or me. "There's one soothsayer born from five thousand fae. Only two recorded in the last three centuries."

"I just didn't imagine you were the one." I wring my hands as I debate what to do with myself.

Ash's expression sours as he drags his palm over Naheli's fur and stars dance around his fingers. "Not a day goes by that I don't regret telling my father that Nera's mate is Sylas of the seelie realm. That prick is not the man I want for my sister, not even if their union could save their kingdom."

"Mates?" I almost laugh, but clear my throat before a sound escapes. I'm too much of a cynic to believe anything of the sort, but then again, I'm speaking to a soothsayer in the flesh.

Perhaps it's time to open my mind to new possibilities—even if they sound ridiculous.

"Fated mates. There's a difference." Ash's expression is unreadable as he meet my gaze. "Hasn't one of the stolen books told you about them?"

There's a bite to his tone, but there's also hunger hidden in the way he looks at me. I must be imagining things again. My cheeks heat, and I don't know if it's from desire or frustration at myself. It takes all my willpower to remain seated. To learn more about the enigma of this world, of him.

The longer I spend with Ash, the more I understand he pushes away anyone that's still coherent enough to want to stay close to him. I have a feeling he's drowning in guilt. Perhaps he even feels he deserves this.

"They haven't." I lean back against the wall. Some roses beside me are still black, and they hum with small whispers, beckoning me to touch. "What is it . . . a mate, I mean? That's not something we have."

Silence descends upon us for a long time. And I don't know if he's going to answer my question, or speak at all. Am I being dismissed, and I'm just too stubborn to accept it?

"A fae takes a mate, much like a human takes a partner. Fated mates are different. The gods write their relationships in the stars. An unbreakable bond that can alter the world."

"And the stars told you Nera and Sylas are fated to be together?" I ask, though it feels like the air has leeched out of my lungs. I study the same stars he's been staring at since who knows when, trying to find something there for myself. "How does having premonitions work?"

"Like anything with magic, Monster. I feel it in my gut, how the stars whisper to me, and if I quiet my thoughts, I can understand what they're saying. Even when I shouldn't."

Like me with the fae language, and the books, the roses, and anything else that has spoken to me before.

Just then, Naheli yawns loudly, stretching on her hind legs and blinking her four eyes at Ash—then me—before sprinting back inside.

Ash dusts off his pants, even though she isn't a real wolf that leaves fur behind, and gets up. "I'm going to sleep. Please make yourself comfortable in my bed. Surely you find it more suitable than your previous arrangement."

While I won't deny that a king's mattress is hard to beat, I am not about to stay here. With him. "About me sleeping here. You weren't being serious, right?"

"Ah, but I was. You see, Monster, when a human stares into a fae's eyes during the Hunt, we're bound to protect you or we fail our side of the bargain. I can't rest if I'm worrying you're running the halls while everyone is asleep."

I press my lips tight and think of one thousand ways to murder Nera and her big mouth. Though I guess it's possible the lunargyres also whispered to Ash. He is the king of beasts, after all.

"I haven't run the halls other than yesterday morning, and now that Nera warned me the beasts knew what I was doing, I wasn't planning on doing it again. I know you don't believe me, but I actually don't want to die."

"You will sleep here, in my bed, and I will take the small chamber next door. It's meant for—company." He clears his throat and scratches the back of his neck. "I'll know if any door in my room opens. That includes the balcony."

"Are you going to sleep in the concubine's room?" I tease, trying to ignore the warmth spreading in my chest. That's too close to trouble, and I shouldn't be flirting or obsessing about why he isn't making me go there instead.

"Yes, very amusing. Now, please put this charm on"—he digs a hand into his pocket, pulls Finley's green stone ring from it, and extends it to me—"and don't take it off until we find you something else."

I reach for the amulet, but it doesn't want to come with me. Its threads recoil slightly from my touch, and it complains rather loudly that I stink. With a frown at the cool piece of jewelry in my palm, I meet Ash's gaze. "It doesn't like me . . ."

He laughs. "It's Finley's. Of course, it won't feel right to you, but it will prevent you from killing yourself until we get to Hedrum."

My skin tingles and . . . what was I thinking before? "We are truly going to Hedrum, then?"

"It seems like we have no choice but to leave as soon as possible. Finley can't be without his amulet. We leave in two days. Try to rest, Monster. The trip is long."

Hedrum, a city of sorcery and magic. One of the few places where humans, sorcerers and fae once lived amongst each other in peace.

But after what Nera said, I don't know if the fae remained there. She said all of them are in hiding. Still, I can't help but smile. Not because I'll get to see a magical city for the first time and immerse myself in a new culture. But because Nera gets her wish for her birthday.

She wants to be free, to live, and I'm happy to be there with her.

CHAPTER 23

Nera doesn't look like a statue anymore, and I stare with wide eyes as she steps into the carriage. Instead of stone features, unblemished pale skin and black hair so long it reaches her lower back. A royal blue dress peeks out from beneath her indigo traveling cloak. Her wings are gone.

The morning light bounces over her skin and sort of . . . blurs, creating a strange illusion that she's glowing. Or at least that's the only explanation my tired mind comes up with this early in the day. Even her eyes have shifted from the beautiful rose gold to a light blue.

She slides over the seat right across from me and drapes her slender, gloved hands over her lap. "It's a glamour to make us look human," she says, giving me a toothy smile. "It lasts for five days before it needs to be strengthened. Since Naheli is staying here, it's easier for Ash to cast the enchantment before we leave."

My wolf friend will remain behind to protect the lunargyres that live in the castle. The cook, a few maids, and others I haven't met. We haven't even left, and I already miss her.

"I knew we were traveling under a glamour," I say. "But somehow I never expected you to adopt the guise of being human. Is the situation so bad that you can't travel as fae?"

"It can be. Right now, most fae who are curse-free hide their nature when traveling the continent, and otherwise stay hidden in their towns around Aphelion." Finley's lips tilt into a strained smile as he studies Nera.

She's looking down at her body and beaming at no one in particular. I don't think she's even paying attention to what we're saying.

Her happiness is contagious, and it's easy to promise myself that I'll do anything I can to help her.

I glance out through the open door. The silhouette of the castle stands behind the thick morning mist, its black towers barely visible from here. "So fae towns aren't all like Eponde?"

"No. We found crystals that help strengthen the wards to hide them from enemies. Now, only Ash and Naheli can find them."

"And me, but I haven't left the castle . . ." Nera says, and her face sobers somewhat.

And we're doing this just to get me an amulet? I chew on my lip, feeling guilty and excited at the same time. "Is it safe for us to travel?"

"I take this trip often. We'll stop in Fairhope first, a magical town of sorcerers and humans who want to stay out of the conflict, and then we'll ride straight to Hedrum, if we make good time."

The carriage dips again, and my eyes shift to Ash as he steps in. I thought he was breathtaking before. I didn't know anything. Destiny and whatever game the gods are playing with me can go to hell. With every trace of the curse gone, there's nothing I don't find glorious about the king of beasts.

His edge of danger remains in the sharpness of his features.

Long, dark lashes frame his now-brown eyes. Sun-kissed skin contrasts against the fur lining the lapels of his charcoal coat.

Beneath the drumming of my heart, I hear a soft, feminine chuckle, and I snap back to reality.

"Are you done gawking, Monster, or did a cat steal your tongue?" He leans against the backrest and closes the carriage door.

"Did you say something?" I swear I didn't see his mouth move.

His lips tilt, just a little. "Finley asked if the ring caused you trouble the last few nights."

I glower at Ash and force my eyes toward his much nicer friend. "The ring hates me, but I don't feel like I'm about to explode anymore."

"Good." Finley nods, doing a poor ass job of hiding his amusement, and leans closer to whisper in my ear. "It's ridiculous, isn't it? The way they glow? You get used to it."

Nera waggles her brows at me conspiratorially. Oh gods. I need to get better at concealing my stupid crush on her brother. I don't even think I can lie to myself about hating him anymore.

Now that all four of us are properly packed inside this box like preserved meat, there's no way to escape him.

We settle into our trip, and I'm surrounded by gorgeous fae while myself looking like a drenched squirrel with eyes swollen from too much sleep. Even Finley looks ruggedly handsome. The carriage would be comfortable for traveling, if I weren't accompanied by giants. As it is, it's cramped and hot inside the cabin.

The roads out of the Kingdom of Aphelion are paved, and transition to gravel the farther we go up the mountains, away from the castle, and onto new lands. Our view out the window changes as the hours pass, the palette shifting from gray to olive hues. The dark forest of the cursed lands fades to grasses and shorter trees, while a thick layer of white clouds remains, as does the mist hugging the ground.

I've been sitting in this same position for hours, and my ass is about to melt into the seat if we don't stop soon. Not that I'm going to be the person to ask how much longer we have—again. Even if everything in me aches. It doesn't help that I'm massively self-conscious about my humanity and lack of grace as I watch Nera sleep. Not so much as a hint of drool on her chin.

It's the same with Ash. He lies so still against his corner, it's like he's become a statue.

At midday, we stop at a shop on the side of the road that looks like it's run by human-eating gnomes. We feed the beasts that pull our carriage disguised as beautiful stallions.

"We have to make it to Fairhope before twilight," Finley tells me as he settles by my side and hands me a green apple.

It has to be because of the slumber.

We arrive at Fairhope by midafternoon, just a few hours before sunset. A small village of twenty or so modest homes, tiny shops with metal signs hanging over their doors, and a large inn with cabins that go up the side of a hill.

The carriage slows in a small plaza with a fountain in the middle and comes to a stop in front of a two-story, white stucco building with wood beams crisscrossing over the walls.

I squint at the brightness outside and meet Ash's eyes as he stands beside the carriage, extending a hand to help me down. The moment my fingers drape over his, electricity travels up my arm and into my chest, like it has every time we've accidentally touched.

This time I'm prepared for it—and it seems so is he. His expression is cool, distant even. Perhaps he didn't feel it at all, and it's just in my head.

A young man approaches the carriage, hands Ash a slip, and blabbers about the feed they give the horses. Finley steps forward, whispering directions to the kid while Nera hooks her arm through the crook of my elbow and drags me toward the building.

"Let's get a table while they explain the strange behavior of our horses to that poor kid," she says with a chuckle.

We cross through arched doors in desperate need of a fresh coat of paint and into a large room where, at the far end, an old man behind a wooden counter hunches over a book, dipping a tattered quill into his ink pot and scribbling away.

He glances at us over half-moon spectacles and dismisses us with a wave of his rather sizable hand. "A warm meal is off to the right. Stefani will sort you with stew and bread. Out you go—off with you."

"Come, Mia," Nera purrs, and pulls me to where the old man pointed. We cross into a dark but cozy room of modest size. Five scattered tables of different shapes and tones of wood fill the space, and a couple of patrons enjoy a meal.

I drink in every detail, from the uneven floor made of gathered river rock, to the rustic columns stained a rich brown. Humidity hangs in the air, saturated with the scent of stew, roasted onions, and butter.

"I haven't been here in so long, but it looks exactly the same," Nera says as we cross to the other end of the room, where the small bar stands. The bartender waves in our direction with a jolly smile that makes his red cheeks shine.

"I can't believe I'm in Fairhope. It's so far north, and across the cursed forest, I just never thought I would see this," I admit, unable to hide the excitement in my voice.

Nera nods, and her expression turns sad, but somehow hopeful. "We have something in common, you and I."

"That your brother drives us insane?"

"Well, that too." She laughs, and we sit at a medium-sized round table that could comfortably seat six, but it's the farthest from the rest of the patrons. "But no, what I meant was that both of us have been trapped, living like prisoners even though we technically aren't."

I mull over her words even after the server, Stefani, comes and takes our order of beer, wine, and a basket of rolls.

"I guess so. Back in Penumbra, I never felt like I couldn't leave—though I guess I couldn't. Even as a prisoner, I feel more freedom here."

Nera's face falls, and she reaches for my hand, hesitating only briefly before she envelops it with her own and squeezes lightly. It's an odd sensation, the coolness of her skin mimicking the stone she is truly made of behind her glamour. "I hope you won't feel like a prisoner for long, that you can see us as a family of sorts, like Finley does."

It's been nearly a month since I came here, and I can admit to myself that I don't feel like a prisoner anymore. Not when I'm working to accomplish something that feels larger than myself. When I feel useful. Plus, breaking their curse, and my bond with Ash, is my new purpose.

"We will see, maybe once I break your cur—"

"Shh." She presses a hand over my lips, and it takes everything in me not to wince, just in case she nips me with her deadly nails. Surely, even if she looks human, the same curse still lingers under the mirage over her body. "Don't say anything about our *situation*." Nera drops her hand and glances around the room, looking far too serious. Then she whispers, "It's hard to tell a hybrid from a human, and even harder to guess who may be hostile."

I nod just as Stefani comes back with our drinks and bread.

"But you . . . glow," I whisper, eyeing the movements of neighboring tables, feeling suspicious of everyone.

"Yes, but most people aren't observant enough to tell."

By the time Finley comes back, thunder rolls above us.

"Why is it storming at this hour?" a man says, tucking his loose white shirt into his kilt. "Get up, you three. We have to run home or we'll freeze out there." The family soon rushes out of the restaurant.

The rain falls with such intensity, I see a small river running down the cobbled roads. Did we bring the storm with the dark magic that surrounds both fae royals? That's why it's always raining at the castle.

"I'm going to get a tabletop game for us to play," Nera announces and takes a large bite of a roll as she gets up. She loosens the ties of her traveling cloak and promptly lays it over the back of her chair. "Birthday week, here we come!"

With Nera gone to do who knows what, and Ash getting us a place to stay for the night, Finley and I remain at the table to wait for our dinner.

I sip on my glass of wine, taking in our surroundings. From the gold-framed pictures hanging on the walls, to the dark ceilings made of rough wood and dried bamboo canes.

"I never asked you. How is it you aren't—affected, like the rest?"

"I wasn't with them that evening, when everything happened, and I've avoided the ailment so far. But I'm still affected in a way, because of my connection with Ash."

I absently rotate his silver ring around my thumb. It's so large it fits loosely even there. The stone snaps at my fingers, not to hurt me, but to let me know it doesn't like my touch. "Where were you when it happened, and how does the ailment affect you?"

"I was in Hedrum." He seems to mull over my other question as he glances at our surroundings. We were mostly alone, except for a group of a few tables back. "I can't divulge what I've learned about the situation to anyone who isn't under it."

I frown, trying to make sense of it. "If you're one of his human 'tributes,' how is it you can go to Hedrum for so long and he doesn't chase you?"

"Ash hates the forced connection, to be honest with you, Mia. I've been with their family for a long time, and his compulsion to hunt me back if I step away has always been less intense than it is with you, I suppose. Before the—disaster, I used to live in Hedrum half of the year and travel back and forth often. I have a residence there."

The wine warms my throat and stomach as I take a long gulp. Ash has told me so many times he will always come for me. It feels wrong I'm the one to get such treatment.

"So it's different with me?"

"Every connection is." Finley looks like he would be happier if someone were beating him raw than talking to me about this. "But that's something you've got to ask him, and not for me to speculate about."

"What's not for you to speculate about?"

I jump as Nera sets a small wooden box on the table. How can someone who's that tall be that sneaky? "Nothing," I say, pressing a hand over my fast-beating heart.

"Gwofs, really?" Finley stares at the box as Nera empties the contents over the table. My curiosity is at an all-time high. She sorts an assortment of gems of varying colors and opacities.

Weird stones I can't place, all shaped into prisms.

"Just because you never win, Finn, doesn't mean it isn't fun."

"I never win because you cheat."

"You can't cheat Gwofs, it's magically bound. If you cheat, you lose. It's quite simple, really. I just have better judgment than you."

He glares at her as she sorts the three types of gems around us. There are four of each type, of varying sizes and with slight changes of colors. Each has a small wave of magic bursting out of it. Finley's ring snaps at my skin as I reach for one. "Ouch."

"You can't play this game while wearing someone else's artifact, I'm afraid." Nera waves in my general direction and continues to sort the stones.

"What are they?" I'm removing the ring before I can think about what I'm signing up for. As soon as I set it on the table, the pressure in my stomach returns, not too strong yet, but a reminder that it's there. Waiting to be let out.

"Galena, wardite, onyx, and fluorite. They are all highly magically conductive, and each contains a spell to detect truths and lies. You pick a stone that feels right, and try to trick it. For example, if you choose a truth, then you have to convince the rock of something that isn't true to you. If you succeed, the rock will spin. Then you win your turn, and it goes to the next player."

"What happens if you lose?"

"You lose a hand," Finley says dryly.

"Hush. And no, you don't lose a hand, but there is a catch. If you lose, the winner gets to challenge you to do something. It can't be life-threatening, but it is magically binding."

I frown and pull my hand back. Not sure I like those odds.

"But if you win, you get to learn a magical truth from the stones themselves."

"What kind of truth?" My hesitation wavers.

"Nothing huge, but you can ask about your own life, maybe even your past."

"Nera." Finley narrows his gaze on the princess. "You're forcing Mia to play your game. You well know that she wants truths about her nature."

"I'm not forcing anyone." She hesitates, chewing on her lip while she stares at me, almost apologetic. I feel like Nera usually gets what she wants. But she's very good at working for it, I'll give her that much. "I want you to play, but not without all the information. I know you want answers, and Gwofs can give you some if you win. But it'll be fun either way, even if you lose. It's a truth or dare game, like what humans have, but with magic. You need to loosen up, Finn."

"So, if I win, I can ask if my parents are my actual parents?"

They both stare at me in silence for a while, and then they both nod. Knowledge is what I crave most, and I don't fear a challenge. I've got nothing to lose.

"Do we have to say our truths or lies out loud?" I'm not sure if I want my deepest secrets out in the open, but to learn about my past, I would do anything.

"No, you hold your stone and think of a truth or lie. The artifact reacts right after. You have to convince it that the truth is a lie, or vice versa. If you make it spin, you win your turn and it goes to the next person. Best out of five rounds wins the game."

Finley scoffs and takes a long drink of his beer. "I'm not playing, Nera. Last time we did this, I ended up drinking an entire bottle of whiskey and was sick for days."

"It's my birthday," she pouted.

"Not for another four days, and you cheat."

"You're such a sore loser." Nera turns her attention to me. "You can't cheat in this game, Mia. If the rocks sense there is magic at play, they will all shift to this." She picks up a rock and shows me a red dot on one side. "And then you lose."

"Alright, I'll play."

I SHOULDN'T HAVE PLAYED. BY THE SECOND ROUND, IT'S CRYSTAL CLEAR that Nera knows how to trick the stones, while I struggle to come up with a half-truth—or lie—that might allow me a spin. A chance to learn a fraction of the truth I crave.

I don't like coconut, I think, remembering that time I had a coconut cake that was all stringy and gross. It reminded me of worms. But then again, I enjoyed the flavor most times. The stone spins after a moment of hesitation, and Finley whistles loudly as he serves all four of our plates with garlic roast and rosemary potatoes.

Where's Ash? He hasn't rejoined us since we split up when we arrived, and to my absolute horror, I miss him. Which I would never admit out loud. Finley assured us he's sorting out a cabin and the horses for the night. Twilight is getting closer, and we have to get to our sleeping quarters soon, before both Nera and Ash are taken by the slumber.

The pressure in my stomach is more present now, a bubbling that's heating my blood as it rushes through my body. Even my face feels warm. Dread fills me when I look at Finley's ring on the table. I don't want to put it back on.

Nera's stone spins again, and I curse my luck. One round left.

"Truth or lie?" Nera asks.

"Lie." I bring the stone close to my lips and close my eyes.

I love the castle. And I envision the lunargyres. All the times I almost died. The never-ending storms and gray skies. The roses. Somewhere deep inside me, I know all these things are connected to the curse. Then Naheli flashes as she fills the rooms with starlight. And I know I've lost this game. Lightning cracks in the sky, thunder follows, and my stone doesn't spin.

By the time Nera stops hollering over her win, I've accepted I might end up drinking an entire bottle of wine and swimming in that frigid lake Finley keeps talking about.

"Your dare is simple." A mischievous light shines behind Nera's newly blue eyes. "I want you to give in to something you've been wanting but haven't allowed yourself to have."

Finley ticks his tongue on the roof of his mouth. "You can't be serious . . ."

"What? It can be anything. Perhaps she's never gotten drunk on whiskey, unlike others at this table, and wants to let loose. Or she wants to go skinny-dipping in the lake, though, fair warning, it's frigidly cold—"

"Or"—Finley slams his drink on the table—"maybe she isn't you, and her wild desires are to escape."

"She doesn't want that anymore." Nera leans forward on the table, waggling her brows at me. "I like you, Mia. Take this chance and do something fun. Don't let fear steal away your life. *Live*."

Something magical spreads in my veins, through my chest. I want to do so many things; the possibilities are endless and impossible to narrow down right now. I open my mouth to tell her this, but I feel something click in the back of my mind. A crawling sensation that matches the energy coming alive in the pit of my stomach.

I want to prove to myself I'm good enough to save Irene, like I couldn't with Father. I want Nera to be free. I want . . . Ash.

A magnetic pull turns me toward the entrance to the restaurant just as he strolls in. He swipes droplets of rain off his shoulder, and his wavy hair sticks to his forehead.

He was caught in the rain outside and looks so . . . kissable.

Oh gods. No.

The chair scrapes under me as I stand in one fluid motion. I want to sit back down, but the little spark of energy inside me challenges that impulse.

I *don't* want to sit back down. What I really want is to go over there and kiss him. My steps are long, and panic bubbles in my gut because magic binds me to move forward, regardless of my reservations.

Oh no, oh no.

We meet in the middle of the dark room, where, being closer to the door, the air is cooler. He tilts his head to the side, eyeing me with curiosity.

He must see something in my expression that makes him drop his guard because he lets me take hold of the collar of his coat and stands still as I fit my body against him. His scent is intoxicating, and this time, I don't chastise myself for loving it.

Pine, mint, and power.

Everything around me falls silent.

I want him.

"Mons—?"

I lift to my tiptoes and press my lips to his before he can finish speaking. The little pressure of the magic pact falls away as I fulfill my side of the bargain, but I remain there, my lips on his as his hands descend to my waist. He pulls me to him and kisses me back like there is no tomorrow.

The air around us grows hot against the cold, and everything feels like too much and not enough. His lips devour me, and he demands more.

Heat bursts between my thighs as his tongue enters my mouth and dances against mine. I can't get enough of this—of him. When we break apart, I tell myself to step away. But I can't, not when Ash lingers, dipping his face ever so slightly until our lips barely graze.

"Do you often kiss unsuspecting people?" He presses his forehead against mine, and his breath washes over me.

"Only when I lose my fucking mind." I shift just a little closer to feel the smoothness of his lips against mine again. Perhaps he will understand the signal and kiss me without holding back.

"That mouth of yours is dangerous," he purrs, and traps my chin with two fingers and his thumb, examining my face like he's trying to find something hiding there.

My blood sings at how right this feels. I have never reacted this way to a simple kiss, so heated I'm ready to throw caution to the wind.

Someone hoots in the distance, and Ash pulls back just enough that I can drink in the sharpness of his cheekbones and his plush lips right before they tighten into a fine line.

"Let's get you something to eat before we need to head to our cabin for the night." His jaw clenches as our surroundings come back into focus. The sound of cutlery scraping over ceramic plates. The slurping of beer. The cook shouting at the server.

Droplets of rain cling to his raven hair. My body is hot, my cheeks flushed with embarrassment, as I come back to my senses and force myself to let go of his coat.

I kissed the beast I'm supposed to hate, and he kissed me right back like I'm air and he's been drowning for years.

CHAPTER 24

We didn't make good time, like Finley hoped when we left the castle. Instead, we stayed a second night at a dingy roadside inn. At least no hybrid would suspect the king of the unseelie to lodge there.

By the time we arrive in Hedrum in the late afternoon after three days on the road, I am too tired, dirty, and slightly itchy to think of my stolen kiss. Nor do I think about what it might mean for me and my changing feelings.

Sure, magic compelled me to ignore my rational thoughts and instead follow my irrational hormones. But when Ash glances my way and my heart skips a beat, it's nothing. I'm just intimidated. When he helps me out of the carriage and our hands linger for a little too long, it means nothing . . . until it does.

He doesn't come to find me again. In fact, I suspect he's avoiding me, which I guess after I kissed him only complicates matters in our hate games.

Hedrum is unlike Penumbra in every way that matters. It's bright and colorful with a blue sky that's now tinted with oranges and sunflower yellows as the sun begins its descent behind the mountains.

The clip-clopping of hooves is our company as we travel narrow streets that wind up and down the hills. Carriages pass by, some horse-drawn others pulled by steam engines. The homes in the distance look deceptively small, though it's a trick of the eye since they grow to two stories high when we finally cross in front of them. Painted in saturated colors, this town stands in rich contrast to the green forest in the distance.

As we enter a small estate hidden behind tall hedges and ornate metal gates, the carriage shakes over the crushed granite path, waking a slumbering Nera.

"We're here." Finley pulls the curtains to the side as the estate comes into view behind the golden trees lining the road.

The wheels screech as we slow to a stop, and the pressure in my gut increases, burning through me as I twist Finley's ring over my thumb, again and again.

"Is it getting worse?"

When I meet Ash's gaze, the longing swirling deep inside me is reflected in his expression. But only for a moment, then he schools his features.

"The ring doesn't like me very much," I admit, and continue with the twisting, hoping it will stop sending out these unpleasant waves of energy and instead help me ease the discomfort. "It's feeling temperamental right now. If I listen to the small voice inside the green stone, it feels cheated to not be on Finley's magical hand while inside this manor."

"You can hear it?" Finley looks panicked, and his gaze shifts to the ring.

"I, uh— Yes? Can't you?"

Finley takes a sharp breath, and his brows pinch. "I don't hear a voice, or feel any obvious intentions. Not like it's alive. I just feel an affinity toward it, which lets me know it's mine."

Nera strokes my old pendant through the layers of her high-neck dress. "I can't hear them either."

I sink into the bench, but no matter how small I make myself, I can't escape their scrutiny. Why am I always the strange one? Even surrounded by magical beings.

"Let me make sure Marlena knows what to expect," Finley says, already halfway out of the carriage before I realize what's happening. For the first time in the entire trip, it's he who leaves first. I guess he's eager to be out of this box and inside his home.

The gravel crunches under his boots as he rounds the vehicle, and Ash reaches for the black handle, clearing his throat before speaking. "Nera, I know this is our estate, but it's managed by Finley and his niece. You may remember Marlena. She isn't particularly fond of the fae."

"Oh, I very much know who she is," Nera says. "I think she dislikes all beings that aren't human, no? She hates hybrids too. So this shall be fun."

"But isn't Finley a sorcerer?"

"Yes," Nera says. "But he is all human, Mia. It's the fae blood she doesn't like, not the magic."

Ash rubs his temple like a migraine is building. "She's Finley's only living relative. Be nice, you two." Then he swings the door open and steps outside, where a lady in her fifties awaits, already talking to her much younger-looking uncle.

"Be nice?" Nera scoffs, shifting toward her door. "I think he's telling himself that more than us."

I press my lips into a tight smile and nod. There isn't a chance in this world that Ash, the king of the fae, is less reasonable than either his little sister or me. Even though I'm a ball of nerves and insecurities.

"Are you coming, Monster?" Ash's deep voice makes my skin prickle just as his gloved hand appears through the open door.

I debate not taking it. Truly. It would be easier to avoid the simple touch, which will undoubtedly make me more confused. But then again, these little moments we steal while acting like we don't care are the highlights of my day.

Gripping his hand, I ignore the spark and walk into Hedrum, the city of sorcery.

I smell magic, like old parchment, enveloping me in a warm hug. Even though I'm wearing Finley's ring, that nagging power inside me stirs.

The tip of my pointed boot catches the carriage step, and I stumble, arms flailing. Ash's body blurs, and he moves impossibly fast. One second, he's standing to the side, the next, he's got me in his arms, lifting me up like I weigh nothing.

I collide with his chest and his breath washes over my face. When he slowly settles me on the ground, I don't shift away and his hands linger around my waist. Judging by the quickness of his heartbeat, our minds have gone to the same place. Back to Fairhope's inn, and my stolen kiss.

"I'll have to repay you somehow for all the times you keep saving me," I say, and finally step down, knowing that everyone around us is watching our interaction.

"I'm sure I can come up with something . . ." He tucks a loose strand of hair behind my ear, and the touch leaves a trail of heat across my cheek.

"Alright, you two, that's enough of that. I think I preferred when you bickered all the time," Nera says from somewhere behind Ash's massive back. Her heels click up the five steps that lead to the front door. She passes the rounded columns and enters the manor like she owns the place, without another word.

The woman beside Finley hisses something under her breath. She looks appalled not only by our strange display but by Nera's actions. So much for being polite to our hostess . . .

"Hello, Marlena, I trust you're well?" Ash says in greeting when we meet them by the steps.

"Your Majesty." She dips into a bow that allows me to see all the onyx stones decorating her high bun and matching her elegant black dress. "I was just telling Uncle I wasn't expecting visitors, much less the king himself." Her pale, silver hair makes her skin appear darker than she is. Her tone is polite, in complete contrast to her pinched expression.

"I'm afraid we couldn't send a bird in time to let you know we were coming," Ash says. "But we won't stay long."

"What a pity. May I inquire what business brings you all the way to Hedrum? It has been a while . . ."

"Five years, if my memory serves me right. We came to get an amulet for Miss Mia." Ash waves a hand in my direction before brushing away a golden leaf that floated down from the tree above onto the fur of his coat.

Marlena's gaze cuts to me for the first time. Her eyes are inquisitive, like she's trying to place me. "A sorcerer?"

"A librarian," I say. I'm so used to speaking those words that I don't stop to notice how wrong they feel now. The pressure inside me stirs, and my blood heats.

Marlena's lips tilt down right before she dismisses me entirely. "I'll have the maids ready your usual rooms and send dinner up so you can dine there. It's been a long trip, and I'm sure you're eager to catch up on sleep."

"Thank you for the hospitality." Ash is already walking away, gently guiding me inside with a possessive hand on my lower back.

I should tell him to stop, but I'm woman enough to admit I don't want him to.

The manor's decor is so different from the castle, gaudy with gold furnishings and thick velvet curtains matched to vibrant wallpaper. I would've never guessed it belonged to Ash and Nera. Finley either, for that matter.

Ash shrugs off his coat as the warmth inside envelops us in a sweltering bubble. “Well, this is certainly not how I remember it.” He drapes his coat over the back of a chair just as Finley and his niece come in.

We go up to the top floor together, and there we split, Marlena and me to the right, where the unwed females stay. Her words, not mine. Ash and Finley go left, to the king’s chambers, which apparently take up a full floor of the other wing.

Finley has his own floor, which Marlena tells me as we make our way down a long hall. Past at least ten doors. Maids rush around the place, dusting a table here, a pedestal with a vase there. Some are actively removing art from the walls.

From the corner of my eye, I noticed a maid rolling up a large tapestry depicting a bird and an elaborate emblem. The design looks familiar, though I have little time to inspect it as the maid tucks it away.

“This way.” Marlena’s voice cuts through the noise of people bustling about, and I quicken my steps. “The maids will bring your things. I’m not sure where you’re from, but in Hedrum we have running water, so you may fill the tub when you’re ready for a bath.”

I brought little, just a few dresses because Nera insisted, in case we go to a dance, some nightgowns I found in my room when I arrived at the castle, a hairbrush, and a few grimoires I sneaked out without anyone catching me. The memory of my boldness makes me smile.

Marlena takes me to the very end of the hall, the room farthest away from Ash. I wonder if this is by her design, or if Finley suggested it. To keep us apart and avoid the unnecessary drama of me doing something stupid. Like kissing him again.

She opens the doors, and the room is beautiful. Sparsely decorated compared to the rest of the manor. Maids are already there, opening the curtains and leaving a tray of delicious-looking food on a tea table in front of the large windows that overlook the garden.

After I get some rest, I dream I'll get to curl up in bed with a book and maybe actually read in peace. But even as the thought crosses my mind, my power stirs in my stomach.

Gods, I doubt I'll ever sleep again, especially since Naheli isn't here. How I miss my friend.

I make my way to the table and the delicious array of biscuits, a small bowl of soup, and a steaming teapot. Marlena follows behind me with a severe expression. "Finley suggested that you stay on the king's floor, alongside his sister. I hope you don't mind that I placed you so far from him, but this is the only empty room in this wing that fulfills that request."

I'm already making myself comfortable. I hadn't realized how hungry I am, though we've eaten little since this morning when we left the last inn.

"This is perfect, thank you."

"Is there anything I can get the maids to bring you before I leave?" she asks from the door.

"Actually, I would love it if I could get a mirror. I haven't seen my hair in a long time, and it will be nice to get to for a change."

Marlena's lips tilt into a smile. Then she nods. "Of course, the maid will bring you one at once. Anything else?"

I'd love to see that tapestry with the familiar emblem. "No, that'll be all. Thank you so much for having me."

CHAPTER 25

I stare at my reflection, unblinking, as if at any moment someone will come in and take this mirror away. This is the first time I've seen myself, unfiltered, since leaving Penumbra a month ago.

With mechanical movements, I pat tinted powder over my skin and apply a thin layer of rouge to my cheeks as I focus on the stranger staring right back at me.

Once I was Mia Clementine. A woman who borrowed magic from grimoires and guarded knowledge from ancient races with enchantments and wards. Now I'm Mia, the hybrid, who needs to wear an amulet or my repressed magic could kill me—or worse, hurt someone else. Lied to by those I love. Protected by my enemy.

Except I can't think of Ash as my enemy anymore. Not when he's telling me truths no one else has shared, protecting me, and training me. He's a victim of the hybrids, just like I am.

I stand from the stool by the dressing table and put the ornate silver hand mirror in my trunk, under layers of dresses and fabric. I'm sure Marlena won't miss it. And by the time she notices, I'll be long gone.

I can barely breathe for the tightness of my corset—or the

intensity of my feelings. I spent far too long making sure my breasts won't spill over the low neckline, but I love this dress. And the fact that Nera insisted I have it.

She claimed she can't wear such a garment, but I think she simply wanted me to have something nice. I'm not sure when Irene last gave me a gift.

Skimming my fingers over the red fabric, I smile at the delicate, embroidered patterns stitched into the bodice in shades of dark green and white. I can't remember ever wearing something this elegant—nor this daring.

A knock, and Nera peeks through the doorway, her hair twisted into a crown of intricate braids high on her head. I don't know why I do it, but I step in front of my trunk, hoping she won't see the mirror, even covered by my clothes, and take it away.

There's something suspicious about the lack of reflective surfaces around the castle, and in the inns we stayed at on our trip. Like they disappeared before we ever made it to our rooms.

Coincidence? I don't think so.

"I knew that color would suit you, Mia," Nera says with a genuine smile as she pushes the door fully open and reveals herself, and the beautiful gown she wears, to me. White with silver lace, it makes her look like the moon.

"Thank you again for giving it to me."

Talking about the clothes reminds me of Morgana, who never came back with my dresses. Did she lose herself to the curse before she got around to making them?

Nera nods enthusiastically and we leave my room to head downstairs, where Finley and Ash await us. It's past twilight now, and our plans for the night were sorted earlier when we went out to get my amulet only to find most establishments were closed in preparation for tonight's lunar celebrations.

So with the silver moon shining upon us, I make my way into a new city, surrounded by the fae I grew up fearing, to go to a magical market. The celebrations sound exciting, though I've read little about them even with all my years of studying old customs. All I know is they last a month, and apparently, we caught the tail end of it.

"I don't know what to expect out there," I admit, while trying to ignore my heated blood as my power, brought out by my nerves, hovers way too close to the surface.

"Lots of dances in the bigger establishments or manors, delicious food from other parts of the kingdom, and of course, drunken fools attempting to get your attention." Nera threads her gloved arm through the crook of my elbow, and we make our way down a long corridor to the receiving room. "It'll be nice to see the full moon in my regular form. Well, without my wings and ears, but still. I feel almost normal."

We spill into the round room at the front of the manor where Ash and Finley wait for us. Everything goes quiet.

Ash is casually leaning against the wall, and his brown gaze drags over me as if memorizing every inch of my body. Time slows and I burn. I want to memorize every inch of him too.

"There you are. I thought I was going to have to come and get you two." Finley steps forward, signaling a couple of maids I hadn't even noticed to bring us our coats.

Mine is a little dirty on the bottom edge, and the black fabric stands out against my red dress. I shrug it on, careful not to damage the curls I spent most of the afternoon perfecting.

Ash steps forward and offers Nera his arm. He wears a black outfit with a wine-colored vest that almost matches my dress to perfection. He styled his hair back, though an errant strand has escaped the constraints of hair product and curls over his forehead.

"Nerala," he says with a smile. "I hope this is what you wanted."

"It is. Thank you."

Their faces draw close, like they are sharing a mischievous plan, and they're both smiling. Like there isn't a curse weighing them down. My heart aches for them.

It takes all my willpower to look away and back at Finley. I curl my hand around the crook of his elbow, and the cool air of the evening envelops us as we leave his manor.

"Now, Mia, best not to get too close to me. I'd rather not get my ass beaten when Ash decides he's had enough of me touching you. The fae can be . . . intense when it comes to relationships."

"That's ridiculous. Plus, it's not like that between us—"

"Is it not? You could've fooled me with that kiss. Or should I remind you that the dare showed us what you truly desire?" Finley keeps his voice down and gently pulls away from me until there's at least a foot between us.

Blood warms my face, but I focus on the positives: One, Ash is far enough from us, there's very little chance he can hear our conversation. Two, while mortifying, I like talking to Finley when he seems so free.

We cross through the front gates and join the people walking under the gas lamps, dressed in their finest clothing.

"When they said chivalry was dead, Finley, they were talking about you," I tease, but keep my hand loose around his arm. I wasn't lying. There's a chill in the air that burns my cheeks.

"Chivalry is for those who don't have to fight a two-hundred-and-some-pound fae who's bonded with an ancient spirit. I already tried to win that fight and came out soulless."

"True," I say. "What a pair we make. Two fools who lost part of our souls for trying to stop Ash when he was wreaking havoc."

"Yes, it's a lesson in being humble, that's for sure," he whispers near my ear, his face a bit strained as he stares around us, as if expecting someone to jump out of the alleyways. "How's the ring working for you? Is it still hostile?"

"Yes." In response to my words, I feel a distinct zap of energy bursting through me. The cool silver ring eases it immediately, but the pressure in my stomach remains. "Thank you for allowing me to use it. How does it feel for you to not have it?"

"I hate every second. But it's reminding me what a privilege having power to wield is. How do humans live their lives without it? Using matches to light a fireplace is archaic."

"Fire spells are my favorite to cast," I admit.

"I don't like how dependent I've grown on magic to do everything, but I miss having it."

"I miss it too." My fingers twitch ever so slightly. Using my magic with Finley's ring is tricky, and most of the time, it suppresses my power, stubbornly refusing to let it out.

"You miss it? Haven't you been able to use magic with my amulet?"

"It doesn't allow me a full flow of power when I try, and then when I need peace, it allows too much, so I can't sleep for fear I might explode."

"What an ungrateful piece of tin." My head snaps toward the sound of Ash's voice. He and Nera waited for us. "Perhaps put it inside a dark drawer for an hour or two to see if it learns manners."

Nera drops Ash's arm and strolls to the other side of Finley, taking hold of his free arm. "I was asking Ash where the best celebrations will be tonight. How much has the town changed in the last five years?"

"You know I live with the two of you, right?" Finley says. Unlike with me, he leans toward Nera, as if her closeness is something he's used to. Then he pulls out an invitation from his jacket pocket. "We got this invitation to the Vanderbilts' dance."

Nera's brows shoot up, and her smirk turns mischievous. "Really? Is your niece going to the dances now?"

Ash groans, shaking his head as he continues forward, shoving his hands into his coat pockets. Feeling like a third wheel,

I rush after him, but hear Finley say, "They usually send it to everyone on the street. I thought you might like to go."

Once I'm by his side, Ash clears his throat and glances my way. "Are you actually feeling like you might explode?"

I shrug, not trusting my voice as we cross a plaza on a beautifully paved path between two rows of large trees. His arm brushes against mine, and our hands linger so close—I want to close the gap but hold myself back.

"Why is it such a big deal if someone recognizes you?" I ask instead. "Finley mentioned in the carriage Hedrum is more neutral toward the fae? I'm sure there are people here who support you."

He nods, but we walk quietly for almost half a block before he speaks again. "It was safer at the beginning, but now, Hedrum is crawling with hybrids, which is why I didn't want Nera to come. They hide as nonmagical humans. Usually they're trying to find a fae who hasn't perfected the glamours. Those who weren't close to me when the curse took effect. It makes them easy prey."

"Is that why you stopped coming here five years ago?"

It smells of campfire, like everyone in town has their fireplaces lit. I enjoy that, even with two cursed fae hidden behind enchantments, the night remains clear of rain.

"No. It's because Nera turned to stone and lost her mind briefly during that first blood moon. After that, I focused all my time on trying to break the curse and avoided the politics of it."

"I never expected the fae to become prey for humans. You always seemed so powerful," I confess as we turn to go down a hill. Street vendors have set up carts between the shops on either side of the street and are selling flowers, food, and various knickknacks.

"Perhaps that was our downfall. We believed ourselves to be untouchable for so long we grew too comfortable. But the power that lies within a repressed society, power willing to incite organized chaos? That's enough to bring a kingdom to the ground."

I mull over his words and feel empty. There's no good side to a war when innocents die for the decisions of those who hold power.

"Are the seelie also affected by the curse?"

Ash is quiet for so long, I don't know if he can say anything about it. It might be a detail in the confines of the curse . . . but then again, if I ask the right question, it seems they can answer me.

"No," he says at last. "It only affects the unseelie of Aphelion."

His kingdom. An act of war to eradicate a race shouldn't be so specific to him. Not unless it's personal. I tilt my head and drink in his expression, the shine behind his eyes. He wants me to keep asking questions. I'm getting somewhere.

"Is the curse directed at your family?"

He looks around us, but we're mostly alone as we walk down the street, and those who are nearby are shouting at each other and laughing drunkenly. "Yes."

My heart lurches.

Continue, his eyes beg me, though his lips flatten to a line. I think back to the prophecy.

The hybrids will come under a blood moon to the unseelie halls.

At first, I thought it referred to a mob who marched into the castle and brought dark magic with them, but what if the person was already inside? What if they were close to him?

Another tribute of the blood moon, like me. What if the prophecy refers to the both of us? Two hybrids coming to the castle, though I'm not intent on their destruction. Quite the opposite.

"Was the hybrid someone whose soul you took?"

Even under the pale light of the full moon, I see how every ounce of color in his cheeks fades. "Yes."

Adrenaline rushes through me as I open my lips to continue my line of questioning, but something moves behind him in the window. Black swirls form around his blurred reflection, like what I saw in Eponde. Long, fingerlike, and drifting closer and closer to me through the surface of the glass.

I turn back to Ash, then to Nera, who still holds Finley's arm, but they both look normal. Glowing even.

"Is everything alright, Monster?" Ash lifts a brow and searches my face. I'm afraid if I tell him what I see, he'll pull me away when I'm so close to finding something. I suspect what I'm seeing in the reflections is a manifestation of the curse itself.

There has to be a connection with the lack of mirrors in the castle. What if the hybrid got rid of them all? What if I can use a reflection to break them free? I just have to figure out how to sever whatever connection there is.

A group of young men stumble around us, breaking my line of vision to the shadowy figure. I watch them stroll down the street, abusing their massive jugs of wine. The last one from their group turns to Nera as he passes, howls at her, and moves on with a manic cackle.

"Drunken humans are so predictable," Ash says flatly, and offers me his arm. "Come, Monster, let's get you an artifact that actually works for you."

CHAPTER 26

I shift my new amulet in my hands, feeling the gentle power that graces my fingertips. The small voice differs from my old necklace, but it's warm and friendly, unlike Finley's ring. I never expected magical jewelers could craft a sorcerer's amulet into something as simple as a hairpin. I'm happy I was wrong. Smiling, I trace the gold petals that make a flower with a beautiful ruby set in the middle. It's fitting that somehow I ended up with a magical artifact shaped like a rose.

"I can't believe you found an amulet in that shop," Finley says.

Both men have been very vocal about my ability to sense magic items as we walked past the jewelry stands on our way to the market. The shop manager, an old woman who could have been five-hundred-years-old, was delighted to be rid of such an insignificant item, and for such an exorbitant price.

Ten gold coins. It would have taken me months to save that much with my librarian salary.

"Are you happy with it?" Nera asks from my side as we both examine the rose-shaped pin.

"Yes." I secure it in the waves of my hair, and I already feel a hundred times better than I did with the ring. "I like that it's small."

Much more than that, I love the gentleness of its voice. But I keep that last thought to myself. I'm quickly learning that being able to hear objects isn't normal, even for magical beings like the fae.

We walk down the busy streets to the address of the lunar dance. It's the only invitation Marlena saved, and it's not terribly far from the manor.

Hedrum is even more breathtaking at night than it was through the carriage window. The gas lanterns spill their yellow light onto the paved roads, and people make their way from shop to shop wearing their finest colorful clothing. The buildings change from markets to homes encased behind manicured hedges. Music drifts on the air, drowning out even the shouts of the sellers we leave behind.

Finley fetches the invitation from the pocket of his coat, unrolls the thick parchment, and reads in silence before pointing to our left, where a river of people flows. "Seems that's our host."

We stroll past brass gates stained with age, held straight by thick white columns. Greenery spills onto a stonework patio where guests with tall flutes of champagne mingle while a guard checks their invitations.

I know I've changed on a deeper level the moment the elaborate crown molding, chandeliers, and curved stairways don't shock me. I guess next to the castle, this place seems almost mundane. Even a month ago, I would have gawked at the elegant details, or the painting on the ceilings.

The music of multiple violins drifts through the dance floor. There's no way the sound of these instruments would travel so easily over the loud conversations and the clicking of crystal glasses without the aid of magic.

Nera's gloved hands wrap around Ash's bicep. "Come, I've been waiting for this for far too long."

"I thought you hated dancing with me . . ." he says, but he lets Nera drag him into the crowd of dancers in the middle of the room.

I always dreamed Irene and I would be close enough to be friends, like they are. A part of me is jealous of their relationship. And another part realizes how broken my family was. Full of secrets, snide remarks, and manipulation.

Finley and I remain on the edges, watching the couples twirl around the dance floor. The two fae hide in plain sight as they enjoy this moment away from their curse.

Finley dips his face close to my ear, and his voice is barely loud enough to break through the noise, so not even the crowd behind us can hear our conversation. "I can't believe all these people are celebrating a fae holiday when we're struggling in the castle the way we are. It's not that I think people should never have any fun because fae are fading into madness or turning to statues, but looking the other way while it happens seems cold. I just wish—I wish Ash did more to fight this."

My heart tightens as I take in Finley's expression. There's a lot of anger there—shame too. It's plain to see as he watches the festivities around us.

I clear my throat, hoping to lighten the mood. "I've never been to a lunar celebration before. Were they always like this?"

"No, they were better when everyone could roam without being hunted. Regardless of species. It's why Nera wanted to come so badly."

"I'm glad we could come," I admit, meeting Ash's gaze as he and Nera cut through the crowd. Time slows and even the music fades. And then, in the quiet that follows, I hear small voices that don't speak the human language. It's not my new amulet, but sounds similar. Not a person, then, but a magical object.

He is here . . . I think the whispers say.

Ours.

He's here.

Every hair in my body rises. Ash breaks his eye contact and returns his attention to Nera. The music resumes.

I glance around, trying to find the source, but all I can hear are the stringed instruments and my loud breathing. It's like someone is playing a joke, and I'm failing to find it funny.

"It's your new amulet working better than my ring?" Finley asks, pulling my attention back to him.

"It's like night and day," I say, though the pressure in my stomach is building again.

"How does it work? Does this one also speak to you, but it's less hostile?"

Wiping my sweaty hands over the skirt of my dress, I take a deep breath to calm my nerves. I don't want to sound crazy, but then again, Finley doesn't appear to be judging me. It's more like he's actually curious—worried, even.

"Your ring wasn't necessarily hostile. Its alliance is to you, not me, which made it unhappy to be on my hand. I don't know how it works, to be honest."

"I've never met someone who can understand magical items as you seem to, but strange gifts are given to those with mixed blood." He clears his throat. "Did mine tell you anything unusual?"

"No. I sense waves of feelings, and sometimes I can understand them. Like when my mother's necklace refused to part from Nera the night she almost killed Ash, but it still helped me restrain her."

Finley hums, not saying anything else. We stand in silence for what feels like an eternity, but I want to dance. Perhaps that'll help drive away the tension in my body. I get the impression he won't ask me though—not after how hesitant he was when I held his arm earlier.

Finley stares over my head, and his skin has gone a shade of green. "I'm going to get us something to drink. Wait here." It's as if he found someone in the crowd. My heart leaps and I turn to follow his retreating shape, but I can't see anyone in particular, and soon his body blends with everyone else.

Now that I'm alone, I can follow the pull of the strange voices. They feel distant yet persistent, coming from somewhere in this house. And I've heard voices like this before, back in the library when the stolen grimoires called to me.

What if there are fae books? I crane my neck to find Ash and Nera still spinning across the dance floor, whispering to each other. I stand there, hoping one of them will glance my way so I can beckon them over and share what I'm feeling.

But then, what if I'm wrong and I steal this moment away from Nera, this small reprieve from her reality, for nothing? I can't trust I have a handle on whatever this is. I reach for the pin in my hair, and it buzzes against my fingertips, whispering something that feels like reassurance. Perhaps I just need to inspect the area casually, make sure I'm not imagining things.

He is here . . . they say.

I squeeze myself through the sea of people, across the dimly lit dance floor, following the voices blindly. I pass under an archway with ornate carvings painted in olive greens and into a wide hallway decorated with paintings of humans. Here, away from the crowd, I can hear their whispers more clearly.

My amulet vibrates against my skull as I step into the emptiness ahead.

There are no guests here, not even staff handing out glasses of wine, so it's much easier to discern the strange pull that's brought me to this place.

He is here.

Ours.

He's here. Not a human language, but the same as the forbidden books in Penumbra.

I know without a shadow of doubt there are fae grimoires stashed away in this place.

My amulet's shaking intensifies with every step that draws me closer. The hair on the back of my neck stands up as I reach for a door handle and push it open. The light of the hall spills into the dark room, illuminating carpeted floors, and a strange tangled sheet moving . . .

A moan pierces the shadows, and I freeze. Not a sheet, but almost-torn-up clothes. In the darkness, two bodies move together over the couch.

My face burns as I step back into the hall and close the door softly. I doubt I went unnoticed, they just didn't care enough to stop. I press my cool fingers to my hot neck, and my helpful brain feeds me an image of Ash's naked chest. And a memory of the softness of his lips.

I shouldn't be here, prancing through the empty halls of a stranger's home by myself, especially if they have stolen grimoires hidden somewhere. I make my way back to the dance. I should let Ash know what I'm hearing, and perhaps he'll have a better plan for what to do. What if he gifted the grimoires to the owner of this place? I could get us kicked out of these celebrations and ruin Nera's night for no reason.

By the time I'm back, three songs have passed, but the space is as busy as it was when I left. I spot Nera and Finley dancing, though they're far from me and keeping their gazes cast down. I lift to my tiptoes and try to find Ash in the crowd. It takes embarrassingly little time to find him, leaning against a wall, drinking from a glass of red wine, and talking with someone.

He is a light, and I'm a moth drawn to it.

"What do you say we go somewhere a bit more private,

Hellion?" the woman purrs, and her hand goes to Ash's chest where she straightens his already-straight cravat.

Hellion? Isn't that the kind of spirit Naheli is? My stomach hardens, and I'm walking closer even while my head shouts at me to turn around and go the other way.

From where I stand, he is the perfect picture of relaxation, shoulder against the wall as he leans down toward her. I watch as Ash's nostrils flare, and then his gaze snaps to me. I freeze, paralyzed by his intense, unreadable expression.

With the glamour both fae royals used to blend in, their eyes changed from metallic shades to common human colors. His were brown when we left Finley's manor, but now, they're back to gold.

His jaw clenches as he tears his attention from me and returns it to the woman in front of him. I purse my lips and straighten my back, ignoring the ugliness brewing in my chest.

If anything, I should tell him about the crack in his glamour. Maybe he doesn't know.

"Can I have a word with you?" I choose not to use his name, just in case there's a reason he's going by another.

The woman turns to the sound of my voice, sharply. If looks could kill, I would be dead now. And she looks and looks. From the tip of my boots all the way to the amulet resting right above my ear.

"Who are you?" she asks with murder in her eyes.

"Yvette, this is my sister's best friend, Monster."

My expression falls. Is he serious . . . ?

The woman lifts a perfectly manicured blond brow at me, and the corner of her lips twitch. "Monster? What a peculiar name, or is it a pet name?"

"Does it matter?" Ash says, sounding bored. My blood boils as it collects in my face. "She came with us from the plains to celebrate Anna's birthday."

Hellion, Anna, the plains? Is he changing their names on

purpose because she isn't someone to trust? Or because he wants to bed her without forming true ties?

"How wonderful for *Monster* to travel such a long distance! I bet it would be difficult to travel with a man such as yourself," Yvette coos, already turning to dismiss me.

I think she means it as a compliment?

A dry laugh escapes my lips before I can stop it, and I straighten my back to be at least as tall as Yvette. "I'm Lia, not Monster." Alright, not my best attempt at a new name, but I can barely think straight with the storm of feelings inside me. "Apparently, Hellion isn't bright enough to remember it."

I glower at him, and his eyes shimmer with amusement. "What is it you want, Lia? Anna was looking for you."

And here I was, thinking of him as a victim just a few minutes ago. Worrying about his glamour, but I'm just being dismissed.

I do my best to ignore the pain in my chest and the stinging in my eyes. There isn't a chance in this world I'll allow myself to rage-cry in front of them. I came here for a reason, and it has nothing to do with interrupting them in the middle of . . . whatever this is.

"I-I need a minute, in private." I hate how my voice wobbles, even as I try to communicate through my eyes that this is important, but I'm not sure I'm quite successful. "You know what? Never mind."

I weave through the crowd of partygoers that fill every inch of the floor, talking loudly while drinking wine and spirits. I crane my neck and spot Nera's shimmering white dress alongside Finley's royal blue coat. They're walking away from the dance floor, toward the door.

Something is off. I feel it drumming inside my stomach. If Ash wanted me to go because it was unsafe, why would he remain?

The whispers of old magic coming down the hall beckon me. I

can't decipher much of what they're saying other than the same few words over and over again.

If I leave now, I'll never get another chance to see if there are fae grimoires here, possibly stolen ones. If Ash thinks a book in the Penumbra library holds the answers to break his curse, what if these do too?

I chew on my lip and know I won't be the one putting anyone in danger. Not anymore. I make my way around the edges of the dance floor and follow Nera and Finley as they get closer to the door.

"Hey, pretty." I hear a voice from behind me, close enough for his breath to fan over my exposed shoulders.

Still, he could be talking to someone else, so I lengthen my steps to catch my friends before they leave.

"Hold on a second, red." A hand grabs my wrist and holds me back. Not too hard, but firm enough I can't keep going without pulling him alongside me.

My skin itches as I turn to meet his gaze. Brown eyes, a round face reddened by the heat of the room, and possibly alcohol. "Please, unhand me."

"Don't be like that," he says with a crooked smile, but doesn't let go. "I've never seen such a pretty thing as you in town. All I ask for is a dance, that's all."

My power burns through me, prickling over my skin. A fire spell crouches in the back of my throat. "I won't say it again . . ."

"Why so serious, red? I'm just having fun." He tilts his head and zeros in on my amulet, which is now shining so bright I can see the glow it's casting over my face. His expression remains friendly. His eyes, however, say something else entirely. Sharp like a hunter. "Are you a new sorcerer in town?"

"Don't let her big eyes fool you into believing she's defenseless. She will burn you alive if you don't let go." Ash's voice cuts like a sharp knife. Round Face and I turn to meet the king of beasts as he glides toward us, hands deep inside his coat pockets, and his face twists into something dangerous. "If you want to keep that hand, then I recommend you remove it from her person. Now."

It's not an empty threat, and Round Face knows it as much as I do. He drops my wrist so fast it's like I actually burned him. His face loses the redness that was there before, and immediately he's backing away, muttering something that doesn't sound like an apology before he disappears into the crowd.

Ash moves quickly, grabbing my hand and pulling me behind a curtain and into an alcove framing a silver suit of armor.

I pull my arm away once we're safe in the darkness of our hiding spot and only the scent of dust and wine accompanies us.

"I thought I told you to go to Nera?" His jaw tightens as he points in the general direction his sister and Finley disappeared.

"I was trying to. It's not like I had a lot of time, and I find it peculiar you followed me here after being such an ass. Where did you leave Yvette?" I turn away from him and peek around the curtain. Not sure what I expect, but it's not him pulling me back.

We're so close his breath warms my face as he leans down to whisper, "We have to leave. When Yvette wakes up, every hybrid in this place is going to be looking for us. If your friend wasn't one himself."

My breath stumbles out of my lips as I meet his eyes, and now I understand the underlying panic there. The pressure in my stomach bubbles more insistently the longer I stay here, and my amulet drums quicker.

Thump, thump, thump.

It's giving me a headache.

"Hybrids, here?"

He nods, and I'm not even surprised. Not with how I've been feeling.

"What do you mean when she wakes up? Did you put her to sleep?"

His throat bobs, and he leans against the wall, peeling the curtain back and studying the moving bodies on the other side. His face darkens. "I was looking for you when I realized this place is crawling with hybrids, but you'd disappeared, and Finley didn't know where you went."

Guilt churns deep inside me. "I felt something like I did back in Penumbra, when I was in the library there, and I was coming to tell you that perhaps they're holding fae grimoires here . . ."

"And—" Ash pauses, turning to me. "They feel like the ones in your library?"

"They don't speak the human tongue . . ."

He rubs his jaw, considering. "There's an enchantment in this place that makes the glamours fail."

"Is that why your eyes are gold?"

He nods. "I noticed Nera's eyes changed when we were dancing. I asked Finley to get her out while she still looked human and went searching for you. It's not a coincidence Yvette, if that's even her real name, found me shortly after."

He's here. It's the same words, over and over.

"She knows who you are?"

"That I'm the king? No. I rarely go anywhere without Naheli, so they would expect her to be here as well."

It makes sense. Ash has power like no one I've seen before, but after he bonded with the spirit, he has to be almost invincible. Unless he was forever cursed, and his people all turned into beasts.

Cold rushes through me, and my fingers grow numb and clammy. It's getting harder to ignore the magical whispers. "Why not leave with them? It's dangerous for you here."

"Hybrids rarely attack in crowded places like this. There are many powerful sorcerers in Hedrum who still speak in support of the fae. Plus, the hybrids don't want to appear to be the aggressors. It goes against the narrative. I was hoping to draw them away and give you enough time to escape."

"Everyone out there looks human. How did you know?"

"Not all hybrids pass for human, Monster. Yvette smelled like fae to me."

"You would know, since you were close enough to count the freckles on her face." Heat flares through my veins. It's entirely unpleasant. I shift away from him, ready to have some space, and I hate the shadow of a smirk that graces his features.

"If I didn't know any better, I'd think you're jealous."

I scoff. "Please—"

"What is it, Mia? You hate me one minute, the next you're kissing me, then you act like nothing happened but get mad when I speak with another woman?"

"I wasn't mad that you were speaking with her." I know the lie isn't fooling him—nor me. "I was mad because you treated me like I meant nothing."

I hate that the truth always pours out of me with him.

"I acted like an ass because I can't fake not caring about you." Ash's eyes cut to my lips. "I'm tired of pretending I'm not thinking of you every waking moment. Of how much I want you to laugh with me. I almost gave away who I am in front of everyone here when that bastard put his hand on you. So no, Mia, I won't leave you here because there's a small chance they saw you come in with us, and they will torture you to get to me. Especially if they know you're mine."

My heart doubles in speed, and I stare into his eyes. Him speaking without reservation tears away every flimsy layer I had protecting my heart, and now I worry it's truly his.

I'm not ready for that, but I don't think it matters . . .

He's here.

Our king is here.

CHAPTER 27

He's here. Our king is here.

My thoughts stall, and I watch with widened eyes as Ash moves the curtain and studies the party on the other side. The books were always talking about Ash. They must have a connection to him and feel him nearby. Could this mean they're from his personal library? Written by him, or by an ancestor?

"We really need to go, but crossing the dance floor is risky with my eyes." He bares his teeth right as he drops the curtain. "I left Yvette in an alcove similar to this, but across the room. If anyone from her team finds her, they'll turn this place upside down."

"The grimoires, they're saying 'Our king is here.' Ash, I think we should inspect them. What if one of them is what you were hoping to find in Penumbra?"

"You can hear them so clearly?" Ash tilts his head, as if he's trying to hear what I heard, inspecting me in a stretching silence. "Interesting . . ."

I press my lips tight and consider claiming I was exaggerating. I don't want another person I care about to judge my behavior and think I'm weird. Or worse. He may not believe me, like Irene back home. "I know it sounds strange . . ."

"Mia, I'm a cursed fae who dreams of stars telling me a future that may or may not happen. I don't think it's strange. Where are you hearing them?"

A loud, clearly inebriated group walks in front of us, unable to see us hiding in the shadows of this alcove.

"Down the hall," I whisper as they pass.

His hand wraps around mine and he drags me close so quickly I can barely brace myself before I hit his chest. "We're going to blend in with these drunken fools. We have to move fast, Monster. I don't know how long I have with this glamour."

The enchantment that hides traces of feathers and wings is quickly fading. He pulls me out of our hiding place, and we blend with the party of friends to stroll around the room toward the same archway I walked through before.

Retracing my previous steps, we move with ease behind the group who seems not to notice us and then break off to turn down the dimly lit hall. It's empty like before. Quiet enough I can hear the grimoires' voices.

He's here.

We move like we know where we're going, even if that's a stretch. Ash's belief in my perception wakes the magic lying dormant within me. But unlike all the other times where it makes me feel like I'm losing control, right now, it doesn't paralyze me. It gives me confidence knowing I'm not completely defenseless. With my new amulet, I feel powerful again.

It doesn't take long to find the grimoires as they beckon us forward, right to one specific door. The hinge's screech is the only sound as we enter a dark space that smells like mildew and dust. Ash waves his hand, and from the tip of his fingers a small ball of fire floats to the gas lamps, and with a quiet whoosh, they each light in succession, burning cobwebs that had made a home inside their glass cases.

The newly illuminated space is small, with makeshift bookcases assembled from old crates. Gold magic waves in the air like summer grasses on a windy day. The grimoires' magic.

Ash takes a step forward. His lips parting as he takes in the books. "You were right. These are some of our lost texts."

There are hundreds of grimoires here, and it would take us days, if not weeks, to go through them. "How are we going to take them home without alerting the entire house?"

"Home?" His brows shoot up as he turns to me. "I never thought I'd hear you call it that . . ."

"I don't know what home is right now," I say, and fiddle with one of the long sleeves of my dress. "But right now, the castle feels more like home than Penumbra, where I've been lied to my whole life."

His expression turns dark, and he nods. "I need time to work on the spell that will make it possible to carry these, so let's hope, for our sake and theirs, that they don't come looking for us."

"We aren't that lucky . . ."

"And here I was, thinking you're the optimistic one between us. I happen to believe my luck has shifted lately." He isn't looking at his stolen books anymore. Instead, his focus is solely on me.

He holds my gaze until my cheeks feel like fire, and I turn away to wander the room, trying to find something to look at while he settles near the crates and magic swarms the place. Long scrolls of gold unfurl from his fingers, calling to the books that grow quiet, as if listening.

I take in the rest of the space, hugging myself to fend off the bite of the cold. The walls once had wallpaper, but it's been removed, leaving pieces of torn cloth, glue, and scrapes caused by a dull blade. Whoever did it attempted to cover the broken plaster with dark gray paint, though poorly. Artwork of fae engaged in various activities in mismatched frames leans against the walls. A handful show them riding their horses in the forest. Probably more depictions of the Wild Hunt.

Then there are masquerade balls with fae and humans together, dancing, drinking. "This is peculiar . . ." My voice sounds hollow even to myself.

Ash remains silent, but I can feel his power drenching every corner of the room. Then, to my shock, I notice a plant growing where his magic kisses the walls. Roses, like the ones in the castle.

Except these aren't black, they're bright red, like my dress. I turn around, my eyes wide as I meet his. He told me back in the castle the roses were tied to the curse, but I never thought I would see that connection so clearly.

Ash turns to the new greenery with a frown. "They grow wherever my magic takes a deep hold. I believe it shows her where I've been."

Her.

I piece together the fragments of truth I've gathered.

The one who cursed him was a woman. Someone close enough to Ash to steal his grimoires right out from under his nose. Someone he trusted, who was connected to him from the Wild Hunt. Another hybrid who apparently likes roses—or hates them.

I keep moving and continue inspecting every knickknack shoved into a dusty corner. Every stolen item that once belonged to the fae.

What Ash said makes sense. The roses could be a way for the spellcaster to discern where he's been, to track his movements, but what if it's more than that? What if they can somehow communicate with her?

The edge of an emblem etched in metal catches my eye. It hangs high above the ground over a narrow display case of dull old weapons.

It isn't magical, but the hair on my arms lifts as I recognize the symbol. I know it well. A shield between two olive branches, and in the center, a pile of books. Except with one difference, this one has an owl with human eyes on top of the books, and a glowing star floating over its head.

With Knowledge, Power says the scrolls beneath the shield. The words of the librarians.

I must have stopped breathing, for my vision blurs as I stare at it unblinkingly. Ash's hand rests on my shoulder, and his warmth seeps into my freezing skin.

"Are you alright?" He follows the line of my vision to the wall and the emblem hanging from it. His eyes widen. "That's the strix symbol. Come, Monster, we have to go."

"What's a strix?"

He crooks a finger at me, beckoning me forward as he heads for the door with long strides. I struggle to keep pace with him. "Strix is the name my father gave the hybrids after the prophecy was revealed. It's a bird, a bad omen—and it kills infants. After my kingdom fell to the curse, some hybrids banded together and formed the House of Strix, which has been hunting fae across the realm for the last decade."

"So the fae hunted the hybrids, gave them a name that would scare anyone, and now the same is happening the other way around?"

"It's tragic how that works, isn't it?" Ash looks away from me, but not before I see the shame hiding in his expression.

The ache in the back of my throat thickens, making it hard to speak. "So, whoever owns this house is a strix—or has ties to them?"

He nods as we pause by the door before he cracks it open, just a fraction. The music flows in, soothing, and he closes it again. "There's a group searching the rooms down the hall. They may have found Yvette."

The song outside ends, and a new one begins. I can hear the steps in the hallway coming closer.

The pressure of my power hums near my skin, hot, but not uncomfortably so. It's ready to react. To defend Ash if it needs to . . . I'd rather not think of why my brain went there. Or what it could mean that I feel such a way.

Ash's glamour is fading rapidly. His ears aren't even rounded any longer.

His eyes are sharp, tense as they shift from mine to the door. "If they come in here, they're as good as dead, and if this is a House of Strix, our exit might get messy."

"You said they won't hurt us if there's a crowd. This place is full of people." When I press my hands to his chest, I can feel how fast his heart is beating. "Perhaps we can leave through the window?"

"My wings are tied to the glamour." He hesitates, glancing to the other side of the room. "Which is fading faster than I thought, so perhaps luck is on our side tonight after all and I can fly us out. But I need time."

How can we stall? I run through possibilities, and heat pools deep in my belly when I think of a way. Physical shows of affection make people uncomfortable. I remember how Nera acted when Ash and I remained close after we arrived at Hedrum, which matches how I felt when I stumbled upon that couple earlier.

Fire pools ion my stomach as I remember their moans and the movements of their naked bodies, and I glance at my king. A cold wave snakes through me as those words echo in my mind. He isn't mine—but perhaps I want him to be my *something*. If we make it through the night.

The steps are right outside, and I don't have time to explain. Or to come up with a better solution. But this could help us escape without anyone getting hurt.

"If they're coming here, I think I know how to distract them, at least a little." The words stumble over my building nerves as I move in front of him, reaching for his face with both hands.

"Are you going to regret it?" He searches my eyes, and his tell me he knows what I intend to do. His pulse is hard under my fingertips. It helps that his face is hovering a breath away from mine and he smells like home.

"I won't, but we have to be convincing . . ." I whisper and focus on the voices outside, muffled by the distance and the room that separates us. Then I press my lips to his, and unlike the first time, he's expecting me.

My stomach flips as it did before, and I cover his ears with my hands, hiding them from view. If they're to believe we have been here getting . . . busy, I need to look properly rumpled.

"Mia . . ." Ash pulls back, barely an inch, his gold irises dark, his pupils wide. But he's looking at me like I've lost my mind. Perhaps I have. His hands snake around my waist, and he twirls me around, pressing me against the wall. "Next time you kiss me, I don't want there to be an excuse. Next time, I want you to mean it." His arms cage me in right before his lips take mine.

When Ash kisses me, he holds nothing back. Like this will be the last time, and he wants to savor this stolen moment. I cradle his face and let him take all he wants from me, for whatever little time we have until all hell breaks loose.

The air shifts around me, warm against my skin. The grimoires' whispers grow louder. Leaning down, he lifts my leg and tucks it around his narrow hips. A breath escapes my lungs as he fits himself against me, and even through the fabric of my undergarments, the layers of my skirts, and his trousers, I feel him hard against my quivering center. Desire rushes through me like molten fire, stoked by his silken tongue against mine. He tastes of sweet wine.

My eyes flutter open when he pulls back. He holds my gaze as he traces his hand down my arm, over my ribs, and around my waist.

"Get ready." The swirls of his gold magic move across the floor and up the walls, then over the windows and through the curtains, blanketing every inch of this room.

The candlelight in the lanterns flickers. It's the same power that almost took out the veil.

My heart races for another reason entirely, and I remember that night. How afraid I had been of him, but not anymore.

"What about this room?" I hear a distinctly male voice outside the door, and everything goes dark.

Ash buries his face against my neck just as the door swings open, letting in the chill of the winter night. I tilt my head and meet the eyes of a blond man. His eyebrows arch as he takes a step back. "Ah shit, there's a couple fucking in this one too!"

"What in the hell did Marion put in those drinks tonight?" another says.

"Out," Ash growls.

My hair rises in response just as the door shuts with a click.

"No one can stay in that room," a third voice says.

"She was pretty, man. Let him have her before we have to kick them out," says the first man. "They can't go anywhere. The windows are warded."

Ash pulls away so fast, I'm left holding the wall for fear my knees will buckle and I'll end up on the ground. The room spins, and the amulet drums in my hair.

"It didn't work. They're waiting outside," I whisper.

He grips my hand and guides me toward the windows, his magic coming alive in waves, illuminating our way. "It bought us time, and that's all I needed."

He opens the curtains over three large windows, revealing the bright silver globe hanging over the city. I lose my breath as I stare at the reflection in the glass. Not because it's encased in gold, or that a hairline crack travels from one corner, splitting into ten, then twenty, then a hundred.

I can't breathe because, lurking behind Ash's reflection and blending with the shadows, there is a monster. Made of misty threads, long-limbed and with eyes so dark they suck the life from the room. It snarls at me with a black hole for a mouth.

He's here.

The king is here—I can't look away—*and he brought the curse of mirrors with him.*

The grimoires' voices turn into a screech as they're pulled from their shelves by threads of Ash's magic, and every book twirls around us like a cyclone of worn leather. Their screams are so loud my ears feel like they're bleeding.

The shadow monster leaps toward me, snarling so viciously even the grimoires grow quiet. But Ash doesn't flinch. He doesn't hear a sound. He can't see the curse as it eases out of the reflection. First its wispy clawlike hands. Then the shape of an arm that twists and billows like the shadows.

I pull my amulet from my hair on pure instinct and shield myself with it, commanding it to protect me. The pin allows my power to flow steadily and keep the shadows from expanding beyond its boundaries. The poisoned threads of the curse swell as it continues pushing against my hairpin, and my arm shakes as I struggle to keep it lifted.

"What's happening?" Ash asks, and his power thickens around us.

I can't answer him. If I break focus for a second, I might lose the handle I have on the curse. The glass from all three windows shatters and collapses into a million pieces, taking the monster of shadows with it.

Ash leaps over to the window frame, and his voice pounds in my throbbing ears. "Monster." He reaches a hand to me.

The silver light of the moon draws a highlight over his silhouette as his wings reappear and the rest of his glamour breaks. He lifts me up onto the windowsill, and I wrap my shaking arms around his neck, feeling numb. Scared.

The grimoires are still quiet, and everything swims around me.

"Hold on to me." He dips and hooks his arm under my knees just as five men charge into the room wielding swords wrapped in fire, and Ash leaps into the sky.

CHAPTER 28

The streets blur under us with the speed we glide over the city, carrying grimoires through the air tethered by gold chains of Ash's magic. I tighten my hold around his neck, dipping my face closer to find shelter from the frigid air numbing my skin, and as I breathe in the scent of his skin, I let myself relax in his embrace.

Hoping my amulet will listen and allow me to use a fraction of my magic to warm my skin, I probe at it, but it stays quiet.

It's one of the few enchantments we could learn as librarians, useful to maintain the library's temperature and keep it from getting too cold during the winter months. I feel the spell in the back of my throat, begging to be used to warm my icy limbs. The stone in the hairpin answers dimly, as if tired, but doesn't release the pressure in my stomach.

It just remains like it's been since we left the strixes' house. A ball of smoldering coals I can't quite light.

"You're cold," Ash says right as his hand tightens against my back and delicious warmth spreads through the layers of my dress.

"I-I'm fine." The words fight past chattering teeth as I call on my amulet again, but meet silence.

Ash gaze cuts to me, hard, unyielding, yet I can't seem to stop looking at the sweat dripping down his temple or the straining muscles of his neck.

"It's just, my amulet isn't answering. But please don't use your energy on me. You have to use enough to carry all these grimoires."

And me.

This is not the first time we've flown together over long distances, and I imagine someone like me is not light to carry.

"I'd rather avoid having to use more complex magic to keep you from fading away when you get ill from the cold, especially once we make it to the forest."

I perk up at his words, and adrenaline replaces the numbness rushing through me. "What do you mean the forest? I thought we were going back to the manor?"

"We aren't going back. I'm a beacon to any strix in this city. I don't intend to lead them to Nera."

Of course, we couldn't go back to the manor after what we just did, but I never thought we would fly across the land, just the two of us. "How will Finley and Nera know we've left?"

"Visiting Hedrum was always a risk. It's why I didn't want to come, even when Nera begged to. Finley and I came prepared to escape if needed, though we hoped for the best." Ash clenches his jaw as he turns his head to study the hundreds of books that circle us. "I never expected to find these there. I wouldn't have, if it weren't for you."

My stomach flutters at his words. I feel light and giddy. But even though I'm blushing, I scrunch my nose as I stare at him, unblinking. "Why do you care so much about these books?"

I understand the need to recoup things that are clearly powerful, but why would he choose to take all these grimoires with us instead of disappearing into the night and the safety of the manor? In that room, I wasn't thinking straight. I was excited to have found the whispering texts. Horrified to discover what the strix are, and how their emblem looks so similar to the librarians'.

I was only thinking about buying us time. But right now, I can't believe Ash would leave Nera behind in a city filled with his enemies to carry all these books across the kingdom.

"I know you went to Penumbra searching for them, but surely you don't believe we'll find the way to break the curse in one of these." I gesture to the flapping pages around us, some hovering just three feet away from my face. "It'll be a cosmic coincidence if we do."

"It has nothing to do with the curse, Mia. There's magic that connects them to me lying dormant in each page." He shifts his arm down my back to get a better hold of me around the layers of my dress. "The books are linked to me through my ancestors. Through many generations of kings and queens who've used blood spells to bind those pages to us in order to safeguard our secrets. To keep our history and power protected."

"You and Nera are connected to each book?"

"Nera is not, unless I die. The binding spell is done when we take the crown and kept alive by the continuous gifting of power by each new ruler. The fae are long-lived, so the connection thrives. We lend a morsel of magic, and in return, the ancient power of my bloodline helps protect the castle."

Whatever warmth I had regained drains as I stare at him. "Is that why they were stolen in the first place? To weaken you at a higher level?"

It has to be why they always felt alive. The night we met, Ash felt familiar. Of course, I had been studying his magic for months. That had to be the reason.

He nods and turns away from me. "I initially guessed they had been collecting them to steal powerful enchantments and knowledge. But I fear something much worse."

"What?" I ask, as we fly over the outskirts of the city, closing in on the dark forest's misty ground.

"What if they could craft a connection with Naheli?" he says. "I don't know if the hybrids are aware of this, but they can't have access to her. They are already using my ancestor's magic to craft the veil you love so much."

I clench my hands around his shoulders, looking away as shame bursts through me, foul and repulsive. "Did the scientists use fae magic to craft the veil?"

"They did. It's an ancient blood spell meant to protect the royal kin from being abducted and used in battle. It creates a powerful shield that repels certain fae types. But in order to keep it going, you need one of their—or, in the case of the veil, *our*—kind's blood. An old ancestor designed it to keep the seelie away from our children."

We cross the edge of the city, and the air is charged with electricity. Almost immediately, clouds cover the previously clear sky. A storm brews in the distance. "Is that why you could break through the veil when most lunargyres can't?"

"Yes. I'm the only fae they can't keep away—well, me and anyone from my bloodline. The shield is made with waves of energy that mimic my magic. The grimoires call the beasts there, but the veil keeps them away as it prevents them from scenting humans in the city. Quite the invention they created to stop me from breaking the curse."

I'm going to be sick all over him if we continue with this conversation. What I saw in that machine room will forever haunt me. I went ahead with Skylar's demands, even though deep down I knew it was wrong.

For Irene, I would do almost anything, but I couldn't forsake Ash anymore.

My heart squeezes at the thought, and we fly above the treetops in silence, until rain begins to mist down on us.

"Fuck." Raindrops catch on Ash's long lashes. "We'll need to find somewhere to stay for the night or risk ruining the books."

Thunder cracks, and the storm catches up with us. Reaching for the pin in my hair, I probe at it again with my mind and urge it to wake up as my fingers tingle. I know how to help this time. I've been protecting grimoires for five years, using spells to shield them from moisture, heat, and cold.

I was trained to be a puppet, but I'll use what little the librarians taught me to help the fae. But the pin doesn't answer other than to keep my power from truly bursting out.

We dive deep into the forest and under the thick canopy. The grimoires follow us, some crashing into thick branches, while others expertly avoid them. Their voices grow stronger in the quiet of the woods at night. Forest debris cracks under my feet when Ash sets me on the ground. I left my traveling cloak back in the strix nest, and I'm cold, wet, and completely unprepared to face the night.

Ash unclasps his hands from around my waist and takes a step back. The cold water rolls over the shiny feathers of his wings as he shrugs off his coat and hands it to me.

"Put this on, Monster, or your shaking bones will call every dark creature hiding in the shadows."

I reach for the coat but pause as my fingers graze the wet fabric. "This is just as cold and wet as my dress."

"Demanding little thing, aren't you?" He raises a brow and smirks, this time with dimples. "Didn't the librarians teach you how to use simple spells to dry yourself and keep warm? I've seen you master fire and wind. Surely that would be easy for you."

His magic blooms around us, and the books fall from the air with murmurs of displeasure, but the coat dries in front of my eyes. Ash steps forward again and drops it over my shoulders. Warmth seeps into my frigid limbs.

"I know how to dry myself," I say, sounding a bit more defensive than I intend to. But I want—I *can* do much more . . . if I'm able to wield my magic properly.

"What's stopping you?"

"The amulet is doing too good a job at canceling my power."

Ash tilts his head as he studies me quietly. Without a word, he walks in a random direction. Does he even know where we are?

"Come, there are things here you won't be able to fight off if you can't use your magic." He glances back over his shoulder, and that stupid smirk reappears on his face. "Though perhaps that's the incentive you need to break out of the hold a cheap trinket has on you."

"Cheap?" I gasp, but follow him through the forest. "This amulet cost more than I make in a month!"

"I think you were horribly underpaid. Though if you are unable to cast a simple spell to keep yourself from dying of hypothermia, then perhaps it's expected."

The heat that comes from my bubbling temper overtakes me rapidly, and my power rushes through my body as I step over a fallen branch. I shrug off his coat, and my amulet vibrates against my head. My whole body hums with pressure. "You're the biggest prick I've ever met in my life—"

I've tried to maintain a level of civility with this fae. Surely, I can't actually have feelings for him, because right now, every cell in my body wants to shove his coat up his—

"Well, look at that. It seems anger overrides whatever your faulty amulet is doing."

I stop. It isn't the cool air hitting my bare shoulders that calms me down, but that I'm glowing all over. My fingers, my arms. Like a candle is burning beneath my skin. My dress is no longer wet, and everything around us is silent. I can't even hear the rain anymore over the rush of blood in my ears.

"Mia," he calls, and I blink my confusion when I meet his eyes. I expect to find the same cruelty he was spouting before, but his face is gentle and understanding. "I believe you can break through the spell and unlock your powers when you experience raw emotions."

"How do you know?"

"Because back in Eponde, the day you almost exploded, you were scared. That's when you lost control. Wasn't it? You saw a shadow creature and your magic broke free. It would make sense it might when you're angry as well. Or sad." He beckons me forward with a wave of his hand, his brow wrinkling as he takes his coat from where it's scrunched in my grip. "It's possible your parents had the necklace crafted especially for you. A way to counteract the swing of intense emotions. The particular spell that's binding your power could be of your own doing, as much as theirs, but your first goal should be to try to access and control your magic when you aren't in control of your emotions."

I take in a deep breath that smells like wet soil, moss, and rain. Thunder rolls over us, shaking the ground beneath my feet. "Would you help me?"

"To lose control of your emotions?" His voice comes out throaty. "Or are you asking me to help you learn to control your power?"

"Both?"

"Put the coat back on, and I'll think about it." He shakes the water off his hair and continues moving through the forest like he's been here before. Perhaps he has. "Let's find somewhere to rest before twilight. We have to meet Finley and Nera in the mountain's crossroad, near Fairhope, in two days."

CHAPTER 29

"I can't keep going," Ash grumbles from where he leans against a nearby tree. He slowly lets his body slide down its trunk until he sits between two large roots. Dragging a hand over his face, he stares up at the tree canopy as morning twilight falls upon us.

"I'm happy to rest for a little while," I say, hoping my panic doesn't show.

He scoffs in response, like I've done a poor job at finding us shelter before slumber takes ahold of him. "If anyone comes our way, and I mean *anyone*, you run west until you hit Fairhope. Don't look back." He points vaguely over his shoulder in a direction I can't quite make out through the fog. His eyes close as his breathing deepens.

A month ago, I would have run. But that was the Mia that thought Penumbra was her home. A human woman who loved her job and wanted to continue learning forbidden magic right under the head librarian's nose.

Now, panic spreads in my chest as I urge time to pass quickly and for Ash to wake up. I'm decent at warding spells, which would be useful to protect us from the creatures of the forest.

I believe your magic is unlocked by strong emotions. Ash's words circle in my mind.

I'm full of powerful emotions right now, and yet, I can't seem to get my magic to work. Nor my amulet.

I close my eyes and focus on the noises in the darkness around us, the memory of the shadow creature in Ash's reflection, and I hold on to the fear that unravels through my veins. My power brews in my stomach, and it doesn't take long for it to tingle in my fingertips. I spend a few minutes grasping at fading threads of magic, and it feels like an eternity before I can finally weave a warding spell and pull it tight to keep us safe.

Ash was right. My hairpin did nothing to aid me, and in the end, I'm able to channel enough magic to erect a ward by using the panic rushing through me.

Thirty minutes later, Ash quietly studies the golden shield around us. He doesn't say much, but I see a flash of pride in his features right before I let the spell collapse. I'm tired, hungry—cold—but we continue traveling under the trees by foot until midday.

When the storm finally clears over us, we fly the rest of the way to the Crossroads. I don't know what I expected, but it wasn't a small abandoned town that reminds me of Eponde. Tucked into the shelter of the forest, it's a long strip of boarded-up shops and statues frozen throughout. Tree roots have come through the paving stones of what was previously a plaza. If I close my eyes, I can imagine it in its full glory, but dread snakes under my clothes and crawls over my skin.

Dark magic.

Mist covers the ground as we walk in silence through a metal gate and into a small building that seems to have been a magical market. It's a structure of gray stone and dark wood with clay shingles covering the high-pitched roof. A sign hangs crookedly over the door, the paint so worn I can't read its name. We pass tables tipped on their side, partially hidden by tall, dry grass. Like the castle, wilderness has taken this place.

"Was this a fae town?"

Ash nods and leads me behind the fallen market, down a narrow path, and to a modest house in the back. It's fully encased in evergreen walls, but it feels less haunted than the rest of the village. Without a word, he runs up a set of five long steps to the entrance. The front door is chipped with age, and it stands between two overgrown topiaries in large urns.

He reaches for the brass door handles and pauses before glancing back at me. "Traveling through the kingdom as a fae is dangerous. Even Finley can find himself in trouble because he's tied to me. The last few years, he's been attacked ten times by the strix. We figured they were tracking the royal carriage, so we got a wagon that has no connection to my crown. The hybrids seem to know where he's going, though, and they disguise themselves, much like we do. Since they travel the same routes Finley frequents and don't need to carry amulets, sometimes in order to avoid confrontations, he needs to stay here."

The door screeches as Ash pushes it open, and we step into a receiving room with high ceilings and an ornate chandelier hanging above us. I scrunch my nose at the mold growing in the corners.

It feels like we're imposing in someone's home, even though it's clear from the bed of dust accumulating on the stairs, this place has been vacant for a while. My heart is heavy with emotion, and I clutch at my chest as I step into the living room. Their things are still scattered about like they left in a rush. Or perhaps this all happened after they were gone, and someone ransacked their place looking for valuables.

"It's never going to stop surprising me what happened to your people. Forced out of their homes by a curse. Also, I can't get over that you all lived just like us. You have the same furniture, paintings, books." I wave at a sofa and gesture to the fireplace crafted with river stone, knickknacks accumulated on the mantel under an ornate painting where a spider made a home at some point.

Ash lifts a brow and tugs a white sheet off the couch, wadding it up between his hands before tossing it into the corner. "And what did you think we lived like?"

"I don't know." I shrug. My breath billows in front of my face. "I guess I expected you to live surrounded by white marble and silver things."

His expression remains haunted even as he smiles. "Are you disappointed by our lack of lavish homes?"

"I didn't mean it like that." I tighten his coat, which I'm still wearing, by the belt, hoping it will bring some warmth back. "All the fae homes I've been to are plenty lavish. A castle, a manor, and this is still bigger than my townhome . . ."

Something in this place is uncharacteristically icy, even for the middle of winter, like the house itself is colder than it is outside.

The grimoires pile in through the front door. One after the other, carried by golden magic. Ash waves a hand, and they all line up on the coffee table, across the floor, and even on the couch. I shut the door after every single book has floated in.

"Should I be worried about lunargyres in here?"

"No." Ash picks a smaller grimoire from the pile, pages through it, and his lips tighten. The grimoire grunts in displeasure when Ash puts it back.

"Is the book disappointing?" I ask, but keep the book's weird emotions to myself.

"It's not that . . ." He loosens his cravat before undoing the top buttons of his shirt as he strolls aimlessly around the place. "A fae I knew well wrote it. I haven't seen him in a decade."

Silence settles between us to match the severity of his turbulent emotions. But I don't dare to break it, instead I try to keep myself busy by studying the large painting over the fireplace.

"To answer your previous question: The lunargyres that may have been here moved downstream a long time ago. I imagine they're living closer to your old home, Penumbra. The rest of the fae who used to live here are out in the back, frozen in stone. There have been no living creatures in this house for at least four years. Except for Finley and Amaia, the old hound that belonged to the family. A nightwalker ate her, though."

I stare at him, horrified. "Are you serious?"

Ash steps toward the fireplace, drops a few logs into the hearth, and chuckles darkly. "Monster, you make it too easy to tease you."

Nightwalkers, creatures of fable that live and feed on nightmares. I can see them thriving here if they exist. After meeting Naheli, I'll believe anything is possible.

"That's not funny, Ash. If nightwalkers exist, they must be attracted to dark magic, which you keep mentioning is all around you."

Plus, if I'm frank with myself, I can *feel* the ugly marks of wickedness weaving around us. Tight in the crevices of the wooden floors and deep in the shadows of this room.

"You've been acting strange ever since we arrived here." I reach for the pin in my hair, and trace the smooth beads that surround the stone, a soothing motion that used to calm me when it was my mother's old amulet under my fingertips. But not now. Even as I stand here, wanting to be in control of my magic, I can admit to myself things have changed. I've changed.

Ash's jaw ticks, and his expression turns thoughtful. "I used to come here when I was a child, to see my best friend. Before life got complicated."

He leans against the mantel and a curtain of wavy black hair falls over his forehead, droplets of rain grazing his skin. "Seeing this place in this state is difficult. But we'll be fine for a day or two, and in the meantime, we can work on your magic as you requested."

Ash steps into the dark hallway, stopping briefly to glance back at me. "I'm going to find something for us to eat. Can you make a fire?"

There's a challenge in his eyes, but it isn't unkind. He knows I can cast a fire spell. The trick will be to use magic when I'm so clearly dependent on my broken amulet. I was able to use magic in the forest by focusing on my fear. Now, I can focus on other feelings.

His footsteps disappear in the distance, and wind hisses through broken glass as I kneel by the hearth. I raise my hands to the fresh wood he just dropped in there. Layers upon layers of ash and old charcoal coat the interior of the cave-like fireplace. I allow my sadness for those who called this place home to come to the forefront of my mind.

The knot in my throat thickens as I focus on that emotion and what I felt back in Eponde, when Finley, Nera, and I walked through its streets and saw all those fae frozen in time. My fingers prickle, and I weave the words of the fire spell in my mind. A few sparks burst out of my fingertips, falling into the kindling and producing a decent amount of smoke.

I've never struggled this much to cast a fire spell, but even though the flames take several minutes to catch, this is the proudest I've felt in a long time. When Ash comes back with a small linen sack in one hand and a pitcher of water in the other, weak licks of flames peek through the wood. Warmth blooms in my chest as I watch the fire grow slowly, pushing back the unnatural cold in the room.

He doesn't coddle me, nor does he comment on the fact that I did it. Instead, he lays a spread of dried fruit and aged cheese in front of us, settling himself by my side, and we eat while staring into the fire.

Ash's rumbly voice breaks the silence. "Let's see what else you can do with your magic before we turn in for the night."

I tuck my legs under myself, turning to face him from where I sit on the floor. A thousand questions churn in my mind, but I choose not to get hung up on the idea of where I might sleep in this place. "How are you going to help me?"

He stands from the floor and arches his back into a deep stretch before extending his hand to me. "We can start with you giving me the trinket you use as a crutch."

I narrow my gaze at him. "Are you going to give it back? Last time you took my amulet, it ended up sticking to Nera."

"Come on, Monster, surely you're aware things have changed? Back then, I couldn't have you setting me on fire whenever you pleased." He watches me intently as I get to my feet and brush the dust off my wrinkled gown.

Of all the clothes I could have been wearing to go trekking through the forest, a tight corset and silky dress are far from ideal. I take off my amulet and hand it to him. "I guess you've got a point, though I could reconsider and set you on fire now."

"Perhaps I wouldn't be opposed to burning up for you," he whispers, closing his hand around my amulet and pocketing it.

I meet his gaze and can't decide if the burn traveling through me is magic, or memories of our kiss last night. "So what now? I'm not feeling threatened or afraid." At least not for my life. My heart is another subject altogether. "I'd rather not focus on how sad this place makes me, or I may spiral down somewhere I don't want to go."

Ash circles me, like a predator does prey. "You need to work around the enchantment that's holding you captive and not rely on your emotions."

"Can you break my spell? I've seen you do magic, Ash, and it's breathtaking. I've never met anyone as powerful as you."

"Now, easy there, Monster. Your feelings for me are showing," he says, grinning at my glare. He sobers a little, his expression softening. "I can't. I tried to unravel it while you slept, back in my chambers, with no luck."

"What if it can't be undone? I don't know how I came to have it in the first place . . ."

"There is always a counterspell. No matter the enchantment." Ash tilts his head, an intense curiosity shining behind his eyes. "The night we met, I had you paralyzed, but you unraveled that spell. How did you do it?"

I suspect the answer is going to be disappointing, and say with a shrug, "I asked it to release me."

"You asked the spell to release you . . . and it listened?" Ash's eyes round as he stares at me.

"I take it that's not common? Is it connected to me speaking to artifacts?"

"Possibly . . . I've lived a long time, and I've met no one like you."

My stomach flutters. "I'll take that as a compliment."

"It was intended as such," he says, rolling one of his sleeves up over his forearm. "Other than asking it, do you feel or see anything else?"

"I guess I see the threads that make a spell, and sometimes that makes it easy to break them. It's how I could get through the wards protecting the forbidden grimoires back in the library."

Ash lets out a deep breath and continues his circling. "It's not uncommon for hybrids to possess peculiar gifts. When did you start wearing your amulet?"

"My father gave it to me five years ago." I wring my hands, and the bubbling in my stomach begins.

"How do the librarians find who has magic and who doesn't?"

There's something fuzzy in my mind, like a veil blocking my access to my memories. When I think back to those days—to the specific afternoon I received the letter with my new assignment—all I can remember is being excited, confused, and afraid.

"After we turn twenty, all young adults go to the governor's house and are asked to hold a spherical artifact that detects an affinity to wield magic in simple humans. We were told we aren't true sorcerers, as no magical artifact would bind to us."

I press my fingers to my temple as a dull headache throbs. "I took my mother's amulet to my first meeting with the librarians. My father told me to not let them see it . . . but they must have."

Ash hums thoughtfully, and I know he's putting together his own puzzle with the pieces I'm finally sharing. "The artifact they used to detect your magic, did it turn colors when you held it?"

Somehow, that question makes my stomach sour.

"Yes, it turns blue if someone has an affinity for magic, and remains white if they don't." I add, "Mine didn't turn blue the first time I held it. Let me guess, it's a fae artifact, isn't it?"

He looks mildly sick as he says, "It's called the Nagine, and a race of dangerous, snake-like beings called the Naga created it to track magical humans. My father stole it from them, from where they live in Sylas's kingdom, in order to track hybrids. When I took the throne, I sent someone I trusted to destroy it, but that obviously didn't happen."

I'm thinking a person close enough for Ash to trust them with such an artifact could be the same person who betrayed him with the curse. A hybrid who roamed the castle before me.

"The Nagine needs Naga blood to work properly, but pure fae blood also does the trick most of the time. I never expected it to be used by hybrids, though I guess it could still detect a magical person if they were to hold it in their hands . . ."

I chew the inside of my cheek. Part of me still wants to defend them—defend myself and my old life built in lies. The sensation in my stomach turns uncomfortable almost immediately.

My hold on my power slips through the flimsy grasp I have on it.

"Do you think the librarians put the block on my power?"

"No, I think had they known what you can do, they'd never have allowed you close to my grimoires." He resumes his prowling around me, and I feel our brief history lesson is over. "If you can unravel spells, Monster, then you need to search inside yourself for something that feels wrong. Your power should feel familiar. A part of you. The spell blocking it will feel like a strange invasion in your body."

I close my eyes to focus on the magic I feel simmering within my skin and find it warm.

I search inside myself for something that feels alien. But it all feels familiar, too familiar. Like a hug I received as a child that never let me go. Like the warmth of my father's voice.

I gasp, but don't lose focus as I pull at that buzzing energy in my center—*my* energy—and find threads of magic tightly woven over it. They feel like my own, but slightly different.

A spell made by someone who is part of me, a person I trusted. I tug at the threads again, but they hold tight, and it hurts if I pull too hard.

Let go, I whisper in my head, and the spell wavers a little but doesn't ease.

My breathing turns ragged as I open my eyes, and the ceiling and walls shift over my head.

"Is it working?" I think Ash asks, but there's another voice, one I haven't heard in a long time, that drowns him out.

No. The familiar voice breaks through the webs that cloud my mind, louder than the whooshing of my heart.

Let go, I whisper again.

The room spins, and my surroundings change. One second, I'm staring at the moldy walls of the fae home, and the next, I'm sitting in my old dining room, staring into my father's brown eyes as he leans over the table, pinning me with a sorrowful expression.

"The pain will only last a second, Mia. This is for your own good."

Tears prickle in my eyes, and I hear myself say, *"No, it's not. Don't do this." I'm paralyzed where I sit as a glowing enchantment wraps around my father's hands, reaching toward me. I never knew he could do magic—not like this. He's a scientist, a man of numbers and logic.*

"Don't do this, please. No one saw me do anything—the globe just turned light blue. It's nothing."

A breeze that smells like shadows, pine, and mint breaks through the layers of my memories. Ash. He's close by, even though I can't see him.

"They don't know who you are, and it must remain that way," my father says, turning to the door as if expecting someone to kick it open. His magic suppresses the electric power in my veins. It's a sedative that makes me slump onto the wooden chair.

I can't answer him. Not even as he locks me away with a spell that he hasn't told me how to unlock. An ache squeezes my chest, and tears spill down my cheeks as my mind clouds.

"Please," I beg.

I feel Ash's arms tighten around me.

"We didn't want to do this, Mia. We wouldn't have come here had we known the prophecy existed. You won't remember this. It will keep you safe."

"No. Please."

Ash catches me before I plummet to the ground, his body almost feverish against my frigid skin. "What happened, Mia?"

The feeling of betrayal is immediate and overwhelming. But I'd rather feel this way than afraid to lose control like I did back in the castle. Ash scoops me into his arms and carries me down the hall. Darkness surrounds us, but I'm too groggy to feel scared. Too sad.

"My father . . . he must've been a strix. He helped the scientists build the veil, and we both know what they do to the lunargyres there." My lips thin as I struggle to not break down.

Ash tenses against me but continues on toward wherever he's taking me without a word.

"I think he locked my magic because I'm able to break your curse. It has to be."

"Did he tell you that? You remembered everything that happened?"

A wave of nausea hits me before I can force the words out. "I remember something from that day. He mentioned a prophecy. He said, 'They don't know who you are, and it must remain that way.'"

Ash's jaw clenches, and he stops in front of a black-painted door. "Can you stand?"

After I nod, he sets me back on the floor, and we stand facing each other in complete silence for a long moment before he says, "I've never heard of a prophecy about a hybrid that's not my own, and I've been searching everywhere, including the stars, for an answer. Sometimes I feel I'm getting closer to something, but the words—the prophecy fades before I grasp it."

"Unless." I swallow the deep knot in my throat and try again. "Unless it's a prophecy unknown to the unseelie, and it's protected in Penumbra."

CHAPTER 30

We let the words simmer between us as we stand outside the room. It's a reach to speak of another prophecy when all I have are fragments of memories and little information.

"For years, I felt something was hiding from me behind Penumbra's veil. Something—or *someone*—that called to me," Ash admits, and the intensity in his gaze makes my heart skip.

Is he talking about the person—the woman, if I'm adding up all the crumbs of information correctly—who stole his grimoires and brought them to Penumbra? The one who cursed him? Or does he mean me?

I push aside the ember of hope that begins burning in my heart. If he shares a soul bond with the one who cursed him, then he would be called there by the magic that binds them.

It's not romantic—it has nothing to do with me. I take a deep breath and look away to the dark room in front of us, for fear I won't be able to hide my overwhelming disappointment.

I can't want more than a physical connection with him. It won't end well for me. He's a king, and even if I help him break his curse, I doubt he's looking for anything more than a distraction with a hybrid like me. His people would riot if this meant more.

But the ugly feelings trailing up my body make my stomach churn. Ash's brows lift and he moves closer, as if called by my darkening mood.

"What is this room?" I ask, shifting away from him.

Hurt flashes over his face, and I wonder if I completely misread his previous comment.

"This is where we sleep tonight." He steps into the new room, and I follow him without a moment of hesitation. I don't trust the darkness that welcomes us, but I'd rather be here with him than alone in the light.

He fetches a couple of gas lamps as I wrap my arms around myself and follow the clear marking of wards that line the perimeter.

I take in the thick velvet curtains that do a poor job at hiding the wood boards covering most of the window. He hands me the second lantern, and the flame's soft orange light illuminates the cracked plaster and the cobwebs hanging from the chandelier.

Someone shoved a four-poster bed into the corner, which doesn't seem to belong in such a cramped space.

"I'll sleep on the couch," he says, pointing to the opposite corner where a small chair sits.

I wouldn't categorize that as a couch but choose to not say anything as I inspect the space and the spells that cover the entire perimeter of the room. "I see there are wards on every wall."

"Yes, we set it up for when Finley needs to rest here. It's the room we determined had the least concentrated dark magic. We spent a few days four years ago casting spells to keep creatures away while we're gone."

I see Ash's magic at work. It's easy to recognize with its shades of gold buzzing on each strand, but green traces? Not so much.

If Finley cast protective spells in this place, they weren't very strong, which goes against Ash's claims that he's a powerful sorcerer. I push those thoughts away as I walk to a second door, which leads to a washroom the same size as the bedroom behind me. Intricate panels stained a deep shade of walnut cover the walls. These windows aren't boarded up, and they face the thick canopy of pine trees, their green needles dragging over the glass as the storm outside rages on.

I'm itching to get out of this beautiful—but constricting—gown. I smell like sour wine and the cheap incense the hybrids were burning at that gods-awful party.

I place the lamp on a small marble table beside the copper tub, and admire the black-and-gray terracotta tiles that cover the floor. My thoughts go back to what he said, and I fear my own insecurities ruined what could have been a sweet moment.

What if it could be more? What if I allow myself to live, like Nera said I should, even if it might end in a broken heart? I can't predict the future, but I have a say in the present, in how I treat him. And myself.

I shrug off his coat and drape it over a stool beside the tub. The heaviness in my chest lifts as I twist the handle by the spigot and water sputters first in brown shades, then slowly shifts clear and steaming hot.

I should close the door, but there is something exhilarating about leaving it open. About him knowing I'm getting undressed here, where he could easily walk in.

I reach for the laces of my corset and tug on the elaborate bow that ties it all together at my lower back. I pull harder, but the knot doesn't budge. Shifting my attention, I take off the full skirt and kick it out of the way. I'm left in my chemise, the corset, and the lacy underthings I've been wearing since before the party. Wrinkling my nose, I pull the undergarments off and toss them to the side to wash later.

Then I focus back on the bodice still tight around my torso.

Sweat beads at my temple as I continue trying to get this thing off so I can bathe, but it seems the more I work on it, the more stuck I get.

With a huff, I glance at the open door, seeing movement in the bedroom beyond. I drop the corset laces and take a calming breath. I could burn the fabric to get it off—but then again, I doubt there's something else for me to wear here.

"Ash?"

The shadows move outside as he comes to the doorway, pausing right before he enters. "Is everything alright?"

"Yes. I need help with my corset."

At first, he doesn't say a thing, and when he strolls into the room, a rush of warmth travels up my spine. He is the image of relaxation with the top of his shirt open, so I can see the smoothness of his skin right before it blends with the peppering of feathers on his neck.

In one hand, Ash holds a glass of amber liquid, while the other is deep in his pocket. Whatever foolish thoughts of bravery I had before vanish as he steps closer. His eyes lock with mine, and I don't move a muscle until he's so close I can smell the sweet and smoky scent of his whiskey.

I catch his jaw clenching as I turn around, giving him a full view of the mess I made of the laces. I pull my hair out of the way to give him better access and wait, not breathing. My heart hammers as he shifts closer to me, and his heat seeps through the thin fabric I'm wearing.

"A couple of maids helped me into this thing last night, and I don't think I can get out of it without help."

He hums, reaching to the side and putting his glass of whiskey on the table, next to the lantern. The flame flickers, and I stand perfectly still while he works on the knot.

I expect him to say something, but he's quiet—too quiet for

someone like him. I press my arms to my stomach, holding the fabric against myself as it loosens around my breasts.

When he's done, he doesn't move away. Neither do I. The air crackles with energy, and my skin tingles in anticipation of what may happen next.

When the tips of his fingers graze the back of my neck, I hold my breath. His touch leaves a trail of goose bumps behind as he brushes an errant strand of hair over my bare shoulder. My heart races as I turn my head to meet his gaze. Whatever restraint he had before, is gone.

He doesn't stop at my shoulder, and his touch continues down my arm. I let go of the corset, and as it falls to the floor, it skims over the thin layer of the chemise underneath. Ash spins me around, and his lips come down over mine in a deep, sensual kiss. My body is on fire, and his tongue, tasting of sweet whiskey, fans the flames.

His hands move over my chemise, sliding over my breasts and my hardening nipples. "Mia . . ." His voice is breathless as his lips travel down my jaw and to my neck where he licks and kisses, leaving a trail of heat across my skin. "If you want me to stop—"

"Don't stop." I bury my fingers in his hair and keep his head close to me.

My body craves his touch, and I'm itching to get out of these clothes, to feel his hands on my naked body. A desperate throbbing builds at the apex of my thighs, and I reach for the top of his trousers, loosening the strings that tie them at his narrow waist.

He's wearing far too many clothes. And this should be scary. Perhaps tomorrow it will be.

He inhales sharply when my fingers graze the tip of his cock. Gods, Nera was right. Fae men are built differently.

"Mia," he says my name with reverence, pressing his forehead to mine. His hands skim my back and settle on my hips, but he doesn't move away. "I don't want our first time to be in this filthy place."

"I don't care where we are." My voice comes out needy, almost a whine. "I want this. I want you."

He groans against my lips and kisses me soundly as he lifts me from the floor. One minute, my feet are firmly on the ground, the next I'm spun around as Ash swoops me up and presses me against the wall.

Distantly, I hear the water is still running. I don't care. This feels right.

I move to find some relief from the pressure building in me. He pushes his hips forward, bringing exquisite friction to my aching center. He's so hard. Deliciously so. I barely hold back a moan as pleasure explodes at the contact.

More. My fingers tangle in the waves of his hair as I pull his face closer to mine.

"I've been going mad imagining what you taste like." Each of his words is full of clear desperation. The scent of him makes my head spin, and my skin grows tight and hot. My core flutters.

He keeps me in place with one arm as his other hand glides up the side of my ribs, pulling away the lacy layer of chemise that's bunched where our bodies meet. A breath escapes me, fanning over his lips as his hand trails down between my thighs.

He groans deeply, and it's the sexiest sound I've ever heard. I don't want him to stop. I meet his gaze and see the same hunger reflected there.

"I'll worship every inch of you until you forget how much you want to leave." He pulls my chemise off my body and tosses it to the side, leaving me wholly naked and pinned to the wooden wall. The chill of the night hits the heated flesh of my thighs.

"I don't want to leave you, Ash. Far from it."

He pauses, his lips grazing mine. "Say it again."

"I don't want to leave." My heart is beating so hard I feel it in my throat. "And I want you—I want us."

"I want this—us—too." He swallows, pressing his forehead to mine as his fingers trace lazy circles over my sensitive skin, right beside where I truly crave his touch. A tease, but it keeps the fire burning in my veins as his words sink in. He wants us too, and somehow, this isn't a one-night thing for him either.

"Ash . . ." I tighten my arms around his neck, dragging my fingers over the thick layer of feathers wrapping around the base of his skull. I move my hips to the side, just enough so his fingers actually touch me where I want him. So I can find some relief.

"Demanding little Monster." His dark, sexy chuckle makes my stomach flutter. His thumb finally strokes me in excruciatingly slow circles that send pleasure burning through me. He presses one finger inside me. "Has anyone touched you like this?"

"No," I gasp, and heat flares in my cheeks. I haven't told a soul how little intimacy I allowed myself as a librarian. I've touched a man before, even if at the time I wasn't ready to let him touch me. This feels much different.

Before I can say anything else, Ash is kissing me. He presses two more fingers into me, still stoking the fire with his slow circles, and my breath stutters at the slight burn and the delicious stretch that follows. Harder, faster, setting a rhythm that matches my breathing.

"Ash, I need more of you." I feel like I may explode from the pleasure he's giving me. My power simmers under my skin. Just there as a reminder it comes alive when emotions are high.

"I have to get you ready." His eyes are locked on mine, and he swallows deeply as his expression tightens with the same need I'm feeling. He continues moving his fingers between us, bringing me closer to my release. My body stiffens, and I come apart under his touch so fast I can barely catch my breath.

When the waves of pleasure turn into gentle rocking, I'm done with his hand and want something more. I reach for his trousers, finishing the job I started before by undoing the ties.

My name on his lips sends a shiver down my spine. He pins me to the wall and hooks his arm right under my knee, pulling my leg up so he's pressed right to my heat. His mouth comes to my neck, licking, sucking again as he carefully presses into me until he's fully inside and I'm struggling to breathe against the tightness and the pleasure of being connected in this way.

"Mia." He pushes the hair out of my eyes, his face hovering close to mine, his expression contorted as he holds himself still. "Is this alright?"

I nod, and just to prove to him how right this feels, I rock my hips over his. Ash's eyes roll back and he groans, loudly. His hand grips my waist, and he moves. Slow, deep thrusts, hitting a spot inside me that makes my blood heat again.

Moaning, I writhe against him. Warmth spreads in my core as a breath catches in my throat. The second climax that rolls through me is less intense than the first, but takes me by surprise.

Ash's movements become erratic as the waves of my pleasure die down, and his begin. He kisses me, hard and needy, as goose-flesh roams over his skin. "Fuck, Mia." His voice roughens at the same time his hips buck into me. Deeper. Harder.

My walls clench around him, and his movements drag my orgasm on and on, pulling every ounce of pleasure out of me, until I go limp in his arms.

Ash cock twitches right before a grunt leaves his lips, and he trembles as he comes inside me.

Slowly, the room comes back into focus around us. Water trickles over the edge of the bathtub, spilling onto the tile floor. Steam clouds the windows and hangs heavy in the air. Ash's arms tighten around me, and he doesn't put me back on the ground but instead walks us to the tub, leaving his trousers behind.

He tsks as his feet splash through the water around the tub. "Look at the mess you made . . ."

"Me?" I say, unable to hide the smile in my voice. "I was perfectly ready to bathe until a beast ravished me."

My arms tighten around him, knowing him well enough by now that I can see when mischief glows behind those golden eyes of his.

"That wasn't me ravishing you, Mia. Not yet, at least. I intend to do much more than that." He steps into the tub and finally lets me down, dragging the shirt off his body and tossing it onto the pile of my dress.

I don't think whoever built this house designed the bath for two people, much less one as large as he. But we squeeze tightly as the scalding-hot water sloshes around us, easing the ache of walking across the forest, and everything that happened after.

We stay in the bath long enough that the water turns lukewarm. Ash strokes what appears to be lavender oil over my arms with a sea sponge and presses a kiss to my temples. "You're awfully quiet," he says. "That usually means you're up to something."

I lay my head on his chest, enjoying the gentle beating of his heart as I stare at my surroundings. When I came into the washroom, I didn't catch all the details, but now I drink in the wooden ceiling beams, carved with beautiful designs of flowers and nature. There aren't any mirrors in here either.

I feel too tired and too comfortable to move much. "Ash?"

He hums distractedly, encouraging me to keep talking while still pressing his nose to my hair.

"Why do you look different from all the other cursed fae?"

He stiffens under me, briefly pausing the gentle stroking of his fingers over my skin.

"Was that the wrong thing to ask?" I rest my chin on his chest to catch his expression. “I was wondering why the curse shows up so differently for you when even Nera has turned into stone.”

“I don’t get to speak of what it means very often, not anymore at least.” Ash resumes his stroking, caressing my forearm and then moving to the side of my ribs. It’s not sensual, more soothing and gentle. Still, my body reacts to his touch by warming up again.

His dark lashes shroud most of the gold of his irises as he looks down at me. “This”—he waves his other hand over his neck and pectoral muscles where the feathers have grown thicker in the last few days—“is my spirit form. Or so I was told by my court advisers before they lost their minds to the curse years ago.”

I blink. “What do you mean, spirit form? Like Naheli?”

He nods. “Once, the unseelie lived in the spirit realm, and our true forms were more animalistic. The feathers, talons, and sharp teeth are mine.”

“Then why does it become more apparent when the blood moon gets closer?” I sit up and turn to meet his gaze fully.

“The curse takes its toll on my body the closer to the blood moon we are.” He reaches for me with a pinch to his brows, pulling me back to my previous position, lying on top of his body. I like this much more.

“Naheli lends me more of her magic to keep me sane, and so my true spirit appearance reveals itself.”

My lips round as I digest all this new information. It matches with the legends and what I learned from Finley and Nera. I think back at the gaps in the information in all the books I studied growing up.

Ash stands and brings me along with him. He’s so large he blocks what little light comes from the lantern, his body and wings casting a shadow, and his eyes taking on a glowing appearance.

“So, does that mean Nera will turn into a bird like you if she connects with her spirit?" I grin at the glint that shines in his expression. "What do you think her spirit will be like?"

"My family believed the spirits that connect with us match our temper. Naheli, for example, is calm and reasonable—"

"More like sassy and snippy," I scoff, shaking my head as a drying spell wafts around us, leaving traces of Ash's magic clinging to our bodies. I suppose both things can be true. Naheli is sassy and mischievous, but also calm—and perhaps even reasonable. "You think Nera's spirit is going to be stubborn and strong, craving freedom and adventure?"

"Yes, and it will be what keeps her sane—and safe—when Sylas comes for her. The seelie kingdom is not like Aphelion. The only spirits roaming freely there are evil ones."

I shiver, remembering the creatures Ash talked about. The Naga, serpents that eat magical humans.

"Even the shadows will try to kill you there."

Whatever playful mood I was in is dampened by the horror of Nera's future. Judging by Ash's sulking expression, he is there as well.

"Can we do anything to stop Sylas from taking her?"

He swallows, thickly, before shaking his head. "I'll try anything, if—when—it comes to that. But the contract is binding." He hesitates, pain flashing in his features as we step into the room. "He's her mate, Monster. Even if I hate him, she belongs with him, much like he does with her."

I'm angry at the old king of the unseelie, her father, who gave Nera away in an unbreakable magical bargain with the seelie. I'm furious that if I'm able to lift this curse, I may bind my friend to another prison, when all she wants is to be free.

But perhaps Nera will use her vast power and strength to carve out a destiny for herself. One she wants, instead of the one males are forcing her to carry.

CHAPTER 31

"THE MORE I PAGE THROUGH THESE GRIMOIRES, THE MORE I THINK you're right. The strix must have an ulterior motive to hold on to these." I shut the book I've been trying to read for the last hour and put it back on the table. "Though I guess mastering the art of casting glamours could be useful . . ."

I glance at the cover of the book, reading the name embossed in gold on the first page. *Morla Skye*.

"What did you just say?" Ash turns to me, his face paling.

"That I think you're right, the strix must be up to something?"

"No, the thing about the glamours." He steps away from the window he's been standing in front of, staring at the gloomy afternoon, for at least half an hour. Taking the grimoire, Ash studies the spine with a growing frown. "Skye . . ."

There's a familiarity in his inflection that makes my stomach twist with something ugly. Morla Skye has to be someone he was close to.

"You know her?"

His nostrils flare as he tosses the book onto the table, and it bounces unceremoniously before falling to the ground with a thump.

I blink, watching the trail of magic the grimoire left behind. Ash's jaw clenches tightly, and his face reddens as if he's trying to speak, but can't. His expression is pure, stone-cold rage.

Ice chases the heat of jealousy that previously took over my heart, and somehow, I know who this is.

The hybrid woman who loves—or hates—roses. The one who cursed Ash and his kingdom. It has to be to elicit such a reaction. Someone who was close enough to him to steal right out from under his nose. Someone who lived in the castle and wrote books for his personal library.

If I ask the right question, he may be able to answer. "Is Morla the one who cursed you?"

He hesitates, swallowing deeply before nodding. He tries to speak twice, but fails. Whatever safeguard the curse has, it prevents him from telling me details of who she is and possibly what she did.

"You already told me back in Hedrum she was one of your tributes. But did she become more? A friend—someone close to you?"

His face brightens, like I struck gold with my simple question.

"Unlike most of the souls we take during the Hunt, the word *tribute* fits Skye very well." He takes a deep breath, looking at the ceiling. "She walked right in and offered herself to my father. She claimed—truthfully, it turns out—to be a wielder of great power. My father refused to allow a hybrid to work for him and ordered the guards to kill her."

"Gods . . ." He sounds horrible.

"I didn't want the hybrids to die, Mia, and if I was going to take the throne, I wanted the guards to know I didn't stand behind my father's beliefs. So, I met her gaze and took her instead.

Those we take live long lives, like Finley. And Skye was a partner and a friend for many years."

So they were close, and I don't need to be jealous of a relationship that clearly ended in flames. But my heart is foolish. I stand from the table, reaching for the grimoire that remains on the floor. As soon as I touch it, it zaps me with electricity. Shaking my hand, I try to move past the cramping left behind by the book's outburst.

"Did you love her?" My heart pounds as I meet his eyes.

"Not the way she wanted." There's a softness in his expression that tells me more than words. He cared for her deeply. He just wasn't in love. So when he says, "That was the problem," I know things got very complicated and very sad. I don't need, or want, to hear the details.

But now I know the cause of the curse. A broken heart.

"When did you learn she worked with the strix?" I ask, but he shakes his head.

Not a question he can answer, or perhaps he doesn't know. He has told me a few times her betrayal blindsided him.

"Skye used to hide in the garden while my father hosted dances. She loved to spy on the fae, study our behaviors when we were acting our wildest. Once, a couple of high fae found her snooping on their business, so they paralyzed her and hid her body amongst the statues. She was so pale, it took us an entire day to find her." Ash sighs, dragging a hand over his face and kneeling by my side, picking the book up from the floor where I left it. "Funny how she made sure my people turned into statues when the curse took them."

So it seems Morla wove details of her life into the spell she created. The statues, the roses . . .

I press my lips together and try to sort through all my questions as I study the cover of the book she wrote.

"Did she teach you how to glamour yourself into something else?"

"Yes. She was fantastic at it."

There it is, my old friend jealousy, poking her ugly head back in. I shift my gaze away as I stand and try to hide the horror of the thoughts plaguing my mind. Because I'm not truly great at anything. I can't control my magic without an amulet. I couldn't please my father, or my sister, even when I tried.

So instead of obsessing over an old friend Ash didn't love, and what that may mean for me, I shift my thoughts to something else. Something I'm good at. And that is coming up with theories. Solving problems.

"What about the roses?"

"What about them?"

"Do you think they're a way to spy on you? Make sure you aren't close to breaking the curse? What if they changed color because I triggered some sort of fail-safe?"

"Yes, I think they're something just like that. And when you touched the roses, they sent out a wave of almost-undetectable power that created a fissure in the wards around the castle grounds."

My mouth feels like it's full of sand. I remember it like it was yesterday. Finley left for Hedrum shortly after, and I escaped my room that night at twilight, using the same roses, after Morgana told me about the slumber.

I pause as I pull at an errant string on the sleeve of the gown Nera gave me. Because I never got the dresses Morgana promised.

"Ash, did you send a lunargyre to my room to fit me with new clothes?"

Ash strolls to the table and drops into a chair. Shame tints his features as he shakes his head. "I wanted to, but we lost our tailor a couple of years ago to the curse. Finley promised there were enough gowns in the closet for you to use."

Could it have been Morla who came to me then? My heart rate speeds up, and I'm sweating all over.

"A lunargyre, or at least that's what I thought she was, came to my room and told me you sent her to fit me for a new wardrobe. She's who told me about the slumber . . ."

It's Ash's turn to lose all color from his face. "That's how you knew."

"I didn't want Morgana to get in trouble, so when you asked me how I learned about the slumber, I didn't tell you."

His knuckles turn white as he fists his hand, golden power licking his fingers. "Did she try to hurt you?"

I shiver as I recall her undoing the knots in my hair with her long fingernails. After a moment of going over everything that happened, I shake my head.

"Damn her," he says, and lets out a shaky breath. "Her betrayal has weakened her bond with me, but whatever remains makes it so neither Naheli nor I can feel her coming through the wards. That's why we needed the crystal."

And why Finley was in such a hurry to leave.

"I'm sorry, I didn't know . . ."

Ash's expression softens. "Mia, I don't blame you for trying to escape whatever way you could. You knew nothing about me or Morla, and I hadn't given you a reason to be on my side. It's not your fault."

The weight in my chest loosens, and my affection for him blooms warmly in my heart. I glare at the grimoire on glamours, the one Morla wrote, and think back on the roses that allowed me out of my room all those times.

She's remarkable at spell crafting—I give her that much.

But there must be a weak spot even to hers, because when crafting an enchantment, the spell master must weave into the strands a way to reverse it. My skin tingles as adrenaline rushes through me.

The hybrids will come under a blood moon to the unseelie halls. Plural.

One to cast the curse—one to break it.

"What if only a hybrid can break the curse? That may be why the roses turned and warned her I was there."

"Mia . . ." His eyes pin me down right before he stands, and his tone turns reverent. "You're brilliant."

I may not be a master of spells or of glamours, but I'm going to break them out of this mess.

"There's something else, and I need you to be truthful with me. Ash, does the curse spread through reflections?"

His whole body stiffens. "How did you—?"

"There are no mirrors in the castle," I blurt out. "Not here, or anywhere you frequent. At first I thought it odd, but then in Hedrum, I thought maybe it's a detail woven into the curse to prevent you from breaking it. Perhaps the mirrors shatter when you're nearby."

"Mia"—There's panic in his voice as he reaches for me, then brings me closer to him—"the mirrors aren't the solution."

I'm not sure I fully believe it.

I fight the need to fidget under his scrutiny. His expression settles into something intense and intimidating, and the apprehension shining through makes me sweat. Back in Hedrum, the grimoires said the words *the curse of mirrors*.

Right when the monster made of shadows leaped out of the reflection and at me.

"Have you found one?" he asks.

I shake my head, even as Marlena's mirror flashes through my mind. I tucked it inside my traveling trunk back at the manor, but all those things remain there. There's no point in panicking him more when I don't have it either way.

He lets out a breath. "Please, don't look for one. The curse spreads through reflections, and the reason everyone in my life is dying, dead, or worse, is because I was foolish enough to not realize it."

"But what if it spreads that way, and it's also how we can break it?"

"No." His voice is so harsh I snap my lips shut. "I will not watch you die cursed because you want to help me. You are important to me, and I'd rather you are safe, even if it means I remain this way."

"But what if—"

"Every human and hybrid affected by the curse died within a month," he says. His eyes glide over my face. "There are no exceptions, Mia."

"But Finley isn't dying."

"He's never met the curse directly through reflection. The effects he feels are directly correlated to his connection to me."

He doesn't know that, back in Hedrum, I used my amulet to deflect his curse when it jumped at me. I may have broken my hairpin, but I still did it. I open my lips to tell him as much when the clopping of hooves over gravel echoes from outside.

Ash's head snaps to the window, and he's a blur of black feathers as he presses his entire face against the cloudy glass. The fog parts as a carriage enters through the metal gates out front. Finley and Nera are finally here.

By the time we're outside, Finley's already out of the carriage. His face is strained and filthy. There are scratches on his chin, and oil shimmers over his forehead and cheeks. The beasts pulling the carriage breathe loudly, foaming at their mouths while their reddish eyes pin me down. The glamour has faded, and they no longer look like stallions. Instead, long teeth protrude from their small snouts. Like a bald horse mixed with a boar.

"Finley, what happened?" Ash opens the secondary door, checking on Nera, who I presume is inside. I keep my distance from the beasts, my hair rising as they follow my every move.

"We waited at the manor for as long as we could. I gathered some of our things to give Mia a chance to return, but when she didn't come back, I assumed something happened." Finley's amber eyes land on me, wild and unfocused. There's a small growl from inside the carriage, and when Ash pulls back, I know Nera isn't herself.

"What happened to her?" Was that my voice? I can't tell from the adrenaline rushing through my body.

"Whatever reversed the glamour at the party also affected her—conscious state. She's been fading since yesterday."

I walk around the beasts, getting closer so I can see what's happening to Nera while my heart aches for the devastation in Ash's features. Both doors to the carriage are open wide, and Nera sits, unmoving, inside. Her wings press against the ceiling, and some of her stone feathers have pierced through the wooden roof.

I freeze when her head snaps to the side, her red, milky gaze pinning me down. Her mouth opens as she snarls at me. Ash's golden magic blooms out of him, enveloping her right before he presses a finger to her forehead, and before she can leap out to chase me down, she slumps back. Asleep.

Ash wraps an arm around Nera's waist, sparing me a glance over her body. The agony in his expression is so intense it takes my breath away. His arms shake with strain as he hoists her up before walking back into the small house with Finley following closely behind.

I wipe my wet cheeks and notice the tremble in my hands. Nera is losing her consciousness, even though we're at least two months away from the blood moon. This is the reason she wanted to come to Hedrum. One last chance to have fun before she loses her mind for good. She didn't think she'd come back from it again—and I can't let the curse take her.

It'd destroy Ash to lose her, and she deserves better.

I stand still, thinking of ways I can help, going over old spells I once studied in my mind. But I don't really know enough magic for something like this. The librarians made sure we were kept ignorant. I look at the carriage, and something nags at the back of my mind.

Finley said he gathered some of our things before leaving Hedrum. Perhaps that includes my traveling trunk, where I hid the mirror. I run around the back to the storage compartment and try the handle. Locked. Finley's green magic is all over it.

White magic circles my fingers, and I ignore the pressure in my stomach, its weight like stones. The unraveling spell bursts through me, and the brass lock clicks open.

Inside, there are two trunks. Nera's and mine. I reach for the leather handle, and my muscles scream as I drag it out of the tight space, scraping smooth wood off the sides. Inside, it smells mildly of dust, roses, and traces of magic. My own? It's hard to tell.

I shift through the layers of lacy underthings and dress skirts, and find the silver oval shape closer to the bottom.

I can't break Ash's curse today, even though I want to. I don't know how. But what if I'm able to free Nera from her much smaller shadowy monster? It seems I'm the only one who can see them.

When Ash had me frozen the night we met, I asked the spell to release me. I did the same last night with my father's spell, and regained some of my memories. I might have a chance out of this mess. The prophecy flashes through my mind again.

Only when the king who cries tears of gold loses all,
will there come a new hope, and the one with the black rose will fall.

Not today. Ash can't lose everything before the day is done.

CHAPTER 32

THE SURROUNDING SHADOWS GROW LONGER AND CLOSER AS I MOVE DOWN the corridor to the dining room. I tuck the mirror under the thick layers of my traveling cloak, and pure determination pushes me forward.

A month ago, I was plucked from my city, a simple librarian who knew very little of what was happening out here. Now, I'm on my way to risk everything to save a beast—a friend—who not so long ago, I hated.

New rose canes cover the walls, which means Ash has been using his magic while I was outside. All are blooming with blood-red petals that bring color to the dreary halls. Following the vines, I find Ash and Nera at a long table bearing a small array of food.

"Mia, I'm glad you made it out of Hedrum alive. I have to say, this is not how I hoped to spend my birthday . . ." Nera's voice is deep with lingering sleep, and I jump at the sound of it. Some of the haze from before has left her eyes, but there is a dreamy quality to the way her eyelids droop, like she could fall asleep at any moment.

Today is her birthday, the whole reason we came all the way

here. And unless we do something, this may be her last one. Panic seizes me, the need to help her becomes stronger.

Ash takes a sip of tea, pretending to be at ease even though his knuckles are white and he's paler than I've ever seen him. "I was wondering if you ran away again."

My shoulders ease as I realize he's trying to distract me from Nera's condition, likely because of my inability to keep my emotions off my face.

"I tried, but got lost and had to come back." I plaster a smile on my face, and judging by his expression, I'm not fooling anyone. My fingers twitch as I reach for the back of the closest wooden chair and meet Ash's eyes from across the table. "I figured you needed time to calm Nera down . . ."

Finley moves outside the windows, walking around the carriage, running his fingers over the spindly wheels, and inspecting everything before we depart for the castle.

"I did, but all is well for now." Ash scratches the edge of his chin as he tentatively leans back in his seat. "Why are you glowing, Monster?" He grabs a couple of olives from a plate and tosses them into his mouth, chewing slowly as he looks at me like he's trying to decipher what he's seeing.

Sweat rolls down my temple. "Maybe I glow when I'm nervous and my magic comes out . . ."

My entire face is warm enough to cook an egg, but at least the suspicion in his eyes eases.

"What happened in Hedrum?" Nera leans her stone chin on the heel of her hand, blinking lazily as she studies me, tapping her nails on her cheek. They're much longer than they were before we left the castle. Back when she'd been fine.

"I told you, we found some of the lost grimoires and decided to bring them along . . ." Ash pauses to clear his throat, then asks me, "Where's your amulet? We need to leave within the next half hour."

Instinctively, I touch my hair, but the amulet isn't there. It's in my cloak pocket, waiting for the right moment to strike.

"It's still not working right, so I see no point in wearing it anymore." It's not a lie, but my voice quakes, giving away my unease. I hope Ash thinks it's all about Nera and not because I'm planning on doing something reckless.

"You should probably still wear it, Mia," Nera says, sobering up just enough for worry to etch her features. I think she's started caring for me, just like I do for her.

I glance down to where the small hand mirror remains hidden under my clothes. I can do this.

She continues, "Magical artifacts weaken sometimes, but unless it's shattered, it'll help you when it matters."

Yes, it will.

Which is why I need to get Ash away from here. "I found traces of magic around the carriage when I was outside. I tried to break them apart, but couldn't. I wonder if that's why Nera and the horses transitioned so quickly . . ." I set up the lie, and the words are bitter on my tongue.

As predicted, Ash goes still, his hand hovering motionlessly over his food. His brows pinch as he leans forward. "You saw spells over the carriage—could you tell what kind?"

"I don't know. It's probably nothing, and I know you and Finley throw protective magic on all sorts of things, so maybe it's that?" I shrug and grab a butter roll for my plate, glancing at Nera from under my lashes.

She sits unmoving in her chair. Her breaths shallow enough that, if I look away for even a moment, I'll miss the subtle movement of her chest. Her eyes are unfocused.

It would be much easier if I didn't have to do this alone. I want Ash to stay, but I know deep inside that if he knows what I'm about to do, he'll stop me.

Ash seems to hesitate for a second, then he stands fluidly,

pushing his chair back. "Nera, are you well enough to stay here alone with Mia?"

Nera blinks a few times and tears shimmer in her eyes. When she meets my gaze, I notice her irises are back to the usual shades of rose gold. Her lips tilt into a weak smile. "Don't worry, brother, I won't eat her. She is yours, after all."

I open my lips to protest that I'm not his, but the words don't come as easily as they once did.

Ash glances at me, lifting a brow, as if expecting my usual retort. But . . . while I don't believe in the kind of ownership the fae seem to throw around when speaking about people, I'm not so sure my heart belongs to me anymore.

A breath escapes his lips, and his voice is warm with affection when he says, "Even as a statue, you're the most mischievous creature I've ever met, Nerala."

Rounding the table, Ash approaches me with that ease in his steps I've grown to admire, then reaches for my waist to pull me close. His lips brush my forehead. "Don't get into too much trouble while I'm gone."

My eyelids flutter shut, and I tighten the mirror against my body, hoping he can't feel its shape hiding beneath my cloak. He knows me well enough to suspect I'm up to something, but he can't stop his compulsion to go and check we aren't being tracked.

"I'll try my best," I say and push down the guilt churning inside me.

Nera remains seated in silence, and I wait until his steps fade into the distance. "I know how I can break your curse."

Nera straightens where she sits, and the wooden chair squeaks at her movement. Her brows pinch and loosen as she takes me in. "Let me guess, you're going to do something that could get you killed. Is that why you sent Ash away?"

I hold her gaze as I reach for his abandoned drink and take a sip of the unsweetened tea, hoping the warmth will chase away the cold that's settled into my bones.

"Yes." I shrug. "I don't want him to stop me before I can at least try. It'll be your birthday present."

Nera watches me in silence for a while and smiles again, so her response surprises me. "No."

I blink. "No?"

"When I took you to Eponde, I was being selfish, and I didn't know you. But that's not the case anymore. I can't let you risk your life to help me, because you mean something to me now." The gem of my old amulet blinks along with the rhythm of her heart. Too slow for someone who is alive and well.

Neither Ash nor Nera want me to try to help them with my magic because I mean something to them. Unlike Irene, who demanded I use my magic even though Ash could have killed me that night.

"I can do this. Please, let me try." I pull the mirror from under my cloak and place it on the table. Nera stands, and her chair falls to the ground. I know I have only seconds to convince her before Ash or Finley run back in. "I can see the curse in mirrors, and I can capture it with my amulet."

I take the aforementioned hairpin out of my pocket and set it on the table with a shaking hand. The darkness I met in the hybrid's home dulled my red stone's glow.

"Mirrors are the catalyst for the curse to travel, but I found I can trap it by using a magical artifact," I say. "I accidentally captured a portion of Ash's curse back in the hybrid house. But because his curse is too large, it weakened the amulet. But yours is different. Yours should be a small copy of his."

"How do you know?"

"Because I saw it in Eponde, in a reflection in a window. It's much smaller."

"How did you find the mirror?" Nera asks, and hope shines in her eyes. “Ash and Finley have been destroying them ever since we discovered how it spreads.”

“Finley’s niece gave it to me.”

Nera frowns at that, and for the first time since she arrived, that old spark of something flares behind her expression. “She shouldn’t have done that. If Ash hears about what she did . . .”

“It’s fine.” I swallow deeply and reach for the silver handle of the mirror, feeling my resolution settle in. “Let me help you. Ash won’t have his head in the right place to find a way out of this mess if he’s worried he’ll lose you. Isn’t that why he hasn’t left the castle in years?”

Shame churns in my stomach as I see Nera’s expression fall. I shouldn’t be playing with her guilt to get what I want. But I’m running out of time, and this opportunity is slipping through my fingers.

Nera hunches over and reaches for her untouched glass of water, drinking half in one go before she nods at me. “Alright, do you need me to do anything?”

“Nothing yet.” I stand and shrug off my cloak, draping it over the back of my chair. My stomach is bubbling, an obvious reminder of my locked power, and it reaches up my chest and neck. My body heats, and distantly, I can hear movement from the hall.

Holding the mirror in one hand, and my new amulet in the other, I go over all the things that could go very wrong.

One of them being that I have nearly zero control over my magic, other than being able to speak to my broken amulet. But I know my power’s at its strongest when my emotions are high, and I can work with that.

Especially since Nera, one of my only friends, doesn’t have long before she fades away.

I take a deep breath and lift the mirror to catch Nera’s reflection. While to my eyes she looks like a sculpture made of white marble, the mirror shows her as that beautiful fae I saw in the hybrid house.

Her brows pinch with worry as she looks at me, clearly thinking this is the worst idea ever. The mirror is small enough that I can only see her, until I shift it slightly and catch the shapes of a creature made of nightmares. It holds onto her auburn tresses, and I watch the shadows elongate, forming a narrow face with sharp teeth and red eyes.

The curse snarls at me with a gaping hole for a mouth. The sound pierces the room, but Nera doesn't flinch, which must mean she can't hear it.

I don't cower. Instead, I tighten my hold on my amulet and let out a slow breath. I'm afraid of the curse, but the monster should be more afraid of me and my magic.

I'm the one determining how much I let out.

I'm the one in control.

The pressure in my stomach loosens as I picture Alana, the head librarian, when she told us to never enter the forbidden area. I let that anger feed my power, and it flows freely through my veins.

The memory of Skylar as he loaded his pistol with lead and pointed it at Ash flashes through my mind. Then Irene, telling me the beast in the chamber looked just like the one who killed Father. I remember my father taking away my magic and memories. I've been manipulated throughout my entire adulthood.

This is *my* choice, and with my temper fueling it, my power comes out in slow bursts. The glow that was previously contained to my fingers stretches up my arms.

I meet the curse's gaze with a challenge. "*Don't be shy now. Come out.*"

"Mia." Nera's voice shakes with fear. "What language is that? Who are you talking to?"

It's easy to ignore her when the curse tilts its head. Surprised I can speak to it.

"*She sees us,*" it says, then unravels its clawlike hands from Nera's hair and shifts away from her.

I glance away from the reflection and toward the space between Nera and me. It's empty of monsters in the real realm, but when I look back at the silver surface, the curse is crawling toward me, trailing slimy strings of blackness over the rug.

I ready myself for its attack, calling on my amulet like I did that night in Hedrum. I ask it to trap the curse. Keep it away from me. The stone vibrates in my hand, fast like my heartbeats.

Nera leans over the table, bracing herself with one arm and holding her stomach with the other as the polished surface of her marble body shifts. She's trembling, barely staying upright. "What's happening to me?"

The curse jumps forward and crashes into the reflective barrier between us. Hundreds of cracks spiderweb over the surface as the mirror shudders in my hand, but I feel no fear. Just pure determination.

"*You are ours,*" it roars, and the cracks deepen and expand. Thin strings of black poison reach out toward me. And I learn two things: One, Ash's curse? It never leaves the primary host behind. The larger part of the spell always remains with him. In order to save Nera, I have to trick this smaller fragment into leaving her body entirely.

And two, I can read its feelings. The curse must have an imprint of how Morla felt when she cursed the fae king. Alone and angry.

The mirror isn't magical, so I can't hear its laments as the curse breaks it apart. My amulet shivering in my other hand sounds scared, but determined to keep me safe.

"*I'm not yours,*" I say in that strange language. My tongue feels heavy. "*But if you leave your current host behind, perhaps I can speak with you more. She can't do that.*"

I don't know how I do it, but as my whole body shakes, my skin lights up like a candle's flame. Flickering on and off in a rhythm that seems to put the slimy black monster in the mirror into a trance.

It blinks its red eyes as if confused. It doesn't like it, and I feel its displeasure.

"*If you come with me, you won't be alone anymore.*" I ignore Nera calling my name and the steps that rumble outside.

"Mia!"

I shift my eyes from the mirror to Nera as she flops onto the table. Her arms have shifted from white stone to beige skin. Her fingertips grow pinker.

"*Yes*!" it hisses, and chaos erupts around me.

At first, the shadows push out in an explosion of poison that's only visible to me, shattering the reflection as the curse escapes containment and moves in a cyclone toward me.

I stumble back to the chair behind me, and my world tips on its axis as black swirls of magic crawl over my glowing skin, burning me. Before they can go back to Nera, I lift my amulet to catch them.

Please, hold it, I ask the beating stone in my hand, and it vibrates in my grasp as it begins to suck in the blackness of the curse.

Nera groans, and Ash is almost here. His magic is warm and pushes against the darkness that's extended from the broken mirror.

Every inch of my skin that thing touches burns like acid. I think I hear myself scream, but it might be Nera as she quivers and collapses on the ground. Her skin is no longer stone.

The darkness holds on to my amulet and clings to my skin.

Someone calls my name. Ash bursts into the room, his face contorting in horror. The magic around us keeps him back.

My amulet keeps absorbing the curse until I hear the stone crack.

A screech pierces the dining room, and this time, even Ash hears it. He pales and pushes against the dark shield of pressure with his own magic. I can't get distracted by him, instead I let another wave of my anger feed my power. My body glows brighter.

I *will* do this.

The shadows sneak out of my pin, but instead of letting them return to Nera, I slam my hand over the amulet and grab the slimy mist with my heated fingers. Another screech pierces the room. The voice of the curse dims. It feels pleased. My fingers and hands turn black.

"No!" Ash screams, slamming his whole body against the shield of dark mist.

"*Stay*," I command the curse, and to my shock, it stops trying to escape my broken amulet. The rush of adrenaline fizzles off, and my legs shake as the shadows retreat.

The room spins above me. It feels like I'm falling off a precipice and unable to reach the ground.

Warm arms catch me by my waist and pull me against a hard mass that smells of pine. The pain holding my limbs hostage doesn't ease, even as my heartbeat slows. My vision narrows to nothingness.

"Mia, love, what did you do to yourself?"

CHAPTER 33

I fade in and out of consciousness for hours—maybe even days? Time doesn't seem to matter. In my dreams, feathers rain from the sky, turning into a beast equal parts beauty and horror. It looks like the shadows of the curse, and when I welcome it with open arms, it spares a life.

Molten heat runs through my body, and distantly I hear Ash's voice. "She's burning up. Do something."

It takes a while to understand the patterns of my strange dreams enough to know when a day begins and when it ends. Pain seeps inward from my skin all the way to my bones. But I'm never alone. Nera speaks to me—about me—somewhere in the distance, asking someone questions.

Naheli visits me in my dreams too. There she speaks with a voice that sounds an awful lot like my mother's. Though perhaps that's a part of my delusions, since I can't quite remember the sound of her voice.

"That was reckless, even for you, Miale."

Miale? I haven't heard my full name in an eternity. It sounds like coming home. I must be going mad—I guess that aspect of myself isn't new.

"Am I dead?" I ask.

"No, but you trapped the curse in your body." Naheli doesn't sound amused, and she moves like mist in the darkness.

"Am I going to die?"

"Not today." I can't see her anymore. "Darkness now lives within you. Don't let it take over."

I open my eyes, and it takes a while for my vision to adjust to the new light and surroundings. I'm not in the house in the forest, but lying in a familiar bed with a tree above. I feel terrible. Weak and aching all over. The scent of healing magic lingers around me, notes of menthol and something sterile that pushes away the earthy tones of Ash's scent.

I hate it.

"You're awake," Finley says from the foot of the bed. We're alone, and judging by the orange light of the sunset seeping past the window, it's late. "How are you feeling?"

"Like the Wild Hunt ran me over," I groan, and press my fingers to my eyes, willing my vision to stop spinning. It's then I notice my skin feels odd, coarse, like charcoal. Pulling my hand away, I gasp as I take in my new black fingertips. The color fades into the tan shade of my skin around my wrist. It almost looks like I was burned to a crisp, except I don't feel that kind of pain.

"Does it hurt?" Finley's brows furrow in the middle as he takes a seat beside me, handing me a glass of water that tastes of wild berries and herbs. "We've been trying to figure out what happened and how the curse will affect you. So far, no human has reacted to it this way."

"H-how is it affecting me?" I smack my tongue to the roof of my mouth to figure out why my water tastes different.

"Only time will tell how it'll show itself."

"I didn't expect it to rebound to me," I admit, feeling too tired to even muster embarrassment. "Is Nera doing well?"

"She is better than well. In fact, she's perfect. You saved her." Finley takes the glass from my hand, fills it again, and presses it back, as if he can read how thirsty I am. However, this time I hesitate, eyeing the glass with suspicion before glancing up at him.

"I added a few drops of night brew to your water to help you rest tonight. It seems you slumber a bit uneasy. All lunargyres do as the blood moon grows closer."

Horror washes over me as I settle back on the bed. My limbs feel numb as I stare at a point on the wall. Questions swirl in my mind, and I no longer feel as sluggish as before. "How long have I been sleeping?"

"Four days," he says. "You don't have to worry about turning. The blood moon isn't for nearly two months. . ."

I bring the glass to my lips, taking a small sip and trying to ignore the burning in my eyes. At least Nera is alright. Better than that, according to Finley. "Where are they?"

"Ash is walking the perimeter alongside Naheli. Nera stayed here with you until I sent her back to her room to rest. There's no need for all of us to be here. Besides, she's extra loud, and I can't hear myself think, let alone help *you*."

"Naheli told me I'm not dying." I hide my blackened hand under the sheets and meet his gaze.

"She spoke with you?" He lifts a brow. "I guess I shouldn't be surprised anymore. What else did she say?"

"That I shouldn't let it take me over, and I don't want to, but honestly I don't feel any different . . ." Other than pain everywhere.

Worry still marks Finley's features, even as he tries to smile.

Steps from outside call our attention, and Ash comes through the open door a few seconds later, followed closely by a giant spirit made of stars and night, shaped like a wolf.

His hair is standing up in waves of disarray, like he's run his fingers through it multiple times. "You're awake." He pauses in the doorframe, staying perfectly still as if moving might make me crumble. There are dark circles under his eyes, and I wonder if he's rested at all since we returned home from our travels.

Butterflies flutter in my stomach, and everything but him falls away as he crosses the distance between us with long steps. I scoot my body to the edge of the mattress, and as soon as I swing my legs over to meet him, he's by my side, picking me up before I can stand and pulling me against him where his lips crash into mine.

A soft noise leaves me, and I wrap my arms around his neck, enjoying the way our lips explore each other. I hadn't realized how much I thought I was going to fail, and that perhaps I would never get to kiss him again.

Distantly, my mind registers steps fading away as Finley leaves the room, allowing us some privacy.

"What were you thinking?" Ash whispers against my lips. "What happened in there, Mia?"

There is so much to tell, so I start at the beginning, when I saw the shadow around Nera's body in Eponde. Then I tell him about the night we escaped Hedrum, when his curse leaped at me.

Ash only lets go once he seems sure I won't drop to the ground. Then he pulls away from me and studies my face. "I didn't think about the reflection in the window . . ."

"I didn't mention it because I thought it might be a dark creature, like you said when I went to Eponde. But it attacked me, and my instinct was to ask my amulet to suck the creature in."

"Is that why your amulet stopped working?"

I nod. "When I saw Nera, how she looked when she arrived, I had to do something."

"I thought I was going to lose you." His eyes grow wide, and he gently caresses the side of my face. “No human or hybrid that’s seen my reflection has survived the curse for long.”

I swallow, feeling a prick of worry in the back of my mind. Shifting my gaze to Naheli, I find her lying by the foot of the bed. She barely glances up at me when she feels my attention and huffs before closing her eyes and going back to sleep. So helpful.

“I’m not sorry for trying to save Nera, but I am sorry I didn’t tell you my plan. And that I hid the mirror from you. I thought you wouldn’t let me do it if I told you my intentions.”

“I was so enraged about what Marlena did, I almost burned my manor to the ground. Then I promised the stars that if you came back to me, I wouldn’t go back to Hedrum and show her what it means to stare at my reflection.”

A chill breaks over my body at the menace in his voice, and distantly, I make a mental note to not involve anyone else in my schemes. Ash reaches for my black hand, lifting it before pressing a gentle kiss to my knuckles.

“Mia, why do you think your life is worth less than those around you?”

“I don’t believe that,” I say, pulling my hand away from his just enough to clear my thoughts. “It wasn’t about believing Nera’s life is more important than mine, but that I knew how to help her, and that if I waited, it could cost her everything.”

“And what if the curse killed you? Would that have been alright because Nera survived?” He presses on. “This seems like something you do often. Didn’t you go to that scientist building—or whatever you call it—to save your sister, even though it meant risking your life? Did you ever consider that you’re important? That those who love you want you to *live*?”

I open my mouth to tell him that, if the tables were turned, Irene would have done the same, but close it as doubt creeps in. Would she?

“Nera tried to stop me. She didn’t want me to get hurt.” It’s hard to breathe around the pain that settles in my heart. "Irene didn't. She never asked me to stop, even though you were clearly dangerous."

Was I so lonely in Penumbra that risking my life for her approval was worth it? I blink at the prickling in my eyes, and I can't speak—not for a while.

I'd foolishly gone to the scientist quarters to make sure she wasn't hurt, but I was manipulated into doing what Skylar wanted. And now that I know hybrids exist and stole the grimoires, I can't help but wonder if Irene is a strix—like our father.

I don't regret trying to prevent my sister from being eaten by a beast, even if she wouldn't do the same for me. Nor do I regret saving Nera. But the haunted expression on Ash's face makes me want to be better. I should be careful about my self-sacrificing ways, because while trying to help others might feel right in the moment, it may also hurt those I love.

"It's easy to see why you don't know your worth when your family treats you like you're disposable." Ash struggles to hide the anger flaring in his eyes. He steps closer, eating up the distance that separates us. "But you aren't in Penumbra anymore, Monster. You're here, and you matter to me."

Tears spring to my eyes, and before I can get a word out, he's kissing me again. He cradles the back of my head like I'm something fragile. And right now, that's exactly what I need.

He keeps me close as his soft lips glide over mine in a dance that makes my toes curl. When we part for air, my mind is swirling with emotions I'm too scared to voice, even to myself.

"I haven't been entirely truthful with you," he whispers, and his expression tightens with something akin to nerves. "The night we met, when you met my gaze, I took a part of your soul—"

"I know . . ."

"The thing is, when I stared into your eyes, you took a part of mine too."

"Of your soul?" My heart fumbles as I search his face for a sign that this might be a joke and I'm falling for it. "I-I don't understand?"

"When fae meet their mate, there's a sensation as the bond sets in. It's hard for us to find each other, especially in a world where so many of us are spread apart. It's even rarer to find one in a human or a hybrid."

My blood rushes to my face, and I can barely hear him with the loud thumping of my heart.

"When I broke through the veil, I was drawn to you even before you attacked me on that rooftop. I talked myself out of it, because I wanted nothing to do with Penumbra or a human. I told myself it wasn't the right time to find you." He takes a shaky breath and lowers his eyes to the ground.

I hold myself rigid, waiting for him to finish speaking as I remember how my world shifted when I saw him for the first time. Did I feel the pull too? My stomach hollows, and I take a step back, trying to sort out my feelings as they rage through me.

My ears buzz. "Does this mean I'm your mate?"

Like Nera with the king of the seelie? Something so alien to me, I can't even begin to understand what it means. This isn't something we're taught in human cities, where we're told the fae are gone.

"No—yes?" Ash clears his throat but visibly stops himself from reaching for me when I flinch back at his words.

"Yes or no?" I don't mean to sound snippy, but I don't know what's happening other than that I'm getting more exhausted by the minute. Probably because of Finley's inopportunely timed night brew.

Naheli huffs as she gets up, casting a shadow over us. She tilts her head at us with a judgy expression before she poofs out of the room. I would've laughed if my mood wasn't so fragile.

"Our bond doesn't match the typical mate-bond." His brows scrunch. It looks like he's trying to find the right words. "That's why I didn't tell you before. Usually mates have a connection from infancy. Dreams, visions of one another. Sometimes they share a birthmark. When we met, you stripped a piece of me like I did you, as if you were also hunting me. Like you were part of the Wild Hunt and could trade a part of your soul for mine. It's what happened when I met Naheli."

My mind whirls, and as I take another step back, my calves hit the edge of the bed. Suddenly, the gown I'm wearing feels too tight. I can barely breathe. I *was* hunting him; I had to stop him to save Penumbra. Had I taken a part of him without knowing, like I did the curse?

My heart feels like it's shrinking, and a wave of sadness floods me. "So we aren't mates?" I hate that my voice comes out so pathetic. It shouldn't matter. Before this talk, I didn't even know that was a possibility, but for the briefest of moments, I thought perhaps we shared a sacred bond.

"Mia, even if you weren't my mate, you would be the most precious person to me." Ash's scent wraps around me like a cocoon. "When I'm not with you, I'm trying to get back here, to your side. You have stolen my every thought, my every breath. From the moment you took a part of my soul, and every day after, I've been defenseless against you. You've stolen my heart, and I don't want it back."

My lips tremble. A path of fire burns through my veins, and I press a hand to my mouth to trap a small cry that escapes at his words. Ash wraps his arms around my waist and pulls me to him, horror painted across his features.

It makes sense that even something as straightforward as being mated would be confusing in our case. Our relationship has never fit into a neat box. We hated each other but became reluctant allies, and then more. Now, I feel cared for, loved, for the first time in a long time.

It all makes sense now. The secret conversations Ash and Nera had that I caught pieces of. The attraction I couldn't escape even when I hated him. Even when I thought I shouldn't.

"Please tell me those are happy tears?" Ash searches my face, looking as confused as I felt a few minutes ago.

I nod, laughing, and dry my face with my forearm. "Is our connection why Naheli came to me from the beginning? Why she acts differently with me than with everyone else and even brought me your special book of prophecies?"

Ash's lips tilt into a smile. "That conniving spirit is always up to something. I may have written about you stealing a piece of my soul in those pages and was overwhelmed that you might have read it."

I should be mad he didn't tell me before, but I can't be. Not when our relationship began how it did. I understand why Ash kept me at a distance. Me, a hybrid who coincidentally studied his stolen books.

And I guess me almost dying was a trigger for him. I cup his cheek in my hand, loving the rough texture of the shadow of his beard, and lift to my tiptoes to press a kiss to his lips. I won't say I love him tonight. That little secret isn't one I can part with yet.

It feels too soon. I've lost myself so completely in his world I never want to go back to what it was before.

A yawn tears past my lips, and my limbs feel heavy as I drag my feet back toward the bed. "I need to lie down again—Finley gave me a potion."

One moment I'm shuffling back, and the next I'm in Ash's arms as he carries me the rest of the way. My body sinks into the cloudlike feather top, and he lies by my side, resting his upper back against the headboard.

"It's close to twilight," he says, his eyes also hooded, and I shift closer, draping my arm over him and snuggling into his chest.

Someone would have to fight me to remove me from here, even if Ash is hardly the most comfortable pillow. My eyes slowly drift shut, and I'm off to a dreamless night.

"Thank you for saving Nera."

CHAPTER 34

In my dreams, the curse laments. Its shadows grip me tight, and the ache in my chest festers. It doesn't let go.

A loud moan pierces the early-morning quiet, pulling me from the depths of sleep with a jolt. Sitting up in bed, I breathe through the heavy nausea coursing through my body, focusing on the light spilling through the gauzy curtains. Even the sunlight does little to bring back the warmth that mournful cry leeched away.

There's a crease in the sheets where Ash lay the night before, and golden droplets glimmer on the pillowcase. Why are there golden drops on the sheets?

I rush out of bed and struggle to find my balance on wobbly legs.

Through the window, I see Naheli sitting in the courtyard with her head tilted to the sky, howling nonstop. Even the lunargyres who aren't statues stand around her, like the sound has paralyzed them as well.

Ignoring the protest of my sore limbs, I quickly make my way out of Ash's chambers. My feet pound through the halls and down the wide steps. I've been in this place long enough to know where to go.

It takes longer than it should to notice the roses changing appearance. Ever since I accidentally touched them, they've been red. But now they're all withering away, their petals scattered across the steps. Like a river of blood.

Holding onto the wall for balance, I run down to the second floor, following Naheli's call.

I stop when I hear Finley down the hallway. "You can't possibly think it's a good idea to go on your own. It'll be better if I come with you."

I was on my way to the courtyard, but instead I follow Finley's voice to the main floor and a part of the castle I've never been

The far wall is all windows, giving the space the appearance of a solarium. One that's the size of an entire building.

Outside, nature overtakes the east garden. White bodies made of stone line the place. Not statues, but lunargyres, frozen in time, the weather chipping away at them while they forever slumber in their magical prisons. Life blooms from grayish stems of trees and bushes. Early spring creeps in, taking away some of the bite of our mild winter. My lungs burn as I try to catch my breath, and I move into a room covered from floor to ceiling in weapons.

Swords are arranged neatly on the walls, their mounts made of fine wood and carefully fashioned to cradle each weapon. Some blades curve, others are straight and narrow. Some glow with the magical markings of spells etched into their sides. Others are affixed to bone handles. And they all hang one above another, going up until I can't distinguish their shapes anymore.

Ash secures a belt around his waist and reaches for a couple of daggers arranged on the small table by his side. I stumble into the light, and before I can take another step, Ash crosses the room with the aid of his wings, and grasps me by my elbow.

He wears all-black leather armor, and the small feathers that come up his neck blend seamlessly with his coat. But it's not his strange outfit that stands out the most, but the golden tears streaming down his face, like the day we met.

"Are you leaving?" I blink, and the face of the curse flashes under my eyelids. Hovering underneath my skin, pulled like a magnet to Ash's much larger fragment of it.

He places a hand gently on my waist. "You should be resting."

"Naheli's howling woke me up." I frown. Why didn't he answer my question? "Is there something wrong?"

As if summoned, Naheli's moans travel the long halls to echo through the room, raising the hairs on the back of my skull. I reach for Ash's face and trace my thumb over his cheek, but the line of tears doesn't smear. It flows undeterred by my touch.

He covers my hand with his own, and when he touches his skin, the liquid gold clings to his fingers. "Every time a scientist in Penumbra takes a lunargyre, I cry their blood. It's a burden only I can bear." He takes a ragged breath and returns to securing the second dagger to his belt.

"What's happening?"

"Nera is gone." Finley's voice wavers. He isn't meeting my gaze, but he sets his shoulders like he's readying himself for a fight. "We've looked everywhere, but since Ash is crying blood, he's going out to the forest to make sure she's alright."

A stone sinks in my gut and I reach for the weaponry table, leaning against it as the ground moves underneath me. "You suspect the scientists took her?"

Ash's brows furrow as he holds me by my elbows, steadying me. "It's unlikely they'll be this close to Aphelion so far from the blood moon. Are you feeling well, Monster?"

I nod, not wanting him to worry about me when something might be happening to Nera. "Why did she leave the castle?"

"She sleepwalks when she has dreams of her soulmate,"

Finley says, his nose wrinkling. "It's been five years since Nera had an episode, so we weren't prepared."

I think back to what Ash told me the night before, about the things fated mates share. Dreams, visions. "Why did she stop having them?"

"We don't know," Ash says as he finishes strapping on a shoulder guard. "I suspect it had to do with her shifting to stone, that it disrupted their bond." His jaw ticks. "You look very pale."

Who cares?

Nera is missing. She walked into a forest full of raging beasts, and scientists are hunting the fae again . . . "So what happens if they actually took her? Are you bringing Naheli?"

Surely, he isn't thinking about going alone. I know he's powerful, he almost took out the whole scientist quarters on his own, but if they're coming all the way here, I bet they have something up their sleeves.

"No. Naheli has to stay in the castle to maintain the wards against—" The words die in his mouth, and his frustration is clear in his expression.

"Morla?"

He nods. "Just in case she gets any new ideas." Ash's eyes look past me, over my head to where Finley stands. "And Finley needs to stay to make sure your condition remains stable."

My cheeks warm, and I hear Finley groaning behind me. I can't blame him. Why would he want to stay behind to babysit me, and the consequences of my own actions, when his friends' lives are in danger?

I reach for Ash's arm and squeeze tightly. "I doubt Finley can do much for me, unless he's come up with the cure for the curse and hasn't told you anything about it?"

"Exactly," Finley says. "If this wasn't something to worry about, you wouldn't have sent Naheli to warn everyone who still has consciousness and bring them inside the wards. You think something's wrong and are marching to your own death. Willingly." I hear something metallic crashing against the table, and Finley's face has gone completely red with fury . . . and something else I can't place. "You've given up."

I whirl toward Ash and try to see if what Finley says it's true. What I find is a broken monarch who's determined to not let any more of his people die.

Why would someone who's given up fight an entire group of hybrids and try to destroy their death machine? Why take the grimoires from the Hedrum house and alert everyone he was there? Why protect the castle from a scorned friend who cursed him?

Ash slams his hand on the table, and every blade shakes. Some even tumble to the ground. "I have told you many times I haven't given up. While you may have lost your faith in your king, I happen to still have mine."

"Then I beg you, take the spirit with you." I could be imagining things, but I swear I see a flash of guilt in Finley's eyes. "Mia and I will be fine. I doubt Morla will come for us."

"And leave Mia unprotected when she just absorbed Nera's curse?"

"Don't leave Naheli here because of me." As if on cue, a wave of nausea rolls through me. I press my hand over my mouth, breathing in and out in long draws, hoping to stave it off for just a few more minutes. Ash reaches for my hand, and I hope he can't feel how cold and clammy it is.

Naheli's howls come again, a sound pained and haunted.

Ash doesn't look away from me as he says, "I need to go alone because even though the hybrids from Penumbra rarely come to Aphelion, they may be here now. Nera is powerful, but after she shares a connection with Sylas, she's in a trancelike state for a few hours, which makes her easy prey."

Finley reaches for a blade on the back wall. "I'm coming, with a tracking charm. I'll follow right behind you on horseback. If you're right, and Nera is safe, I'll return as soon as I see you're on your way back."

I meet Ash's gaze with a plea in my own. "Let him. Please. You never know what kind of weapon they may have."

"Like a hybrid who wields fae magic she doesn't understand?" he says. "I think there is only one of you, Monster."

Monster. When he began calling me that, he said it with such disdain . . . Now, the way his voice shifts with a touch of adoration makes my stomach flutter.

"They have guns," I say.

"Alright, Finley. You may use your tracking charm and follow behind, but I won't wait for you." Ash presses a kiss to my forehead and remains by my side for a long time, longer than normal. I glance over his shoulder and watch as Finley leaves the room to get ready to accompany him.

"Do you remember what we thought about the grimoires and my suspicions?"

I nod, and he pulls back but hovers a breath away from my skin, leaning just a little over my cheek. "No one can know that having the grimoires helps them control an ancient spirit tied to a soul weaver, not even Finley. A spirit like Naheli can cause destruction in the hands of the wrong person."

Ash hasn't told anyone about why he truly thinks the hybrids are stealing the books. Not even his friend.

"I should come with you . . ."

"You know you can't, not like this."

"Well . . . if trouble were to arise, how would I come to help you?"

He hesitates, his jaw working. "Would it make a difference if I asked you not to?"

"No."

He sighs, but a shadow of a smile appears on his lips. "If I don't return, Naheli can bring you to me. She can't go into Penumbra, for the reason I stated before, which means you shouldn't come unless you're sure I'm gone and you aren't cursed anymore."

"I'm not waiting until you're dead, and if you're afraid that'll be the case, then maybe don't go?"

As soon as the words leave my lips, I know they're the wrong ones. Of course he has to go. Anger and fear blend in a horrible cocktail of emotions that worsen my nausea. I open my mouth to tell him . . . something, but he's already pulling away from my weak grip.

He pauses right under the archway that leads to the massive solarium and turns to look into my eyes. "Stay out of trouble, Monster. I'll see you at nightfall."

Ice travels through my veins. His expression says so much more than words ever could. He knows something I don't, and it's clear in his eyes. I hear his voice in my mind like I'm listening to a conversation through a wall. *Don't trust anyone but Naheli.*

It's then that I notice three things.

One, Naheli has stopped howling.

Two, that felt a lot like a goodbye.

Three, even though he wasn't sure the night before, he just spoke inside my thoughts. A magical connection.

Ash is my *mate.*

CHAPTER 35

THEY DON'T RETURN AT NIGHTFALL.

The first night, I hardly sleep at all, just wait for them to come back. Naheli remains by my side on the balcony as the storm rolls in. I nearly catch my death that night and wake up to the icy drizzle that's starting to feel like spring. The wolf naps a lot more than normal, and there's something odd to her energy I can't place, as if it's being disturbed. She comes and goes from the bedroom as I regain fragments of my strength.

On the second day, I go to the training room and resume practicing magic. It's too difficult to stay in Ash's bedroom when everything smells like him, and it's a reminder he hasn't returned home. I know myself well enough to understand I'm one bad thought away from making a terrible decision and breaking my promise to him.

On the third day, I know in my gut that something has gone terribly wrong.

I focus on the emptiness around me as I try to find Naheli in the darkness of the training room. We've been here all morning as I practice spells I might need later today, when I go after Ash and into the forest. My steps echo as I ease my way deeper into the shadows. I've been here so many times, I know the nooks and crannies from memory. I keep my eyes open even though it makes little difference, since I can't see what's in front of me, unless I use magic.

During the last couple of days, I've overcome my habit of relying on my broken amulet and instead trust in myself. The darkness in my fingers has extended past my wrist, and it's halfway up my arm by now. It gets worse when I use excessive amounts of energy, even if I remain in control.

I study my surroundings, and I'm thankful whatever made me ill the day Ash left is fading away.

I take another couple of steps, running through my mental catalog of forbidden spells. Most of them are useless to me right now. Because even though in theory I know what they do, I'm never going to use a spell I can't control again. Only spells I've studied enough to truly understand. And it's not really the time to practice new spells.

So instead I focus on the same old enchantments I've been honing with Ash over the last few weeks. The revealing spell is bright as it travels through the room, lighting every nook and cranny where the wolf may be hiding. But I can't find her anywhere. She isn't here.

"Naheli, did you leave?" I ask the nothingness.

As panic rushes through my veins, I feel the shadow of the curse stir, liking my displeasure. Something nags at the back of my mind, the same feeling I haven't been able to shake. I can't stay here any longer. It doesn't matter what I promised Ash.

I secure two daggers in the weapons belt I've been carrying since they left. Being alone in the castle, surrounded by cursed beings, meant I had to be alert and prepared.

A crash echoes from the tall ceilings, the distinct sound of metal warping. My heart hammers in my chest as I run to the nearest window, pushing it open as the humid air hits my face. Fog hugs the castle grounds so thick it's hard to see much of what's happening out there. The metal spikes of the gate twist at strange angles, and beyond that, Finley's wagon lies on its side.

My fingers twitch, and I'm running before I can think straight. They're here! And if they weren't hurt before, they might be now. Why didn't the gate open? Did it have something to do with Naheli disappearing out of nowhere?

I rush down the twisting steps of the tower to the main floor. Air burns in my lungs as I run out the door and into the gray day outside. My skin shimmers, and I don't know what to feel. Hope, excitement—worry?

Keeping my eyes on the moving shapes of bald lunargyres that stalk this place, I cut through the courtyard. So far, in the last couple of days, they've seemed unbothered by me, even when I got a little too close for comfort.

I cross the first, and its eyes narrow in my direction, but it doesn't open its mouth at me. I don't hear their thoughts or feelings like I do with some magical artifacts, not like what Nera described.

Sweat trails down my neck, rolling between my breasts and soaking my dress. I use the momentum of my swinging arms to propel myself forward.

Out here, the musk of roses grows thick, even though I'm running away from where they're most concentrated in the castle. When I get to the gate, I see no one. One wagon wheel continuously spins. The other three look broken from where I stand.

I grip the bars, standing on my tiptoes to get a better look at what's happening.

"Ash?" My voice catches in my throat, and tears spring to my eyes. "Are you there?"

Never have I felt such frustration at staying behind. After what I did with Nera, I was trying to be sensible and not put myself, and everyone else, in danger. I couldn't go with him days ago, I was too ill. But what if . . . I could have made a difference?

"Ash?" I call again.

A horse whinnies in response from where it remains pinned under the weight of the carriage. The other is already running down the road, so far away it's all but a shadow. I look around for a way out. My attempts at opening the gate are futile. It won't budge no matter how I pull and push. The iron doesn't react to my fire spell, and I can't pick the lock with my blades.

I could climb, but that is unlikely to go well. This gate isn't Penumbra's library sturdy shelfs. I look at the bars with apprehension. They twist where the carriage hit them.

It'll be a tight squeeze. I shed my coat, my weapons belt, and my dress, until I'm left only with my cotton slip and my undergarments.

As I push through the bars, I find a barrier holds me back. A shield that's too similar to the veil. My breath fogs in front of my face as I press my body against the thin membrane, and the morning dew clinging to it seeps over my skin like a kiss of ice.

I close my eyes and feel for the makings of this ward. It whispers to remain inside. It sounds a lot like Ash, and it makes me more determined. Pressing my hand to it, I unravel it, like cutting through strands of twine, until the shield has broken away enough to let me through.

No one is in the carriage, though I find traces of blood in the driver's seat and in the back where a large imprint marks the place a body lay over a handful of empty sacks. I help the horse next, lifting the weight of it with trembling arms and a push of the same wind spell that saved my life so many months ago.

The darkness in my arm grows an inch, and I swallow, going back for my cloak so I can hide the traces of the curse taking over my body.

I find four fresh sets of tracks by the edge of the forest, trailing along beside the castle walls. One set of smaller feet, likely Nera's, and three larger ones. I frown as I lean down to study them. I have no clue how to make sense of where they're headed, nor have I ever hunted for anything in my life. But what I lack in skills, I make up for with determination.

If the wards didn't allow Ash in, for whatever reason, I can undo a section of it and grant them entrance. He can lecture me about leaving after they're inside.

I hear voices in the distance as I approach, keeping myself carefully hidden by the darkening skies of early afternoon and our misty surroundings. Finley is the first one I see, specifically his coat and the gentle slope of his wide shoulders. I rush forward, and adrenaline makes my senses sharp with every little twig that snaps under their feet or mine.

My heart leaps to my throat as I draw closer and don't find Ash's wings. Nor Nera's slim body. And the voices are less familiar.

I pause, shifting behind a tree trunk as a crawling sensation runs down my back. Staying in the shadows, I move in, getting closer and closer.

"You almost killed us running that carriage against the gate," a man wearing brown trousers and a white shirt sneers, brushing a hand over his bald head.

I press my body against a tree, attempting to calm my loud breathing as I try to understand everything unfolding in front of me.

"It usually opens for me," Finley says, and his expression is strained as they continue walking the perimeter. "You weren't supposed to come here. The castle won't let you in, I told Skylar as much."

Finley's working with the scientists? I peek out from behind the tree and my heart tears. Had he betrayed us all along? Or was he taken hostage in the forest?

"It will let us in, eventually. The broken king has little time left." A second man laughs, and the sound brings ice to my veins. "We want the gold, and if you want your niece to keep her manor —and you, your freedom—then you will get us inside."

So, that's why we ended up in the strixes' house that night in Hedrum. It's likely why Ash's and Nera's glamours had disappeared. It wasn't a coincidence. Nothing ever is. I grab at my throat and remember drinking the night brew he gave me, and how ill I've been for days.

"I've paid my share for that freedom." Finley's jaw tenses, and I see licks of green magic hover around his fingers. "Nera was off-limits. I only gave her Mia's necklace for you all to locate the castle. Nothing more."

"The bargain wasn't for the princess's life, it was for your niece's," Bald Head says before spitting to the side.

"I have to admit, I was surprised she wasn't a beast anymore . . ."

My blood freezes as I listen to a voice I know well. I shift in my spot, trying to keep my feet light as I peer around the other side of the tree trunk. I'd recognize Irene anywhere. Even deep in a fae forest, hidden under the layers of a thick cloak.

CHAPTER 36

"Your sister broke Nera's curse," Finley says.

I hide again as pain weighs down my heart.

I'm close to the castle. I could run back to Naheli, wherever she is. I could try to get the conscious lunargyres somewhere safe before they get inside. My skin glows as I lose control of my emotions.

"Where is she? Where is Mia?" The clicking of a gun being loaded echoes in the forest silence, and even the creepy crawlies seem to wait with bated breath.

The scent of magic wafts around as Finley's aura comes through to protect him from the threat of gunpowder and lead.

"She's alive. I kept the promise I made when we met in Hedrum. You weren't supposed to come here and shouldn't have hidden in my wagon. There's a spirit in there that will tear you all apart."

Except I don't know if Naheli is even here. Perhaps Ash is too injured, and so she can't remain in this realm.

I may faint.

"If you think for a second I wouldn't come here for her, you're delusional." Irene's voice is bitter and calculating. I almost leave my hiding spot to stop this madness. "She better be alive, Finley. I don't care what blood contract you signed with Skylar, I'll end you."

"Irene . . ." another voice cautions, one I don't recognize.

I glance at the shadows, and everything around me deepens. When I came out here, I never expected to find *this*. I was prepared for something horrible, an injured Ash, but not this . . . betrayal.

"I won't calm down. A beast took her almost a month and a half ago. She better be unharmed and—"

"I didn't think the curse could be broken," Finley interrupts her with a tone torn by shame. "But she did it. There's no need to go through with this. If she's able to break the curse, there won't be any more lunargyres coming into Penumbra. Be sensible."

"We don't care about the curse," the man who spoke before says, disbelief tainting his words. I feel this third person is a strix. Here to murder fae and nothing else. "This has nothing to do with the beasts. The curse is just a way for all of us to see what the fae really are. We won't let them take over the world again, take humans to be their servants, or push the hybrids out of society. Hunt us down like dogs. We're done with them, and the king of the unseelie is just a message for the rest of them."

I watch as Irene's eyes widen just a fraction, but to an untrained eye, she keeps her expression mostly neutral. She knows about the hybrids, about this war between them. Yet, she never told me.

The bald-headed man laughs, showing teeth stained with tobacco. "And the king thought we would let the princess go. Someone once told me the fae were cunning. What a bunch of bullcrap."

Finley takes a step back, shapes of bright green magic swirling around him. I don't know how effective a protective spell from a skilled sorcerer is against a bullet. I shouldn't care . . . But my stomach sinks at the thought of him getting hurt. I can't let them kill him.

"Why did Mia stay here if she is well, Finley? Do you have her locked in the dungeons?" Irene's voice shakes with anger.

Like she cares. I hold a scoff behind tight lips.

Finley doesn't answer.

Irene cocks her pistol. "If I have to ask again, you will have a bullet in your leg. And if you don't answer after that, Rick will put one in every other limb. You won't be able to walk or ride back to your precious niece, and the beasts will have a feast in a couple of days."

I don't even recognize my sister. She was so sweet when we were young.

It seems likely now, I'll have to fight them. What are my odds against three people with guns? I have little control over my magic, and every time I use it, the curse takes more of me. And I can't trust Finley to help, not when we're in this mess because of him.

I don't know what feels worse, that Irene was a strix all along or that Finley, someone who I grew to care about as a friend, betrayed everyone. I take a deep breath and know that, no matter what, I won't put my morals in question again.

I reach for my blade's pommel, tightening my grip on it as I allow a dose of power to trickle past the binds that keep it locked in place. The curse stirs, and I feel a trace of pain reach through my body as I release my magic. Enough so the curse feeds from it, but I have some left to use. There's a good side to this parasitic curse in me. It dulls my power, preventing me from exploding. The bad side is that my arm is all charred skin.

"I'm done with this fool," the strix says, and everything slows as he pulls the gun from his holster and shoots Finley. My entire being narrows to the brass bullet as it cuts through his body and lodges in the tree behind, sending blood, pulp, and bark flying everywhere.

A spell blasts out of Finley's hand as he falls to the ground, but it narrowly misses the bastard who shot him. Magical green flames catch on a large specimen of cedar, consuming it quickly and sending black smoke into the treetops.

Finley screams, holding his stomach. Abandoning my hiding place, I raise my hand toward the man and cast the revealing spell, trying to blind them all and buy myself time to reach Finley. My curse, who feasts on my emotions, eats the light of my power before it comes out.

Sweat pours down my forehead, and I close my eyes and feel for traces of the slimy texture of the curse. If I can unravel spells, this is no different, even if it's scary and painful. I pull at its threads, making it uncomfortable.

When I finally get the revealing spell to leave my hands, it has the desired effect. All the scientists shield their eyes from the brightness that blankets the forest. My heart drums in my ears, but my little win over the curse is short-lived. It doesn't take long for the shadow monster to push back, trying to take control of my magic again.

Its voice is deep and high at the same time as it whispers in the same odd language I heard before. *You're angry*, it coos inside my head. *Make them stone.*

Darkness bursts out of my fingers in waves, and I have no control of how my spell's intentions shift. My vision turns white. Distantly, I hear muffled screeching. Then a loud thump shakes the ground.

I stumble back as my eyes find the man who shot Finley, who is now on the ground, unmoving, and made of pale marble. A statue, like the curse wanted. The bark of a tree digs into the palm of my hand as I barely catch myself before falling to the ground.

Irene shouts, and the second man trains his pistol on me. A

flash of panic rushes through my veins, but I'm too exhausted to do much. This may be how I die, and I keep my eyes on him as he cocks his head.

"Who's this bitch?" His eyes narrow before my sister brings the butt of her pistol down on his head with all her strength, and he collapses, blood trailing from his temple.

"Y-you're here . . ." Irene stares at me with wide eyes as the dust settles around us, and only we remain standing.

My stomach churns at the sight.

The corner of her lips lower into a grimace as she studies her teammates, now mostly dead on the ground. "I thought this would be different, and I didn't expect you to be . . . free."

She takes a step forward and I take one back. My eyes train on the brass gun she still holds in her gloved hand. I wonder how many lunargyres like myself she's shot down. Will she use it on me once she learns I'm not on her side? Once she learns what I've become?

"What you did just now—no one has to know. I'll tell Skylar I found you chained in the castle, and that Finley killed Rick and Alan. We can go back to living normal lives," she says with a wild expression.

Funny how she only mentions what *I* did, not the fact that she cracked her colleague's skull with her gun. But I keep those thoughts to myself.

Instead, I repeat the words she used the night I met Ash. "Tell me, Irene, did the princess, Nerala, look like the beast that killed Father? Or is that just something you tell yourself to justify the horrors you commit so you can sleep at night?" I narrow my eyes at her as I remember how she played on my grief so I'd use my magic.

I can deal with Finley's betrayal, but Irene's . . . I don't think I can ever forgive her for this.

As she looks at me, her eyes widen, and she realizes I'm not supporting her in this. The power that's always present under my skin strains inside me, and the curse seems to have taken a step back.

"But . . . they're *monsters*." Irene holsters her weapon, lets her arms hang to her sides, and takes another step closer to me. "I understand you're upset with me. I should've told you what we were doing, but Father thought it was better to keep you away. He wanted to shelter you from everything. It was a way to keep you happy, because he knew you felt too deeply."

She glances back to the scientists sprawled out on the dirt and leaves, and her brows furrow. She sighs deeply. "I told him it was better to tell you about the machine and the fae and how much we needed to keep our city safe from them. And when the monster took you, I—"

"He isn't the monster, Irene. You and all those bastards in that scientist building are. Every time you hunt a cursed beast to feed the machine, you murder an innocent fae."

"Us?" Her voice pitches high. "Have you forgotten all the people they've killed?"

"Oh, I haven't forgotten. At first, I was trying to get back to you so I could help you with that, and then I realized the truth. It's hardly their fault when they are cursed to be mindless." I pull the sleeves of my cloak down, hoping to hide the corrupted flesh of my arm. "Did Father tell you about the hybrids?"

"The what—?" She looks confused. "Alan just mentioned hybrids, too, but I don't understand it."

"Hybrids are part fae and part human, and they're the ones running Penumbra under the guise of protecting our people." I wish I wasn't so skeptical of everything she said or did. "Can you do magic, with or without an amulet? Was that also a lie?"

"You know well I can't," she snarls.

"Mia," Finley groans from the ground.

I rear my head back as Ash's words come through my mind. *Don't trust anyone but Naheli.*

Did he know something was wrong with Finley? Perhaps his insistence on coming along alerted Ash of something. Perhaps he was wary of how ill I was after drinking that potion. Though, admittedly, I was ill before that too.

Naheli's growls slip through the air, and I can feel her presence all around me, as if she is the forest itself. My hair lifts with the static of her power.

Irene pales and moves away. "What was that?"

"That's the spirit that protects the castle," I say. "She will kill you. It's better if you go now."

"What about you? Won't you come with me?"

"Back to Penumbra?"

"Yes, of course. You always loved the library."

I remain silent for a few moments before I speak. "I'm going to Penumbra tonight. But not with you."

Hurt and understanding flash across her face. "You're going to save him, aren't you?"

I say nothing, but feeling Naheli behind me after thinking she was gone has pushed some of the hurt away. I take a step in the wolf's direction, facing my sister in case she decides she'd rather have me dead than helping the fae.

"Why?" she asks.

"Because . . ." My feelings for him are not something I want to speak out here in this bloodbath with people who betrayed me. "They deserve to live."

"Do you love him?" Her voice is all but a whisper, yet those words pull at something in my heart. I shouldn't have stayed. I should have gone with them, even in sickness.

"You lost your right to know who I love the moment you manipulated me."

"They'll kill you if they catch you."

"I know." I'm that fool who runs into impossible situations when those I love are in danger. But this time I have more information. I also have more power and a bigger task. But mostly, I'm not alone.

"At least take these," Irene says and digs her hand into her cloak pocket. I jump back and cover my chest with my arms, expecting another weapon that she'd use on me.

She presses her lips into a fine line and pulls out a ring with dozens of skeleton keys that shimmer as they catch the dim rays of the sunset spilling through the canopy. "You thought I was going to hurt you?" There's shame in those dark eyes.

"Can you blame me?" My voice trembles, and I glow like a flame. But this time, I'm not afraid. I feel powerful, even in my heartbreak.

"For what it's worth, Mia, I'm sorry this happened. I never thought Skylar would make a deal with the sorcerer. Or that you would grow attached to the beast." She extends the ring of keys toward me, and they jingle as she shakes them in the air. "These will let you in the building without triggering the alarms. You'll have to go down to the basement. We keep them in cages that cancel out their magic until . . ." Her voice trails off, and I think I see traces of horror in her face.

As if talking about it with me is making her realize how truly despicable they are.

I watch as she swallows deeply. But I don't approach her. I don't want to be anywhere near her, just in case she has something up her sleeves that might make it impossible for me to go.

"She isn't a beast," I say.

"Who?"

"Nera, who you took to kill in that machine our father helped build."

Naheli's growl is so deep, Irene falls to her knees, pleading to the darkness. I don't need to turn around to see the horror behind me, for I've seen how the ancient spirits look when they run wild. My sister always thought the lunargyres were the monsters, but the true nightmare is standing right behind me.

And she is furious.

"I'm so sorry, Mia. I didn't know the fae could form such connections with humans. I would've— The king, he bargained for the princess's release. We were supposed to let her go, but Skylar didn't." Tears spring to Irene's eyes as she tosses the keys with enough strength they land by my feet. "I was so shocked he'd been tracking Mother's pendant, I didn't know what to do."

She swipes her face and sniffles. "I saw Finley turn back and suspected he was coming this way, so I told Rick and Alan there would be treasures here and convinced them to come with me. I had to come save you. I thought he had you in the dungeons or something, and it was my only chance to find this castle before the beasts took over."

I don't take my eyes off her as I crouch to pick the keychain out of a pile of rotten leaves. She can cry. She can say the perfect thing that once would've made me bend backward to make her happy again, and I still wouldn't trust her. "And Skylar let you come to save me?"

"No. He was so preoccupied with the king, he didn't notice we left. I swear it." Irene shakes her head. She looks so much like her younger self, before whatever corrupted her made her who she is now.

"I never thought there would come a day where I wouldn't want to see you again." I hate how my voice breaks, that my heart crumples when my sister sobs at my words.

And for a second, I feel like I've taken it too far. But then, the moment is gone and I turn around, ignoring the burning sensation in my eyes, and walk into the shadows where Naheli awaits me. I hear my name and pause.

When my eyes fall on Finley, my heart bleeds again. He presses a hand to his wound and gasps in pain.

In the house in the Crossroads, I could see the imprint of Ash's magic in the wards in the bedroom—but not Finley's, even though Ash said he frequented the place. I should have said something then . . . but I never suspected this.

"Mia, please . . ." Finley's sorrowful eyes land on me as he tries, but fails, to sit.

I hesitate, wanting to leave.

Something breaks inside me. I grip the keys in my hand, shove them into the pocket of my cloak, and make my way to him. I pause a few steps away, glancing down at the bed of leaves around him, and the blood soaking into his olive-green clothes.

My blood curdles. "What do you want?"

"To say I'm sorry." Blood stains the inside of his lips.

"Save it for Ash when he returns." The fae are wicked, but somehow I doubt Ash would truly hurt this man, even after his betrayal.

"I thought this was the only way I could save Marlena. I thought Ash had given up and there was no way to break the curse—"

"But you knew it could be done. You saw what I did with Nera and still fed me the night brew and didn't warn him when you left."

Except somehow, Ash seemed to know.

Finley's arms shake as he pushes himself up, holding my gaze. "I told him what I did right before we got to Nera. He put me to sleep, and when I woke, I was hidden away and they had already trapped him."

"He's in there because of you." My voice shakes with fury and I turn to Irene. "And you. Be glad that I'm not as horrible as either of you, or you'd already be stone, just like him." I point at the scientist that remains paralyzed, his body now made of smooth marble.

Naheli's lying on the ground and tilts her head to greet me. Her expression says nothing, but I can see the edges of her body are slightly fuzzy and fading away. Which has to mean Ash is hurting badly.

She tilts her head to me and growls loud enough I hear Irene's shaky breath in the background. Unlike my sister, I can read the spirit's emotions.

I climb onto her back using her folded leg, and hold on to the fur on her shoulders. It doesn't take long for the mist to turn into a saddle right under me.

The cool mist that makes my wolf friend wraps through my fingers like ropes.

I turn to Irene before leaving, knowing well I may not see her again. "If for once you want to do something for me, then you have to help him."

I pointed at Finley, hoping she understood he mattered, even in his betrayal.

When my sister nods Naheli runs. The trees part to move out of our way. We jump off boulders and large hills, and we ride through the night under the stars.

At twilight, I don't slumber like most beasts, and I have no one here to ask what that means.

CHAPTER 37

THE GLOW OF THE VEIL IS BLINDING AS WE BREAK OUT OF THE THICKNESS of the canopy and into a clearing outside Penumbra. The gas lanterns twinkle in the distance, bathing the streets of the city beyond in light.

The wind howls in my ears as the wolf moves faster, and I tighten my hands on the cool mist of my saddle's horn.

"Naheli, Ash doesn't want you to step inside Penumbra," I begin as the shield's milky-white membrane, separating us from the citizens inside, grows near.

I never thought I would ride through the forest on an ancient spirit, but then again, things have drastically changed. Naheli doesn't slow, and I prepare myself for impact as she leaps into the veil with a howl.

For a time, we are suspended in a heavy substance that burns all over. We're pushed and pulled in multiple directions, and the scent— It claws at me. The curse rejoices at the surrounding death, and that horrible feeling brings tears to my eyes. I glance down at my hand, and even though most of my arm remains hidden under my cloak, I feel the dryness of my skin going all the way up to my shoulder.

Mist bursts from Naheli, sending stars out to form a shield around me. A web of small cracks opens the wall, like it did the night Ash broke through, leaving a hole just large enough for us to cross.

We land on a wet cobble road, and for the first time since we left Irene behind, I hear the ancient spirit panting. Even though there's a crack in the veil, no alarm rings to warn the city the shield is broken. At least when we cross through the streets, we find them desolate.

"Naheli, stop."

She doesn't.

The scientist quarters peeks out from behind the smaller homes at the edge of town. "If the guards see you running through the streets, they'll warn the city, and they might kill Ash before we make it to him. Let me off. Sink into the shadows or become something less . . . magnificent."

She slows down, turning her head to glare at me with her four amber eyes. I guess she doesn't like to be told what to do.

The city is dark, and most everyone has gone to sleep for the night, giving us the perfect cover. I point at a narrow alley to our left and Naheli rushes for it, stopping only after we've dived into the maze of passageways. There are a few flickering gas lanterns on the streets, but not enough to reveal us.

Naheli's misty body shrinks to the size of an actual wolf, and she loses two of her eyes. She'll look convincing to anyone who isn't looking too intently at the fact that small shimmering stars float around her. I don't have time to worry about what-ifs when Ash may be dying right now. The veil stretches up to the sky, undeterred by the fissure Naheli made.

Unlike the last time I came to the scientist quarters, we go through the back door, where there are fewer chances to run into someone. I fish Irene's keys from the depths of my pocket, and it takes me a couple of tries before I find the right one. The metal door leads us to a long hallway and narrow steps up to an unknown location. Irene told me to go to the basement, but how do I get there?

Judging by the area of the city we crossed through, we should be on the eastern side of the building.

I move to the stairs, but my eyes drop to Naheli when she whines. She tilts her head in another direction. Down into the depths of the corridor.

Footsteps creak on the floor above, their voices muffled, and I know this place is crawling with scientists who may or may not be strixes. Naheli's body shifts to mist, and she goes through a narrow door at the end of the hall.

I follow the wolf down stone steps that take us to underground tunnels. The cavernous ceilings haze with distance, and we follow the serpentine underpasses that lead us away from the main building. Moisture skims the rock walls, and my steps squelch with the mess of mud on the ground.

We're getting closer to Ash. I can feel it in the pit of my stomach. The farther into the ground we go, the angrier the wards and more aggressively the spells leech away every ounce of warmth remaining in my body.

They command silence.

They cause pain.

Wind hums through crevices in the heavy wooden doors that line the tunnels, and I glance at Naheli, who remains by my side. She's regained some of her height as she leads me with purpose.

Then her body flickers, like it did back in the castle. Right before she disappeared.

"Are you going to leave?" I breathe out.

She tilts her head, and her four amber eyes pin me down. Her muzzle wrinkles as she peels her lips away from her long canines.

It would be scary, except I hear a hissing sound that forms the essence of words. It leaves her mouth like an icy caress.

"Save him."

And she disappears into thin air, right in front of my eyes. Her magic leaves this place, and I feel it's directly tied to whatever's happening to Ash.

I don't allow myself to descend into a whirl of panic. Instead, I let those words guide me as I repeat them, again and again.

Save him.

Empty cages are spread around a wide, circular chamber with low ceilings.

A familiar voice drifts from an open door at the far end of the room. Skylar's tone has taken on a taunting drawl, but I can't understand what he's saying from this distance.

I unsheathe one of my daggers and keep a mental handle on the power I repress. Using too much would expedite the curse taking my body, but I can't think of how else I'll be able to get Ash out of here. I cross the empty space, passing iron bars and runes carved into the walls.

Through the door, the stench is suffocating. Magic blending with sweat, blood, and something rotten that lingers in the air. The room is dimly lit, which works in my favor as I rush behind tall wooden crates, peering into the crowd that gathers around him.

My heart plummets when I see Ash's black wings folded at strange angles inside a cage that's too small for a man of his size. Golden blood and tears stain his face, dripping down into the darkness of his feathered neck. His hands aren't talons like when he took me during the last blood moon. Instead, they remain their regular shape, except for the black fingernails that mirror the appearance of my hand.

He leans against the back wall, resting both arms on his bent knees, taking deep breaths, and ignoring the group's taunts.

"Did we capture the right beast?" a scientist asks, dragging the barrel of his gun over the bars. I watch as Ash winces at the noise, and I remember how sensitive he was to my screams the night we met. "Why isn't he more . . . beastly?"

"Who cares," Skylar drawls as if bored, leaning against the rock wall with one leg crossed over the other. "He's the same beast. Once we harness his energy, the veil will have power for a long time."

Anger boils inside me, and I glance over my shoulder to make sure no one's sneaking close. I try to form a plan to get him out. No one has noticed me yet, but there are too many of them for me to take care of on my own. I'm decent with weapons, but my magic without an amulet is too unruly to rely on. Back in the forest, I blacked out and turned a man to stone.

I can see at least four scientists wearing their regular outfits, holding guns in their hands.

Perhaps I can hide here and wait for them to leave? I search around, trying to find Nera in a nearby cell—or cage. But she isn't anywhere. Worry pricks in the back of my mind. Is she already in the machine? Power vibrates under my skin, and my fingertips grow warm as I lose control. The curse takes another inch of me, and the skin of my chest turns dry and taut.

I close my eyes to settle my breathing, and I see it, that angry demonic face inside me. Waiting for me to use a spell, so it can take more.

"Honestly, he doesn't look feral to me. I hardly think he's a danger to us." A female voice breaks through the chatter of males, and I open my eyes wide and peer around the corner to find Harper sitting behind a bulky table.

She blends with the shadows, and all noise fades away when she stands on shaky legs, looking as unsure as she did the night I saw her last in the library. "I don't think this is right . . ."

A knot lodges in my throat as I remember how Harper questioned the scientists that night, and how mad it made me. She called their attempts weak. I couldn't agree more, even as I worry about her being here. Why is Harper in this cave prison? Did she know about this all along?

"At least the hybrid is smart . . ." Ash says. He looks and sounds tired. Iron shackles wrap around his bloodied wrists, and his clothes are torn in many places. Roses grow from the corner of the room behind Harper's desk, and their blooms are all black. At some point, Ash regained enough energy to call the roses, which could be the reason Naheli came back.

The hybrid. Singular. Could it mean the scientists around us have no magic, just guns?

"I should've expected the librarian's stomach to be too weak for her to do what's needed for the greater good." Skylar's lips peel back as he throws a glare at Harper, whose eyes round with fear. "Do I have to remind you how important it is to protect our city from *him*, after he almost destroyed the veil last time?"

Harper shakes her head, sucking her lips between her teeth. "No, I understand."

"It's why you're here, isn't it? To be punished for allowing Irene's sister out of the library during the last blood moon, which got her killed?"

Whatever color remained in Harper's face drains away. She clears her throat and speaks after the snorts of multiple men die off. "Yes, I know why I was called here."

"Good," Skylar says. "Now that it's settled, keep the ward around the cage up. When it failed last time, he killed two people."

I hear Ash's bitter laughter drift through the air, and silence follows for a while before Skylar's voice breaks through again. "Am I funny to you, beast?"

"Funny? No." Ash leans over his knees, his golden gaze fixed on the scientist with a lazy, unafraid look. "Predictably dull? Yes."

The hollowness in his tone pulls at something within me. I creep forward in the darkness, while letting out a fragment of my power. There are five scientists and one librarian in the room. I doubt Harper will truly hurt me, and if I'm able to wield fire, I might scare them enough to run.

"Do we even need him alive?" a scientist in the back says as he rolls his sleeves up over tawny arms. His knuckles are stained with golden fae blood.

I take one step out of my hiding spot, flames licking my fingers, and a hand covers my lips.

A needle sinks into my neck.

A man hauls me up against his body, and I scream and fight him with everything I have.

But just as I reach for a new spell, I meet a wall. Something that completely blocks me from accessing my magic.

"What do we have here?" Skylar's steps echo off the low ceilings. His nostrils flare while he studies me.

I gulp for air, and my limbs grow so heavy I slump into the body that holds me.

"I found this shadow hiding behind the crates," the man behind me says, and his sour breath stinks of ale. His arms tighten around my torso, squeezing so tight I can feel every inch of his rounded stomach press into my back. "She had a weird light coming out of her fingers, so I sedated her."

I glance over Skylar's shoulder, and Ash's face grows slack when our eyes meet.

Skylar grips my chin roughly and twists my face to meet his eyes. His expression is severe as he takes in my dirty, sweaty face, partially covered by waves of my hair as they stick to my cheeks. Then slowly, his brows round up as he puts together who I am.

"I never expected to see you again, darling. I guess I was wrong about the beast killing you." He studies me with renewed interest and a dash of annoyance.

Harper's red cloak comes into the edges of my blurred vision as she calls my name. "Release her at once," she says, reaching toward me with extended arms.

The brute behind me grunts and takes a step away from her and closer to Skylar.

"How are you here?" the latter asks, ignoring Harper and fixing his gaze on me.

"She escaped a week ago," Ash says, waving his hand like I'm the worst pest he's ever had to deal with, but the words don't match the panic in his eyes. It reminds me of what he did back in Hedrum. "I thought the forest would take care of her. I guess I was wrong."

He shakes his head almost imperceptibly. Everyone studies my reaction, like they're about to cast a judgment that could cost me my life.

I understand. Ash wants them to believe there isn't a connection between us. That I was his prisoner all along. I hate that he has to protect me when I came here to save him. My disappointment with myself at this failure sinks deep into my soul.

"I-I came here to see my sister." My voice slurs, and tears prick my eyes as I look around at the expressions of the men behind Skylar, all in varying states of horror and hope as they take me in. The sedative they injected me with sinks deeper into my very being. "Please . . . I've been away from home for too long."

Except Irene isn't here to save me. I left her back in the forest, near the castle.

"I can take her to Irene. She is probably in her room," a man says from the back, stepping forward to reveal a head of red curls and a pale face covered in light freckles. I fight to remain awake as my vision blurs. The strange sedative doesn't quite knock me out, just makes my limbs so heavy I can't move.

Skylar lifts a hand and his eyes tell me he isn't buying our act. "And you just came into the building? How?"

"The same way I did last time," I lie.

"And somehow you found the tunnels underground?"

I sob, letting my frustrations out through the tears rolling down my face. "My spell didn't work on the front door like it did last time, so I came through the back and got lost. I've been walking for days, fighting beasts in the forest . . ."

Almost everyone's faces shift with compassion, and I know I've won most of them despite my poor performance. Perhaps if they took me to Irene's room, I could wait until the sedative wears off and I'm able to walk again.

Skylar's eyes move slowly down my neck and pause on my chest. But there is no lewd intent in that horrible, distant gaze, just triumph. He grabs my blackened hand and lifts it so everyone can see.

Gasps resound around me as torchlight drags over the dry patches of my dead skin.

"It seems some of the dark magic the fae uses is running through her as well. Mia is likely turning into a rabid monster herself, and since we don't know how it'll affect a human, she can't be left out to attack us."

Even Harper takes a step back, like being near me would allow the curse to spread to her, like a disease.

The corner of Skylar's lip ticks. Somehow he knows we're lying. I don't know why he cares this much. Last time he saw me, I was ready to hurt Ash for him.

"Take her out to one of the back cells. No one upstairs can know she's alive—especially Irene. Once we deal with the king and the princess, we can figure out how to cure her."

Skylar looks at me with a knowing smile. The bastard thinks he's won, and I'm not so sure I know how to get out of this mess.

Naheli? I beg inside my head as I'm dragged back toward the circular room I came from. But the spirit doesn't reappear.

"Is she going to be alright?" Harper asks.

“Of course. We’re not the monsters here.” Skylar pulls his gun out of his holster, holding it down casually as his brown gaze travels from Ash to me. “Now, librarian, make sure the beast can’t open the cage again.”

It was a threat, even if it wasn’t worded that way. Harper pales and moves toward Ash with long steps. She mutters something under her breath to him, but his face is fixed on me. The spell Harper uses is not one I’ve ever heard of, however it slides across the room and tells me its meaning.

Bind. Repress. Silence.

It’s the same magic I felt when I first arrived, and blue swirls move across the cage and around Ash like a cocoon of silky strands.

“Wait,” I beg Harper, or anyone who will listen. I gather all my energy as I surge forward, escaping from the cage-like arms keeping me trapped.

The movement catches the man behind me by surprise, and I collapse to my knees on the hard floor. “Please, he isn’t a monster,” I say, ignoring the pain flaring from the point of impact as I talk to the scientists, Harper, and Skylar.

They look at me with everything from pity to fear—to hatred. My eyes meet Ash’s, and he implores me to remain quiet.

“No,” Ash whispers, frozen in place.

Harper continues chanting, undeterred by my words.

“Please, you can’t kill all the fae. This is wrong . . .”

But Harper doesn’t stop, and the spell thickens around him. Subduing him further.

“Please, Harper, I love him.”

I clamp my lips shut, even as the words ring true. *I love him.* The fae king who drives me mad, and makes me smile at the same time. Who challenges me, and teaches me about my power, about life. He took me from Penumbra and showed me the truth.

Ash reels back, and his eyes widen.

Everyone falls still as magic churns from me to him. Threads of red that wrap around his body and pour from his open mouth when he calls my name. Light bursts from his eyes and fingers, heating the cave to sweltering.

My ears drum as I crawl forward, taking the chance in the chaos to get closer to him as his body transforms until it's made entirely of gold. The smell of magic mixed with roses drives away the previous stench in the room, and every feather covering his face and neck retreats.

When the light fades away, all that's left behind is his true self. A beautiful fae king hunching inside his cage.

Admitting my love for him broke the enchantment.

His curse is gone.

CHAPTER 38

Ash shrinks a couple of inches, and when the light dims, he's back to his fae form, breathing heavily and holding his body with shaking arms. He stares at me with something so pure and wonderful my heart skips a beat. Then his expression turns to devastation.

Because, in breaking his curse, I outed myself and my alliance with the fae. Losing any of the support I previously had. Loving him—admitting it out loud—could mean my death.

Chatter explodes around us as the scientists behind Skylar talk. Someone shouts, "Fae whore," but I can't tell who said it.

The same red-haired man steps forward, crossing his arms as he glares at the others. "This is Irene's sister and Killian's daughter. These are people we have been working with for years. Let's not act like she's a villain because she fell for a fae. She's not the first human to do so, and she won't be the last."

"Plus, she's clearly cursed. What if the beast has her under a spell?" another one says. "Let's take her to Irene, and I bet she will keep her safe until this whole thing blows over."

Another person agrees, and the environment shifts.

"Or perhaps we shouldn't be using the king in the machine at all," says another louder voice. This man is older, with a salt-and-pepper mustache and a balding head. "This feels wrong."

A shot is fired, leaving my ears ringing. The man who spoke last falls to his knees. He presses his hands over his heart, and dark blood spills between his fingers before he collapses. Dead.

Skylar trains his gun on the redhead, his expression severe. "This isn't up for discussion. We are part of the guards of Penumbra, and we *will* defend it. If anyone else is ready to die for the fae, speak now—or walk yourself into a cell and save me the trouble."

The man who injected me with the sedative picks me up from the ground. My head sags, and all I'm able to do is stare at the dead man on the floor. His blue eyes gaze at nothingness as his blood halos around him.

"Gale and Heath, take the body to the mortuary. I'll run the report," Skylar says.

The toxin doesn't take away my conscious state, just my ability to move my arms and legs. Is this what they use on the fae before putting them in the machine? Horror sinks its claws into me as a group drags the body away.

How many scientists have been killed for speaking against what goes on here?

A dull prick of my power pokes from under my skin, but it's so muffled I can't seem to grip at the threads to wield it. The darkness covering my arm remains, and the slimy shadow inside me stirs, still palpable if I probe hard enough.

Ash is free of his curse, but I'm not.

Harper watches stiffly as they drag me back into a dark cell in the circular room, but she does nothing to stop them. I can't blame her after what happened.

"My father helped build that machine, and Irene works with you all. This is how you treat their family?" I scream to anyone who would hear me.

"You're tainting their name," Skylar sneers. "Siding with the fae over your own people. Wheel the king into the machine room."

I'm left speechless as the scientists pour out, dragging Ash's cage on a dolly. Harper remains behind, not meeting my gaze.

"I'm sorry Mia, I just—" She hesitates, following the shapes moving down the long tunnel with her eyes. "I don't want to die. Skylar will kill me, like he did Kyle. I hope you'll forgive me."

And then she turns to leave me alone in the darkness of this cave.

"Wait, Harper," I say, attempting to crawl over the wet rock, over the filth I'd rather not know the source of. She pauses, not lingering too close as Skylar awaits nearby, his gun still in his gloved hand. I lower my voice so he can't hear me. "Where is Nera, the princess? Where are you keeping her?"

Harper hesitates, but then her eyes shift to where the rest of the group is headed. "The fae siblings are always together."

Skylar lets out an exasperated breath and steps in. "Enough chatter. Go on, librarian, I'm running out of patience with you."

Harper shakes visibly and leaves without looking back.

He steps closer to my cell, and I try to lift my body so I don't look like a trembling child while he stares down at me from above.

"You thought yourself so smart," he croons. A cruel smile graces his features. I once thought him handsome, but truly, he is the most horrid being I've ever seen. "So you freed him from his curse, and you thought people would change? You see, Mia, when fear is present, it drives most of our decisions. Whether they fear a beast or a gun, it makes no difference."

There's a blur that could have been a figment of my poisoned mind, but when Skylar smiles, he's no longer the man I know—but a woman with golden hair and familiar features. I've seen her before. Where?

A shape-shifter? *No*, a glamour. Cold grips my chest as I stare at him with a wide mouth.

He loads his pistol slowly, making sure I see every brass bullet. "We laced these with iron and salt. A perfect combination to kill fae and hybrids. Except I can't kill Ash. I've tried so many times. The night he took you, I had no reservations. But tonight will be different, and I'll be free at last."

"*Morla Skye*," I say.

His gaze flashes to me, and his smile is knowing and wicked. "In the flesh. How did you learn about me? Ash wasn't allowed to speak my name."

The contents of my stomach curdle as Morla's glamour falls back, revealing her fully to me for just a moment. She thinks I'm going to die here.

"Why curse all the fae if you only hate him?"

"Hate is such an ugly word, and I didn't hate him for such a long time. Quite the opposite, darling. But if he refuses to be mine, then he will be no one's." Skylar's eyes turn manic, the glamour keeping her looking like him shifts, and for another moment her beautiful face is revealed to me again.

I reel back. "You're crazy."

"He makes me so," she growls, and takes a deep breath to calm herself. "You know what happens to those of us bonded to the fae?" She doesn't wait for my response. "We can't ever move on, we're always tethered to them. They, however, couldn't care less if we—their tributes—are killed. If we never return home."

Something tells me Morla has a hard time controlling her temper, much like earlier when she shot Kyle. So I remain silent. Perhaps she won't kill me, and waiting for her to leave is my best option.

"Was he able to tell you about the curse?"

"No."

She laughs, like my ignorance about it is music to her ears.

"Even if he could, he doesn't know all the details. You see, the curse is simple. After what I did to him, and what the hybrids did to his kingdom, I was sure he would grow to loathe our kind. So I added that only a hybrid could break it. Of course, it was unlikely he would allow one so close to him again."

"Is that why you wove your roses into the curse? So they'll send you a signal when a hybrid is nearby?"

Morgana came to me not long after I touched the roses for the first time. She sent me to die out in the halls that night.

"Yes." Morla's cocky expression falters before she schools her features. "I've been dying to know more about you, Mia. When you broke into this building during the last blood moon, you had your amulet like any sorcerer does. I didn't expect you to be a hybrid or I wouldn't have had you help us."

Skylar had been curious about my necklace the night we met. My father told me to never take it off, to let no one see it. Perhaps being protective about it allowed me to sell the lie better.

"Why hide behind your glamour and your gunpowder? Why did you even need my help if you're this powerful hybrid?" As soon as I speak, I regret my choice of words. Goading her is the wrong move.

Her lips peel back, and she snarls as she levels her pistol on me. She fires, and my ears ring with the loudness of it all. I jump back. My heart collides with my chest, but there's no pain. No bullet.

"Pity." She ticks her tongue, looking at her pistol with a frown. "I guess I truly can't kill you. It must be because your soul is connected to Ash, as mine is."

So that's why she tried to use me that night to harm him so her people could plug him into their machine. I wonder if she tried when she came to my chambers in the castle as Morgana.

"It doesn't matter. You don't matter," she says, more to herself than me. "It'll all be over by the end of the night."

My head throbs as I work to put everything together with my sluggish mind. "So you broke the man you supposedly loved. Congratulations. That makes you the worst person in the world."

"He played me like a fool and made me believe there was a future where I could be more than a so-called friend of the unseelie prince. But he made sure I understood how I, the hybrid, wasn't good enough for him. I was shoved aside, unable to form connections with anyone. Our kind, the hybrids, hated me, even after I cursed him. To them, I will always be the fae king's whore."

So she hid under Skylar's glamour.

"Ash has nothing against hybrids," I say. "That's not why he didn't think you were good enough for him. If you ever loved him, please stop this. You don't have to hurt him, Morla."

"You *would* think that, wouldn't you? He chose *you*." She spits as she speaks, and her saliva spills like poison down her chin.

And to think I felt jealous of this woman when I learned about who she was back at the Crossroads. I thought she was powerful, and I wasn't.

But I am good enough, even when I struggle to handle my magic. Not only for him, but for Irene and my father. I never needed to prove myself, and Ash showed me that.

"You probably think you won, but you didn't, darling. You see, I also wove a caveat into my curse. If Ash falls for the hybrid who loves him, then she'll die." Morla is looking at me with such triumph it makes me sick to my stomach. "That blackness consuming your skin is his love, killing you."

"No." I hug my arm to my chest. My mind is quick—but my movements are slow. "That happened when I removed Nera's curse, not because of you."

I wasn't about to tell this woman I absorbed the curse and every time I close my eyes I see its black face. Morla doesn't need any more fuel for her madness.

"Do you think that's how the curse works?" She laughs prettily, loads one more bullet and spins the barrel of her gun. "I crafted the spell myself, and if a human or hybrid is affected by it, they turn into monsters and die within hours. But your curse is different from the rest, isn't it? It's likely that when you saved Nera, it made Ash admit his feelings for you."

Ash and Finley told me they'd never seen anyone reacting to it this way before.

Something dark lurks in her eyes, and when she lifts her head, the glamour falls back into place. Morla is back to being Skylar. "Time to go. I have a very important guest to attend to."

I glare at his back as he strolls into the depths of the tunnels. When I can barely distinguish his body from the shadows, he pauses.

"Did you know Ash's father used to starve the hybrid rebels down in the dungeons? No one came around to feed them—except for me. I hope for your sake your curse takes you quickly. I hate the idea of starving. Don't you?"

CHAPTER 39

My concentration is the only thing stopping me from fading away. The sedative is strong, and time is blurry.

I blink my heavy lids and think of Morla's words. Could it be true? Is Ash's love actually killing me?

A dry laugh escapes my lips, because I know the answer to that question. My black hand, and how far the curse has advanced in the last day, show me I have little time left to help Ash and Nera. Which means I need to get out of here.

I grip one of my shackles and try to make my other hand as small as possible as I attempt to pull it off. The iron scrapes my skin, and the spell that clings to the rough texture of it zaps me.

But I don't stop, even as I feel my energy—whatever little remains of it—dwindle further. These chains were poison to Ash. That has to be the reason he appeared so ill, and why Naheli was flickering even as she led me here.

To a normal hybrid like me, it stings, but it's not life-threatening. What really hurts me is the spell woven into the metal. That the magic smells like Harper. Scared and unsure.

The sedative and the curse together quickly consume every

ounce of energy I have left. I can't free myself this way. And if I fall asleep, who's to say if I'd ever wake up? The curse has extended up my neck, and I feel it creeping to my chin.

Dread sinks in, and I know I have to unlock my father's spell in order to access my full power. It's the only way I can get out of here in time.

I follow Ash's teachings. My magic feels familiar and warm, in contrast to the curse's dark and slimy texture. I push the darkness aside and chase the threads of what belongs to me, locked away by my father years ago. This time, it doesn't take me long to find the blocking spell woven tightly over the center of my being.

Familiar but foreign.

I close my eyes and imagine what it would look like if I could see it, and I reach beneath the enchantment's layers. My repressed memories seep through as soon as I tear through the membrane. They flood my mind, and his words flow as I unbind myself from him.

"This is for your own good," my father said. "They don't know who you are and it must remain that way."

I can't remember how I answered him. I pull another thread of his spell, and more of my magic streams through me. The curse gloats, consuming everything it can get its hands on, but I don't let it distract me from my task.

"We didn't want to do this, Mia. We wouldn't have come here had we known the prophecy existed. You won't remember it . . ."

They wouldn't have come to Penumbra, a city full of hybrids and stolen grimoires.

". . . it will keep you safe."

I pull away a few more strands of his spell, and a sob escapes me. I won't ever feel my father's warmth again. He's been a part of me even after he was killed. The pressure in my stomach increases along with the heavy throbbing inside my head. The spell snaps, unleashing the rest of my memories of that afternoon with the force of a dam bursting open.

"I won't remember what?" I challenged my father, barely speaking past the knot in my throat. But somehow, I knew he was going to take this memory away. Just like he intended to take my magic. "All the librarians have little magic. We have this order to protect the—"

"That's a lie, Mia. Your peers can wield power without amulets, and certainly without grimoires sharing whatever little power they may have from the king," my father scoffed. "Your power isn't like theirs, and when they find out what you are, they will kill you."

"Who will kill me?" I hated how afraid I sounded. My father's words sank deeper, and I looked at him, shocked and uncertain. "What am I?"

"You're the one who will destroy the curse keeping the fae away from this place." He swallowed deeply. His magic tightened around me, and my power dulled. Everything in my body, except for my head, was paralyzed on this chair. He continued, "And the strixes will kill you. They've infiltrated the librarians, and the scientist quarters. It's dangerous for you to be so close to them. We didn't know you'd be drafted into this role or we would've left."

I sobbed loudly, hoping Irene would come in and stop him from doing this to me. "If I'm unable to access my magic, I won't be able to do anything in the library, including defend myself."

"You'll have your mother's amulet. It'll allow you to access your power to protect yourself in an emergency, but more importantly, it'll make them believe you're a sorcerer, not a hybrid."

"How do you know what they'll do to me?"

"Because I'm a member of the strix, and if you weren't my daughter, I would be forced to kill you."

My eyes widened as I stared at him, seeing him for the first time. Ice crawled over my skin, and my power dulled further. The man in front of me wasn't the warm and caring person I thought he was. Not even a scientist working to protect the people of Penumbra from the Hunt.

I didn't know what he meant by hybrid or strix, but I knew he was a man capable of murdering an innocent for some reason. And no matter what that reason was, it wasn't good enough for me.

I glared at him as he finished the spell, and his magic wrapped over my own, dulling it so much I could barely feel it. "I don't know what the strixes are, Papa, and I don't know of the supposed prophecy . . ."

He seems conflicted as a spell swirled around his hand. The wisps of white reached for my head. I pushed against the chair's backrest, and the legs scraped on the floor as I watched the approaching enchantment with horror.

Even with my power nearly gone, I could feel the spell's intent. It wanted me to forget this ever happened.

"You know what I'm doing, don't you? You understand what this spell is going to do?" His expression turned to one of regret. "This is why I must do this, pumpkin. You're a sunderer. Someone who possesses the gift of understanding and unraveling any spell. The prophecy speaks of a hybrid who can unmake the curse, and your mother and I believe that's you."

The spell wrapped around my head, and my thoughts blurred.

My father pulled a note from his trouser pocket and slammed it on the table in front of me. "Mia, you've unmade spells crafted by your mother in this house without knowing it. You speak of magical things like they have emotions. You are a sunderer of sorcery, and the strix will kill you first and ask questions later."

The green ink of my mother's sprawling calligraphy stood out against yellow parchment, and as I read on, something sank deep within me.

Black feathers will rain from the sky, leaving pools of poisoned ink over the land. From the darkness, a beast will appear, with sharp teeth and magic that brings death to us all.
The curse of mirrors will ravage the land for forty blood moons and at last,

A hybrid bound to the Fae King, will rise as fate demands.
Brought by destiny to break the chains that hold his realm in thrall,
The Sunderer shall bring death to those who caused his fall.
And death will be her constant friend, by shadowed hand and breath
As she walks beside him, through the dark, unyielding path.

I met my father's dark gaze, He turned away, grabbing the prophecy and tossing the parchment into the flames of the woodstove by our side.

My vision narrowed and nausea grew within me.

I remember waking in the middle of the night, calling for mother while those words spilled from my mouth.

"She always told me it was a dream," I said. Yet her face always turned ashen.

My father's spell blurred my thoughts a little more.

"Your mother risks facing the gods' ire if she doesn't record the prophecy. She's heard it from you time and time again and we can't simply ignore it anymore. She must leave soon, and take it to the ministers of sorcery. The house of strix will find out soon enough you exist, they have people everywhere."

"It was just a dream."

"No, Pumpkin. Your power is too unique to be a coincidence."

"I'm not a soothsayer."

I was angry . . . But I couldn't remember why.

My father looked at me as he sat and reached for his cup of coffee, giving me a trembling smile.

"

You're not, but he is."

Sad . . . Though I didn't understand why.

"Papa?" I blinked, turning around to take in the kitchen table. I was so cold, even though the warm summer air wrapped around me.

"Mia, are you paying attention, or are you daydreaming again?"

He frowned at me as I looked down at my cold breakfast and my half-empty cup of black coffee.

"Sorry—I'm here," I said, and I tried to ignore the headache. And the weird emptiness in my chest. "What were you saying?"

"Never look a fae in the eyes, Mia," my father whispered. "They'll see it as a challenge and will never let you go. It will mean your death."

I gasp for air. The muddy ground spins around me. My entire body shakes as I try to clean tears from my face.

My parents were always strixes. They feared for my life and hid me in plain sight. My mother disappeared right after. I wonder if they were intending to escape together at some point.

Did he know Ash would eventually come for me, because we were mates? I was always dreaming of his broken prophecies.

Magic flows through my body, warming my cold limbs, undeterred by the curse. Even the remnants of the sedative evaporates. White light flashes from my fingertips, and the lock of the shackles snaps off as I wield the unraveling spell so easily, it's like breathing.

I lift my hand toward the cell's door and wield another. So much power courses through me, the curse can't consume all of it. The darkness on my skin recedes—just a little—as the gate twists and opens with a squeak.

I walk out of my cell enveloped in a ball of light, with death—my curse and companion—trailing closely behind.

CHAPTER 40

Orange torchlights guide me as I follow the breeze to the end of the tunnel. I walk away from the lingering scent of stagnant water until I find drops of blood—*his* blood. Gold and freely flowing on the ground. I follow his tracks up the smooth, slippery steps.

This is familiar. I came down this stairway with Naheli. The tall steps make the ache in my body worse as I run up them, two at a time. My magic—and a healthy dose of adrenaline—aid my strength. I'm tired, but I will endure.

It takes me a while, but eventually I make it to the machine room, chaotic and buzzing with the clamor of scientists rushing about. Morla didn't leave anyone guarding the halls, likely not expecting trouble. Steam rises from the brass pyramid in the center, occluding most everything from me. Hiding behind the curtain of shadows provided by the hallway, I wait for the perfect moment to sneak in.

I spot two cages on the other side of the massive room, hastily pushed against the stone wall, with a group of men lingering nearby. One is Morla, under the guise of Skylar.

They speak loud enough I can hear them from where I stand. "After tonight, we'll be free," someone says.

Fool.

My stomach sours when I find Ash through the smoke. He's slumped over, holding onto the bars of his cage. I imagine he's whispering comforting things to Nera.

No one's looking my way. My breaths are shallow as I step over puddles that remind me of the first night I was here. Body pressed against the wall, I inch closer and closer.

I have no plan other than possibly using my revealing spell to blind them all. Then perhaps using fire to get Ash out of his cage. We can both figure out how to help Nera after that. Perhaps once he's free of the shackles, he'll regain enough strength for Naheli to return. It's not ideal for her to be here, but I need help. Especially since I don't know who's a hybrid hiding behind a human disguise.

I watch intently as Skylar rounds Ash's cage, his arms behind his back as he speaks to the group of men. Harper stands meekly to the side, her gaze averted to the ground in shame. She hates this . . . I'm sure of it. Perhaps if the scales tilt enough, she might help me? Even though she's in this mess because of me. My heart grows so heavy with guilt that I can hardly breathe.

But if I focus on the bad things, I risk being frozen by them. Instead, I think of Skylar and his lack of magic, other than the glamour that hides his true appearance. He seems to rely heavily on weapons.

Did crafting such a curse zap Morla's power completely?

"I said to weaken him further," Morla says with Skylar's voice to Harper, who visibly flinches at his command. "I don't want him talking or moving at all."

"And here I thought we were having fun." Ash's words drag through the noise.

I crouch down, hoping my squeaking soles won't call their

attention. Steam rises in the distance, and scientists shout as metal clanks and hinges hiss.

Harper shakes her head, and strands of her silver hair stick to her shiny skin. "I-I've already done all I can. The laws of librarians demand I don't hurt living things. I can keep him subdued so he won't hurt you all, but I won't injure him . . ."

Even though Harper growing a backbone would've normally made me happy, I fear for her safety. Morla is bloodthirsty, and has a gun strapped to her belt. Skylar looks around and surveys all of those that surround him, watching their every move.

Most of these people didn't watch Skylar kill Kyle down in the cave. Most probably think this is the way to protect Penumbra, but seeing the fae looking so unbeastly is making them question the whole thing. I watch as a few scientists shift closer to the cages, their faces set in hard expressions.

"Whatever." Skylar pulls a pair of fine leather gloves from his pocket. Slowly, he puts them on as he walks toward Ash. "Load the princess into the machine first. The king gets to watch until he repents for every life he took for granted." He points at Ash, who says nothing in return, though I see him stiffen. His head lifts, and he stares at Skylar like he's seeing him for the first time.

Did he figure out who's really behind this? Perhaps her glamour flickered, like it did down in the cave?

I step over hoses and wires. My eyes flit across the room, searching for something I can use as a distraction, and then Harper's gaze fixes on me.

Time seems to slow as I wait for her to turn to Skylar and tell him I escaped. Without a word, she tilts her head toward a sliver of space nestled between the wall and a rounded column shrouded in darkness. But I don't have time to move into the shelter of shadows because they're loading Nera's cage onto a dolly.

I grab a metal tube from a crate beside me and press my hand to the cool column, my cracked skin whitening over my knuckles. Their cruel laughter makes this all much worse . . .

My search for a distraction resumes until I find a brass box with square doors and a keyboard at the top. Liquid pumps through translucent tubes, feeding the main body of the pyramid.

It looks important . . . I should destroy it.

I creep closer, crouch nearby, and wait. The ticking gears bring an idea to the forefront of my mind. Steam hisses from the box and goes quiet in a one-minute cycle. Steady like a clock. If I time it right, I should be able to destroy whatever this is—I pat the box—without alerting anyone I'm here. If I stop the machine, it'll draw everyone's attention, and I can get Skylar away from Ash.

Sweat drips down my temple, and I tighten my hold around the tube. As I count down the minute until the machine makes noise again, enchantments I once studied flash in my mind.

. . . Twenty . . .

. . . Nineteen . . .

. . . Eighteen . . .

The veil's energy shoots up to the sky, illuminating everything around us.

Some of the scientists look downright ill as they try to maneuver Nera's cage over the mess of things scattered on the floor.

. . . Thirteen . . .

. . . Twelve . . .

. . . Eleven . . .

"We should get the princess out of the cage. There's no way we'll fit it through this narrow space . . ."

"Didn't you learn a thing from what happened in the forest?" Skylar says. "The moment she isn't surrounded by iron, she'll wake up and kill you like she did to Maurice and Lio."

That almost brings a smile to my face. Of course, Nera isn't defenseless, even stuck in a trancelike state. She's feisty and powerful.

. . . Five . . .

. . . Four . . .

I hold my breath and shove the tip of the tube into the seam of the elaborate panel, prying it open. Sparks fly, landing on my skin, but I ignore the burn as I push until metal screeches and I see the gears turning inside. I call for fire, and let it run wild in the chamber, melting the wire casings first before growing hot enough to melt the copper wires inside.

Flames burst from the hole, and black smoke billows out of the exhaust pipe jutting from the box. An alarm goes off somewhere, and I rush to the spot Harper showed me earlier. It's a tight fit, but I manage.

The machine sputters and then stalls.

I wipe at my forehead and watch as Skylar and a few of his men turn to the pyramid. The veil flickers off and on.

"What's happening?" Skylar screams and I hear the hurried steps of the few who are still following his orders, but more and more seem to back away, disappearing into the shadows themselves.

I press my body against the wall and hope the shadows hide me as someone runs by quite close. I have minutes before they realize someone tampered with it and it wasn't a random explosion.

Seeing my chance, I jump at the only opportunity I may have. I'm by Ash's side so fast, but he's already shifting toward the cage's door. He doesn't look surprised to see me—nor does he say a word.

The unraveling spell comes to my mind easily. Something I've used on dozens of occasions, but for the first time, it doesn't work.

I try again, and panic surges through me when nothing happens. Not a click.

I hear Skylar's clear voice in the distance before a shot rings out and something buzzes over us. I jump in place and then slam the tube I used before into the lock with all my strength. Which isn't much considering all the power I just used.

"I-I can't!" I slam it again.

"Mia, you've been escaping your room in the castle for weeks. You already know you can unravel spells. *Use your gift.*"

I lift my eyes and meet his golden ones, and the knot in my throat loosens, even as I reach for the door with shaking hands.

Another shot hisses by, and it lodges itself in the wall in front of me. Rock fragments rain down on us, but Ash's hand wraps around mine on one of the bars, and I don't look back.

"Focus, Mia," Ash urges. So tired. So weak. "You can do this."

I look at the lock and see the strands of Harper's old spell, thinly woven over the metal and into the keyhole. A great enchantment meant to deter even those who wield sorcery. But not me. I pull at it, hurrying it to let me in and ignoring the running steps behind.

I swing the door open and step in, over his golden blood dried on the floor. I reach for his manacles—

"Stop!" Skylar's deep voice falters into a more feminine sound. He grabs Harper by the throat, yanking her back to his body where he presses the barrel of his gun to her temple. She screams as the metal burns her skin.

Even Ash stills beside me.

The veil gurgles as it continues to fail.

"I'll kill the librarian unless you step out of the cage, Mia."

The blood drains from my face as Harper's expression turns into a silent plea. But even through the layers of her fear, I see the resignation in her slumping shoulders.

She knows I can't. If I do, they'll kill Ash—the man I love—and his sister. They'll kill *me*.

Skylar presses his nose to Harper's moonlight hair. "Are you going to choose the fae, the creatures who killed your father? You'll choose them over your friend, who may I add, is here because of *you*?"

"I'm sorry." I don't look away from Harper, and my heart tears as I move my hand to Ash's shackles and snap my fingers. My spell breaks through the lock.

I hear a few shouts of protest just a second before the shot echoes in the room and Harper's blood splatters over Skylar's cheeks. He lets her fall to the ground. Lifeless.

The screams that follow match the turmoil inside my body, and my vision blurs with tears as I push the iron away from Ash's ankles. Only when he's free, I heave but, by some miracle, manage to not be sick all over the ground.

I doomed an innocent to save the man I love. I'm a monster. The curse devours my insides as despair takes ahold of me. But I won't let Morla take more from us, and before I fade away, I use my sunderer power to unravel what makes my curse. I steal some of its darkness and blend its magic imprint seamlessly with mine. It hisses as if in pain, and I feel myself grow stronger as its anger becomes my own.

I look across the room, feeling the curse rush to my skin, savoring the possibility of freezing them all in stone. Naheli was right, this curse never wanted to kill me. It likes a host that speaks back. It craves death, but not necessarily mine.

Instead of light, I become darkness. A spell forms in my mind in threads of red and black. Something new that encompasses all the betrayal and sorrow Morla, the strixes, Irene, my father, and Finley caused. The enchantment tastes of a strange mixture of smoke and mint. It wants to cause destruction, to turn their hearts to granite.

I lift my arms, and the spell blasts out of me so fast it pulls me forward. Unlike in the forest, where I had no true control of what I was doing, here, I launch the spell at the five men running at us. The first turns to stone so fast, there isn't time to scream.

The second gets caught mid-run. The other three jump out of the way of my power, but I catch their legs and throw another swirling spell their way, finishing them off. My energy dwindles, but still, I turn two more to stone.

Ash gets up from the ground, and I don't need to face him to know he's regaining his power. I can taste it in the back of my throat before waves of gold grow from behind me and stretch until I can see them from the corners of my eyes. In the corner the shadows morph, and from them, a wolf appears. This is the first time I've seen Naheli look mostly like stars. Her eyes glow the same color as Ash's power.

He presses his hand to my waist and guides me out of the cage, and it's then that I notice I'm floating at least a foot above the ground. Our powers blend, mine in black and his in gold.

His words caress my ears, the fae tongue clear. "*Keep Nera safe, Monster.*"

Then he steps around me, just as Naheli jumps to devour those who were foolish enough to stay and fight. Skylar's face turns so white it looks like he's made of marble himself. The pyramid cracks, and the veil sputters one last time and then fails entirely.

Many of the scientists run screaming from the room, just as the bells of Penumbra ring loudly outside. The lunargyres—or the fae—made it into the city, probably called by Ash and Naheli. For the first time since the cave downstairs, Skylar's glamour fails him and his features flicker from his, to Morla, then back into Skylar. The few lackeys that remained by his side falter and step back.

I rush to Nera, narrowly dodging a piece of the pyramid as it crashes to the ground. I undo Harper's spells, and Nera's skin regains its color rapidly as I drag her body over the ground and out of the iron.

Once she's out, I turn to Ash as his golden magic envelops Skylar in a tight cocoon before throwing him into the metal pyramid. His bones crack, a cry escapes his lips, and then his glamour fades completely, leaving Morla pinned to the metal. Pale and staring wide-eyed at the man she supposedly loved. She has no power left, not after cursing Ash with something so vicious it damned his entire kingdom.

Morla lifts a trembling hand and tries to cast something. Nothing happens. Ash strolls toward her, unconcerned.

"You can't kill me," she hisses, and blood sprays from her shaking lips.

"You were always so bright and cunning, Skye. And you're right, but while I can't kill you, I can punish you." Ash stops right beside her, and the room falls silent as the wolf spirit stalks over to them, her aura filling the space with indigos and purples. A growl shakes the glass of the dome ceiling.

"Naheli, is another story, and I'm afraid you've made her *furious*."

I want to look away as Naheli's power engulfs Morla. But I force myself to be present, to watch what happens when one lets darkness take over. She screams and her face shifts into the faces of many people. Old and young. A shape-shifter like I've never seen before, and likely, never will see again.

Her breaths slow as Naheli becomes the sky inside the machine room. Wind blows my hair over my face, and the glass cracks above us. Only when the screaming stops do I open my eyes again and focus on Nera, who stirs at my feet.

I press a hand to her feverish cheek, and notice for the first time, my skin is no longer black. I inspect my hand, my arm, my chest, and find there's only a small black dot in the center of my palm. A big part of my curse disappeared when Morla died.

When I look inside myself, and at the power that makes me, I find a trace of that darkness, what I wove into my core so I could use its power.

And that black slimy monster will forever be a part of me, like the memories of this night.

"Mia?" Nera's voice is soft, and it pulls me out of my thoughts.

"You're safe," I say.

"No, I'm not." Nera swallows, her eyes wide in panic as she stares at the dome above us. "He's coming for me."

"He's dead. Skylar is dead." I comb her hair back in a soothing motion that used to calm Irene when we were young.

Thinking of my sister makes the knot in my throat reappear, and I know I can't speak again. Not for a while.

Ash rushes through thick plumes of smoke, and Naheli remains behind, near Morla's body where she's pinned to the metal wall with ropes of gold.

I sprint to meet him, and his arms wrap around me in a tight embrace. His heart thunders under my ear.

"Mia." He pulls back, reaching for my hand as his eyes search every inch of my bruised skin. From the top of my head, down my arms, and pausing to inspect every finger.

He visibly relaxes, some of the tension in his face and shoulders melting away. "I thought the curse had taken most of your skin."

"I pulled it apart, and I used it to wield a stronger kind of magic." I look down at my palm and the black dot that remains. "I'm afraid I've accidentally woven it into myself. The good news is, Naheli told me it doesn't want to kill me."

"That ungrateful wolf." Ash wraps his hand around the back of my neck and brings me close again. "Of course she told you that and not me, the fae she's bound to."

"What now?" I meet Ash's gaze, ignoring the surrounding destruction. I wonder if he expects more trouble, though I doubt it, not with him and Naheli on the loose.

"We go home . . ." He hesitates, and his expression sours. "That is, if you don't want to remain here, in Penumbra."

I blink. "Why would I want to do that?"

"Well you were keen before, and we made a deal. You're free. If you stay, I won't come back for you." He lifts my hand and brushes his lips over my knuckles. "But I beg you to come with me."

I smile and know what Morla said back in the cave is true. He loves me. Against all odds, the king who was forced to hate the hybrids fell for one, as I did for him. And so, when our prejudices about and anger at each other grew into pure, genuine feelings, his curse was broken.

"This isn't my home. You are."

Ash pulls me to him, and his soft lips devour mine with an all-consuming kiss. He presses his forehead to mine, interlacing our fingers.

I don't know what we'll find in the castle. Whether Finley will be there, or Irene. Whether the lunargyres are now fae, who will want to try to return to Eponde to resume their lives in a broken city.

Ash looks over his shoulder at the spirit who takes up most of the space with waves of darkness and starlight. "We have to make one last stop at the library to collect my possessions, then we can go home."

CHAPTER 41

Sunrays kiss the top of the forest as we glide closer to Aphelion. The rain clouds and heavy mist have parted somewhat, leaving the castle visible where it stands tall behind the conifer trees. The light gray stone and dark wood accents hazed by the distance are beautiful in the morning light.

Emotion clogs my throat as I tighten my arms around Ash's shoulders and bury my face in the crook of his neck. A mild scent of blood lingers on the dark fabric of his clothes, which are torn and tattered from the torture he endured.

Now that we've left Penumbra, all my emotions barrel into me. The betrayals, the lies, Harper's death . . .

"Are you alright, Monster?" Ash's voice is tired. He tightens his grip around me as we head toward the courtyard. Thousands of grimoires circle around us, carried by the same golden enchantment he used when we escaped Hedrum. Nera isn't far behind and also carries her fair number of books with her. Their power, especially when combined, leaves me in awe every single time.

"I should ask you that question . . ." My chest squeezes when I spot Finley's carriage by the gates. Empty and tilted on its side.

Did he survive his gunshot wound? Should I care? "When you left, you told me to not trust anyone but Naheli. Did you know Finley—?"

On our way out of the library, Nera had been worried about Finley and the fact that he wasn't there with us. It was me who told her what happened. Both siblings have been quiet ever since.

"After Hedrum, with the strixes' party and the mirror incident, I suspected something was wrong with Marlena. I didn't think Finley would be involved with Skye, but he was acting particularly off when I left that night, like he knew I was about to get attacked."

When Finley begged Ash not to go looking for Nera that night, did he already know Morla was waiting for him, hiding under the guise of a scientist?

"He told me to tell you he was sorry, that he didn't see how else to save Marlena," I say, even though I don't want to tell Ash what else Finley said before I left for Penumbra. In the end, he betrayed us all, and we almost died. But, I'm also not a petty person at heart.

Shame churns deep in Ash's features as he avoids my gaze, nodding. "I'm sorry you had to find out what he did when I didn't come back. After Skye betrayed me, I don't have an excuse for how I let this happen with Finley too. And you and Nera got hurt because of it."

"It's not your fault someone you trusted blindsided you." I rest my hand on his cheek, shifting his face so I can look straight into his eyes when I say, "We were both betrayed by those we loved, and ultimately, believing people are good separates us from them. Finley betrayed us because he didn't think there was a way out of this, but had he trusted you . . ."

My voice shakes as I think about Harper. Maybe her last moments in this world wouldn't have been inside the machine room. I wonder if she knew about the strix and the hybrids before everything happened.

"Is the bond going to make you chase after him?"

"Eventually . . ."Ash hesitates. "Though perhaps his actions fractured our bond long before I suspected him. It may be why I didn't feel the need to chase after him, or to protect him, for the last few years. I'll eventually find him, and he will have to answer for what he did to us."

We go down to the courtyard, while the chilly breeze of the early morning hits my cheeks. I'm tired, but I can't help but smile as the grimoires move over us and toward the castle. "You won. You destroyed the veil and recovered your grimoires."

It had been relatively easy since I knew the way in and the schedules the librarians kept. The evening guard never suspected the fae king and his sister would come steal all the forbidden texts.

"*We* won, Monster." Ash places me on the ground, and I'm already missing the warmth of his body as he steps away. "I must admit, I didn't expect you to set that librarian's cloak on fire. But that was a wonderful distraction."

"I gave him three warnings," I huff.

"Please remind me to never make you that angry, or you might set me on fire . . . again." Ash chuckles and reaches for my hand. When I face the castle, the air catches in my lungs.

From afar it was beautiful, but now, as I stand in front of the glorious stonework, it leaves me speechless. With the curse gone, some of the grime and lichen that had made a home on the stone has faded. The magical roses that previously climbed the walls are gone—withered and brown, shriveled into nothingness.

We step forward just as Nera lands behind us. She wears a dirty nightgown that has seen better days, the tattered edges streaked with mud and soot from the city, much like her pale skin.

The grimoires she carried pour into the castle as a side door swings open and fae of all shapes and sizes rush out.

Some have wings, others shimmer with the light—similar to Ash and Nera. All of them clamor at us, their expressions alight with joy and reverence.

I stiffen beside Ash. How are they going to react to me, a hybrid in this place which not so long ago was cursed by one?

"Don't be nervous, Monster. They're mostly harmless—but I was told once that the fae want human pets, so I'd be careful if I were you."

"Have I told you I hate you?" I glare up at him, remembering when I uttered those words at him.

"Once or twice." His grin—with fucking dimples—could blind a person. "But it's the other words you said back in that dump of a city that I choose to focus on."

My cheeks warm because I know which words he's talking about. We haven't spoken about my love confession in the cave, and I don't think we need to dwell on it. I spoke my truth and showed him how I feel. Just like he's done for me.

"Your Majesty." A tall fae is the first to reach us. He bows, giving us a clear view of his beautiful silver hair tied back with a black ribbon. He places his palm over his heart in a gesture of reverence. When he straightens, his ebony eyes shift to me briefly before they go back to Ash.

A small smile graces his thick lips. He doesn't look more than thirty, but something in his eyes screams that he's much older than even Ash. "You did it. You broke the curse and saved us all."

"I didn't break the curse. Mia did." Ash turns to me. My stomach flutters. "I believe you've met Alaris, Mia?"

I gape at the cook and can't speak. Of course, he doesn't look like a bald mole anymore, but I never expected him to be a handsome man either.

"Thank you, miss." Alaris straightens his coat and smiles at me. “I knew from the first time you came into the kitchen that you were going to play a big part in His Majesty’s future.” With that, he steps back so others can greet us.

“Sir, where are our families?” someone asks from the back. A fae with pink hair that’s matted by grease and still has sticks poking out. “Was Eponde affected?”

“I haven’t gone back to Eponde yet.”

“Sire, are the hybrids returning?” another says.

“Is *she* a hybrid, like Morla?” Pink Hair says, in a harsher tone.

I wince. Ash’s gaze cuts to whoever spoke and everything around us grows dark with his temper. His aura thickens in a way that would have been terrifying a month ago. There isn’t a doubt in my mind this show of power is a warning for my sake.

“She’s my mate, so no, she isn’t like Morla.”

Silence descends after that and the fae with pink hair falls back behind the others. All of their eyes follow me, more with curiosity than not.

“Are the wards strong enough?” someone else shouts, cutting through the tension.

Ash places his hands on me and pulls me behind his body, giving Nera a look over his shoulder. Like I wouldn’t know he wants me out of here while he deals with his people.

“I just came back from Penumbra and haven’t been to Eponde—or any of our cities—yet. You are free to go and see if your families are well.”

Nera tucks her hand into the crook of my elbow and pulls me into the castle. “Boring politics,” she says, though her brows pinch in the middle. “Let’s go inside so we can get clean.”

I look back at Ash, who nods at me with a tight smile. Then he faces his people, and I let Nera guide me into the castle.

“Will he be alright?”

“Oh, yes. He was born to handle this,” Nera says. “You will learn, too, as you are bound to be their queen.”

I stumble on my feet at her words. Had Nera not caught me, I would've kissed the marble floor. Her smile is sad, but gentle—and true. "Don't be nervous, Mia, you're going to be an amazing queen."

"You're just saying that . . ."

"Have you met me?" This time her smile reaches her eyes. "You went to Penumbra and saved us. You're powerful and amazing. They will grow to love you, like we did. You just have to give them time."

Inside the castle, fae are everywhere. Some are cleaning. Others seem a bit lost, talking with each other in hushed tones. All look at us as we walk by, bowing at Nera and staring at me.

I never knew there were so many lunargyres in the castle, though I guess it makes sense. Many were statues out in the gardens, and many—Ash told me—lurked in the shadows. Perhaps some of them have seen me around during the last month and a half. And to them, I'm an outsider.

I glance at where the roses used to be, and a part of me mourns the loss of the plants. Another, bigger part of me is happy they're gone, since Morla used them to spy on us.

I rest my hand over Nera's, squeezing it tight as we step onto the floor where Ash's room is. "How are you doing?"

"I've been better." She shrugs. "But don't worry about me. I'll get over what Finley did . . . and what happened in that horrible place."

Naheli waits inside Ash's room. I guess it never occurred to me, but this is now my bedroom as well. The wolf spirit lies on the bed like we didn't just come from battle. Her dark indigo fur buzzes with static. I stop right inside the doorframe before Nera can leave.

"I don't suppose I could borrow a few dresses from you? I've been waiting for Morgana to bring me some new ones, but since she was Morla all along, I have nothing to wear."

"You keep destroying the ones I lend you." Nera's mischievous smile takes over her features. "Plus, if you are without clothes, then perhaps I will get a nephew or niece early."

"What?" I stare in horror at the back of her beautiful wings as she walks down the hall, waving me off and cackling like a maniac.

She just reminded me that Ash and I were together back in the Crossroads house, and I didn't take the birth control potion the day after.

CHAPTER 42

FOUR AND A HALF MONTHS LATER . . .

THE BLOOD MOON HITS DIFFERENTLY IN THE FAE LANDS, ESPECIALLY SINCE I stopped fearing it and grew to understand it. Three months ago, the celebrations were small as Aphelion healed from ten years of the curse, and we waited for those who'd left to return home. Tonight, though, the unseelie indulge in their revelry.

Fire burns in a clearing right outside the castle's walls. We aren't too far from where I saw Irene and Finley last, but even though those memories weigh my soul down, they don't take away my excitement for the Wild Hunt celebrations.

Fae circle the bonfire, dancing in white clothes with gold paint smeared over their skin. They're all wild with something I can't name, though I feel it may be contagious. The drums in the circle have my heart skipping beats and my stomach fluttering with anticipation as I watch Ash dance in the firelight with our people. Naheli sits behind him, so massive she's at least six feet taller than he is, and he's already tall himself.

Her magic—and that of the spirits of the Hunt—blends with every shadow around us. I hear the whispers of spirits I can't quite see with my human—hybrid—eyes. But the fae can.

"Your Majesty, would you like more wine?" A fae approaches me with a tray of drinks. She's wearing the same white clothes as everyone else, and her shining skin tells me she was probably dancing recently.

My heart jolts at her words. "I'm not the queen."

I can't quite get over that I'm now considered one to the unseelie, even though we haven't had the ceremony yet. I guess that to the fae, being mates is an unspoken, binding contract. It takes everything in me to not touch the delicate silver crown resting on my head.

Not the queen's crown, but that of the king's mate—which apparently is the same.

"Not yet, I suppose." She smiles when I accept a glass and take a tentative sip. "How do you like the Hunt, ma'am?"

The sweet wine goes down the wrong way, and I pat my chest as I cough. "It's not what I expected . . ." I admit, feeling my face grow warm as my eyes find humans and hybrids dancing in the woods with the fae. All of them bear the mark of the unseelie. Eyes that are just a little different, with similar coloring to the fae who claimed them. I've never worn the mark of Ash's tribute, like Finley and Morla did.

Our bond's always been different.

"Did you expect us to run through towns and take humans?"

I'm nodding before I can stop myself.

"We did, before. Once His Majesty took the throne, though, we transitioned to celebrating in the forest with the spirits."

I imagine that may be the reason fewer sorcerers have been reported being born back in Penumbra in recent years. I look at Ash again and bring the wine back to my lips. He moves with the sound of the music, and even from where I stand on the edges of the dance circle, I can spot the feathers stretching up his forearms and getting lost under the rolled-up sleeves of his shirt.

He meets my gaze from across the crowd, and my core flutters with the heat—the intensity—in it. I clear my throat and down my drink in one go, and distantly hear my new fae friend excuse herself, as Ash stops dancing and prowls toward me.

I take in the lusty daze in his eyes, and the peppering of black dots, feathers, over his neck. Like when he was cursed. I wonder if his spirit form reveals itself even slightly during every blood moon. Not that I'm complaining. I quite like his feathers and wilder nature.

"Monster, why aren't you dancing with us?" He leans against the tree behind me, caging me in.

"I'm tired."

I haven't been dancing at all, and he knows it. I'm too caught up taking in every little detail of what goes on around me during the Wild Hunt to care about moving my body—not in that way.

"Liar," he says and catches my chin with two fingers, tilting my head up so his mouth lingers close over mine. "You're just curious about what the fae do tonight."

"Can you blame me? I grew up hearing about this." I press my hand to his chest and love the beating of his heart. "I was expecting for there to be some hunting going on . . . This is a little disappointing."

"You want to be hunted?" When I meet his gaze, I know his head is in the same place mine just went to.

Liquid pools between my legs, and I find it hard to speak, let alone meet his challenge. "Like you could catch me . . ." I say, sounding a lot less sure than I mean to.

His lips hover so close, I can feel them graze over mine. "It'll be so easy. I could do it in the dark."

I push aside the hunger burning inside me. "Is that so?"

He opens his lips just briefly before I call upon the revealing spell and blind him with it. Sneaking under his arm as fast as I can, I narrowly escape him, weave between a few fae who complain about the sudden brightness, and then I'm sprinting over leaves and sticks toward the castle.

My heart pounds as I dart through the shadowy corridors. The air burns in my lungs, and I struggle to catch my breath, but I push myself to go faster. The rhythm of the drums outside keeps me moving. Even here, deep in the castle, I can hear the laughter of the drunken fae I left behind. My dress smells like a cocktail of fae wine and smoke from the campfire that has been burning since midday.

I turn a corner, and my gown sticks to my sweaty skin. Studying every single nook and cranny around me, I take in the new paintings that decorate the halls, the arrangements of white roses in tall urn-like vases.

I'm easy prey. He'll quickly find me here.

I stumble onto a long, secluded balcony on the eastern side of the castle, where I've never been before. The night air brushes against my flushed cheeks, and I move away from the glass doors but freeze when I see a woman standing alone, leaning over the baluster. I recognize her voice, though unlike before, it's soft and rushed as she speaks to the shadows.

"Nera?" My voice wavers, and I forget everything as I step closer to my friend.

She gasps and straightens to her full height. She didn't hear me coming, which is odd for her.

"Mia, you scared me," she says, placing her hand over her chest as she breathes deeply. "I'm just staying out of sight of the guests."

How did I sneak up on her when I'm still breathing harshly from my run here? I raise my brows. "Are you well?"

She wrings her hands together, glancing at the shadows in the corner before turning back to face the castle grounds. The red moon overhead bathes us with its magical light. I don't think

Nera wants me here. I take a step back and know I'll have to find a new hiding spot.

"How are you liking your first blood moon with the fae?" she murmurs.

Nera doesn't like to be coddled, much like me. So instead of asking her what's happening, again, I look around, trying to find pools of magic that might tell me if she's in trouble.

There's something odd about the shadows in the corner that reminds me of how it feels right before Naheli materializes, like something is between spaces. I squint at the darkness but find nothing there, no threads of magic or makings of a spell.

The hairs on the back of my neck rise and my heart doubles its beats as I feel Ash getting closer.

"He's hunting you, isn't he?" Nera chuckles, though she scrunches her nose at me. "There are things a sister doesn't need to know."

I swallow deeply. "I swear something's wrong with you all on these three nights. You aren't yourselves during the blood moon. It's like it makes you all crazy."

"Something has made us crazy, but it's better that we let loose on our grounds and in our cities than pour into the human ones and wreak havoc there. Isn't it?" She pauses, glancing at the door. "If you don't want him to catch you so soon, you better go. I can feel him coming."

These fae siblings are weird. If I didn't know better, I'd think they're twins.

I turn to leave. There's no way in hell I'm going to let Ash catch me so fast. Not after he gloated that it would be so easy he could do it in the dark. The cocky bastard.

I slip back into the halls, and the lanterns flicker with a wave of golden magic. His enchantment bathes the entire place in darkness, and it takes all my concentration to undo it before I trip over something. His next spell freezes me in place, and I undo it almost immediately, but the distraction gives him enough time to put out the lights entirely. Unlike him, I don't know where each lamp is located, so casting a flame to relight them is nearly impossible.

I call on the revealing spell, and light leaves my extended fingers. I hear his chuckle before I see him. I try to jump away from the sound, but arms wrap around my waist in an ironclad hold and whirl me around.

"Monster, you're mine." His voice is velvet as he pulls me into an alcove, where I'm tucked between the immovable wall of my mate and a statue of a fae that could be a lunargyre from my nightmares. Ash presses me firmly against the cool stone wall. Before I can cry out, his lips claim mine in a searing kiss that burns away my resolution to escape.

I melt into him as he leans over me, and the heady taste of his tongue on mine feeds the mix of adrenaline and excitement rushing through my body and pooling in my core. Ash's kiss turns fierce. A silent promise of what's coming if I let him—if I don't escape him.

I've been chased by shadows and bathed in the light of the red moon, and now I'm about to be devoured by the fae I love. I'm happy—even if my ego claims otherwise—that he caught me. This time, and the first time.

Ash's breath is hot against my skin, a stark contrast to the unyielding cold stone at my back. His hands roam from my waist, grazing my ribs, before he cups one of my breasts. A shiver runs down my spine, and I scrunch the collar of his white shirt with one hand, lifting to my tiptoes so I can get more of him.

"Better," he growls softly, his lips trailing a path from the hollow of my throat to the sensitive flesh in the crook of my neck. "You're driving me crazy." His voice shakes with the intensity of his desire, and my core flutters in response.

With his front pressed to mine, the hard edge of his cock digs into my stomach. He nips at my collarbone before slipping a hand lower, lifting the layers of my dress to expose my legs to the night's air.

His taunting goes unheeded, as if the very notion of being caught only adds to the thrill of tonight. He meets my gaze, and mischief flickers in those golden eyes, right before he kneels in front of me. He pulls my skirt up and leans in to plant a kiss on the sensitive skin of my thigh.

"Ash—" My voice is a plea, half warning, half wanting more. "We're still . . . in the hallway."

His low chuckle vibrates against my skin, and when he lifts his head, his lids are heavy with desire.

The words *I don't care*, come through my mind even though he doesn't say them out loud. "Then you better be quiet."

My blood boils, and he trails his tongue closer to my throbbing heat. I'm shivering with need as he gets closer and closer to where I want him, and I gasp as his mouth finds the bundle of nerves at the apex of my thighs. He pulls the lace of my undergarment aside and traces his tongue over my sensitive flesh. Pleasure travels through me. Grasping his hair, I try to stifle a moan, but I don't think I succeed.

I hold him in place as his tongue slides inside me, and I tremble where I stand, trying to not move for fear he'll stop or I'll call attention to what we're doing.

His fingers glide to my entrance, and he pushes one into me, his lazy movements feeding the flame building inside me but not quite pushing me over the edge. I arch my back as he pushes a second finger into me and pumps faster, curling them to find the spot inside me that drives me insane.

"Please," I say, and he sucks my clit into his mouth. I buck against it, a moan leaving my lips as an orgasm takes me by surprise.

I writhe against his face, chasing the last waves of pleasure taking my body. Even my fingers can't keep holding my dress up like I've been doing thus far.

He stands and leans in close to whisper in my ear, "You riding my face is the sexiest thing I've ever seen."

He scoops me into his arms, and we leave our hiding spot in search of a more private place where we can finish what we just started. His study is cloaked in darkness, save for the red moonlight that slips through the window. The door closes behind us with a loud crash, and I barely notice the traces of golden magic on the door and walls. A spell to keep everyone out.

My insides quiver with anticipation for what's coming. Ash sets me on his new wooden desk, and something falls to the ground, shattering on the marble floor.

My cotton dress felt breathable in the humid heat of midsummer, but as he unties the bows over my shoulders and pushes the fabric down to reveal my breast, he has to peel it from my skin.

His face turns dark with hunger for me, for us, and when he speaks there's a touch of reverence in his words. "You are so beautiful, Mia."

He sheds his shirt before closing the distance between us with a hungry kiss. I close my eyes, drinking in every stroke of his tongue and how he feels pressed against my bare skin. Reaching for the top of his trousers, I undo the ties at his narrow waist and wrap my legs around him, bringing him closer until I feel him at my entrance. I need so much more of him.

I slide my hands over the smooth surface of his chest and up to the beginnings of feathers by his neck. Gods, I love him in all his forms. I love his beastly form and his breathtaking fae beauty. I love him when he's mischievous and when he's vulnerable and sweet. "I love you, Ash."

He pulls back slightly to meet my gaze, and there is a softness in his sharp features only I get to see. My heart swells with happiness when he drops a gentle kiss to my lips. "And I love you, Monster."

He grins, and my breath catches in my throat. Emotions overwhelm me as he presses slowly inside, stretching and filling me whole. I groan, holding tight to his wide shoulders as he thrusts in a maddening rhythm that sets my blood on fire and makes my insides tingle.

His lips travel away from my own to skim over my jaw and neck, his breath leaving a trail of goose bumps across my skin. "Touch yourself, Mia. I want to feel you come around my cock."

Those wicked words make my core tighten around him, and I obey without a question in my mind, immediately finding the sensitive spot between my legs, right above where he enters me. The pleasure intensifies as I circle my clit with my fingers, matching his pace and closing my eyes so I can feel *everything*.

My second orgasm barrels into me, hard, stealing a moan from my mouth. I didn't allow myself to be loud back in the hall, but right now, alone in this place, I let myself be free. Ash groans, quickening his pace as he moves inside me, dragging out the waves of pleasure taking over my body.

He stares into my eyes when he pushes deeper, his pace becoming erratic as he chases his release. I cradle his face with both hands and bring his lips to mine, kissing him right before he sucks in a deep breath and comes inside me. His movements slow, and we're left breathing heavily while I wait for my heart to stop trying to escape my body.

"Become my queen, Mia."

It's not the first time he's whispered those words to me, but this time they don't send fear coursing through my veins.

But I still enjoy teasing him too much when I can. "Maybe one day I will, but not yet."

He pulls back enough to drink in my messy, sweaty state. His side smile spikes my heart rate so it's once again beating too fast. "You're a wicked little human."

"Only for you."

Living with the fae these last few months has settled my nerves. I know there's a lot to rebuild in his kingdom—my kingdom as well?—and that the strix are still out there, plotting their revenge. But my being a hybrid who may—will—become the queen of the unseelie will send a message that change can be possible through love, not war. That we can live together in peace.

That humans don't need veils to keep those they love safe, and that the Wild Hunt can happen without the fae taking tributes for sport. Things can change, and Ash and I represent that.

Because, against all odds, I fell for the fae king—and he fell for me.

The End

EPILOGUE

NERA

"I THOUGHT SHE WOULD NEVER LEAVE . . ." THE SHADOW SAYS FROM THE corner of the balcony just as Mia goes back inside. The blood moon shines over me, casting a red light across every surface, but it doesn't reach him where he stands.

There's something wild, magical even, in my blood tonight. His, too, I imagine. Something that allows me to stay grounded in the now and not fade into a panic about his visit. Losing myself to fear is what he wants. He loves to watch me squirm.

"Was that Ash's mate? The one I kept seeing in your dreams?" His dark voice brings some comfort with its familiarity. I hate that I missed it—that I missed him—while stuck in my stone form. But now that I'm here talking to him again, I miss the distance the curse wedged between me and the seelie king.

"That's none of your business," I snarl to the nothingness. "Why are you here? Couldn't you be happy only terrorizing my dreams?"

"Funny, I don't remember our last encounter the same way . . ." he says, tapping one long finger over what I assume is his face. He lacks his usual cruelty. "Didn't you say how much you missed me and begged me to not leave?"

I hope my cheeks will return to their normal color, or at least that he won't notice how flustered I am by the memories of our last meeting, when I was so happy to see him again after five years of silence. When I definitely lost my fucking mind. Sylas is someone I've never forgotten about. After all, it's written in the damned stars.

I desire to see him. To fight with him. I crave his touch . . . Not even when the curse had sunk its claws into me did I forget the sound of his voice, or his smooth movements . . . or his brutal personality.

I take a deep breath. This is only a fragment of him. A shadow. His shadow. Surely he can't see those details.

I swallow deeply as Sylas moves closer. Even now, his scent tickles my mind, a memory I shouldn't have, since we've never met in person—not really.

"You took something from me last time we met, Nerala," he says. "I want it back."

"I didn't mean to. You can have your shadow back. I don't want it."

This man has been a constant voice in my mind since I can remember. Except now . . . he isn't in my head. Not since the night the scientist took me, and while I held onto the memory of him, I accidentally—and in a panic—stole his shadow.

Fuck. Ash is going to kill me if—when—he finds out.

He's here. He has come for me.

A clear male form takes another step forward, and his translucent body shifts with the night sky.

I press myself against the railing, and the cold stone digs into the shapes of my wings.

"It seems you won't let me go, and I guess our time apart has ended."

"No." My heart skips a beat. When I think I'll be able to speak without giving my horror away, I say, "I'm not coming with you. I don't want you, nor do I want your shadow."

He chuckles and steps back into the corner, tilting his face to the moon, and briefly, that magical red light graces his handsome features. For a second, he isn't a shadow but a male—and he is here.

"Traveling the continent during the blood moon will speed this up. Ready your things and tell your brother I'm coming."

GLOSSARY

- ***Shyene:*** Spell used by Mia, and crafted by the King of the Unseelie—Ash—to weaken an adversary.
- ***The Veil:*** White energy bubble that protects Penumbra from the beasts of the Hunt. Uses an ancient blood spell meant to protect royal fae kin from being abducted and used in battle.
- **Blood Moon** happens every three months. It marks a time where the veil in between the mortal land and the spirit lands thin enough and the fae can ride with the spirits. Used by the riders of the Wild Hunt.
- ***Scientists,*** *a group in penumbra who* maintain the veil.
- ***Librarians,*** a group of magical people in Penumbra who protect the magical grimoires; forbidden to wield their power.
- ***Strix,*** a bird, a bad omen; the name Ash's father gave the hybrids.
- ***The House of Strix,*** a group formed when hybrids banded together to hunt fae after Aphelion fell to the curse.

- ***Hybrids,*** part human part fae.
- ***Naga,*** snake-like beings who live in the seelie kingdom.
- ***Drawl,*** bald horse mixed with a boar. Massive, winged.
- ***Hellion,*** type of spirit made of night and stars. Can shift sizes and travel across planes.
- ***Nightwalker,*** fabled creatures that live and feed on nightmares.
- ***Lunargyres,*** beasts created by the curse. They hunt for humans during the Blood Moon. Have different appearances.

WANT MORE?

If you loved Ash, Mia and their crew, please consider leaving a review! It helps me find other readers like you 🩶:

While I've you here, sign up to my newsletter to see an exclusive NSFW art of *the* bathroom scene *wink wink*

Keep reading to find more to see what happens next with Nera and Sylas, a loose Hades and Persephone retelling with a Peter Pan twist.

Every seelie queen that fell in love vanished. I won't be next.

Princess Nera's fate was sealed in blood the night her father traded her hand to secure her brother's crown. Years later, she believes the cruel seelie King Sylas has forgotten about her, until he comes to collect what he's owed by the ancient deal. Her.

Now she's trapped in his court of nightmares, haunted by creatures that feed on her dreams and make her doubt what's real. To make matters worse, Sylas hates her, and she's determined to be a thorn in his side for as long as they live.

But when those same creatures threaten the kingdom, the unlikely couple must work together to stop them—an act that brings Nera dangerously close to the feelings she swore to avoid. Their love could unleash a greater evil, which will force them to choose between letting her to vanish or allowing the kingdom to fall to ruins.

Untethered *is a sexy gothic romantasy with a morally gray love interest and a slow-burn romance, perfect for fans of Hades and Persephone's.*

To those who helped me along the way...

To my amazing alphas, betas and CP:
Helen, Sarina, Courtney, Ali, Victoria, Jourdan and Teresa.
Thank you! This book wouldn't be the same without you ♥.

To my street team, the Unseelies. Thank you for making this release a dream.

To my ARC team, thank you for giving this book some of your valuable time.

To my editor, Anna. Thank you for working around my shifting dates and word counts, and for cleaning my messy words but keeping my voice 🥀.

To Nicola and Chase. You two inspire me daily.

To my family, thank you for supporting me while I became a grumpy gnome that hid in her cave for days on end.

About the Author

Abbey Fox is a Dark Fantasy Romance author who loves to write imperfect but powerful heroines, morally gray heroes, gothic worlds full of mystery, and stories with plenty of swoony moments.

When she isn't working on her lusciously dark tales of fae kidnapping their love interests, she enjoys tending to her indoor jungle and drinking café lattes that are mostly milk while dreaming of Mediterranean home decor. She also loves doing art, and many of the pieces found inside this book—including the cover—were created by her.

Keep up with Abbey by signing up for her newsletter to receive information about her new releases, current projects, latest artwork, and other extras right in your email.

www.abbeyfox.com

Also by Abbey Fox

The Wicked Kingdom Series:

If you love fated mates, a shadow daddy and a slow burn romance:

The Curse of the Crow

The Curse of a Kingdom

The Curse of the Fallen

The Curse of the Shadow God (Prequel)